C. Hope Clark

Hope Clark's books have been honored as winners of the:

EPIC Award, Silver Falchion Award, Imadjinn Award,

and the

Daphne du Maurier Award.

Murder on Edisto selected as a Route 1 Read by the South Carolina Center for the Book!

"Ms. Clark delivers a riveting ride, with her irrepressible characters set squarely in the driver's seat."

—Dish Magazine on *Echoes of Edisto*

"Award winning writer C. Hope Clark delivers another one-two punch of intrigue with *Edisto Stranger* . . . Clark really knows how to hook her readers with a fantastic story and characters that jump off the page with abandon. Un-put-downable from the get-go."

—All Booked Up Reviews on *Edisto Stranger*s

Edisto Storm

The Edisto Island Mysteries – Book 12

by

C. Hope Clark

Bell Bridge Books

This is a work of fiction. Names, characters, places and incidents are either the products of the author's imagination or are used fictitiously. Any resemblance to actual persons (living or dead), events or locations is entirely coincidental.

Bell Bridge Books
PO BOX 300921
Memphis, TN 38130
Print ISBN: 978-1-61026-275-0

Bell Bridge Books is an Imprint of BelleBooks, Inc.

We at BelleBooks enjoy hearing from readers.
Visit our websites
BelleBooks.com
BellBridgeBooks.com
ImaJinnBooks.com

Cover design: Debra Dixon
Interior design: Hank Smith
Photo/Art credits: © Mikhail Kokhanchikov | Dreamstime.com

:Lesd:01:

Dedication

Dedicated to the first responders of Edisto Beach.

Prologue

Sunday afternoon

IN THE WINDOW'S reflection, Arlo straightened his button-down shirt and ran fingers through black curls he'd flaunted for as long as he could remember, a never-fail asset. Then he walked into Wainwright Realty. The young receptionist straightened then, after an up-and-down analysis of him, smiled. "What can I do for you, sir?"

He went out of his way to acquire that kind of look from people like her. His hair long on top but neat and clean on the sides. Tight enough to admire, loose enough to entice a run-through. His shirts ran one size smaller to embrace biceps, the buttons not quite gaping across the span of his chest.

Coming closer, he leaned and touched fingertips on her desk then, ensuring her eyes followed up his forearms, in feigned afterthought, he pulled back. "Sorry. The name is Arlo Adkins. I believe you're holding a rental especially for me."

Her tight grin broke free. "Let me look. Would you like to sit?" She motioned to a red upholstered chair a few feet over.

Sliding it closer, he accepted, noting every last item in the beach office's décor ran red or yellow or a combo of both. Somebody in here was a jarhead.

"You don't look like a Marine, honey," he said, making her blush enough to match her cropped red sweater.

"No, sir. That's my boss. She retired from the Marines." She seemed to be taking longer than necessary to find a simple reservation.

"Once a Marine, always a Marine," he said. "I was a Ranger."

"You sound like her." She spun back around, showing him her computer screen. "Here you are. *Seas the Day.*"

"I try to," he said.

Her coyness slid into a look of bafflement. "Pardon?"

"Seize the day. You said seize the day. It's a good way to wake up and embrace life, don't you think? After experiencing people shooting at you, you learn to embrace that concept."

Blinking, she took a second. Then a laugh escaped her, and, though embarrassed again, she clearly warmed to him. "Seas the Day, silly. S-E-A-S," she spelled. "Not S-E-I-Z-E. I bet that's what the owner meant when they named it. Don't you think?"

He gave her his own brand of coy, recognizing an IQ just short of the temperature outside. "That's really sharp," he said, letting her feel good about herself.

"Two weeks, right?" she said.

"Yes, ma'am."

"You and two others?"

He nodded. "All three of us are Rangers. This is how we reconnect. That sandbox overseas was a nasty place. We each did three tours, one of us four, but once we returned to the States, we realized we'd forged a connection. Now we meet annually to tell war stories and feel real again." He gave her a mild wince, like he'd suffered . . . they'd suffered . . . and this was their love for each other.

"Ooh, forged," she said. "That's a powerful word. Doesn't getting together make you think of the bad things, though? I'd be afraid of stirring up nightmares or something."

"Oh, no. This is how we keep the nightmares at bay, honey." He stopped himself. "Hope that's not insulting, you know, to be called *honey*? My apologies if it is."

"This is the South . . . honey," she said. "It's all good." She glanced at his left hand for a ring.

When her look returned to meet his eyes, he winked, and damn if he didn't for a second feel he was going to have to catch her before she swooned. But she didn't, and there she sat, waiting for him to flirt back, the keys forgotten in her hand.

"Is it okay for me to move into the house now?" he asked, pointing at the keys.

"Oh, oh." The keys jangled as she lifted them up for him. "These are for you. There are only two keys, so you guys will have to share. I hope that's okay."

He touched the key tag, making sure to brush her hand in doing so. "We've shared way more than keys over the years. I'm sure we can manage."

She didn't immediately let loose. "Call me if you need anything. Any time."

"You," he said, then winked. Not a fast one but something more filled with meaning. "You are a sweetheart. I know where to find you, Miss Semper Fi."

"You sure do," she said, giggled lightly, and let go.

He left without looking back, feeling her gaze on his slow amble.

Outside he undid his shirt buttons, letting the shirttail fly free, his Toby Keith tee exposed to the breezes coming off the water two blocks over. Having nailed their rental, he'd done his job. His two buddies, however, had work to do. This was *vacation* number thirteen.

And to think they once thought they'd never fit back into the States.

Chapter 1

Callie
Monday morning

POLICE CHIEF CALLIE Jean Morgan craved escape from the office. *Craved it.* Edisto Beach streets beckoned on such days as these, days that God sculpted to perfection. Short of the hiccup in June with a lady who died in the surf, this summer had proven superb with less issues from top to bottom. Whether tourist or native, the community had behaved.

This was how a cop stationed to a beach was supposed to live. The temperate, intoxicating September weather with its eighty-degree days, blue skies, and fewer tourists. *God bless school starting.* You could change the name from Edisto to Eden, to include jungle, snakes, and splashes of nudity.

The vacuum sound of the front door alerted her that someone had entered the station, but Callie wasn't called about the visitor. That meant the station's lone admin Marie efficiently handled the issue. Bummer that there wasn't a good event to beckon the chief of police out of her meeting and outside. Meanwhile, Callie remained confined to her desk.

The newly elected councilwoman seated across from her had arrived without notice, cramping Callie's plans to drive the streets with windows down, taking in the fall weather.

Being police chief subjected Callie to such drop-ins from the power base that could make or break her future. Liking or disliking such moves mattered little, and as always she rolled with the flow. She'd been meaning to have a tête-à-tête with this woman anyway, but they'd kept missing each other to the point Callie wondered about the woman's intentions. Maybe the councilwoman felt the same about her. Time to test each other and see how they got along, because the police department and the town council most assuredly had to work simpatico.

Donna Baird hadn't come dressed to impress, more dressed to be genuine, like any other day of the week. She wore cargo capris, thick-soled sneakers, and a pastel polo, a beige boonie hat over a faded dark-blond bob of a haircut—the totality of a uniform of sorts she'd become noted for. Her dark tan spoke of a love for the out of doors, the ensuing wrinkles an indication she didn't care about the ramifications of such love. No wedding ring. No jewelry whatsoever. Her partner, a harlequin Great Dane, sat politely at her side, his head almost at the level of his owner.

But that didn't mean Callie knew her well . . . or trusted her. Not yet. People who involved themselves in politics usually fell into one of two categories. Too altruistic to be practical, or too opportunistic to care about the people they served. She recognized this opinion as rather tainted, but she had a few years of experience to support the opinion.

Politics ran towns, and politics hired the police department, so regardless of why someone ran for office, Callie had to get along.

The council lady had replaced Brice LeGrand, killed just under a year ago protecting the safety of the beach, as proclaimed so eloquently at his funeral. The handful of people who'd witnessed the murder remembered the shooting differently, but his multi-generational Edistonian heritage justified such respect. Callie missed exchanging grievances with him, arguing about how he could do her job better. Sadly, he'd died proving he couldn't. Her win didn't feel like much of one.

"I know I'm not Brice," said the councilwoman, the dog observing her as she spoke. "However, in spite of all the nobility and honors heaped upon his memory, I sense he wasn't a real fan of law enforcement."

Callie couldn't help herself. "An understatement for sure, Ms. Baird." But then she caught herself. "However, Brice is gone." Despite her past clashes with Brice, she continually caught herself defending his memory.

"Call me Donna. Hopefully you won't have me shot if we butt heads over something."

The humor fell like an anchor. To Callie, anyway. Donna, however, laughed as if she'd rocked a comedy house, not noticing that Callie barely managed a smile.

Callie understood she hadn't been the cause of Brice's death as did everyone in town. He had been the creator of his own demise.

She hoped this woman read people better than this when it came to the town's needs.

"But Brice is water under the bridge," the woman said. "May I call you Callie?"

Callie dipped her chin. "Sure. Or Chief. Either works."

"Ooh, I like *Chief*. Anyway," Ms. Baird continued, "I'd like to be a friend of the Edisto Beach Police Department. Someone who has their back, who understands their needs and their challenges." She leaned in. "I promise not to write traffic tickets like my predecessor."

Callie wished Donna would quit bringing up Brice so they could move forward.

"I appreciate the gesture," Callie said. "We'd welcome your support."

Callie maintained a wish list of department desires, the biggest being more chests wearing badges, but she was wise enough to feel this woman out and give her time to settle into the job first before timely planting seeds as to what was needed.

Donna Baird had won the special election hands down, and with that much clout already, her visit to the station was welcomed, her efforts to reach out promising. So far, so good.

No question Donna was well liked on the beach, a retired large animal veterinarian often seen walking her Dane named, humorously, Horse. Apparently, he had campaigned with her, imprinting the ticket on everyone's minds all the way to the polls. Donna had never held office before, but being retired, she had needed a hobby, an interest, and when someone suggested she run for Edisto Beach Town Council after Brice died, she'd leapt at the opportunity. So did the voters. She won seventy percent of the vote, a total of 490 out of the 700 who voted, Horse, no doubt, having given her an edge with animal love overriding political persuasion.

While being a dog owner could take an election, it didn't make you an astute public servant. Time would tell.

Callie had been waiting over these last few weeks for a queen-bee mentality of some sort to rear its head via Donna Baird, but thus far the veterinarian seemed to be a genuine community enthusiast. If she continued acting that way, fantastic. If her enthusiasm weighed in for Edisto Beach police, even better. Callie could use a cheerleader on town council.

"What can I do for you, Donna?" Callie said, needing to get out on patrol. Donna had arrived at straight up eight, forcing Callie to push Thomas out without her. After a busy summer, and with the weather so gorgeous, she'd put herself on patrol and let the others have a day off. She'd rather not test fate with only one officer on the streets.

"This is what you can do for me. Technically, it's for us." Seemed that Donna came with purpose. "I'd like to do a ride-along with you or one of your officers. I'd prefer to see firsthand what you folks are up against as well as learn what they do well. More people need to understand you. I waited until I understood my job as an elected official before coming here, and I didn't want to lay this in your lap on a busy tourist weekend. So, is today possible?"

"Oh." *Shit* flashed through Callie's mind, but she checked herself. This could be a good thing.

Donna's head tilted to the side, measuring. Funny, but Horse seemed to do the same. Though an impromptu request, Callie couldn't see a problem with it. Brice wouldn't have asked politely. He'd have made a demand, assuming he'd even wanted to ride along and learn what her officers did for this town.

Stop it. Now she had to quit comparing the new councilwoman to Brice.

Question was whether to put Donna with Thomas or take the woman along with her. It might look rather unappreciative to delegate the job.

"I was about to go out when you walked in," she said, decision made. "Care to come along?" Then she glanced at the dog.

"Oh, Horse is trained, and he's used to riding in the back," the councilwoman said. "And as long as it doesn't get hot, he doesn't drool. I keep his teeth brushed, which helps a lot."

Good to know.

Callie rose from her chair. "Then let's go."

Donna grinned like a kid on her way to visit Santa.

When they walked into the lobby, Marie couldn't take her eyes off the beast lumbering through, hugging tight to Donna's left. "What's his name again?" Marie asked. She owned a cat.

"Horse," Donna said, as if introducing her favorite grandchild to the preacher on Sunday morning. "I was a horse vet. Since I couldn't have a horse at the beach, I went with the next best thing."

"Hmm," Marie said, not daring to reach out to pet the animal. Instead, she turned to Callie. "BOLO for a College of Charleston student who disappeared yesterday."

Callie's son, Jeb, attended College of Charleston, as did Sophie's daughter, Sprite. They'd been an item almost since they first met three years ago. Sophie Bianchi was Callie's next-door neighbor and the island yoga expert. Although some called her a witch—behind her back— thanks to her so-called abilities to speak to the other side, Callie loved the fact Sophie knew everyone who lived in the area and kept up with the latest. Her ability to pry information out of people came in handy.

Marie continued. "Sent you the details on the girl. And I'm keeping an eye on the weather. It's showing personality."

Callie nodded in silent understanding. A lot had been going on in the Atlantic this past week, and the year's predictions had called for a busy hurricane season. The season ran from June through September with August and September the peak. However, predictions had fallen flat up to now, which only made Callie pay closer attention to see if the shortfall would wind up pounding them all at once here at the end. While this was her favorite time of year otherwise, the threat of hurricanes was real on coastal islands. One paid attention to storm systems developing as far east as Africa and how they behaved as they headed west. One of those could turn into a Hugo, Matthew, Helene, or Milton causing serious damage, each hurricane in its own way. Such storms meant potential for incredible property damage and a hard pounding to the island economy, and, of course, a threat to human life.

Each day during those four months meant one eye on weather predictions. Donna, on the other hand, flashed a puzzled expression at the two ladies' unspoken insight. "It's gorgeous outside. Part of the reason I came in to ask for a ride-along. What better way to spend the day and appreciate what Heaven has bestowed upon us."

With a smile, Callie turned to explain. "It's hurricane season. Nobody usually worries, especially on days like this, but the town has to watch developments far in advance. Right now two tropical storms are playing tag in the Atlantic. Nikki and Owen. We are going to get part of Nikki."

The storms were on a first-name basis around there. Matthew, Hugo, now Nikki, without the word *hurricane* before their name. They were like black-sheep relatives who didn't take much explanation. Everyone who lived in coastal regions of the Carolinas and the whole of Florida was on a first-name basis of each storm they'd experienced.

Donna's expression melted into one of concern. "Shouldn't you be putting out warnings?"

"We do." Callie started to tell the woman that *we* meant the government, to include the newly elected Ms. Baird. There had been discussions at the council meetings. Donna had been to two meetings. The one when she was sworn in, and one a couple weeks back. Hurricanes were discussed, but the woman was green in the job with only three years of residency, none of those years having seen much of a hurricane scare.

On the town website, in the monthly newsletter, even the Chamber talked about preparedness. "We started in June with notices," Callie said . . . reminded. "We had a Hurricane Emergency Preparedness meeting at the Civic Center in conjunction with the county back in June, and again in August. And everyone with a phone that pings off the local tower can be texted with notices. There's the CodeRED app as well that we advise everyone to sign up for." She started to take this further into the Incident Command System, the beach's Emergency Operation Plan, and the monthly staff meeting with Colleton County, but it wasn't her place to educate the councilwoman on everything top to bottom in this their first visit.

With a little uptick of her mouth, Donna seemed to acknowledge the efficiency. "Well, let's hope I don't have to see how well it all works."

"I hope you don't either."

But she had another question. "What about renters?"

"The CodeRED app, travel insurance, the information packets they get from the real estate people, the news . . ."

"A lot of moving parts, one could say."

"Yes, ma'am."

Donna brightened. "Well, label me impressed. And my apologies for not being at either of those public meetings. I will be from now on."

There'd been only twenty-seven residents at the August meeting. You could only do so much for people. "Good. Let's see if I can impress you some more. Let's go." The three left the station, took the narrow sidewalk to the parking lot and entered the patrol car to begin their crawl through town. Horse hopped in the back as if he belonged there.

"How do you like the job so far?" Callie asked, taking Murray Street out to Palmetto Boulevard, almost immediately having to make a hand motion to a speeding vehicle, the driver braking, not expecting to see a cop in their eager effort to get somewhere.

"I'm seeing this job with potential for having fun and doing good," Donna replied. "Unique collection of guys on council. Never paid much attention to them before I decided to run." Her gaze covered the intricacies of what comprised the front seat of a police cruiser. "But everyone's likeable enough. No shortage of desire to keep this beach intact, minus the attempts to transform it into something more commercial. People look at life through so many different lenses."

"That non-conforming attitude makes us special. Can you give me a second?" Callie pulled into a drive. "This owner is out of town. I promised to keep an eye on his place."

She exited the vehicle, quickly doing a once-over around the property, pulling on doors, checking locks, then soon returned, noting the dog stooping down to look out the driver-side back window at her. His breath fogged the window.

Donna waited for Callie to do her belt. "Did you do that for me, or do you have a list of homes you babysit? I can't see you doing this for everyone."

A test already. How about that. "Everyone who asks us gets checked. Some are more paranoid than others. Some have had bad experiences in the past. Some rarely leave and don't feel comfortable with their house being empty with tourists running about. No rhyme or reason really, but it's amazing at how natural it becomes to canvas homes, and unless we have a larger-than-normal day of accidents, mishaps, or tickets, we're able to cover a lot of ground. We develop an inherent knowledge of which houses belong to locals and which to lessors and which fall in between. Some are more secluded and more prone to break-ins. Rentals are also monitored by the agencies, the cleaning crews, and so on. The weekly turnover, believe it or not, means less break-ins. Doesn't hurt that the beach sees us out and checking."

Donna bobbled a brow, seeing the logic. Maybe the woman really wanted to understand the lay of the land and how it was protected. The ride gravitated from reserved to more pleasant, and Callie grew accustomed to Horse's breathing in the back.

The dog's continuous breath also gave her a flash of thought about how a pet would work for her out here. Then she thought of the endless hours she was away from the house and Mark's long days.

She wondered if Jeb ever wished she'd let him have a dog.

Speaking of him, a text came through . . . at a glance she saw his name. She waited until they came up on a stop sign and glanced down, just in case.

Call me when you get the chance. Very important but not an emergency.

He knew how to code a message, not wanting to pull her from a dire situation to call a son who only wanted to talk about his grades or a conversation he'd had with his grandmother. She put away the phone and pulled on through.

They traveled the better part of three hours. Callie let Donna check a few houses, educating her on what to watch for. A tourist waved them down only to ask about camping on the beach. *Only in the state campgrounds,* they were advised.

A block later, a local beckoned. He took a backstep at the sight of Horse in the back seat. "What the hell is that?"

It was difficult to tell what kind of creature the dog was with his body filling the shadows behind the cage divider, his face smashed against the glass. He might not drool in terms of Donna's drooling measurements of the various breeds, but Horse left enough gloppy wetness to show he had it in him to compete.

The councilwoman rolled down her window. "Hello there. I'm your new town council member, Donna Baird. Horse back there is my partner. Who might you be?"

The gentleman grinned wide, identified himself, and shook hands when Donna gave him hers. "You're that new politician with the dog," he said.

Yep, branding in action.

"What can we do for you?" Donna asked.

"A tourist parked in my private drive to get closer to the sand, the idiots. Total *tourons*," he added, using the relatively new moniker given to tourists deemed to be morons, considered a rather invasive species.

He motioned to his home on the land side of Palmetto, in the middle of the five-hundred block where a Suburban filled one side of his drive. "The son of a bitch probably thought nobody was home since my wife took one car and the other one is in the shop. I walked back from lunch at El Marko's to find it there. Other than walk up and down the beach screaming for the owner of a silver Suburban, I have no clue how to move it."

"A love-hate relationship, these tourists. Don't you think?" Donna said. "We need their money, but oftentimes you gotta hate their manners."

The man thought a second. "Gotta agree with you there. These restaurants would cave without these damn visitors, as rude and unappreciative as they might be."

"I hear you," she answered back, then turned to Callie. "Is there a ticket or something we write for this? I'm by no means familiar with all things legal, but do you have a suggestion, Chief?"

Brice would've snatched up a ticket book and written the citation himself. This woman had finesse. Callie almost couldn't say no to what hovered between a request and a nudged order.

Her phone buzzed with another text, and a glance down said Jeb again. *Call me.*

Callie would but now was not the time. She hit the automatic reply, *Busy. I'll call later.*

This was the middle of the day, and he knew she was on duty.

As for the situation before her, she didn't have the staff to continually write tickets. However, this type of situation warranted tickets more than most. There was a fine line between maintaining peace between the tourists and the residents, but vehicles that parked in drives like this were usually day-trippers. They drove over without spending a dime, their own drinks, food, suntan lotion, etc. bought from their local stores rather than the ones on the beach. The one- and two-week visitors were the ones who brought the income, plus they parked where they rented.

Callie left her vehicle on the curb, pulled out her ticket book, and promptly left the SUV a remembrance from Edisto Beach under the windshield wiper.

"What the heck do you think you're doing?" yelled a man around forty, high-stepping his way across the hot pavement.

But before Callie could address him, the owner pushed forward. "Giving you a damn ticket for parking in my driveway."

"I didn't think anyone was home," said the violator.

"Doesn't give you the right to park here," came the reply.

Callie moved in between them. "Whoa, wait a minute." She turned to the owner first. "Mr. Pope. I'll need you to step back over there, please."

"But—"

"You heard me. Let me handle this."

Pope reluctantly stepped about fifteen feet into his grass, his scowl going nowhere.

"Now," she said, returning to the visitor. "We have beach accesses for parking."

"The ones we usually use are filled. Nobody was using this drive, so what's the harm?"

"It's private property, sir."

"It's on the beach."

"There's parking for visitors like you, parking for renters at their rentals, and parking that belongs solely to the homeowners."

"What if I move the car? Will you take back the ticket?"

This one was earning his ticket big time. "No, afraid not."

Instead of accepting his consequences, he stared daggers at Mr. Pope. "You rich bigwigs who can afford to live here got no business keeping us regular people from visiting what Nature gave everybody." He jabbed a finger in the air toward the other man. "You ought to have a *no parking* sign up, old man."

Callie moved between the violator and Pope. "Accept the ticket, sir."

But no, the fuss continued. "My wife is pregnant, and I have two small children who can't walk for blocks. Not with the wagon, the chairs, the towels . . . Have some consideration."

"Move the car, sir. I'd hate to have to tow it, and you don't want to push this minor incident into something that necessitates your wife driving those small children home by herself."

He huffed once, twice, those consequences settling in. "You'd arrest me?"

"I could, but I'd rather not."

"Fine. Direct me where to park." He marched toward his driver's door. Mr. Pope took a few steps further back, arms crossed, his smirk proud for all to see. The driver snatched the ticket from his windshield, hopped in his seat, and cranked up. His window went down. "Well?" he said. "Direct me where to park."

"Wherever there's a spot at any of the accesses," she said, backing off to give him plenty of room.

The driver backed up abruptly.

"Whoa!" she yelled as another driver on Palmetto swerved to miss. Then she marched up to the driver's side. "You're testing me, sir. Take your temper down a notch and find a legal place to park."

"We aren't coming back here."

"Your prerogative, but if this is the way you drive and treat others, we'll be okay with that decision."

"Bitch," and he backed out and drove on, clearly watching his mirror. Callie let him go.

Her phone rang this time, and she took it, keeping eyes on the SUV, hoping to see where it wound up parking. "What is it, Son?"

"Didn't you get my texts?"

"Yes, and you said it wasn't an emergency. I have a quick minute. What is it?" She glanced back at her patrol car to check on her passengers. Mr. Pope had walked over to talk with Donna through the window.

"That girl that disappeared? Surely you have a BOLO on her."

Her son had the glorious perk of being related to a cop and having the ability to talk the lingo. With his father having been a US Marshall and Callie a former Boston PD detective, Jeb had a decent grasp of the culture.

"Yes, we all have the information on her. She disappeared from College of Charleston. That gave me a start. You didn't know her, did you?" Girls this age often reappeared. Nobody had seen her get taken and there'd been no ransom note.

"Yes, Sprite and I know her," he said. "She lives in Sprite's dorm."

That grabbed Callie's ear. "How well does she know her?"

"Well enough to get interviewed by the cops," he said.

That snagged her whole attention. "Since you know her, then what do you think happened?" Her son was level-headed and had proven himself mature beyond his years, especially during her deep-gin days when he'd been the adult in the house.

"She was taken, Mom."

"What do *they* think?"

"Without a ransom note, they can't say."

"No cams?" *Must not have been.*

"They show her leaving the library, going a few blocks, but then nothing. She never arrived at the dorm. Listen, Mom, she was a hard-core student, never accepting anything less than an A. Her father pushed her for sure, but she also pushed herself. She wouldn't just disappear like this. Sprite's afraid to walk to class, so we're tag-teaming wherever we go."

God had blessed her with the perfect son, and Callie reminded herself of that almost every day. "Good for you."

Callie ran through the steps, observations, and interviews the detectives would be doing right now, but she also knew that, absent any evidence of abduction, those detectives would have this voice in the back of their minds saying the girl could've struck out on her own.

"Damn right it's smart, Mom. Someone tried to grab Sprite yesterday."

Chapter 2

Callie
Monday mid-day

WHAT THE HELL? Jeb's news almost knocked Callie back a step. "What do you mean someone tried to grab Sprite?"

"Someone talked trash to her from a van and tried to get her to come closer. She screamed and ran. She was shaking when I found her." His voice ran almost an octave higher than the norm. The life of someone he loved had been threatened, and having dealt with that before, he was having none of it now.

"Does her mother know?" Callie asked, trying not to be heard by Donna and the resident, Mr. Pope.

Of course Sophie didn't know. She'd have come straight to Callie, her zen fractured into a million pieces. Her baby girl meant everything to her.

"God, no, Mom. We weren't going to tell Miss Sophie if we didn't have to."

Whoa. "Not the right call there, Son. You do not hide things like this from a parent."

But Jeb stood his ground. "You know how she is about negative news. She loses her mind, and she'd take Sprite out of school. Instead, Sprite stayed out of class the next day, just the one day, and I calmed her down. She's back in class with our tag-teaming setup."

"Jeb, still. . ."

"Just a minute, Mom. With Langley taken, and it being all over the news, we feel we *have* to tell Miss Sophie now."

Okay. Better. "Tell me you reported Sprite's scare to the campus police," she said.

"We did, but like Langley, there was nothing on a camera anywhere. Sprite didn't think to use her phone. Police took a report, but after Langley disappeared, they came back to us with a detective. They just left. I kinda wanted to talk to you before they interviewed us, or before they left, but you didn't text me back."

"Dang it, Jeb, you could've led with that in your text!"

He might be damn independent, but he was still only twenty-one.

"Damn it," she whispered. Even so, she wasn't sure she could've told them to do or say much differently than they did, short of informing their own parents sooner than they had.

Likely tired of peering up, the councilwoman had gotten out of the patrol car to continue the conversation with Mr. Pope. She kept one eye on Callie, attempting to judge what emergency might be going on.

"Would you tell Miss Sophie?" Jeb asked. "We don't want to come home this week and have to do it."

Too early for fall break. Not yet time for midterms. She agreed it was better to either phone Sophie or Callie do it face-to-face. "I guess I can do it. Y'all stay in class."

"There is no class later in the week, Mom. The school announced probable closure for Thursday and Friday because of the hurricane. What are they predicting for you? We're trying to consider where to go, and I'm not thinking the beach."

That college would shutter sooner than most schools because of its location on the Charleston peninsula, barely one mile from the city's point overlooking the Atlantic. With Hurricane Hugo, every street in Charleston disappeared underwater, and most of everyone's first floor.

"Go to your grandmother's," she said. "She's far enough inland, and she'd appreciate a visit."

Mayor Beverly Cantrell would be up to her ears in hurricane plans for her own constituency, too, but Middleton was twenty-five miles from the water. Low enough to endure serious flooding and the tornadoes that such a storm spawned, but high enough to avoid most serious damage. It was Callie's emergency go-to place as well. The house was on high ground, as high as Lowcountry properties went, in the center of town.

"Chief?" Donna said, having walked over since Mr. Pope had gone inside. "Something wrong? I can leave if you like. Horse and I can walk."

Callie held up a finger to say she'd be right with her.

She attempted to absorb this news from Jeb. It had happened. He'd handled the situation, and he'd handled it without her and done well doing so. Still her instincts were to do . . . something.

"So, you are telling Miss Sophie, right?" Now he sounded more like the little boy asking his mother for help.

Sophie wouldn't like the news, and she damn sure wouldn't like her daughter going to someone else about it first, not much unlike Callie hearing her son had handled a very grown-up situation without her assistance.

"Yeah, I'll tell her." Yeah, this she could do. He'd dealt with everything else quite well, so how could she say no? They said their goodbyes and hung up. Then she had to make the mental shift back to the aftermath of the parking incident.

"You all right?" Donna asked.

"Yeah. An issue with my son at school. He's at College of Charleston, which means hurricane decisions. We're good now." She nodded toward the Pope residence. "Is he good?"

Donna beamed. "Oh, he's lovely," she said. "Thinks you're a badass and I'm the queen of town council."

Callie enjoyed the chuckle. "Then let's get back to work. Thanks for tending to him while I was busy."

"If that's what the job is about, I'm thrilled," the councilwoman said, getting in her own side of the car.

While she was glad to hear that, Jeb and Sprite remained on her mind and, therefore, the missing girl. When she returned to the station, she'd make a call or two. There probably wasn't an abduction, and even if there was, Edisto Beach wasn't much of an abduction destination.

"Ready?" Donna asked, bringing Callie around.

"Absolutely." Clicking her belt and letting Marie know she was back on the road, Callie tallied her morning's progress—resident officially appeased, a day-tripper properly educated, and the novice councilwoman satisfied. Making someone think you've done something on their behalf always worked.

Donna watched her sideview mirror as they put distance between them and the drive. "That was really fun."

"The people are what our jobs are all about. Both yours and mine."

"Excellent teamwork, but I don't see your position one of writing parking tickets all day, Chief."

"I would hope not," Callie said. "But, if we're lucky today, you won't have to experience the more gruesome issues we have. Shark bites, drownings, a heart attack in a hot tub." *Someone getting shot.*

Donna winked. "While I've been exposed to a lot in terms of bodies and calamities as a veterinarian and could handle gross events better than the average councilperson, you are correct. I'm content for you to do your job, and I'll do mine. There's a division of authority we can each respect, I say."

Callie hunted for a small warning hidden in there, but she wasn't sure one was meant.

"Care to grab a meal at El Marko's?" Everyone knew Mark, and Donna had lived on Edisto long enough to be aware of the commercial entities on the beach. Callie left off the fact she lived with the owner. Everyone knew that, too.

"El Marko's? My God, woman, I've eaten a hundred of those mini-quesadilla appetizers. Sometimes I come in for a beer and just that. So sure, let's do lunch."

Yeah, lunch could become a more regular thing with Ms. Baird, especially with the department in dire need of staff. Six uniforms just weren't cutting it anymore.

Donna had bought a place on Portia Street, not far ahead, and once they delivered the Dane to his home, appropriately named *Sea Horse*, Callie did a U-turn on Palmetto. Seven blocks later they parked beside the small strip mall where El Marko's occupied the unit on the west end. With this being Monday, and from the number of cars in the lot, the place was busy.

Sometimes lunch came and went without a stop for Callie, and she and Mark didn't see each other for the entire day. Theirs were long days. She arrived at her work around seven most mornings, the winter allowing her to slide those times around with less activity on the island. He opened the restaurant at eleven. She got off well before he did, meaning she often ate dinner there just to see him. He came home within an hour of midnight, and after an in-and-out shower, fell into bed, waking her for some cuddling and light conversation before crashing. They tried to keep their Sundays open, but tourism had a way of being a demanding taskmaster.

Callie escorted Donna to her VIP table near the kitchen, hoping Sophie wasn't working right now. Not with Jeb and Sprite on Callie's thoughts. "You mind sitting here?" she asked. The table was smaller than the others, a cross between cramped and intimate, depending on who else ate with you. Stan, for instance, her old boss from Boston who'd followed Callie to Edisto when he retired, could take up a sizeable chunk of the table's real estate.

"This is just fine," said her guest.

No sign of Mark. She'd meant to check in on him earlier than this, but Donna's request for a ride-along had distracted her.

He'd been dragging for a week. He ate less, declined alcohol, and she'd seen him drinking straight out of a bottle of Pepto Bismol three times. An ulcer crossed her mind, and she'd mentioned the possibility to him, but he wrote his symptoms off as a bug he must've picked up.

"Should you be working with food?" she'd asked him just this morning. The last thing he or the beach needed was a reputation for food poisoning . . . or worse, Hepatitis A. Eateries went under at the slightest indication of either.

He'd felt the need to defend. "My standards are higher than that, Callie." Not "Sunshine," his cozy nickname for her in times of endearment. She didn't question him about his bug again.

The waitress took their order, and the same waitress brought the order to the table. Mark usually delivered as his excuse to take a break with Callie.

"Where's the boss?" she asked, after the waitress inquired as to what else they needed.

"Oh, he went home, Chief. About two hours ago. Said his stomach was upset, and he didn't want us to catch anything. Miss Sophie is closing tonight."

Donna paused, prepared to box up her meal.

Callie read her. "No, he'd have called if it was important. Enjoy your meal. I'm famished. How about you?" Meanwhile, she shot him a quick text.

"Starved," the councilwoman replied.

The place hopped with diners. Concerned for Mark, Callie didn't dawdle, though, and with Donna having ordered her beloved mini quesadillas instead of a full meal, she didn't waste too much time eating.

"Think he's okay?" Donna asked after consuming her last bite. The doctor in her had clearly recognized Callie's concern, and the fact she'd checked her phone three or four times to find nothing.

"Do you mind?" she asked Donna, indicating she needed to make a call.

"Not at all," the councilwoman replied. "I need to check my messages as well."

Both took to their phones.

It didn't take a minute for Callie to hang up and remove her napkin from her lap. "He's not answering. Mind if I take you back to the station? I can give you a raincheck or pass you over to Thomas, if you like."

"Drop me off at the station," she said, holding up her own phone. "They're calling for the council to meet in a couple hours, so I might as well hang there." The government complex housed everyone, from town council to the police station.

Callie didn't ask about the purpose of the meeting. If it was important, she'd learn soon enough, but her guess was the hurricane.

She dropped off the councilwoman and drove straight home, a mile away on Jungle Road. She slid maybe a foot or two coming in on her gravel drive, telling herself not to worry.

She bounded up the two-dozen steps to her front door, and called, "Mark?" louder than she intended. Not immediately hearing him, much less seeing him, she trotted further in, thinking he might be in the kitchen, his favorite room of the house. Instead, she found him on the sofa, but just as she laid a hand on his shoulder, he jumped up and ran to the guest bath, the closest. His immediate retching drew her up short.

The mic on her shoulder voiced attention. Marie.

"They want you at council meeting at three," she said. "Hurricane Nikki got tired of playing with Owen. She's decided to visit South Carolina. The governor is notifying all coastal towns to start preparations."

"Got it. Gotta go."

But Marie wasn't done. "There's a fresh BOLO about that College of Charleston student yesterday, too. They are looking at it as an abduction now."

A motherly stab of concern ran through her all over again at how close her son and Sophie's daughter were to this incident. She'd have to find time to tell Sophie, sooner rather than later.

"Pass it to the officers, Marie. Got my hands full at the moment. Call you back."

Her phone rang before she could return the radio to its mount. Sophie. She'd probably been watching the news.

But Mark had risen to his feet, wobbling his way to her. She let the call go to voicemail as she met Mark halfway and assisted him to the sofa. "Want some water? Ginger ale?" The fever coming off of him left no doubt he was ill.

His black curls clung to forehead and temples; his pallor foreign to his Cajun complexion. His hands shook when he let go of her. "No, just get me to the hospital, Callie. Something isn't right."

He doubled over, going to his knees on the floor.

Sophie called again. Then Donna.

But right now her choice was the emergency in front of her, not whatever might be on the other end of the phone.

There were no ambulances on Edisto, one of the few downsides to living on the beach. In the time 911 sent one from thirty miles away, Callie could deposit Mark at the St. Francis emergency room herself, blue lights guaranteeing a faster arrival, badge pushing the professionals to hop quicker. First responders took care of first responders.

That's what she repeated to herself while assisting him into her cruiser. In between talking to him, her knuckles tightened at ten and two on the steering wheel, her foot fighting not to push the pedal to the floor.

Mark had taken a bullet in his former life as a State Law Enforcement agent, one that remained in his leg, so he was accustomed to weathering pain. Struggling to remain sitting up, he clearly wasn't weathering this very well.

She scooted across the causeway, out of town, and sped up, "How long have you been nauseous?" She'd asked him before, but a stomach spasm had interrupted his reply, his moans cutting into her heart. He couldn't sit straight. He couldn't lie down. He could barely talk.

"Four, maybe five days," he managed, one hand gripping the door handle, the other braced stiff-armed against the dash.

Why didn't you tell me was thought and discarded, because chastising a man in his state wasn't right. Besides, she knew the answer. Mark was an independent soul, a cop shot in the line of duty. He took care of himself like she took care of herself. Both were tough, and their likenesses drew them together. But they also served as a reflection of how much that mentality could infuriate the partner on the other side.

Behind her body cam, her uniform, and her vest, beneath all that made her strong and impervious, her heart hurt like a big hand squeezed it hard. She'd backed Mark on some simple, quasi-precarious situations in the restaurant. He'd been her backup for assorted crimes on the beach. Both he and Stan, though retired, often came to her aid, whether accompanying her to sordid situations or directing parade traffic.

But she couldn't pull a gun or slap cuffs on this. Scared, she despised this lack of control. He was hurting. For all she knew, he was deteriorating, spiraling into some deep place someone might not be able to pull him out of.

For God's sake, she had just found Mark Dupree. She ought to be praying for God to take care of this man, but instead she cursed, thinking how dare a higher power rob her of someone who got her, welcomed her, loved her. The two other men she'd loved had been murdered. She'd earned the right to have this one.

No, no, she took that back. *Just do what you can do, Callie.*

She was already doing that, though. She drove him toward a place that could tend to him, and she could get him there faster than anyone else, which made her speed up more.

She covered the forty-five miles in thirty-five minutes, half the trip on a two-lane road. Her preemptive radio call had someone waiting when they arrived, and after a whirlwind of them taking him back while she handled the admission, she stood alone, her breaths shallower than she'd like, in the middle of the ER waiting area with nothing to do but wait. She wasn't good at waiting.

Didn't take long for her phone to explode. A police chief couldn't slip away without someone noticing, and the fact she'd left the island, blue lights flashing, would make more than a few curious.

She had already called Marie as she crossed the causeway, but Marie—pinnacle of the station and able to manage the sudden manpower loss—was still due an update. No doubt the station's Wonder Woman had already radioed Thomas, asking him if he could handle things solo until the next shift.

"They took Mark back," Callie said before Marie could say more than hello. "No news yet. He's in so much pain, Marie. I seriously need to wait here."

"Thomas is fine on his own," she said before Callie could ask. "But the town council meeting is in about an hour. Want him to go in your place? Or me?"

Of all days to have one uniform on duty. "I'd rather you go, but we can't shutter the station."

"Of course we can," replied the office manager. "I'll put a sign on the door, leave a number to call, and say where I am, which is literally right next door."

Born and raised Edisto, Marie held a place in the hearts of the island's unofficial royalty—those inhabitants with deeply embedded roots in island dirt. The older residents understood more about Marie's past and why her family had crumbled due to the shortcomings of certain parties in authority. Since an old police chief had promised and failed to take care of the child, there had been an unofficial agreement about tending to Marie. Callie honored that sacred duty, a duty that came with the Chief of Police title since that one so long ago had let down the girl's family.

In her own right, however, Marie was damn good at what she did. A treasure trove of facts, island genealogy, and deep-closet skeletons as they related to every family on Edisto ground. Clearly Edisto was where she was meant to be.

Callie defaulted to her judgment about the meeting without hesitation. "Sure, go ahead. Do that. If council doesn't like it, tell them to stick it." She had no patience for politics now. Her mind was down the hall, through those double doors, fighting not to think of a dozen disastrous diagnoses that fever, nausea, and stomach pain represented.

"They'll be fine with me," Marie said. "Anyone you wish me to call?"

"Let the mayor and council know ahead of time so it's not a shock when you walk in. I'll call everyone else. Half the beach has tried to call me already." She quit counting at a dozen texts and eight voice mails.

She hung up from Marie, debating whether to call Stan or Sophie first. Mark had no family, Callie being all he had. Stan was Mark's best friend. Sophie was Callie's, but also Mark's hostess. That's when she remembered the waitress at El Marko's stating Sophie had been asked to close that night. That decided her next call.

She took herself outside after letting the desk nurse know. Even with a phone to one's ear, anyone close could hear Sophie in the best of conversations, and an episode like this would take the spiritualist-slash-yoga-maven's volume to another level.

"Soph. Mark's in the hospital." Callie let that sink in, allowing the subsequent prattling of phrases, questions, and exclamations play out, because Sophie never let you get a word in edgewise.

"What can I do?" the woman finally asked.

"Can you handle the staff? Arranging who opens and closes El Marko's?"

"For how long? I mean, is this going to cross into my morning yoga classes? I have a business, too. I mean—"

"We're talking a day or two, I imagine." Or so she hoped . . . she prayed. "Be there for me on this, okay?"

If push came to shove, Callie guessed she could open herself, assign staff, leaving after she was done at the station to work the evening to midnight hours. She knew the drill.

"Of course," Sophie said. "Sorry. This is just so sudden. He's so . . . solid. I'd expect you to get hurt before him."

Sophie . . . ever saying the wrong thing at the wrong time.

"Let me go. Got irons in the fire, Soph. People to call."

"Want me to tell Jeb?"

How ironic Sophie asking to call Jeb when Jeb had not long asked Callie to call Sophie.

Jeb would want to know, but Callie thought it better to have more tangible details before stirring him up. Chances were high that he'd come home straightaway rather than wait until Thursday and go to his grandmother's. While he attended college, barely an hour away, classes started just two weeks ago. She didn't need her hand to be held or nearly as much care as her son was prone to think, even if he had begun to let down his protective guard about his mother when Mark moved in and filled the void, giving her son assurance she'd be okay.

Jeb was a natural caregiver. Sweet, admirable, but his propensity for worry stemmed from a family history of death and setbacks. He'd even put his education on hold for a year when she couldn't seem to climb out of the bottle a while back.

"No, Soph. Let's get answers first, okay? Promise me you won't bother him. You know how he is."

Sophie hesitated then agreed, and Callie vowed to call Jeb the minute she hung up. Callie had her doubts Sophie could contain news this big, especially with Jeb dating Sprite, but hopefully she'd keep her word, for a while, anyway.

She disconnected from Sophie and hit the instant dial for Jeb. He was calm. He was assuring. He was better than she was during personal times like this, and she wondered where he inherited that from. "I'll let you know when I know his status," she said.

"You better," he said. "Call if you need me."

A little relieved after talking with him, Callie then notified a couple of restaurant staff, Stan, and a few others.

She hung up and glanced at the lobby clock. Damn, she should have heard something by now. She jumped up and ran to the front desk, inquiring as to Mark's status. Surprisingly, they ushered her back, saying something about having called her name once before.

Mark looked pale. He lay at a forty-five-degree angle on a gurney behind the third curtain. "Hey, you," she said, coming to the bedside. "You don't look like you're in as much pain."

"They give you stuff for that," he said, his smile lazy and slow to spread. Still, he looked exhausted. "They tell you?"

"No. Been on the phone taking care of the station and El Marko's. What did they say?" She ran a hand over his brow then down his temple to his jaw. She couldn't describe the relief she felt at him not wearing deep furrowed wrinkles of agony.

The curtain flowed back, the top grommets zinging along the rod. "Appendicitis," said a deep voice belonging to the doctor's coat, the dark complexion made even darker against the stark white. "They're getting things ready for him now." He came over, looked closely at Mark, then stood back. "Is this your main squeeze?" he asked his patient, before reaching to shake Callie's hand. "Isaac Holt." He studied her name pin and the insignia she wore. "Edisto Beach, huh? My grandfather used to live out there. Wish he'd never sold his place."

"I've heard that a lot. Appendicitis?" she asked, her way of telling the doctor to get back to the details.

"Bad enough to take him right in," he said. "Anything about his health I ought to know that he might've forgotten to tell me in his current state?"

"He has a bullet in his leg," she said.

"Yep, he mentioned that."

For the life of her, she couldn't say if he had any other underlying conditions. No pills in the medicine cabinet at home. That could mean either he ignored his health or he was pretty damn healthy. She leaned toward the latter. "Nope. Nothing I'm aware of, and I'm all he's got," she said, smiling back at Mark's stuck-on smile from the meds. "He's a good guy."

The big doctor chuckled. "Ain't love grand?" He turned aside, spoke to someone waiting outside the curtain, then came back to her. "Well, tell your sweetie goodbye. Give us an hour or two, then we'll let you see him again. Prefer you hang around."

"Trust me. I'm going nowhere."

Then like that, in a blink they adjusted the bed, disconnected the items measuring vitals, and whisked him off, again leaving her alone. Despite the noise and activities around her, the emptiness swept back in.

"Here, let me walk you out," said a nurse when Callie hadn't moved. They started back toward the double doors, then to fill in the quiet, asked, "You keep up with the news?"

Guess it was the uniform.

Callie glanced over and up at the middle-aged woman in pastel scrubs. A solid build, she had five inches and fifty pounds on Callie. "Been preoccupied. Something break in the last few hours?"

"One of our surgeons," she said, hitting an oversized black button that automatically opened the doors. "Dr. St. James. His daughter's gone missing. Didn't come in last night. Student at College of Charleston. We're all praying for them."

"I'll keep an eye out," was all she could think to say, not caring to open a conversation.

The nurse gave her a pat on the arm. "We'll come get you when your husband's out of surgery."

Husband. The word held such a warmth about it. She and Mark spoke loose words about the topic at times. Moving in was practically tying the knot as far as they were concerned, and sharing closet space seemed to scratch that itch for both. Still . . . she hadn't corrected the nurse because she hadn't wanted to. She liked the sound of the word.

Maybe the bat-out-of-hell drive from Edisto with him groaning in misery had awoken her. She wanted this man. She never wanted to lose this man. No doubt he adored her based on all the crossroads they'd navigated these past eighteen months, most of the obstacles hers. Maybe once he was out of here and healed, maybe on the side porch one Sunday, or during a walk down Botany Bay, she'd broach the subject.

Realizing she stood in an area with a dozen people seated, each trying to remain entertained by the television mounted in the corner just over her head, she moved aside and assumed a double seat meant for larger people, to keep from banging her utility belt. Her uniform received side glances from everyone for a while, but when she didn't leave, she ultimately blended in as one of them.

The news was on. Football, right now, a major topic this time of year, then a few other local fall events. Someone was arrested. A fire in West Ashley. Then up flashed the face of a girl around twenty, beautiful as only the young can be.

Langley St. James. Pre-med student. Missing from Copely Hall. Suspected kidnapping.

Charleston wasn't far from Edisto, but who left the mainland for an island when kidnapping someone? One way in. One way out. Edisto wasn't a kidnapping destination, so her concern about the girl wasn't high on Callie's radar. She didn't feel it necessary to hit the streets knocking on doors and flashing a photo.

Mark and a hurricane ranked higher on her scale of possible problems at present.

She leaned over, head in her hands, and tried not to think about the worst that could go wrong.

Chapter 3

Arlo
Prior Sunday evening

THE RENTAL WASN'T bad. *Seas the Day* was located on Arc Street, a one block, narrow road connecting Billow and Neptune Streets. Minimum street traffic since you basically had to be going to one of five houses there to even travel it. Walking distance from the beach but far enough away from the nosey.

Arlo Adkins approved, and since finding the rentals for their vacations was his job, enough said. The three Rangers had developed a sixth sense about them, ever looking over their shoulders. That vigilance struck some as skillful. Others pitied them, assuming PTSD, when in truth, they just didn't want people in their business. They needed their style of rental to accommodate their personalities.

He scoured sites continually for the next great adventure. He used *adventure* loosely since they didn't believe in tourist buses or cruise ships. They might kayak the Mississippi. They might hike the Appalachian Trail. They might fish one of the thousand lakes of Minnesota. None of their adventures involved hordes or even mid-sized gatherings because of their shared claustrophobic distrust of strangers.

Leonard Lowe, Bruce Bardot, and himself. Thrown together overseas, he'd immediately marveled at their double-letter names, and over beers one night, they tried using LAB in a nickname to no avail. Double Lab. LLAABB, and they'd laughed at the stuttering in saying that. Well, he'd laughed more than the others. Bruce hadn't much of a sense of humor, and after innumerable failures, he considered a smile good enough. But even Bruce threw out a few names, with everything sounding lame, until they got liquor-drunk one night. The name evolved from Lab to Labrador, to just The Retrievers.

The name made perfect sense, as if it really mattered. It was a joke between them. What had mattered, though, was the unifying result. Only

Arlo noticed that each of them, in his own way, floundered solo. Admittedly, he needed them more than anyone he'd ever needed.

He never wanted to be like Bruce, though, who married and divorced barely two years later, his wife claiming his mind had never left the Sandbox or his buddies. She tired of playing second fiddle to something invisible. Arlo kind of understood where she was coming from.

Bruce was calm. Too calm, she said. From his days of studying the endless horizon for the enemy and, as a medic, mending those who didn't watch closely enough, he'd developed the patience to watch paint dry and keep his cool. Eerie at times. Soothing at others. Depended on how well you knew him, and currently, those who knew him well included only two people, Leonard and Arlo.

Bruce had scouted the house already, finding the two porches right away. The back faced due north, a large copse of trees blocking the view to a pool and another house. Then beyond that, Whaley's Restaurant. The secluded feeling of being behind trees gave him the peace and protection of not being watched himself. Bruce preferred to do the watching.

The front porch faced south, to the road few cars traveled, with the ocean two blocks over, visible if you peered between two older homes on Palmetto, then two others on Point Street. Waves audible if you listened. He didn't sit still until he'd had an intricate, well-studied lay of the land, at which time he'd calmed, at peace with the address.

Arlo gave him whatever he wanted. Leonard didn't care. Bruce's silence represented an inane patience. Arlo recognized his needs and obliged him with first choice of room each time, attempting to pick a rental—his own assigned task—that contained a room with a wide view.

Leonard stood three inches above the others, and right now he carried the first load up the two flights of exterior stairs, a duffle bag as big as he was and half his weight. Arlo never bothered to assist. Leonard likened himself to the He-Man, the strong one. Living areas in Edisto houses stood fourteen feet above ground, just in case of storms, and those stairs stoked his incessant need to exercise. He came into the house, went back to Bruce's room, and deposited the duffle gently on the bed. The rule was to take care of Bruce first, and his large duffle was the first to be brought in. Its cargo was precious.

Upon his return to the States, Leonard had worked side jobs, unable to settle into one full time. He spent every free moment taxing himself in the gym, on the track, doing whatever wore him out so he could sleep at night. He carried muscle atop of muscle and prided himself on completing a Murph Challenge within forty minutes—a workout performed by athletes on Memorial Day, in honor of Navy SEAL Lieutenant Michael Murphy who died in Afghanistan in 2005. Leonard pushed himself monthly, always seeking to cut a second off his time. He went nowhere without his twenty-pound vest, because one never knew when he would wake with the urge to hit the road to do his mile, then his hundred pullups, two hundred pushups, three hundred squats, finishing with another mile. Sometimes all three joined in. Most often they gave Leonard the time he needed to test himself alone.

Arlo—"Pretty Boy," they occasionally called him—didn't mind his buddies' quirks, and honestly, he didn't mind preening a bit. Gave his self-assurance a little icing, you know?

He'd decided that they needed to meet more and more often until their getaways had evolved. One didn't do what they did overseas without bringing baggage home, and they understood each other and where their cracks were. So now they traveled together throughout the year, an unofficial family. He'd never told them how much this soothed him. He never asked them how they liked it. The unsaid was that this worked for reasons that didn't need to be discussed.

Their financial needs were few, and their *permanent* address was a small rental duplex in Franklin, Tennessee, that had been Arlo's residence for a few years prior. No income tax in the state. For all Uncle Sam knew, all three lived there. The government got squirrelly when you didn't plant roots, so the men gave the Feds something tangible to tamp down any curiosity.

While Leonard unloaded the rest of their things, Bruce set up his bedroom, and Arlo turned the rental into their temporary home. He relished doing the cooking, and he had a system. They rarely stayed anywhere long. Nine days tops. They preferred six. They'd done this so many times they read each other's minds as to when it was time to pull up stakes and scratch their itch to be gone. Edisto, however, booked in terms of weeks, so two it was.

Their routine was so ritualistic, they were set up in thirty minutes.

"Making a call then I'm hitting the beach," Leonard said. "Been dying to put in two miles on sand. How long is this beach?"

"Four miles," Arlo said.

"Then four it is." He snatched up his own bag and disappeared into a bedroom, and in two minutes, he returned in shorts, shoes, and no shirt. He bounded out the front door, phone to his ear. They might not see him for an hour depending on how he felt running, whether he ran the beach once, or twice, or more. Driving caused pent-up energy, and he had to release it somewhere.

"I'll be in my room," Bruce reported, turning to leave.

"Well, my work here is done," Arlo said. "Time for me to grab groceries. You good alone, man?"

Bruce looked back with a stoic, are-you-shitting-me glance then left the room to sit in his—to think, to look out the window, to go to that place he always went to for enough hours in the day to keep him sane.

From the outside looking in, they were a tight camaraderie forged by the deployment of war. Beautiful men. Polite. Patriotic to the point of envy. They unintentionally captured the female eye and intentionally kept them at arm's length. They grabbed the occasional booty call, but permanent was not in the cards, and once a woman learned that they usually left them alone.

But on the way to the grocery store, Arlo pondered whether to grab that real estate receptionist and enjoy a couple hours with her. Dinner. Her place afterwards. He doubted she would say no.

Chapter 4

Callie
Monday evening

SHE COULDN'T SIT here and mope and dream up bad scenarios, so she called her support guy. Her old boss Stan said he'd hit the road and join her, but she told him to hang around the restaurant just in case. She called Thomas despite Marie having also done so, and he assured her he had things covered. She started to call her mother, then didn't.

Mother—as in Beverly, the adopted one who'd reared her—would insert drama Callie didn't need right now. But she could call Sarah later, her biological mother who lived two doors down from Callie on Edisto Beach. Again, best to do so with good news, not reason to fret.

Weird how the mother she didn't know about until a couple years ago had become the one she'd run to in time of need, and the one who'd raised her had taken a back seat. Emotionally, anyway. She ought to feel guilty about that. Sometimes she did, but being around Beverly usually dispelled the guilt.

Recognizing the fact she was just searching for something to do, Callie quit making calls. She had no news anyway. She leaned back in her seat, seeking a comfortable position, then before settling too far, reached for her phone and searched for the name Langley St. James.

A few local news sites popped up, most of them displaying the same canned story. Pre-med student. Junior year. Honors college. Came from Porter-Gaud, a private high school in downtown Charleston where she'd graduated second in her class. Her father was Justin St. James, thoracic surgeon, fifth generation Charlestonian. Mother deceased five years ago.

Langley was reported missing by her roommate early this morning, when she didn't come home. Being such a diligent student, the fact she'd failed to show up for Anatomy Lab underscored something wrong. The roommate reported to the RA of the dorm hall, who reported to the college's powers that be, who contacted Dr. St. James and the police. No ransom yet, per the press, not that the press would know. Kidnappers frowned upon their business being on news networks . . . assuming this was a kidnapping.

Callie wondered who'd leaked the news story so soon with a ransom in limbo.

If the case were hers, she'd be asking the obvious questions. Did Langley have a boyfriend or girlfriend? How did she get along with her father? Had she seemed upset lately? Why didn't someone call last night? What had been done to check her usual hangouts, study places, and friends?

Charleston had a decent police department. Callie expected them to perform with optimum efficiency. Still, focusing on Langley had given her some respite from worry.

Twenty-five minutes ticked by. The town council meeting should had started. She pulled up multiple weather reports to see how serious the storms looked. Nikki had grown, and though still a rough tropical storm, her shape had concentrated. That's what storms did. They played around in the Atlantic until conditions ripened such that they acquired shape and grew, or they thinned and dissipated, with insufficient power to do much more than rain.

In Callie's history on this earth, she'd experienced a myriad of tropical storms and stunted remnants of hurricanes along with the tornadoes they spawned and the floods that destroyed homes. She had vague memories of the granddaddy of them all, Hurricane Hugo, that drove straight into Charleston and came up through Middleton when she was eight.

She barely saw her parents for weeks after with all the clearing and construction and aid relief required for so many residents. A blue tarp covered their own roof for five or six months before overworked roofers could get to them on the waiting list, her father refusing to put his needs ahead of his constituents. She remembered an elephant-shaped watermark on her bedroom ceiling for the longest time before Beverly had the entire interior repainted. A true Category-5 hurricane. Those weren't common.

After Callie moved to Boston and married, Edisto experienced a taste of Frances and its four-dozen tornadoes across the state, but Matthew was the worst in 2016. She'd offered to come down and assist in the cleanup of *Chelsea Morning*, her parents' beach house, now her own residence. Being four blocks off the beach, it fared better than most. Just flooding and wind cleanup, while the houses along the water had septic tanks exposed and carried off a block away. Palmetto Boulevard was buried eight feet under displaced sand. It took the better part of a year to clean up the town with the Corps of Engineers' assistance. However,

Irma followed on Matthew's heels the next year with the highest storm surge since Hugo.

Edisto and Charleston hadn't been harassed much since. At least not with anything scary. It was easy to get lulled into complacency.

Hurricanes were a part of Carolina living, and most of them wound down before hitting the state with only rain. Natives went with the flow, knowing full well how to prepare and, since Hugo's harsh lesson, how to evacuate.

Callie had not experienced one in her tenure as chief. She hoped she never had to.

She kept hitting the replay button showing time lapsed predictions of where Nikki would make landfall. The storm had covered a lot of ground today and proven she no longer wanted to play, taking her role as a menacing storm seriously. Per all the predictions, she would make landfall in Florida, South Carolina, or North Carolina, with one forecast as far north as Virginia. That was the problem with these things. You often didn't know until the day before, maybe two, if you were lucky, whether you had a potential disaster on your hands. It's why so many people held hurricane parties and remained in their homes. Odds were you only got rain, but on the off chance those odds went against you, you could lose everything, including your life.

The empty lot on the beach across from *Windswept*—Mike Seabrook's house on the land side of Palmetto—had once had a house on it. Matthew swept it off its foundation and halfway out to sea, giving *Windswept* a clear view of the ocean and higher tax value.

The thought of taxes reminded her that Marie ought to be in the thick of the meeting with town council now. Callie wished she were there, especially with Donna Baird on board. A pending storm would provide this new councilwoman a true test of her leadership. Not quite fair her being tested by something so serious so early in her fledgling tenure, but her constituents would have to hope she was up to the task. It's what they elected her for.

The clock said ninety minutes had passed since they'd wheeled away Mark. Dr. Holt said an hour . . . or two. In a stupid flash of alarm, Callie wondered what the problem was, then told herself the doctor was only being thorough.

Only an appendix, right? She made the mistake of doing a search on her phone for the procedure. One hour. Everything said one hour. So why wasn't Mark's procedure one hour?

She'd endured stakeouts for hours at a time, where the slightest flick gave you away, so you learned not to shoo a mosquito or move quickly. So why couldn't she be patient for a simple surgical procedure? Unless it wasn't so simple?

Two minutes to the two-hour mark. Had Mark, hiding his discomfort, exacerbated his condition to the point of dire . . . or worse?

Think of something else. The missing girl, the suspected abduction just flashed on TV again. No sign of her anywhere. No ransom call, note, or text. Not Callie's immediate business, though. Mark came first, and the hurricane second. Plus, the officers under her would be routinely aware of BOLOs. The description was out there, the updates readily available even though she'd expect them to be more attentive to the storm.

For the longest time during this wait, Tropical Storm Nikki continued as projected, moving east but at no pace to be concerned about . . . until about ten minutes ago. Forecasts began to shift, more of them pointing to a landing swath between Savannah and Myrtle Beach. What had been a wide array of forecasts, scattering the projected landfall up and down the eastern seaboard had tightened to a funnel directing winds to South Carolina, to include Edisto and Charleston.

An urge to head home zinged from head to toe, warring with her concern for Mark, but Marie hadn't called, probably still in the meeting. *And where the hell was the news of Mark's procedure?*

"Chief Morgan?"

She jerked around, biting her tongue on the words *About damn time.* She stood, fighting hard to appear patient. "Yes?"

Two hours to the minute. She'd about built up steam to go hunt somebody. She'd never seen herself as one of those family members, but she got it now.

"So sorry, ma'am. We—"

Her heart hit her ribs like a fist. "Sorry about what? What happened? They said an hour."

The nurse smiled and held up her hand. "No, no, I'm just saying sorry for the wait. He's out of surgery and waking up. Would you like to come on back?"

They'd waited until Mark woke up to get her? "Thank you," Callie said, and tried damn hard to walk at the nurse's pace instead of strong-arming her to the wall to get through.

They'd had an unexpected ten-minute delay in starting the surgery which had led to a domino effect of other things. No concern, they said.

No concern. Right. No harm done except for her imagining him dead in a corner with nobody remembering to come tell her.

They traveled down one hall, then another, then into the recovery area, her gaze scanning every curtain, every bed. Finally, there he was. He seemed to be attempting to clear his head, his blinking in slow motion. She rushed to the bedside. "Mark?"

"Cops can be the worst," said the booming voice behind her. "Great in a crisis for everyone else, but not so much when it's their loved one."

Guess she wasn't so good at hiding the panic.

But she liked that voice. It sounded certain and comforting. She didn't argue with his assumption about cops and their private feelings, because he wasn't far from right.

Dr. Holt patted her lightly on the back. He had big hands. Big enough for Callie to fathom how he was a good surgeon when a scalpel would be like a toothpick in that grip. "He was lucky," he said. "That little do-nothing piece off his intestine had a slight leak to it."

Callie flashed concern, but the doc waved his big hands in assurance. "We just had to take some extra time to ensure no infection had escaped or at least traveled very far. You don't want to shortcut that. But he ought to be fine. He's on antibiotics and a few other drugs, as you can tell, and your average doctor might say he could go home as soon as he's alert, but honestly, I'd rather that be tomorrow. You have a problem with that?"

How could she have a problem with that? This gentle giant had just saved her guy. "I'm eternally grateful. I'm totally good with him spending the night." She was totally good for two nights. His appendix had leaked. What happened to being safe than sorry?

"As a result of your little setback, shouldn't he stay longer?"

Her phone vibrated with a text, then another. She really wasn't interested in doing cop work now, nor did she want to update people about Mark until he was awake and talking.

"Ordinarily I might say yes, if we had the beds to spare, but with this hurricane coming down on us, we'll get slammed. It might be safer for him to go home and prepare for the storm, don't you think? Rather than have family back and forth in this weather?" He smiled a big toothy smile. "Honestly, he's good."

She didn't like the use of the word ordinarily. "Are you sure?"

"Yeah, it'll be all right." He looked at his watch. "Got a few others to see to. I'll leave y'all alone." Dr. Holt was gone.

"Sunshine?" The voice came out raspy. Mark swallowed and tried again. "What's going on?" He frowned with sluggishness, unhappy with his word choice.

"Hey," she said, running a hand around the side of his face and holding it there, letting him know her presence. "I'm here. They took out your appendix, but it was leaking, they said, so the procedure took a bit longer. They want to keep you overnight. I'll be right here the whole time then take you home tomorrow."

He smiled, then he didn't.

She snatched her hand back, afraid she'd caused an issue. "Are you in pain?"

"No, no," he mumbled. "You shouldn't stay. The station . . . the restaurant."

"Both taken care of," she said, gently returning her touch. More texts hummed through, proving her a liar. Then a call.

"You better take that," he said around numbed senses.

She lightly chuckled. "Guess you are coming around." She lifted her phone, caller ID the police station. "Chief Morgan."

"First," Marie said. "How's Mark?"

"Out of surgery. Appendicitis. He will be released tomorrow but has some recuperating to do. At least they didn't cut him wide open."

"Glad to hear good news. They were asking about him at the council meeting. Speaking of which . . ."

"Wait." It was after six in the evening. "Why are you still at the station? Did the council meeting go long?"

"Have you been watching the weather?"

"Off and on. No sound on the television. I see Nikki flexing and becoming a threat. Landfall later this week. Why?"

"At the meeting, they said the governor wants us to prepare for a hit. Most of the forecasts show Edisto getting hammered. Whether it makes landfall in Charleston or Savannah, we're right there."

"Prepare as in . . . what?"

"Suggest people leave the coastal areas."

Wonderful. Guess she hadn't been totally tuned in. Truth was she'd just been watching the pictures, the sound turned down low, her mind elsewhere.

"Council will be meeting again tomorrow. They want you there," Marie said.

"Did they give you a difficult time?" Surely not.

"Not me personally, but I can take whatever they dole out, Chief. The new councilwoman, Donna Baird, however, was extremely nice, and she came to your defense. Said you were too busy saving Mark's life. That shut them up."

She most likely had done just that. "I'm leaving in a little bit. Have to return to get Mark tomorrow. I'll get back here first thing but don't have a release time quite yet."

"Meeting is at noon," Marie said.

Somehow that didn't sound doable. An hour to Charleston. An hour back. Mark's release anytime in the morning. That didn't count the restaurant opening at eleven, with setup taking an hour beforehand. "I'll do my best. Time you went home." No point in spending overtime they'd sorely need for the storm days. She sent Marie on her way with thanks, and she hung up.

They were initiating the hurricane plan. Callie had two officers on duty tomorrow in addition to herself. No more one-officer staffing for a while, until long after the hurricane came and went. She saw overtime on the horizon and a full-on presentation at the council meeting tomorrow, especially with the new member showing signs of sway in Callie's direction.

She turned back to Mark.

He gave her a feeble grin. "I see it all over your face. You've got the beach tugging at you. What is it?"

Bless this man. Here he was laid up in surgical recovery asking about her. If that wasn't something to love, what was?

"How upset would you be if Stan retrieved you tomorrow? They want to release you then because of the storm. I want them to keep you, but they might get busy with Nikki."

"I don't mind in the least," he said, slowly but gaining in awareness. "I'd rather go home as soon as possible anyway. By the way, make Sophie open El Marko's in the morning."

In the morning meant eleven for the public. Ten or so for staff. "I'll do my best," she said.

"If you can't, you can't." Even doped up he read her concerns.

However, he didn't need to be worried about her, the restaurant, or what may or may not happen on the beach. He just needed to get well. When she got him home, she'd prop him up in the living room and cuff him to the sofa if he tried to step out and help. She needed him well, not handicapped by a setback from working too soon.

She kept him company until they moved him to a room, then she ensured he was settled in for the night. It didn't take long for him to doze off after she kissed him and told him to rest. At almost nine, she made her way to the parking garage, sat in her car, and studied hurricane projections.

Damn it.

This was Monday night. Nikki's landfall was loosely expected for Thursday night. If an evacuation was suggested, they'd warn people to make preparations for such forty-eight hours ahead of time to then proceed thirty-six hours ahead of time, meaning roughly noon Wednesday. The middle of the day. Good.

Most residents understood the dangers of hurricanes. Tourists usually ran scared of them.

Hurricanes brought attention, for sure, but King Tides and lower-grade tropical storms could flood just about anything on the beach and a major chunk of the island. The houses in the beach town rarely exceeded ten feet above sea level, so a storm surge of that many feet, meaning a storm at high tide, could destroy property. Luckily history had blessed Edisto over the years, with it usually missing the major storms due to geographically being tucked in like a cove along the coastline between Florida and North Carolina. But beach towns invariably got hit. Maybe every fifty years. Sometimes every ten. Sometimes two. But people around when it happens only care about what happens to them then, not what the odds are.

Callie's brain scrambled to review a list of the important communications. When the station was closed, they had a recording. The station's phones would be swamped with calls on what to do, what's required, and how the police department would take care of anything and everything that interrupted people's vacations. Forget that everyone who lived on the island had hurricane preparedness pounded into their heads year-round, and visitors were informed to get travel insurance and, especially during June through November, to study up on what to do, where to go, and how to manage. They had apps for this now. Any cell phone could be pinged with warnings and directions. Funny how technology took over when Nature got angry.

The human-nature side, however, was not to worry about a crisis until caught in the middle of one. Callie had a lifetime studying human behavior to validate that.

One good thing, this didn't appear to be a Category Four or Five. Not yet, and hopefully never. But with Edisto being on the opposite end of a major span bridge, the McKinley Washington Bridge over the Dawhoo River, the public was told to get safely on the other side before winds exceeded forty miles per hour. One major gust when driving across the apex of said bridge and no telling where your car could wind up.

Come Wednesday, day after tomorrow, she'd have to set up a roadblock, usually around the Edistonian, on Highway 174. People would be allowed to leave. Nobody would be allowed to enter. The worst would be rental owners who'd be wanting to see to their real estate before the hit. They'd be turned around, angry as hornets.

Technology would notify everyone, negating the need to go house to house, though she and her officers would make rounds, answering questions, warning folks to leave.

She pulled out of the hospital garage and headed home, over the speed limit but short of lights flashing, her mind still tumbling. She wanted to reach the restaurant and see that it had been closed properly. While staff remained, she hoped to see that it had a sufficient contingency plan for the next day. Enough of them had to be available for the crowd, and there would be a crowd. Amazing how people didn't seek shelter off the beach until mandated to do so, but they'd be all abuzz about the pending weather and flittering around excited, comparing stories, seeking people who'd weathered the storms before to see if they were doing things right. And they'd do it over drinks and good food.

She had to ensure the restaurant opened around eleven a.m. and make the council meeting at noon. She prayed no other calamity reared its head and that the citizenry and guests didn't lose theirs.

She used Bluetooth to place a very overdue call. "Hey, boss. Need to update you."

"I was about to feel hurt you might be putting me last, Chicklet."

After having visited Callie in her earlier days, when gin was her daily coffee and depression her diet, Stan had moved there to tend to her, then fell in love with the place. He started the Hawaiian shirt trend that Mark had copied. Their shared taste in wardrobe and careers in law enforcement had bonded them, and a day didn't go by without Stan occupying a place at El Marko's bar or grabbing a bite at the tiny VIP table near the kitchen.

Callie updated him on the surgery.

"I could have taken him . . . but I get it. So, what is it you need from me other than a shoulder?"

"They want to release him tomorrow, if you can believe that. After surgery! All because of the storm." That fact still gnawed at her.

"Chicklet, they wouldn't let him go if he wasn't able. Besides, I'll watch him."

"So," she started, hating to ask. "Can you pick him up tomorrow and bring him home? Between the restaurant and another council meeting . . ."

"Say no more. Besides, I've got much more mass for him to lean on, just in case."

She still felt like a heel. "I hate asking. I hate more not being there for Mark."

"I know you do, but he'd want me if he couldn't have you. I'm more than happy to play second fiddle here so you can keep the home fires burning and the dangers at bay."

"What would I do without you, Captain Waltham?"

"What you always do, Chicklet. Get things done. Go ahead and check this box and move on."

She loved the nickname. It was endearing and long-standing, going back to when they met. He lived on Big Red, an old-timey chewing gum that left him smelling of cinnamon. In the guise of bringing an apple to the teacher, in the early days she'd brought him the wrong kind of gum. Because of her mistake, along with her diminutive five-foot two size versus his six feet and accompanying mass, he'd nicknamed her with a gum name that defined her.

The nickname gave her a small sense of peace each time he used it.

That was all she needed to tell him, honestly, but they didn't hang up. Instead, he kept talking until she crossed the Scott Creek Causeway into town limits, and once she parked at the restaurant lot, he met her at the entrance with a smothering hug.

"I ain't waiting tables, but I can wash dishes," he said, as they took note of who was there and what had to be done in Mark's absence. The time was only ten thirty, but Sophie had just gone home according to the wait staff.

This was why Callie kept El Marko's on her to-do list. Sometimes Sophie's priorities only made sense to her. Mark could fire the woman, but everyone loved her too much.

Chapter 5

Callie
Tuesday morning

TUESDAY MORNING. Callie rose early, pre-dawn but the air warned of exceptionally warm temperatures. She hadn't slept well. The emptiness of the other side of the bed and the upcoming day's expectations made her restless.

She had to prep and check on staff at El Marko's before its doors opened at eleven, and, of course, half of the beach ran around like crazies about the pending storm reminding her she likewise had to get to work. Right now, they were excited. Tomorrow they'd be wary. Thursday they'd be losing their minds.

El Marko's first. For an hour she made calls and donned an apron to help prep its kitchen. She'd woken Sophie and begged her to get in there and substitute for Mark, but Sophie insisted she needed to tend her nine a.m. yoga class first. Yoga was as sacrosanct to her as law enforcement was to Callie. She promised to appear by ten thirty.

Callie was forced to ask Mark's right-hand staffer Wesley to come in early. She'd pay him double time out of her own pocket, if necessary, but being the good young man he was, he agreed to be there in thirty minutes. She should've called him instead of Sophie to begin with.

He arrived and grabbed an apron before saying a word. "Is Mark all right?" He wasn't accustomed to seeing Callie running point. When fully staffed, they had a system that often required little more than an hour of prep time, but Callie couldn't rely on everyone showing up, or how many diners would appear, or which staff might bail to prepare for the storm.

All of which made Callie wonder at what point to close the place. She wasn't about to do that without Mark's input, but that decision could wait until he was home.

"He had surgery, and he'll be okay, but he won't be a hundred percent for a couple weeks," she said.

"On top of having Nikki come to town, too," Wesley said, now armed with a knife adeptly dicing onions and peppers at a speed she wouldn't dare risk.

Wesley dumped the diced pieces in a bowl and commenced dicing another stack. "Well, tell him we got this. I know who to call and who can come in, Callie. You have a town to police."

Wesley's main source of income was El Marko's. The man would work every hour Mark gave him. To think that Mark had met him when Callie accused Wesley of stealing a four-hundred-dollar sweater. Only someone else had stolen the garment and given it to him as a gift. To make amends, Mark had hired him on the spot, and Wesley had been incredibly loyal.

It was after eight o'clock. Before turning the restaurant over to Wesley, she rang Sophie. "I'm gone. Wesley's here. Try to get here before eleven, please."

"My class . . ."

"You bailed early on me last night," she told Sophie before she could whine. "I can't afford that today. Mark can't afford it."

Sophie's silence meant she'd clouded up, but Callie had no time for dramatics. "Mark is incapacitated until after this storm. This place is his livelihood, and he's adjusted schedules around you and your yoga, not to mention your dates, more times than I can count. He relies on you, loves you, and swears by you, and this is not the time to prove him wrong."

Callie envisioned those coral-colored fingernails balled into fists and going to Sophie's hips.

"I might have a house to board up," Sophie said. "You know how it gets around here. Soon you won't be able to find anyone to do it for you, and I'm not standing on those extension ladders to do it myself." Callie understood how dangerous it could be shuttering these houses that rose two stories off the ground. The beach wasn't to that point yet, but Sophie tended to err on the side of caution. Her storm shutters were custom, and she had a system of how they went on and off.

"Promise me," Callie said. "Ten thirty."

"I'll try to—"

"Promise."

"All right, I promise. Guess I can coordinate my shutters from my phone."

Callie hung up and headed to the station. This was Tuesday morning. Nikki wasn't due until late Thursday night. By tonight, however, once they entered that forty-eight-hour window before landfall, people should be making their plans.

Surprisingly, Sophie and the long-time residents were the bigger issue in times like these. They had their emergency kits, their plans, and made their decisions on how to weather a storm without input from anyone else. They preferred to ride out a storm, protecting their real estate. An occupied house had less chance of being vandalized. Residents had endured Mother Nature enough times to not underestimate her, but they also felt they could read her better than most.

Callie pulled in two officers, putting the others on stand-by, with Officer Annie Greer coming in on her own. Having lived over an hour inland her whole life she'd paid attention to hurricanes but never endured the brunt of them. This would be her first. "I'd rather be busy than wait for something to happen," she told Callie when she magically appeared. "Pay me or not, I'm here to help."

Callie nodded toward the lobby full of people. "Can you answer questions? I know this is your first hurricane, but you've been trained. You've lived your whole life in South Carolina. Care to dive in?"

"Sure," the young officer said, bellying up to the counter dividing the public from the desks. Marie motioned for the next person to go to Annie, and the line moved faster.

People entered this station to ask questions and fuss. People lined up at the gas station to fill up their vehicles and every gas container they could grab, and they complained about others getting more or cutting in line. The Food Lion, not long ago Bi-Lo, not long before that Piggly Wiggly, had all cash registers going full throttle with people grabbing and hoarding what they felt were essentials. For some, that was beer, chips, hot dogs, and charcoal. For others, it was the proverbial milk, bread, and anything in a can. The wine shelves were emptying fast along with—thanks to memories of COVID—toilet paper. Sometimes you couldn't make rhyme or reason out of why products like shampoo and cake mix were grabbed three or four at a time. Half of these people would change their minds and leave the island anyway, but they told themselves they had no idea how bad things would be up the road.

People bought like they expected the apocalypse.

This is what hurricanes did to communities. The shift in barometric pressure altered folks' personalities. People wanted to be told what to do or hated being told what to do, and if you dared do the opposite, they cursed you for not reading them appropriately.

It wasn't as if people weren't schooled on what to do and when to do it.

By noon, Mark hadn't arrived home, Stan texting that the doctor had been delayed with an emergency before Mark had been released. Callie finished reading, put away her phone, and entered the council meeting.

The mayor opened. "Florence, Matthew, and Irma," he said, slowly studying each person as if looking for sinners on Sunday morning to preach to. "Not a one of them bore directly down on Edisto Beach, yet most of us remember the damage. That cone they love to show on television and news sites doesn't mean if you aren't in it you won't see damage. Wind, storm surge, flooding, and tornadoes occur outside the cone. And a myriad of hazards can occur. Remember, we're in Zone A, people."

Zones were relatively new. Zone A meant first evacuated. The state's Emergency Management Division had created a website that was rather elementary in explanation of zones, hazards, shelters, etc. to include an interactive graphic that showed how dangerous flooding was with a three-foot surge, then six, nine, and more as compared to a man, a car, and a house. Just the three-footer could take a grown man off his feet and sweep him away.

Callie sat patiently, listening to words they'd all heard, studied, and experienced. She had attended tabletop emergency responder scenarios with Colleton County where they studied sundry storm surges and how far inland they'd spread and the damage they'd inflict. Most recently, they'd run through a nineteen-foot surge, never seen before but still possible. They had to be aware of what might occur.

That level of a surge would put the entire island of Edisto, almost seventy square miles, under water. That explained part of why there were no serious shelters on the island.

"We're in OPCON 4 right now," the mayor said. "By tomorrow we expect to slide into OPCON 3. Don't be surprised if this storm increases that we don't just leap into OPCON 2. If that occurs, we convince these people to leave. Mandatory evacuation starts when—"

"Excuse me, Mr. Mayor," Callie interrupted. "We can no longer mandate evacuation. Pure voluntary."

"Of course, of course," he replied. "But we can try."

"We can strongly suggest, yes."

He wasn't fond of being corrected, but he moved on. This man had been a friend of the deceased Brice LeGrand, and though he wasn't nearly as caustic as Brice had been, he seemed to still carry a small torch to poke at Callie on occasion. But he was a gnat compared to Brice's stings.

"When the storm makes its approach, then throughout and after, we follow the Incident Command System which will keep us in touch and in tune with the county and state as to what is done. The Edisto Beach Police Department, along with the Colleton County Sheriff's Office and the Edisto Beach Fire Department, will control people movement in and out of the disaster area. Remind people with special medical needs about the Colleton Medical Center in Walterboro. For those not continuing through Walterboro toward North Augusta, the regular shelters are in assorted locales in Walterboro, Ruffin, and Cottageville."

Everyone in the room was aware, but the mayor was getting this information on the record. Some of it might've been specifically for Donna Baird's ears, but kudos to him for wanting everyone on the same sheet of music.

"Be aware of the re-entry levels afterwards, because you know as well as I do that people will be asking you to bend those rules when the time comes. They'll ask you how they can get back in earlier and want an exception."

Callie added, "And if they can't see how they can get back and tend to their property, enough of them will stay behind and risk the storm. So be not only informative, but also understanding, and particularly suggestive of evacuation. Re-entry protocols are for everyone's safety."

"And ask everyone to sign up for CodeRED," Donna said. "To me, that's about the smartest thing I ever saw to provide alerts. I've lived here for three years and wasn't on it until Chief Morgan explained it to me." She smiled at Callie, who returned the gesture in thanks.

Callie knew all of this. So did the rest of the room short of Donna, but the mayor continued. The radio stations, the television stations, the websites. The phone numbers. A reminder that homeowners had special stickers identifying them when it came to coming and going.

"Food Lion is struggling already," said a councilman.

Not a soul was surprised. "Nothing we can do about that except stop people from looting, fighting, or causing problems," the mayor said, nodding at Callie.

Another member spoke up. "Yeah, they're out of ice. The storm isn't for two more days, and they're out of friggin' ice."

Again, nobody surprised.

"They should get another delivery later today," said another.

Nothing covered here was news to anyone, except for Donna, maybe. Storms were part of island life. Nobody was ever surprised at what might happen or had happened in the past. It was what it was. Coastal living in the Carolinas came with such weather, and to move here, or travel here, without being aware of the potential, was simply naive.

Two council members got hung up on the occurrences from the last storm, wondering how to prevent such damage in the future, but they might as well have been talking to the wall. Predicting hurricane damage was like picking the right lottery numbers.

Callie imagined where Stan was right now with Mark. She'd sure like to hear when Mark would be home.

But she had to be here. Her presence, and that of the fire chief, gave assurance to the others. When the storm hit the fan, so to speak, she and her people, along with the county and their people, would kick into gear. Civilians like these liked to act authoritatively, but when anything went south, they couldn't tell up from down.

The rehash of what to expect and what was expected of each person there, took around ninety minutes. Callie hung around just in case there were questions.

Donna came up to her afterwards. "So far I'm finding these town council meetings dry as dirt and preaching the obvious. Did I miss something?"

"Most of this was for your benefit," Callie said under her breath. "In case you hadn't noticed . . ."

"I'm the only female on the council," she finished.

"And the newest." Callie smiled at the oldest tenured councilman, who nodded in his exit. "Just give them a little grace. Especially now. Some of them don't work as well under pressure as you might think. Did you do emergency surgery on animals?"

"Many times."

"Then I suspect you handle pressure just fine and better than most of these gentlemen. Call me if you have any questions."

Truth was Callie had never kicked the beach's full emergency plan into gear. Since she'd held the job, there hadn't been much more than a tropical storm or two each year; most of the bigger storms hit Florida. Last year the Sunshine State had taken a massive beating multiple times, and woe be to them for it. However, storms hitting land to the south before they reached South Carolina, lost energy and saved the Palmetto State from its own beating.

Projections weren't as positive for that happening this year.

They parted, and Callie returned to the police station right down the hall. They kept a couple of television screens up on the wall to keep abreast of breaking news, and in times like this, they would split screens to keep four channels alive.

As she walked in, she instinctively glanced up. The weather channel showed the hurricane path, still over two days out. Another channel spoke of politics. A third, however, flashed up that same photo of the pretty girl, Langley St. James. She paused to see where that case had gone, to see if she'd missed anything over the last couple of hours.

"Yeah, timing sucks for that poor girl," Marie said, noting Callie's interest and using the remote to turn up the volume. The words *College of Charleston Coed No Longer a Suspected Kidnapped Victim* scrolled across a caption at the bottom.

"She came home, I bet," Callie said.

Marie nodded. "Yeah, sounds like an honor student without a lot of common sense. Or there's some family stuff we aren't aware of."

"Can you turn that up again?"

Marie did just as Dr. St. James took a place in front of a microphone.

"This is an apology to the community. My daughter finally contacted us and said she is safe. Thanks to everyone who tried to find her, and who thought she was abducted. I cannot thank you enough."

The screen flipped back to a reporter's desk at the station as they recapped, practically *tsking* at the stress this girl caused her family.

Marie turned the volume back down.

Callie was still somewhat intrigued. Since when did they put a family member behind a microphone to call off a search? "Marie. Can you back that up to the father, please?"

Marie could run everything technical in the station, so Callie hadn't attempted to learn. Besides, Marie kept the controllers locked in her desk.

The father reappeared.

Callie moved closer to the screen and studied the man as he gave his short announcement saying his daughter was safe. "Pause it."

Marie did. "Why, what is it?"

"Not sure," Callie mumbled, studying the doctor's expression.

Officer Thomas Gage walked in.

"Thomas," Callie said, using hand gestures for Marie to back up and replay Dr. St. James. "Tell me what you think about this?"

He came up beside her. "As in, what?"

"This is the missing girl's daddy. Watch him and listen, then tell me."

Again, Dr. St. James gave his message. Marie stopped it at the end, freezing the man's face.

"I'm seeing one less thing for me to worry about," he said.

"Don't disappoint me, Thomas."

He studied the still picture, hoping to impress his boss or learn something new. "I think it's weird he felt he personally had to quickly get in front of the cameras. Charleston P.D. would've had this covered. They would've told all LEO the BOLO was cancelled, and his attorney could have issued a statement on behalf of the family to the press." He thought a bit. "Maybe he felt sheepish. He's got money. He knows people. Maybe this is his way of apologizing for going off the deep end about a daughter who acted like a typical teenager."

"She's twenty," Callie reminded him. "You're only bumping thirty."

He gave her a faux scowl.

Thomas was a respectable thirty, though, but she loved messing with him. He had more of a detective head on his shoulders than the other older officers. He and Annie were the kids on the team, the same age. The rest of her team bumped retirement age, tired of thinking very hard anymore. They'd come from other police departments, hoping to ease into retirement at the beach. They'd never done hurricanes before coming to Edisto and expected a slow pace.

"Some kids are less mature than others," Thomas said.

"True that on maturity," she said. "And, like you said, no point pursuing the issue any longer. One less thing on our list."

Though something niggled her about the father, she couldn't put a name to it. Could be nothing but a father being a father. No point wasting more gray matter on it. Callie had a hurricane to tend to.

"Thomas, you and I will be the last ones off the beach. That okay with you?"

"Sure. Why me?"

He knew why, but he liked hearing it.

"You're the youngest, the most experienced when it comes to island living and its storms, and if push comes to shove, you're the most physically capable."

"Yeah," he said, pointing two fingers like guns at her. "Just like I thought."

Marie laughed from her desk.

Phone pinging, Callie glanced down at the text. Stan had just deposited the love of her life at home. Time to take a moment for someone other than Edisto Beach.

Chapter 6

Callie
Tuesday afternoon

CALLIE HEADED home to *Chelsea Morning*. The Town of Edisto Beach officials had sent out a formal notice last night about Nikki, and it appeared people were heeding the warnings. There would always be some who didn't, but the grand majority did. Everyone got the notice in their email, on their phones, and it was posted on the assorted Edisto websites and social media.

State of Emergency Declaration
A State of Emergency has been declared for South Carolina in response to Tropical Storm Nikki.

Primary Threat
The most significant threat posed by the storm is extreme rainfall and flooding, with predictions of 20-30 inches by this Friday. Additionally, a storm surge of two to four feet is expected.

Precautionary Measures
Electronics and Vehicles: Unplug all electronics and golf carts under your house.
Flood Safety: Avoid driving or walking through flood waters.
Boats and Trailers: Ensure all boats and trailers are secured.
Road Closures: Be prepared for potential road closures.
Travel: Plan your travel accordingly this week due to expected statewide flooding and the possibility of evacuation.

Resources Available
Sandbags: Available at the Fire Department.
Sand: Available at the Jungle Road Park Parking Lot next
to McConkey's Jungle Shack.
Stay safe and take all necessary precautions.

In the mile it took to reach *Chelsea Morning*, Callie surveyed properties and noted the increase in attentiveness. A couple of residences already had hurricane shutters over their windows. Some cleaned up their lots.

Neighbors helping neighbors, and she noted real estate trucks with tools and plywood in the back heading toward rental property that agencies managed for owners who lived too far off to tend to their houses themselves.

Sandbags were going up, especially at the addresses on the lower side that often flooded. The point end could be the worst, but the first six blocks past The Pavilion could flood and erode as well.

Most people were already bringing in items that could morph from lawn décor into missiles. The simplest item from a garden gnome to a strand of pine straw could penetrate trees, siding, wood, even glass. The shift in the air's pressure from low to high created a vacuum effect with high winds that turned any item into a projectile. Most never believed such stories until they saw them.

One woman hauled containers of what looked like gasoline or pesticides out of her storage area. Kudos to her. Most people left such chemicals in their storage unit on the ground floor, unwittingly poisoning flood water. She apparently had done this before.

Callie pulled into her crushed-shell-and-gravel drive. Her personal car was strategically placed to hug the house between pillars that propped the first floor off the ground. Mark's car did the same on the other side. It was times like these one understood why resident parking was beneath a beach house. When your dirt is only eight feet above sea level and the storm surge is twelve feet . . . well, one's house soon becomes an island. Better the car flood than the residence. But, of course, it was preferable one got off the beach before flood waters arrived.

None of her own items were put away yet. Another line on her to-do list, but her own place might have to wait until she'd seen most of these people across the big bridge to safety.

She parked at the foot of the two-dozen steps—just a few feet from Stan's vehicle which parked behind Mark's—and took the stairs two at a time as long as she could. Hand on the knob, she turned it to enter.

Locked. What did she expect. All three of them were cut from the same cop cloth.

She unlocked and entered. "Mark?"

"We're in the living room," Stan hollered. "Got him set up all nice and cozy in the recliner. A drink at his side, the remote within reach."

She didn't know whom to hug first, but since Stan was between her and Mark, she addressed him, barely able to reach around his ample girth. He was twice her weight.

"Thanks, big guy, for taking care of my main guy," she said with a second squeeze, then let him loose, having done her duty. She knelt in front of Mark. "How are you feeling?"

"Sore. Beaten up a little. Not as bad as I thought, though." He shifted place in the chair and winced.

"Bet you'll have a good deal of that for a few days," she said.

"Can't lift anything over ten pounds for at least two weeks. They have to release me to do more." His smile dimmed. "How are you going to handle taking everything in and locking things down before the storm? Aren't we supposed to evacuate?"

"We've been told to prepare, not do it. Not yet. They're still watching Nikki to see if she veers north enough to avoid us. Gotta love the Outer Banks of North Carolina, you know?"

Edisto had missed a lot of storms in its history, only for either Florida or the Outer Banks to take the hits.

She pushed one of his black locks out of his face. He needed a bath, but for now he'd make do with just rest. "In hindsight, I'm not so sure we shouldn't have sent you to my mother's house in Middleton. Stan, too. That's where Jeb and Sprite are headed."

"As long as the restaurant is open, I'm needed here," he said, shifting and wincing again.

She stood. "Look at you. What good would you be there?"

"I can sit at the VIP table and answer questions."

"And wear yourself out? No. I have Wesley in charge right now, and I was about to run over to see if Sophie showed. She gave me a hard time last night about going in early."

He gave a brief grin. "She always gives me a hard time. It's who she is. Once she's there, she's great. It's just getting her to show up. You know her. All it takes is some shiny distraction." He winked in an attempt to appear put together. "I love her. You do, too." He started to ease forward.

"No!" she exclaimed, an internal alarm giving her visions of pulling something loose. "You stay right there." She peered at Stan.

"I can watch him," he said.

Mark scowled. "I don't need a damn babysitter."

Stan chuckled. "Honestly, my man, they did say you had to be supervised for at least the first twenty-four hours. Callie has her hands full. I don't. Besides, I'm bigger. I can put you in your place." He winked. "And help you to the bathroom."

She planted a sizeable kiss on the Cajun and stepped back. "Hate to go, but . . ."

He waved her away. "We get it. Go on." Then he held up a stop-sign hand. "No, wait a minute. All I have on the hurricane is what my phone says."

"Thursday night," she said, going right to the point. "Near midnight. Tonight at the same time puts us in the forty-eight-hour window for preparedness. The thirty-six-hour window, at noon tomorrow, means we start the push for people to leave or batten down the hatches."

She wasn't going to ask him about shutting down El Marko's until she'd judged his condition, but clearly, he had his wits about him. "When do you want to close the restaurant?" She had her own recommendation, but he was the owner.

"Close of business today," he said. "No, let's say eight tonight. These people have homes and families, too."

Good. Even better than she was going to suggest. "I'll pass the word. You both have CodeRED on your phone?"

Stan held his up, showing her. Mark nodded.

"Good." She kissed him a quick one this time, patted Stan on the arm, and left. The minute she set foot outside, though, she felt a rise in tension. Cars drove a little faster. More residents up and down Jungle Road moved around outside. While it was supposed to be too soon to feel Miss Nikki, Callie swore a tingle danced in the air of something forthcoming.

On the way to El Marko's, she saw tourists packing up. *Good.* She and her officers would spend now to Thursday night convincing people that hurricanes didn't discriminate. Rich or poor, resident or renter, young and old, Nikki would arrive to see how many of them she could mess with and prove who was boss.

Darn, she meant to tell Mark about the abduction, but he'd probably heard. Especially with the doctor being assigned to St. Francis where Mark left his appendix. She was just so accustomed to talking shop and cases, but with him not up to speed, he could just sit back and recu-perate.

Thank God for Stan.

Thinking of him, she took a side street to check out his place. Nope, he hadn't done anything to prepare either. A lot of places weren't ready, but again, not in the forty-eight-hour window. Tomorrow would be more hectic as the official countdown began. The number of things she'd like to see done on this beach had no end, but all she could do was follow the hurricane preparedness manual, use the good sense God gave her, and do the best she could to keep these people safe. Property could be replaced. People couldn't.

The restaurant came into view. *Damn.* It was two thirty and the place was slammed. Everyone must have been attempting to get a good meal before everything closed. A few of the restaurants had already shut doors, the rest posting signage about closing early.

Inside, Sophie played both hostess and waitress. Callie had known the woman way longer than Mark, but congrats to him for having trust in her. Callie's trust came with a hint of doubt; however, admittedly, if pushed to do the right thing, Sophie usually did.

Sophie laid hot dishes on a table about eight feet away then rushed over, releasing a hard breath at the sight of her neighbor. "Any chance you can grab an apron?" she asked, her eyes still darting around the room for anyone waving for help.

"Think about what you just asked, Soph." Then, not giving her friend the chance to respond, she said, "No. We are handling the beach in preparation for the storm. If I waited tables, town council would fire me on the spot."

Sophie didn't like that. "Then what about Mark? Any chance we could prop him up in the kitchen?"

"Oh hell no. He can barely stand."

"Stan?"

Callie laughed, not seeing the big man maneuvering hot food be-tween these tight tables. "He's watching Mark, who cannot be left alone."

Wesley peeked out of the kitchen, found Sophie, and waggled a finger, telling her they had orders ready.

"Gotta go. I sure wish Sprite would get her ass home and help," she said.

"She and Jeb are going to my mother's house in Middleton." The conversation with Jeb about Sprite's scare, the school closing, and meeting with Charleston detectives rushed to the forefront of her mind already saturated with obligations. This, however, was not the time to cover such details with Sophie. The point was Sprite was fine. Callie had to admit, however, if the shoe were on the other foot, she'd want to know the details of what she knew.

Sophie froze. "How do you know that?"

"Spoke to Jeb. He asked whether to come here or go to Middleton. I sent him to Mother's, and you know as well as I do that he and Sprite are of one mind."

Another deep sigh. Then from across the room, Wesley called. "Sophie!"

Callie quickly added, "Close the restaurant at eight. Tell Wesley, please. Won't reopen until after the storm."

A nod, then the red broom skirt, turquoise gauze top, and dangling beaded earrings swished and were gone.

Callie exited before someone snared her inside, but someone instead caught her outside. "Chief Morgan." The receptionist from Wainwright Realty stood there in her red-and-yellow glory, huffing as if she'd run across the street from Janet Wainwright's headquarters.

Callie glanced up to see the old lady Marine leaning from her porch, watching to make sure her receptionist reached the chief. "What is it, Natalie?"

"The boss needs to talk to you. Told me to not let you get away." She swallowed and took another breath to slow down. "You aren't going to leave me hanging here, are you? Please don't send me back to her empty handed."

The plea was so damn pitiful Callie wouldn't dream of returning this poor girl back to face the wrath of the retired Marine having unsuccessfully executed her mission. "Come on, Natalie. We can't fail to follow orders."

"Thanks, Chief." The poor girl didn't even look both ways before crossing, probably expecting Callie to take care of that, too. "I didn't need boss giving me extra work tonight, which she would have just to *encourage* me to do better next time. See, I met the nicest guy," the girl said. "He's a renter, and after I treated him nice when he checked in, he came back and asked me out last night." She was downright giggly.

Callie hid her smile. "Good to hear. Have a good time?"

"Excellent time! We're going out again tonight." Another giggle, but she kept one eye out for Janet, still watching from her storm perch. "Don't tell Janet."

"Oh, God, no."

"And your guy might not understand hurricanes, Natalie. Don't let him get so stuck on you that he sticks around for some all-night hurricane party in the name of getting to know you."

They reached the other side, heading to the stairs. "I already told him, but he and his friends are going to ride it out."

"Where are they renting?"

"Arc Street," she said.

Callie had to think about that one. They rarely checked those houses. If she was correct, Janet managed all five houses on the short street. Being all the way down Palmetto Street, almost to the sound and three blocks back off the water, they weren't in the worst path if a tropical storm hit. But a hurricane could hurt any property in the town to some degree, and the people who stayed through a storm shouldn't be novices assuming the storm was little more than a hard rain.

"What's his name?" she asked the girl.

That drew her up short. "Why?"

"I try to keep up with who might be sticking around."

Natalie looked up at Janet, who was waiting hard, if there was such a description. Janet did everything hard, calloused, and Marine-like.

"You aren't rushing my tenants to leave, are you?" Janet yelled down from above, interrupting the conversation.

Callie paused to allow Natalie to answer her question. "Again, what's his name?"

"Arlo," she said. "Adkins. He's ex-military." The grin slid back. "He is so sweet."

Callie tucked away the name as a house to check and took the stairs to deal with the military veteran in front of her. She'd deal with the other one later. "Your people driving you nuts?" she asked looking up at the real estate broker.

Janet waited until Callie reached the porch. "Weather people say it's not a direct hit on us," she said. "I've got tenants wanting to stay, but they're asking my opinion."

"Tell them to leave, Janet."

"It's not my place to give that advice, Chief. I refer them to their TV and government officials."

"I know you won't tell them to leave, which is why I'm telling you that you should. Matthew's cone wasn't a direct hit on us either and look at the damage from the storm surge."

"There is no mandatory evacuation, Chief."

Ironic Janet using the same line that Callie herself had earlier used with the town council.

"No, there's *suggested* evacuation. Anyone I see will hear a speech about how there's a certain point where everyone, including police and fire, will be off the beach. If someone who remains behind gets hurt, can't find water, whatever, they're on their own. No magical helicopter hovering, waiting for people to wave and ask for help. They're stuck until we come back and scout for Nikki's damage."

Janet looked away, watching down the street where people moved in and out of the Food Lion parking lot, hunting for a place to park. "People get their noses out of joint when they lose money on a vacation. They don't often come back."

Callie countered. "The dead never come back."

When the Marine's cool sarcastic side glare didn't have the effect on Callie as planned, she said, "We don't have people dying in these storms, Chief. You know it and I know it."

"Because we send them packing. People haven't died on this beach from a storm in many a decade. Don't let your stubbornness break that record."

They'd never had this conversation before. In the three years of Callie's tenure, they hadn't had a reason to. The mild seasons were greatly appreciated, but now the beach was due a storm, and Callie was learning quickly who took hurricanes seriously and who didn't. Who held which opinion was surprising to her.

"Excuse me, Ms. Wainwright." Natalie still waited in the wings, one ear out for the phone to ring, the other listening for the best time to speak.

"What is it, girl?"

Callie didn't turn to look, not wanting to see Natalie wilt when Janet delivered whatever caustic answer would result from the poor girl interrupting.

"Um, it appears a lot of businesses are closing early today. I was wondering if I could take off a little early, too?"

Janet's silent admonishment should've given the girl her answer, but the delivery didn't take. Then the poor naïve child gave an explanation, almost making Callie shiver for her. "I have a date," Natalie said, "and he was asking if I could get off early to catch a meal at a restaurant before they shut down. Everything's closed tomorrow."

"Have people been calling today with questions about all this hulla-baloo?"

"Well, there have been some calls, Ms. Wainwright."

"More than normal?"

The girl's gaze dropped. "Maybe. I didn't count."

"If you were a Wainwright renter, and you've never experienced a hurricane, would you not call the local broker you used to make the reservation and inquire on what to do with the house, how long to stay, and if they can come back and make up the rest of their vacation at another time?"

Natalie didn't respond.

"Would you want your money back? Would you want instructions on how to file your travel insurance?" Janet's words sped up, in a crescendo. "Would you want to feel like someone had your back when the shit hit the fan?"

Natalie got the message. "I'll work until five, ma'am."

For God's sake, it was only three thirty.

"Kids don't have a work ethic anymore," Janet said as Natalie disappeared inside.

And some bosses don't have a heart, Callie thought, excusing herself. Janet was going to do what Janet wanted to do. She'd lasted decades with this style of hers. All Callie could do was her own job, and if someone needed questions asked or a suggestion on whether to stay or leave, she'd respond the same, whether or not there was a Janet Wainwright in the equation.

Chapter 7

Arlo
Tuesday afternoon

A DAMN HURRICANE wasn't going to stop them from this, the Re-trievers' most recent adventure. He had come in around midnight last night to find Leonard asleep and Bruce sitting on guard, his duffle bag still on his bed, open. He stared out the back window, through the porch toward the trees. He usually slept on the floor or in a chair.

That receptionist, Natalie, had proven to be fun last night, and Little Miss Innocent had shown him moves between the sheets. Way more moves than those of just a quick learner. Enough so that he'd hoped to revisit her this evening, but her text said not until six thanks to an unforgiving boss. Well, she worked for a Marine, so that was that.

Regardless, they had planning to do, but now—of all times—Bruce had decided to nap when the three of them needed to talk. That's how Bruce slept, in spurts. His nap wouldn't last long, and they rarely disturbed one.

Leonard had just come in from another run, slowed down. He had expelled enough energy to give him the calm he needed. He was known for thinking too much. The exercise toned that down most of the time.

Arlo was the most normal of the three, or so he envisioned himself. He had his demons, and they appeared mostly in his dreams. Sure, he sat with his back against the wall in a room full of people, and he watched their hands. He flinched at loud noises from planes, fireworks, and, of course, firearms. Everything stayed locked, and, not just him but all of them tended to rotate who slept because one had to remain alert most of the time.

So right now, at four in the afternoon, Bruce slept, lying lengthwise on a sleeping bag on the floor, parallel to the duffel bag on his bed. One couldn't see the weapons, but Arlo was aware Bruce had at least three in the room, in assorted clandestine spots that made for easy access.

"Leonard?" Arlo called, hearing noise in his kitchen. He oversaw all things domestic from food to laundry. He'd grabbed enough food to last them two weeks in case they couldn't get back into the store. That hurricane out at sea had the beach throbbing which suited them fine. Less attention on them.

Who noticed the three Rangers on an obscure street nobody navigated? Leonard was the one most exposed to notice with his shirtless runs along the water with his tan and physique. But he wasn't a conversationalist, so nobody had the opportunity to know him. He was just a tall, good-looking guy always alone and ever jogging on the sand.

Leonard had fixed himself a sandwich with six slices of ham and three of cheese and was popping open the top of a beer when Arlo entered.

Leonard held up the can of beer. "What is this shit?"

"Hey, these idiots around here are raiding that Food Lion like ants on syrup. I got what they had. There's a hurricane coming, or hadn't you noticed?"

"Hadn't noticed."

Arlo glanced back at Bruce's room. He still lay prostrate on the floor. As if he were dead.

"Was hoping to wait till Bruce got up, but we need to talk."

Leonard motioned with his sandwich, chewing. He swallowed. "He'll be up in less than an hour." Then took another bite and spoke around the food. "You seeing that girl again?"

"Maybe."

"You and your libido, dude. But you do you. Don't need to see you jerking off around here."

"Fully intend to spend time with her, my man"

Brow arched, Leonard smirked. "What about the hurricane?"

"If it hits here, it will be Thursday night. They are suggesting people evacuate."

Leonard snorted a laugh. "Well, that ain't happening."

Arlo had to grin at the absurdness of that, too. "Check the storage room below. If there are hurricane shutters, we put them up. If not, that means the real estate people will likely want to come secure the place, which we cannot afford."

Taking another monster bite, Leonard chewed, listening.

"That's part of why I'm seeing this girl again. She works for the company we rent from."

Another snicker from the big friend. "You keep telling yourself that. I won't be waiting up for you to come back early with boards and hammers."

Arlo grinned, another glance back to Bruce's room. No change. "You clue him in when he wakes up, all right?"

Leonard nodded.

"And make sure he eats. I bought that nasty smoked cheese and sardines stuff just for him. Surprise, nobody was hoarding those in their hurricane scramble."

Nose scrunched, Leonard reared his head. "I know I ain't eating that shit."

"Anything on the news?"

"Let me check," he said, forcing the rest of the sandwich in his mouth so he had two hands. His big fingers clicked, as he finished chewing and pulled up the local news station.

Hurricane mostly. "See? I keep up," he said, flashing the screen toward Arlo.

"What else?"

Wherever they visited, they kept up with the locals. Where the action was, what the weather was, what news could keep attention off them.

The next story that rolled across the slideshow was Dr. St. James and his notice to the public that his daughter had made contact, and she was safe. He apologized profusely about using police forces that were better utilized for the hurricane.

"Kids," Arlo said, scoffing once. "Anyway, he's convincing. Bet there are some people pissed at him."

"Not our problem," Leonard said, putting away the phone and finishing the beer he'd set on the counter.

"Anything else going on around here?" Arlo said, reminding Leonard he was the guy to keep up with the news, especially local.

"Nope." Leonard left to take a shower.

Maybe Leonard was too focused. When he exercised, he could channel his attention to too fine a point.

He hadn't paid attention to the hurricane?

Arlo guessed since his own chores weren't so demanding he could tackle hurricane tracking. And hurricane preparedness, though when they got the boards here, Leonard would be given the lion's share of that *exercise*.

Arlo showered and left a little early, hoping to convince Natalie to take off at least thirty minutes earlier than she said. And if she feared her boss that much, maybe Arlo could convince the jarhead herself. Wainwright. The owner. The first name escaped him.

He pulled into the Wainwright parking lot and bounded up the stairs two at a time, again taking a second to straighten himself in the window's reflection before going in. Natalie was already smiling, probably having seen him through the window.

The phone rang and she flinched, jumping to take the call. The person on the other end apparently had more than one question, and with Natalie occupied, Arlo took the chance to walk around the lobby. When he reached a double-door entrance, he dared to try the handle. Unlocked. So he further dared to poke his head inside.

The white-cropped hair all but shined against the mahogany desk and dark-curtain backdrop. Janet Wainwright looked up from her papers. "Can I help you?" Not that she sounded like she wanted to.

"Hello, Ms. Wainwright. Hope I'm not disturbing you."

"You are, but now that you have, what can I do for you?"

Arlo stepped in but didn't venture far. "Just wanted to meet the Marine that runs this beach."

She hadn't moved an inch. "And why would the Marine bother meeting you?"

No wonder Natalie snapped to during working hours.

"I was Ranger," he said. "Three tours in the Middle East. That goes for my two friends as well. We rented a house on Arc Street through you. When I heard we had a military mind running things, I had to see her for myself."

Janet gave him a humph. "Well, I'm the Marine. Thanks for your service, but we're rather busy. Is there something wrong with your rental? Are you leaving because of the storm or not?"

"We plan to stay," he said. "I'd be happy to secure the place. We're more than fit enough to handle hard work. Tell us what to do and we'll do it. Not only for our place but a few more, if you like. Just an offer from one military mind to another."

Janet sat a little straighter. "I'm supposed to warn you about sticking around, you know."

"As you should. We are rather independent sorts, though—handy and capable."

She studied him. Then she studied him longer.

He let her, understanding the sizing up.

"The boards should be in the storage room beneath the house, Ranger. Feel free to install them. My nephew will be in touch with you about three other houses. Can't ask you to do much more than that." She paused. "Much appreciated. Afraid I can't reduce your lease, though.

That's between you and your travel insurance. These rental owners rely upon me for their livelihood."

"Understood, ma'am." He opened one of the doors but remained standing in place, stiffer now, waiting for more before being dismissed.

She noticed. "So, what else?"

"Any chance you can thank me by releasing that pretty little thing at the front desk so I can treat her to dinner? These restaurants keep threatening to close early, and no telling when they'll open back up."

Janet fought a smirk. He could see it in the corner of her mouth. She saw how he'd played her, and she'd let him.

She pushed the intercom on the phone.

"Yes, ma'am?" came the soft voice from the front desk.

"You can go home. But I need you bright and early tomorrow. Early if possible."

"Yes, ma'am."

Janet hung up, gaze returning to rest on Arlo. "Well, go on. I'll expect your house and the other three to be boarded up no later than Thursday noon. That clear, soldier?"

"Loud and clear. Thank you, ma'am." He turned and left, pulling the door closed behind him.

Natalie met him in front of her desk, purse in hand. "What did you do?"

"Just showed her I was a good soldier. Now, where do you want to eat?"

Chapter 8

Callie
Tuesday evening

TUESDAY EVENING. Callie clarified the shift change before taking off to El Marko's. The day had been filled with questions from anyone and everyone, and Marie had more than her share of visitors, but nothing was deemed serious and nothing that a short conversation couldn't handle. Even fewer tickets. The last one Callie wrote had been that day-tripper at Mr. Pope's house. She wouldn't have written that one if she hadn't had Donna in the car . . . or she might've. That guy was a genuine *touron*, as the beach called irresponsible tourists.

Tomorrow she'd set up the noon roadblock, letting people out and not letting people in. Tonight was the lull. Everywhere she went, televisions showed the Weather Channel with its various projections, past hurricanes, and ad nauseum explanation about what would happen with this or that storm surge or a particular wind speed. Inside or outside the cone. North or south of the eye when it hit. On and on. Over and over. They called themselves *informing the public*. Callie considered them alarmists. Hell, even weather people had become drama queens.

She arrived home, ran inside, and on the way to the bedroom hollered at Stan and Mark in the dining room, "I'm gone as soon as I change!" Then she tossed her uniform and assorted attachments on the bed and grabbed jeans, a polo, and her dressiest sneakers. On the way out the door she stopped long enough to check on Mark.

"Headed to the restaurant," she said. "You okay?"

"Sore. Tired. Frustrated," he said from the dining table. Stan had him playing cards.

"He's fine," Stan said. "Bored but fine. Only takes him to stand and move around to remind him why he's not supposed to. He had a nap, and he had dinner. I've all but talcumed his butt."

Mark threw her a tight-lipped reaction to that. "He's overkill on this babysitting stuff."

"Good," Callie said, the kissed him on the mouth before waving goodbye, tapping Stan on the head in thanks as she scurried by.

Six thirty p.m. When she arrived at the mini mall, El Marko's was slammed. Walking up to the front door, she counted a dozen people outside on the waiting list for dinner. The pleasant eighty degrees came with just enough breeze to push hair out of your face, making nobody mind the delay. Half the restaurants had already closed. No wonder El Marko's had more business than normal.

She entered, scanning the terrain. Sophie and one other girl waited tables. Callie understood the routine enough to know that the girl helped cook in the kitchen between acting as waitress. Sophie, on the other hand, doubled as waitress and hostess, because everyone had learned a long time ago that she had no business helping in the kitchen.

Sophie ran up and pushed menus and a damp rag into her hands. "The second someone stands, wipe the table and seat someone else." In other words, *do Sophie's job before some other employee had a chance to claim her labor.*

"Let me check with Wesley first." Callie zigged her way around tables to the kitchen where three guys were throwing food together, one washing dishes in between. "Where do you need me most?" she said above the din.

"Can you cook?" one young man asked.

"Hell yeah, she can cook, she can wait tables, and she can hostess, but I'd rather my cousin quit serving tables and get back in here," Wesley said. "Put the chief out front to make nice. They know her and won't be as inclined to fuss."

This was why Wesley was Mark's favorite.

Callie reappeared in the dining room and took to work, much to Sophie's delight.

Sophie maintained the door, letting Callie clear the tables. She had barely finished wiping one down before a couple arrived to fill the seats.

"Chief!"

Natalie was chivalrously seated by a handsome man in his late thirties, maybe older. He took care of himself, that was for sure, and could almost be a young version of Mark.

"Hey, Natalie. Who's your date here?"

The gentleman hadn't allowed himself to sit, having seated his date first. He reached out a hand, and Callie tucked away her rag under her arm to receive his greeting. "Arlo Adkins, ma'am. Did Natalie say, *Chief?*"

Callie chuckled. "She did. Cop by day, waitress by night."

"No, she's not," Natalie said, tugging the shirttail of her guy to go ahead and sit. "I heard the owner is sick. She's filling in for him because they're an item out here. They live together on Jungle Road. The house is called—"

"Anyway," Callie interrupted. "Yes, I'm helping out Mark." She let her gaze gloss over of the room, telling the couple that she had work to do. "Y'all have a good dinner. Hope you enjoy it. Nice to meet you, Arlo."

She removed herself. There were tables to tend, plus, any longer and Natalie would've given the man an encyclopedic discourse of all things Callie Jean Morgan.

The evening wore on, and by eight it became apparent that El Marko's wasn't closing early. She made a command decision to shut it down at ten, putting a sign on the door that diners would not be seated past nine thirty. That would pacify anyone waiting that they'd be allowed to eat. Anyone new could decide to move on.

The sign did its duty. Diners started thinning, and by nine thirty, there was no line and the dining area was only half full. Natalie and Arlo, however, remained, chatting like fresh lovers do, too enthralled with each other's newness to worry about something as frivolous as time.

The number of diners thinned until all that was left was the couple and one other table. Callie returned to them. "Anything else I can get you?"

"I'd like two of your biggest platters to go, please," Arlo said. "Is it too late? I know we've sort of monopolized this table."

Callie smiled like a waitress should. "No, you're fine. And yes, I'll get that order put right in. Honestly, I just ordered the same thing to go as well. Smart minds think alike, I guess." She thought she'd run the two platters home to Stan and Mark then scoot back to the restaurant to help clean up.

She placed Arlo's order as, coincidentally, her own was ready. "Be right back, Soph. Taking dinner to the boys."

"Sure," Sophie said, breathing as if she'd climbed Mount Rushmore. "I'm exhausted and get to clean up the mess, while you get to loaf off."

Callie motioned for her friend to follow her through the kitchen and out the back door. What she had to say wasn't for other ears.

"What the hell is wrong with you?" she said, the door propped for reentry with her foot.

Sophie spread her arms wide. "This! The storm, the restaurant . . . my daughter. The universe is upside down, and I don't know how to function." When she finished, she kept breathing hard, her emotions loose and untethered.

Barometric pressure changes impacted normal people, whether they believed it or not, but with Sophie, it could turn her inside out. Sophie wasn't fond of the unexpected, and she frustrated easily, but what was that extra worry about Sprite who should be safely out of the storm's path?

"Hey." Callie rubbed a hand up and down Sophie's arm. "I see how storms could mess with your . . . otherworldliness stuff, but what's going on with Sprite?"

She realized this was going to take more than a moment. "Wait here," she said, needing to take care of the two remaining occupied tables inside. "Be right back." She pointed and reiterated, "Don't disappear on me."

Callie took maybe two minutes to deliver the now-ready take-out to Arlo and Natalie, then another two to handle the charge. *Wham, bam, done.* She saw them out and locked the door; the dining room now empty, she ran back to the rear entrance.

Sophie was gone.

Back inside, she asked Wesley if he minded if she delivered food to Mark and Stan and run right back. Of course he didn't, and with them closing with one less person, she made the trip extra quick. She barely had time to set the bags down, take a good look at Mark to ensure he was okay, then dart back.

While closing at eight would've been nice, closing at ten wasn't bad. By ten thirty, they were done and gone. Callie drove around a few blocks to take note of which places had been vacated and who had boarded up. She remembered Arlo, and Natalie saying he and his buddies were on Arc Street. She hadn't been there in ages, so she trolled down and took a look. Nothing had been boarded up, and they might not be since they were located four houses back off the part of the beach called Bay Point.

Lights were on in *Seas the Day* as well as one other house on the street. The other three were vacant.

Arc Street was, as one would imagine, an arc. Five houses with the Arc Street address, then nine houses across the street, whose front doors faced Palmetto instead of Arc. The Palmetto address gave them greater value.

Callie made the circle down Palmetto then back around Dock Site, to Lybrand, then to her own street, Jungle Road. Stepping out in her drive, she sensed the change in the air.

They'd had more than the normal rip currents today, and they would do nothing but increase until Nikki came and went. Nobody'd gotten caught in one today, but tomorrow was another opportunity. The beach had warning signs at most access junctures, but with the awesomeness of the ocean panorama, one tended to pass them by, caught up in Mother Nature, and not see signs about currents, trash, and dogs on leashes.

She let herself inside. Mark slept in the recliner, Stan on the sofa, snoring loud enough to keep anyone awake but an exhausted Mark.

In the kitchen, food wrappers and bags were in the trash and dishes were cleaned and drying in the rack. She smiled. Like kids, they'd gotten full bellies and eased off to dreamland.

That was when she realized how tired she was, the weight of her arms and legs like anchors. Her day had started just after dawn and ended at midnight. Way more rushing about than the norm, and with the world having slowed down finally and heavy breathing coming from the living room, she too was succumbing to drowsiness.

She'd need to talk to Stan and Mark about moving inland before the storm. Tomorrow was Wednesday. Nikki was due Thursday at midnight. The television remained on, like before, on the weather channel. The hurricane wasn't expected to reach a Category Five, they said. Not even a Four. Maybe not a Three. She'd take any break she could get, but even Category Ones at the wrong kind of tide could send enough flood waters with just enough wind to cause millions of dollars of damage.

Because of the intense damage left on October 8, 2016, by Matthew, that name had been retired from use for hurricanes. Extreme rainfall and flooding killed twenty-five people in the Carolinas, all but one due to water. Over ten billion in destruction.

Callie wouldn't sleep easy until Nikki came and went, regardless of the number she was labeled.

Except for tonight.

She straightened a blanket over Mark and took herself to bed. She fell asleep in seconds, but visions of wind filled her dreams most of the night. After waking up a half-dozen times, she rose at a quarter to six. Dream pieces clung to the periphery of her memory, making her almost feel as if she dressed for battle.

Chapter 9

Callie
Wednesday morning—forty hours before the hurricane

SHE WENT TO BED Tuesday night exhausted but satisfied with having performed all the hurricane preparation she could.

She awoke with Mark beside her, and, with her mind darting about, listing her responsibilities, she almost got up. Her clock read seven, the time she normally showed at the station, so she'd managed an extra hour of sleep, but Mark's presence, and the peace on his face allowed her to steal a few more minutes of rest.

Half an hour later he awoke to see her watching. He smiled.

"How do you feel?" she asked, satisfied to run a hand down his shoulder and arm, afraid to hug.

"Honestly? I'm scared to move," he said. "The second I do, I'll be reminded. Then I'll have to move around to get the aches and pains out only to plant myself back in the recliner."

She shrugged. "Sort of what happens when doctors slice and dice on you. You're not supposed to jump off the operating table and run a mile. Six weeks till you're back to almost full speed. Want me to help you up?" She rose, planning to assist him anyway.

He stifled moans as she managed to sit him up. When he stood, however, his loud groan brought his babysitter hollering from the other side of the door.

"Is that noise from Mark's appendix or sex he shouldn't be doing?"

Callie grinned at the big man hanging around for his friend.

"I don't know. What do you think?" Mark tried to holler back, but the lack of strength behind his words didn't fool anyone.

With Mark on his feet, and her accepting he was mobile enough, she went to the door and let Stan in, not caring in the least she wore a thigh-high nightshirt. The man had seen her totally naked before, during a weak moment when they almost let their relationship cross the line.

They'd never spoken about it since that night, when a timely phone call brought them to their senses.

Stan escorted Mark to the bathroom, and Callie checked her phone. Nothing urgent, but she was shrewd enough to recognize they hovered in the lull before the storm, literally. Outside would be gorgeous, for a while. Wind would pick up by nightfall but nothing to be too scared about. Today was when people would leave, board houses, and relocate boats further inland or further north or south, depending upon how the forecast continued to take shape.

Speaking of which, she checked the weather. The storm increased, expected to graduate from tropical storm to hurricane, they said. It would hit Florida first, but it would ride up the coast rather than jam itself across the state and lose strength.

That could mean a lot of wind and rain for Edisto.

She ran things through her mind. She and two other officers, Russell Wiley and Ben Benoit, along with Charleston Sheriff's deputies were scheduled to handle the roadblock. When it came to hurricane comings and goings, one couldn't project the myriad of behaviors that would come out of assorted tourists, day-trippers, rental owners, and residents. That didn't count the island residents who lived outside of town and off the beach. The spectrum ran wide from generations of historic names to freshly relocated retirees, and they all had visions of vandals infiltrating during that void of a time between the storm and when safety assessment teams allowed reentry.

Much of the bigger island, the folks away from the beach, would choose to stay put. Evacuations weren't mandatory in South Carolina. The properties on marshes and those overlooking the Atlantic would roll the dice in terms of safety and jeopardy for human life. Midnight Thursday was the projected landfall between high and low tide, during a neap-tide time of the month. Neap tides occurred with the sun, moon, and earth at right angles, with a lunar high tide and a solar low tide, meaning they partly cancelled each other out. Smaller tides. The smaller the tide during a hurricane, the smaller the storm surge.

If Nikki stayed tropical or Category One, and with this being a neap-tide season, the damage could be way less than otherwise. Thank goodness for small favors . . . hopefully. Callie would take that.

Mark and Stan reappeared. "You need to get ready for work," Mark said, frustrated. "I think I'd rather be shot in the leg again than this."

"You'll live, Cajun." Callie kissed him and hustled to shower and assume her duties. Didn't take her twenty minutes to be done and out.

Mark, the master in the kitchen, had used his buddy to assist him in fixing a fruit smoothie for her, with a scoop of protein powder. "You will forget to eat, especially with the restaurant closed. Drink this. Come by here on your way to the roadblock, and I'll have lunch for you."

She took the shake, drinking half on the spot, him watching like a mother requiring a child to drink her milk before leaving the table. Almost wiping her mouth on her sleeve, she reached for a kitchen towel instead.

"Stan, once Mark gets settled, please take a shower, and do whatever you feel you need to do at your house. He seems good, and after all this moving around and after he eats, he'll nap. Use that time to your advantage. I'll call and check in. Don't be surprised if Sophie shows, which reminds me, you want me to leave the door unlocked for her, or—"

Mark scoffed. "Come on, Callie."

She knew better. All three of them being LEO made the question stupid in thought, much more spoken aloud.

"She can wait for me to get to the door," he said.

"I can give her a key."

"Give Stan the key, but not her."

Despite her quirks and all her flaws, flightiness, and pouting, they loved her. Knew she meant well, but in the middle of the beach's busyness, she'd lose the key somewhere. Or so Mark was thinking. Callie could read his mind pretty darn well these days since he'd moved in.

Leaving the men to themselves to make their own agenda, she left. There wasn't time to go into when Mark would leave the island. Stan would be more than willing to take him, but he, as well as she, probably wanted to give him this day to recuperate. Nikki wasn't due until tomorrow midnight. Ample time. If push came to shove, the men could leave when she did. Mark couldn't drive, which meant leaving one car behind. She'd let her officers take the patrol cars to safety.

Outside, Sophie's beau of the month, Buck, was installing shutters next door. "You can do mine any time you like," Callie yelled across the distance.

"Got ten more ahead of you," he yelled back. "I'll see what I can do."

But Callie waved him off. "You take care of your business. If you find time, good. If not, it'll get done."

He gave her a thumbs-up and returned to his task.

Being almost eight thirty, Sophie would be at yoga. Storm or no storm, she'd hold her classes to be right with the universe.

Callie got in her patrol car and was backing out when Donna Baird pulled in and waved her to stop. Callie rolled down her window. Horse was in the back seat, his big head poking outside his own window. No fear of him jumping out an open window. That massive chest wouldn't fit through.

"Hey, Chief."

"Hey, Donna. Something up?"

"No, not really. I have a favor to ask. And if I'm a burden, just say so."

"Won't know until you tell me. Shoot."

Horse woofed, and Callie jumped.

Laughing, Donna reached back and patted the beast. "He recognizes you," she said. "He's your buddy now."

Callie grinned, wondering what she'd done to merit such affection. She'd never considered herself a dog person. Beverly never let her have a dog growing up, and she'd always lived with a fellow law enforcement officer with odd hours, so she'd never gotten one herself.

Callie redirected attention from the dog back to Donna. "Your favor?"

"Can I accompany you to the roadblock today?"

At first thought, the request wasn't out of line. Donna hadn't been a problem yesterday and could possibly have proven an asset in hindsight. Nothing invasive or overtly pushy about her.

On second thought, this could be a politician placing herself in convenient situations to be seen, maybe to curry favor for future elections. Yes, she'd be learning how Edisto worked, and a hurricane wasn't a daily occurrence, so the education of the beach's evacuation and preparation procedures was opportune, but still.

"Don't you have preparations to make?" Callie asked.

"Done them," she said. "Honestly, I keep my hurricane preparedness up to date all the time, short of battening down the hatches. I'm single. Doesn't take much if you stay on top of it. Frozen bottles in the freezer. Clothes washed. Keep an inventory of my belongings, along with video, for insurance purposes. My important documents are in a fireproof box to be grabbed. I rarely keep objects loose outside anyway. Just a couple of lawn chairs already locked up. My sister lives in Orangeburg, and I know the back roads."

She kept talking as if she had to prove herself, while Callie pondered the pros and cons of letting the new town representative come along.

"Okay, agreed," Callie said. "But I can't let you ride along this time. I have no idea what will come up or how long I'll be there. You might want to come home sooner or proceed from there to your sister's place. I just ask that you remain out of the way and don't step into a situation. I can't afford for you to be more trouble atop of what may already occur."

Donna held up three fingers in Girl Scout on-my-honor style. "I promise. Where and when?"

"I'm leaving around eleven thirty," Callie said. "See you there. I'll let my guys know. If the other council members have an issue, that's on you."

"Agreed," she said, and eased back into traffic, the dog looking back at Callie.

Maybe she should've petted him.

A couple of hours later, she left the station, Marie handling the foot traffic fine. A lot of people had already left, the rest busy doing what they'd inquired about the day before.

She'd texted Mark about coming by around eleven, and when she arrived, he met her on the porch with a brown-bag lunch ready. Stan's car was still there.

Callie heartily kissed Mark. "How are you feeling?"

"I'm going to hear that a lot for a while, aren't I?"

"Yes, sir."

He flexed his shoulders and back a little. "Doesn't take much to hurt, but I'm okay. I stay tired."

Nodding, she expected him to sleep more today. He was the type to do too much then crash. Do it again and crash. "Stan still here? He been home yet?"

"He's in the shower," Mark said with a chuckle. "I watched TV while he napped this morning. I think I need to agree to naptime to get him to leave and get his own affairs in order."

"Whatever you guys need to do." She peeked in the bag, unable to tell what he packed. "Does it need to be on ice?"

"Not if you eat it within the hour." He sat in a porch chair. "Can you sit a minute?"

"Barely a minute," she said, taking the seat beside him.

He sighed, focusing on the street for a second. "I don't want to leave you here. I stay until you go. That's tomorrow afternoon, right?"

"I'll leave when people are gone or anchored in, when I can tell that I can't help any longer. But I also need to keep looters from sneaking back in as long as I can."

"Time?" he asked.

"The storm and people's behaviors will dictate that. I imagine no later than around eight or nine tomorrow night," she said.

He nodded, not happy. "This sucks."

She shrugged. "It does, but we cope. Wesley took care of the restaurant. Keep him on the clock for his extra effort," she said.

His agreement was animated, head bouncing until even that little movement impacted his wound, and he winced and stopped. "I'm not worth a damn to anyone when I ought to be out there." He did a backhanded motion toward nowhere in particular. "Helping everyone." Then he flipped a motion to the house behind him. "Can't even take care of this place."

"Pouting doesn't look good on you, Cajun." She rose, which made him rise. "I've got to go," she said, leaning in for another kiss.

Then she was down the stairs. Halfway, she shouted back up. "Call me if you need me. Either of you."

He nodded okay, and she trotted down to the gravel drive.

Sophie waved down from her porch. "Is Mark okay?"

"Yeah. Check on him if you like." Mark would kill her for that. Callie glanced back up to see if he'd heard, but he'd gone inside.

But Sophie didn't reply, instead she stared down as if she had a bone to pick. What the hell? Was she still pissed?

God, Callie didn't have time for this, but in the seconds she wasted having the thought, Sophie came down, and the march in those sandaled, size-ten feet said she had hard words to share.

Chapter 10

Callie
Wednesday mid-morning

SOPHIE HEADED toward Callie, apparently on a mission, and Callie quickly radioed her uniforms at the roadblock, just in case Sophie's intentions took more than a few minutes. Callie expected her day to be full of unexpected interruptions. How many times today would the thought, *Hurricanes made people crazy*, enter her mind?

As hard as Sophie stomped, however, her steps couldn't be heard through the soft ground of silt, sand, and grass, a metaphor for how Sophie argued. A lot of energy that didn't make much noise.

"Why didn't you tell me that Sprite was attacked on campus?" Sophie stopped an arm's length away, one hand on a hip, the other pointing a finger. "You of all people should not keep secrets from me."

Callie let her get it all out.

"About my child, of all things," Sophie continued. "Someone tries to steal my baby and you keep it hidden?"

No wonder Sophie had walked away from the restaurant yesterday. She knew. From her own daughter, probably, which was how the news should've been delivered anyway.

"They asked me to find a good time to tell you because they were afraid to," Callie said. "The hurricane, then Mark's emergency, well, since they and the missing girl were safe, I didn't see the urgency in it."

"But they told you!"

"And they should've told you themselves, Soph."

There it was. The anger was half in fear for her daughter and half from the sting of being left out. Callie could fully understand both, but she thanked God for having a son instead of a daughter.

"Bothered me too when Jeb told me after the fact, but they handled it like adults. I'm rather proud of them. However, it sort of hurt my feelings being told after the fact, too, Soph. We have to face they're growing up. There was nothing I would've advised them to do differently."

Then the dam broke. Fat silent tears rolled down Sophie's cheeks. "But . . ." She sniffled.

Callie pulled her into a hug. "I was going to tell you. How did you find out? Sprite call you?" She'd have wet spots on her uniform, but that was okay.

"The news."

Callie pulled back. "Wait, they didn't tell me that what happened to Sprite made the news."

Thomas honked as he passed by. Both waved and smiled like normal. So typical Edisto.

Callie turned back to Sophie, wondering if there was more to the story than Jeb said. She wouldn't break into tears like her friend, but she'd be pissed.

"No," Sophie said. "I saw the story about the kidnapped girl. When they said she lived in Copley Hall, I called Sprite to see if she knew her. She said she did, going on and on about the girl, and then said she could've been kidnapped instead of Langley. I squeezed the rest out of her." She inhaled long and deep. "Is this how it's going to be, Callie? A constant argument over which family will dominate with these two kids? When they are married, who gets the invitation first to Thanksgiving? Who hears first about them expecting our grandchild? Who do they visit first on Christmas?"

"Whoa, Sophie. Take a few breaths."

Sophie could get wound up and prattle on for ages about a topic that deeply affected her, taking it to another level, and nothing would affect her more deeply than her daughter. And extrapolating her worry into projections years ahead was typical Sophie.

Short of losing a child, nothing hurt a mother more than a child omitting them from their lives. No doubt this would happen repeatedly from here to forever. Probably for both of them.

At Jeb's age she'd moved to Boston all those years ago, to snub her parents. Now, being the mother of an adult child, she better understood that pain . . . and, therefore, Sophie's.

"Look at it this way, Soph. Sprite is safe. She's with Jeb and Beverly for the storm. You're invited to stay there, too, you know."

Wiping under her moist lashes, Sophie looked for mascara on her fingers. "I'm staying with Buck."

Callie thought about that. "But he has a condo in Wyndham."

"He also has a house in Columbia."

Okay. Good. Everyone would be safe. The shock of Sprite had been diluted. "I've got to get to the roadblock, Sophie."

"Edistonian?" she asked.

Callie nodded.

"You can leave, but you can't get back in until after the storm, right?"

"Right. When are you leaving?"

Sophie tried to peer down the road but apparently wasn't seeing what she looked for. "Buck's got a list of houses to secure, but we might be last minute getting off the beach."

Sophie had an island sense of when to leave, anyway, so Callie wasn't worried about her. "Here, give me a hug then wish me luck dealing with everyone. Mark's upstairs with Stan. Feeling some better but still dragging."

Brows arching, Sophie's buoyancy returned. "Then let me go visit them." She took off, like a kid with a new distraction. "Ta-ta."

Assuming he married Sprite, Jeb could have a way worse mother-in-law than Sophie Bianchi.

Before anyone could wave her down, Callie hopped in and headed toward Highway 174 and the rest of the day's fun.

Thomas and Annie managed the beach streets, and Marie ran the station. She left a guy off duty to have at least one uniform on call as backup and fresh.

Cars were already piled up ten deep when she arrived at the Edistonian. A Charleston deputy, a Colleton deputy, and two of Edisto Beach's own were already in place, querying the purpose of those trying to access the island's beach, and educating those leaving about the prohibition against re-entry. No two cars would come with the same story; each had an excuse as to why they should be exempt from whatever rules were in place.

She waved at Deputy Don Raysor, the Colleton SO deputy assigned to Edisto Beach since they were so low on manpower and the county was so dependent on the beach's property tax dollars. The county would fall under the poverty line without that income.

But before she positioned herself on the road, Callie went inside the Edistonian, making the manager aware she was there and would be there into the night. The woman gave a faux appearance of being put out by all the activity, but Callie was familiar with the owner, who had not only wholeheartedly approved, but was plum delighted that people turned around in his parking lot. Half would stop for gas, others just to shop because they were there.

Back outside, she could see the gas was going fast. Some filled up just because it was handy, whether they'd been detained or turned around. A Grand Central Station of cars. Coming, going, turning around, parking, backing up, you name it.

Callie trotted over to assist with the traffic and chose to relieve Deputy Raysor.

"Hey, Doll," he said under his breath, his nickname for her, dating back to her first arrival when they hated each other. He'd called her that to get under her skin. Now it was a cute joke between them.

"How many have you locked up, Don?"

"Forty-seven," he said, his jokester grin wrinkling up under his eyes. "I'll be here until five, then I'm to return to Walterboro, they said. Are you okay on the beach?"

Raysor's love was everything Edisto. The beach, the island. He loved it all. He knew every inch of it, and every one of its people. Name a hurricane over the last forty years, and he'd worked it in some form or fashion.

"I can try to get them to leave me down here," he said.

But Callie shook her head. "We've got this. Your people need you in Walterboro. We're leaving by dark anyway. My officers will be gone by supper time. I'm buying time to let Mark rest up. Thomas is leaving when I do."

"Our Cajun doing okay?"

"Yeah," she said. Horns honked five cars back. Guess drivers didn't like seeing uniforms talking to each other when they ought to be directing drivers.

"Time for my break, Doll." He lowered his voice. "Don't shoot any of 'em. I've had to stop myself twice." He chuckled and left.

Callie took in the system her team had set up. Three on each side of the road, to speak to each driver. Councilwoman Donna stood off to the side, geared up in sunglasses and a wide-brimmed straw hat. She'd left Horse at home, thank goodness.

Callie's first stop was a commercial truck, headed to Food Lion with assorted groceries to restock what was fast becoming bare shelves per the grapevine. People would buy groceries whether they needed them or not, whether they were leaving the beach or not. Many stocked up because they didn't know what supplies would be available when they got to where they were going to ride out Nikki. But Callie's role was not to read into that or judge the need. Supplies were supplies. She let him through. The man would be out of there as soon as he could anyway.

The next car had an emergency access decal, meaning they were a full-time resident or a part-time resident who didn't rent out the property. The decals were specifically attached to a make and model vehicle registered with town hall. Not shared. Not bounced from car to car. Stuck in the corner of the windshield for times just like this.

Long-term renters and owners of rental properties would be assigned temporary emergency stickers that were hurricane/event specific. The beach wasn't doing that yet. Not at this stage of the game.

The window went down. "Hey, Mr. Addison," she said, recognizing the man who lived on Marianne Street full time. She looked in the car and saw the back seat filled with food and emergency items. "Prepping for tomorrow?"

"Prepping for after," he said. "Won't be able to get this stuff later, so I'm stocking up now and leaving in the morning."

"Sounds good. Thanks." She waved him through.

The next car, however, made for edgier conversation.

The guy in his thirties had his lady friend beside him and another couple in the back, all dressed in bathing wear, a cooler wedged between the couple. "Wanted to spend the day watching the weather. Figure the beach ought to be wide open and less congested. We won't get in anyone's way."

Callie would address two dozen or more of these before the day was out, with the other officers on her side of the road dealing with likewise numbers.

"The governor ordered evacuation, sir, so we cannot allow access."

He pointed to the car she'd let through ahead of him. "But you had no problem with him?"

"He lives on the beach, sir."

"An evacuation is an evacuation," he argued.

She motioned to the parking lot. "You can turn around there. Thank you." And she moved on toward the next car, keeping one eye on the first. He hesitated, probably after having a flash of an idea to make a break for it, then turned into the Edistonian to do as told.

Another car came up, no decal. "Sorry, sir." Odd she hadn't seen any women drivers yet, but these were early times.

"Left this morning to get a few things the beach grocery store ran out of. Need to get back to my family."

"You're a renter, sir?"

He nodded, as if that was all he needed to say to get through.

"Address? Name? Proof of rental?"

His mind seemed to go blank. He showed his driver's license which Callie snapped a pic of. She handed it back, waiting for the rest.

"Um, it's back at the rental," he said. "With my wife, her sister, and three kids. What does it matter?"

Calm as could be, she relayed the message she'd have to say repeatedly before the day was through. And tomorrow. "First responders need to know where to check for people afterwards. We're leaving y'all on your own tomorrow evening. We don't stay here either."

He froze. "What does that mean?"

"It means if you get hurt, if you run out of water, if snakes come in your house, if a boat breaks loose and rams into the rental . . . the list goes on and on. . . there is no immediate rescue. There will likely not be communication either. But if we know who you are and where you last were, we can identify you."

She purposefully glanced down the highway, to her right, letting this guy know that others needed to be addressed. "Information, please."

He relayed the rental. A Wainwright rental. Janet was likewise keeping up with who was leaving the island and who wasn't, at least concerning her properties. The real estate agencies proved to be good intel during storms.

"We'll be gone by morning," he said.

"Sounds like a smart plan, sir. Move on, please."

An hour later she stepped aside from checking cars to check in with Thomas at the beach.

"Rip tides are something fierce today," he said. "Had two close calls. One swam their way out of it; the other got hauled in by someone on a float. I'm telling everyone I see that the currents are bad and to stay out of the water."

"Those people ought to be leaving," she said.

"Tell *them* that."

"Frankly, I hope you are. Annie, too."

"Yeah, we are. Told the beach patrol to warn the heck out of people, too."

The town had not long hired civilians to scout the beach. Said "officers" patrolled on ATVs, watching for litter violations, protecting turtle nests, educating the public on the dangers of the rip tides, hunting for the temporarily missing, and in extreme situations when the uniforms weren't present, providing safety assistance such as CPR if someone got swept under. They helped Edisto PD quite a bit, but Callie still could use a few more officers.

"Keep me updated," she said. Thomas was capable, but she'd be the one accountable if a serious accident occurred while the force was busy on a roadblock. She wished there was a simple switch to turn on and off, closing Edisto access.

She returned to the traffic, which wasn't letting up.

Day-trippers galore were refused. Her first reporter approached, a familiar face—Alex Hanson, granddaughter of Mrs. Hanson, who lived across Jungle Road and two doors down from *Chelsea Morning*. The grandmother had lived on Edisto since she was a girl, and last year took in a mentally challenged young man, Monty Bartow, to live with her. Both needed someone, and they gave each other company. Alex's years on the beach and relationship to her grandmother practically labelled her as a native, too. Before she graduated from being a novice blogger to television reporter with WLSC in Charleston, she lived full time on the beach. The station she now worked for adored her connection with all things Edisto, and she used it like a trump card anytime she could.

"Gotta go get Grandma and Monty, Chief." She still drove her old Volkswagen, and Callie would not be surprised if she used it to trigger the memories of the residents, easing her back into people's good graces and confidence. Surely in Charleston she drove a vehicle with more panache. Or could it be that this one still carried a resident sticker. Several years old, but still valid.

"When are you leaving?" Callie asked.

"I don't know. Whenever I can get her put together."

Callie looked the tiny car over from hood to fender. "And you intend to pack her, Monty, and their things in this?"

Alex looked around the interior of her car, feigning she hadn't contemplated that yet. "Why, yes. She travels light. And my place has all they need. Monty's simple to manage."

"You're carrying them from here to Charleston where they're evacuating as well."

Callie liked this girl, but there was a small piece of her she had never trusted. Alex was an opportunist. The young blond girl rolled her eyes, ever a lover of drama. So, Callie pushed. "You sure you're not sticking around to report on the storm?"

"I'll do a spot or two," she admitted.

This is the part Callie didn't like. "Don't you try to ride out this storm, Alex. And don't you dare make your grandmother ride it out."

"I won't."

Alex could be lying through her pretty straight teeth.

"Let me see your driver's license."

Alex hesitated but pulled it out, and Callie snapped a picture. Not that she needed it, because she could identify Alex, could pull up her license at any time. Taking the picture was for effect.

"What was that for?" she asked.

"To identify the body," Callie said.

To which Alex laughed. "Nice try, Chief. But I have a decal. You know Grandma. My license is in one of your databases. Can't fool me. I need to get to the beach. The longer you keep me, the longer it takes us to leave."

The girl was right. Callie let her through, praying her need for a story didn't outweigh the need to move her grandmother to safety.

Cars kept coming, each with a different tale to tell. The other reporters were no-brainers. Some threatened to call the mayor. Others said they'd have her job. Others accused her of violating their Constitutional rights. Most turned around, but a couple of them set up beside the Edistonian, interviewing people turned away and those simply refueling. Clearly the reporters were attempting to fill their quota of news by filming human-interest pieces about how scared people were about the pending catastrophe. Surprisingly, Donna Baird made herself available for interview, probably wishing she had the dog.

Another phone call. Janet Wainwright. Callie walked away again, just in case this was an emergency.

"Chief, I have a complaint. I hear you're stopping my people from coming back to their rentals and telling them they have to leave."

"Janet, I'm busy out here. I suggest they leave before the storm. And those without proof of having a rental are questioned. Only one specifically gave me a hard time, and I let him through."

"Well," the Marine said, the *tsk* coming across the line loud and clear. "He felt interrogated."

"Better that than a Wainwright renter found dead in a Wainwright rental. Think about how Alex Hanson would report to WLSC about that."

Pause. "Is that bitch on the beach?"

"Yes, ma'am, retrieving her grandmother."

A groan. "I'm calling bullshit on that. She's looking for stories."

"She's probably doing both, but no point in giving her fodder for a story, Janet. Keep your renters safe and your rental owners clear of any lawsuits."

More silence.

"Gotta go, Janet."

The Marine hung up first.

Callie's watch said five p.m. Her bag lunch had long been consumed; her feet ached, sick of the asphalt. She turned around three more cars when her phone rang for the tenth time since she'd arrived.

Beverly, her mother/mayor from Middleton. "Just how many people are you sending to my house?" she said, exasperated, without so much as a hello. "I have expectations. I have responsibilities. I haven't put clean sheets on any of the beds. Who says I have room?"

"Mother—"

"And Jeb . . . what the hell, Callie? You've put my grandson in danger?"

Oh, good Lord. "Hold on. Need to take care of this first."

A driver waited not six feet in front of her. Thank goodness this one was patient. "Sir, what is your business on the beach?"

"Went to Charleston for bread and stuff."

"From where?" she asked.

"Our rental. Me and a couple of buddies do this every year."

"Callie?" Beverly called out.

Phone back to her ear. "Mother, hold on." Back to the driver. "Long way for bread. Are you riding out the storm?"

"Thinking about it," he said, then nodded toward bags in the front seat. "More than bread, though. Might be a six-pack or two in there."

Beer did go quickly during these times. "I suggest y'all pack up and leave, sir."

"It's only a Cat One, ma'am."

She liked the use of *ma'am*. "Some of our worst flooding happened during a Cat One. Which house?"

"Don't remember the address, exactly. One of my buds handled that. It's over where the beach turns a corner. Not sure what you call that area."

"Bay Point. Which street?"

He shrugged.

"Rental agency?"

"The Marine," he said. "But we only brought one car. Even if we leave, I'd have to go in and get them."

Callie glanced across him at the bags.

"Callie? I can't wait all afternoon," yelled her mother.

"Go on through," she told the driver. "But think about leaving, please."

"Yes, ma'am." And he pulled away.

This time she walked away from the highway, back to the store. Then she cursed, realizing she hadn't snapped a photo of the license. Damn Beverly's impatience.

Donna Baird had finished with television journalists and wandered the parking lot, speaking to people. Callie reached the end of the store, the side facing some farm acreage that had been allowed to go unused this year. "What is it, Mother? I've got a hurricane to manage."

"As do I," she said. "Never put me on hold again like that."

Callie bit her tongue. The least the woman would do was ask if it's a bad time. After all, her daughter was chief of police. "You've got me now."

"Gotta go now," Beverly said, biting each word.

"I said you've got me, so talk," Callie repeated. *For God's sake, you're wasting both our time.*

"If you're coming, you better get here. I'm not here to play hostess to your people."

"Let Jeb do it. You're always grooming him to walk in your shoes."

"Don't sass me."

Callie sighed. "I'm not. Honest. But I'm swamped with obligations, Mother, as I'm sure you are, too. Can this wait?"

"Absolutely, it can wait." And Beverly hung up.

Chapter 11

Arlo
Wednesday afternoon

LEONARD ENTERED via the back door, the quickest and more clandestine entrance to the house. "Yo," he said. "Anybody home?"

"Very funny," Arlo said, coming out of the kitchen. "What took you so long?"

Leonard threw the three bags on the counter. "Let's see . . . I had to scout the area, I had to stop at a grocery store that wasn't picked clean, and then I had to deal with the roadblock coming back onto the island. So, nothing, really. Just bee-bopping around taking my time enjoying the sights, Pretty Boy. West Ashley is a busy place. Further than I thought."

"We drove through there on the way here. I pointed out the spot."

"Groceries are not my job, though."

"We have one car. We stick to our strengths, dude. But it didn't kill you to pick up a few things, and I don't remember us needing beer."

Their assignments were not negotiable, and Leonard knew it. Leonard was the point man of the trio when they were on adventure. Arlo was more of the advance man, handling car and venue rentals, but because he reserved everything online, he rarely saw people other than maybe some receptionist who caught his eye. Upon leaving, he dropped off keys in off hours when the adventure was over. It was easy to travel invisibly these days.

Arlo started unloading the three bags. The kitchen was his duty, and he had to practice what he preached. Bread, peanut butter, and two kinds of jelly in one bag. Three six packs of two kinds of beer in the other. Bruce didn't often drink, so the brands suited the other two.

"How's he doing?" Leonard asked, while at the same time glancing around the corner into Bruce's room. He sat in a chair, looking over the bed, over the top of the duffle bag, out the window into the trees. "I swear, I don't know how he does that, man."

"Be glad he can do that, *man*." He went to put the beer in the fridge.

"Hey, hand me one of those," Leonard said, reaching out.

Arlo eased one out of the cardboard carton. "What was that about a roadblock?"

"In front of that convenience store between here and that big bridge, they must have six or eight uniforms stopping every car trying to get here. Told them I left y'all here without a car, so I was your only way off the beach."

"True that." Arlo looked inside the third bag. Not groceries. "Everything go okay?"

Leonard laughed. "With that mess out there? You'd think being in hurricane alley, these people would have a grip on how to handle this weather."

But Arlo wasn't as comfortable with difficult situations as Leonard, who rarely felt pressure. The tallest of the Retrievers had no sense of fluster. He thought through everything he did, analyzed whomever he spoke with, and, despite his size, managed to blend in. He loved slipping up on people and getting by others without being seen. He was little more than that handsome guy who jogged the beach.

Arlo held up the third bag. "But *this* went smooth?"

"Yeah, man."

"You weren't seen?"

Another chuckle. "Not on your life."

This difference between them wasn't a rub, but it was still . . . a difference. One worried little. The other worried they didn't worry enough. Leonard could be a hint flippant, which was why Arlo made initial reservations. Leonard picked up the drop-offs, because he didn't get rattled.

They had their strengths, but nobody was perfect.

Both protected Bruce, though . . . who always protected the duffle bag.

Arlo studied the third bag's contents, Leonard watching, holding his beer.

"All there?" Leonard asked, shifting his weight to lean against the stove.

"You don't know?"

Leonard shrugged, making him take a noisy slurp from the can. He swallowed and cleared his throat. "Not smart to count it on site. And so what if it's not the right amount? What am I supposed to do about it if it's not?"

Guess he was right. If the bills fell short of $300,000, what could he do about it? Call the doctor and demand he come back, meet Leonard, and cover the shortage? Nobody ever shorted them a dime.

Because to do so meant taking the chance that the person holding your loved one would be angered and retaliate, and retaliation meant only one thing. Two actually. One, not getting your loved one back, or two, getting them back dead.

Arlo threw the bag into the top freezer of the fridge, uncounted. He started toward the bedroom to check on Bruce, but then he remembered what he'd promised Wainwright. "Hey. I obligated us to board up three or four houses. To include this one."

Leonard plopped on the sofa, the television already on the Charleston news. Remote in hand, he started to change the channel, then got caught up watching the weather lady tapping her screens and buttons to explain assorted predictions for tomorrow night.

Leonard sat forward. "We're riding this thing out, you say?"

"I think it's best. If we dump her now, no telling what'll happen to her, so we do it on our way out of town after that storm sweeps through. It's not like we're directly on the beach. This thing has got to take out four rows of houses to reach us." Arlo waited for the weather lady to finish, and the topic to change to how the locals tend to their boats in times of hurricanes.

"Did you hear me?" Arlo repeated. "We've volunteered to board up a few houses. No later than noon tomorrow, she said."

His tall buddy turned. "Who is *she?*"

"The lady we rent this house from. The retired Marine drill instructor, dude. I sort of had to promise we'd assist with boarding."

A brow went up. Leonard was brawny, but he wasn't dumb. None of them were. Fact was, they considered themselves Mensa-level brains, and intellectually they had tested higher than ninety percent of their Ranger cohorts at the time. They could see details like nobody's business. They could read people. They'd successfully managed a dozen adventures, starting with one a year, progressing to one every four months, each pulled off without a glitch.

"Why'd you have to make her a promise? To stay here in the storm?"

"Nah. She had no problem with that. The police do, but supposedly they can't force us off." He clicked his tongue. "There's more than one reason to date the real estate receptionist, my man."

"Then why the promise?"

Arlo gave a mild shrug, meaning the reason was obvious. "The Marine said for her to let her receptionist leave early and go on a date with me last night, I had to agree to being the labor she needed for a few houses. The boards are already at the houses. They are custom and supposedly easy to install. You and I could do that and be endeared by the Jarhead."

Bruce remaining at the house went unsaid.

"Don't like you making friends with the natives, dude. When do we do this?" Leonard asked.

"Noon tomorrow. We rise at dawn and take care of business."

Leaning back on the sofa, Leonard finished his beer, resting the empty on his knee as he squeezed the can, turning it in circles to squeeze it afresh. "You sure we don't leave tomorrow?"

"I'm sure."

"Won't they come knocking on doors? To urge us to leave?"

"Maybe."

"Do they come inside?"

"Not without our permission," Arlo said.

Bored with weather, Leonard rose and meandered toward the kitchen. "Did you cook anything while I was out?"

"No. Made sandwiches. In case the power goes out, they'll keep. Don't whine about it."

"Then I need another beer."

Arlo sighed. "If you expect those beers to last through the storm, you best go easy on them. Hey, take a sandwich to Bruce. Otherwise, he'll starve."

Chapter 12

Callie
Wednesday night—thirty hours until the hurricane

AT HOUR PAST DUSK, Callie dismissed her officers at the roadblock as did Charleston County, leaving a Charleston man working into the night. She was but a hundred yards from her drive when she received a call from Jeb. Bone tired, she answered . . . because it was Jeb.

"Hey, can you talk right now?" he asked as she parked in her drive.

She tried to hold back the sigh that he might take the wrong way. She loved it when her son called, but she hated being this weary when he did.

"Everyone okay?" she asked.

"Yeah, yeah. Nothing like that."

"Y'all all settled in at your grandmother's house?"

"Yep, she gave me the blue guest room. Gave Sprite the yellow. She asked me how many more were coming, and I said you and Mark, maybe Sophie and Stan. Possibly Sarah." He still couldn't call Callie's biological mother Grandma or Grandmother or anything endearing. He would forever see Beverly as the real deal.

Beverly likely sicced Jeb onto her for a head count. "Yes, your grandmother barked at me this afternoon. But Miss Sophie is staying in Columbia with Buck. Sarah is going to Atlanta. Mark, Stan, and I will be coming, but at the last minute. She should not be surprised at any of that. If it gets too tight, I'll bunk with Sprite. The yellow room has a king. Mark would probably prefer the recliner anyway."

Jeb gave a small grunt. "Well, you know how she can be. She grabbed some lady and her daughter and made them clean the house like it was Christmas. Felt sorry for them," he said. "How's Mark?"

Callie felt sorry for most people who had to work under Beverly's oversight, but that was not her problem. "Mark is . . . better. I'm bringing him with me late tomorrow to give him more time to rest."

"That's good," Jeb said. "Okay, business taken care of. Now can you talk?"

"You already asked that, and I am talking. Have you got something more specific on your mind?"

"Yeah, but I need your full attention for this one."

"To be truthful, Son, I'm spent," she said, disconnecting her belt and leaning back in her seat. "Doubt I'm good for much more than yes-or-no answers. Not to discount your concerns, but can it wait until morning?"

The call went quiet.

"Jeb?"

He sighed. "Yeah, I suppose so."

She repeated herself. "You sure everyone there is fine?"

"Yes. I know you've got your hands full with the storm. We can talk tomorrow."

"You sure?"

"Yes, ma'am. Love you."

"Love you, too, Son."

Taking a minute before dragging herself up those stairs to the house, she felt silly thinking she wouldn't worry the rest of the night about what bothered Jeb.

Thursday morning – day of the hurricane

THE NEXT MORNING, Callie awoke to an empty bed. Feet padding across the planked floor to the living room, she found Mark stretched out in the recliner snoring, his blanket half puddled beside the chair.

Stan went home last night, bless him. He needed his own bed. But he'd promised to return for half the day then go home the second half to finish tying down his own place. Therefore, she had to tend to Mark before she dressed for work.

"Hey, guy." She stroked his leg. Slowly his eyes opened, and he sucked in a deep breath and started to stretch. "Don't—" she warned, but too late.

"Owww, oh, son of a bitch!" he said, jerked awake by the protesting wound, the stitches unforgiving.

Just watching him hurt. "You all right?"

"That sure as hell woke me up. Almost peed myself."

That unexpected visual threw her into a belly laugh, and he couldn't help but chuckle as well, flinching and trying not to.

"Come on," she said, reaching down to help lower his legs. "Gotta get you taken care of so I can go to work. Stan said he'll be over later."

"I need to move more anyway." His humor was replaced with a scowl as he stood. "Why the hell does this hurt so much?"

"Don't ask stupid questions. You're still not allowed to take a shower. Need help?"

His first steps looked painful, but he seemed to ease into a better rhythm the closer he got to the bath. "No. Let me do this myself."

Since he wasn't showering, she did, one eye on him making slow, creaky movements around the bathroom as he tried to wash in the sink. His limp leg seemed to hurt him more, but there was nothing she could do to make his healing any easier. Time alone would put him back to right. That and not overdoing. After he finished puttering around this morning, he'd park himself back in that recliner and probably drift off watching the weather people spit statistics as they gave best- and worst-case scenarios about Nikki.

She got dressed about the time he managed to, and she met him in the kitchen, pretending not to notice his stopping at one point to ponder whether to head to his chair or get something to drink. After directing him to go sit, she fixed him toast, two eggs, a banana, and coffee, then set a large thermos of water beside him.

"Have I told you lately how much I love you?" he said.

"No, remind me."

"I love these eggs, this toast, this . . . coddling."

She smiled. "I'd hope you loved me for more than that."

"I've forgotten. As I heal, you'll have to remind me."

She leaned over and kissed him hard on the mouth. "One step at a time, Cajun. Don't want to pop any stitches." She'd already set up his phone charger and anchored his phone to the side table. She tapped the screen to life to double-check the connection and ensure he had a full charge. "Call if you need anything. I'm on the beach today. I can get here from anywhere in two minutes."

"Gotcha," he said, this time his smile looking good on him.

She hated leaving him, but with her other officers on the roadblock, she and Thomas would have to oversee the beach town today. Then the beach patrol would go off duty around six.

Today everyone would be less forgiving of people attempting access, and they'd hold people more accountable. No coming back if you left Edisto. No getting on unless you were a resident. Period.

Outside, the air seemed charged. Soft gray clouds moved to what might appear gentle to visitors but hinted at something more ominous to Callie. There was a scent in the warmer-than-usual breeze that lingered, sometimes pushing in a small gust as a warning of things to come. The hair didn't quite stand on her arms, but a small, cautious crawl of wariness did in her core. These weather events crept in incrementally until they were suddenly there in full force. The coast ought to thank the heavens at the onslaught coming in the middle of the night.

Despite the weather's eerie sensation, she couldn't get Mark off her mind. He didn't look any better than yesterday. He was supposed to have a post-op check tomorrow, but with the storm, no medical offices were open, and they'd postponed him to next Monday, just short of a week from when he had the surgery. No fever, though, which was the big thing they were supposed to watch for. If he spiked one, they were to go to the ER. She could only imagine how backed up and under-staffed they'd be.

She pulled up to a stop sign, poised to turn onto Palmetto. She made sure nobody was behind her and texted Stan. *Let me know when you get to the house.* Then she added. *No rush.* Not that she meant it. Then she typed a second note. *Watch for fever.*

A couple of palmetto trees across the road danced more than usual. The owner hadn't kept the dead fronds tended properly, and those would be the first branches to fly off in the evening's winds.

Then just as she started to turn, Stan called.

"Just tell me to go over there," he said.

"I didn't want to push."

"You have a funny way of showing it in your texts. Is he not doing well?"

How would she answer that? "Um, he's probably fine. Of course, he hates aching and being limited. I fed him breakfast and left him in the recliner with water."

"Sounds like you left a pet."

"Stop it. You know better. I just hate him being alone."

He gave a humorous grunt. "I'll be over there in a half hour." He gave another deep Stan chuckle. "I like how you two are getting along, Chicklet. Does my heart good."

That did more than anything that morning to make her feel better.

They hung up. She drove two blocks before she met Thomas driving towards her, coming out of Whaley Street. They matched up driver to driver, windows down.

"How's Mark?" he asked.

"Sore, tired, and fussy."

His laugh came with a nod of understanding. "I hear fussy often means they feel better."

She could hope. "How're things looking?"

"Actually, people aren't doing half bad this time. We're going to have our share of people sticking around, but what can you do? All in all, we're good. I've had to move some yard furniture and grills at empty houses. If I can't store them someplace, I do what I can to tie them down with whatever I can find. Amazing at how many of these storerooms aren't locked. The outdoor showers work pretty well as storage, though."

Thomas was a commonsense kind of guy. More so than a couple of her older guys. Though young, his ability to think on his feet was why she wanted him with her to the end during these last hours before landfall.

Like a kid with a walkie-talkie, Thomas also loved using his loudspeaker, which he'd start doing later in the afternoon, repeating the warning over and over to make sure everyone had one last chance to be safe.

They moved on, back to watching for problems, warning people, offering assistance when needed short of packing people's cars for them. They would also attempt to note who remained behind.

About an hour into her day, Callie spotted Donna walking her dog on Palmetto Boulevard, his gentle gait even with hers. Callie pulled over to the curb. "Hey, aren't you leaving?"

"I'm packed but didn't see the rush. Wanted to walk Horse until he was worn out anyway."

Callie gave a lighthearted scoff. "How many miles is that going to take?"

The councilwoman laughed in kind. "A while. He keeps me in shape, for sure. But I'm greeting people. Hope you don't mind, but I've been advising them on the protocols of a hurricane."

Callie didn't mind one bit. Donna certainly took her new role on the council seriously, quite refreshing not only after Brice's shenanigans, but also considering the existing members. They did their jobs, but they didn't act particularly enthralled with their responsibilities.

"Just spoke with Arthur Wainwright," Donna said, looking over her shoulder, toward the west end of Palmetto. No telling which house that might be. "He's running himself ragged, poor guy." With a pinched expression, she peered at Callie. "Does Janet treat him okay?"

Horse took a step toward the car, Callie watching. "Yeah, she might be a little hard on him, but he's her only heir, and she wants him to earn his inheritance. She feels it's her duty to train him to step into her shoes, as big as those are." She winked. "Not that Janet intends on going any-where anytime soon. The kid's only twenty-three, but she'd go to the mat for that boy. I've seen it."

Horse took another step. Callie looked at Donna for permission.

"Sure, he likes you."

Callie extended her hand. Horse came over and laid his massive head in it, peering up at Callie with eyes the size of half dollars. Curling her fingers, she lightly scratched his chin and felt her heart melt. "He's sweet."

"Most Danes are," Donna said. "Good watch dogs, but very soci-able. Gentle giants."

Horse readjusted his head, asking her to scratch a little to the other side. She did until her extended arm tired of supporting twenty pounds. As she retrieved her hand, sliding it easily back in the window, Horse gifted her with a tablespoon of warm slobber.

"Oh, sorry. That means he really likes you," Donna said. "That and he's warm from walking."

Luckily Callie carried clean-up supplies in the cruiser.

"Where's Arthur?" she asked, dabbing between her fingers with a paper towel, a wet wipe at the ready on the console. "Want to get a feel for how many of their renters are sticking around." And if Arthur didn't know, she'd go see the Marine herself. Janet would've contacted all her renters, for sure.

"He's on Thistle," Donna said, pulling on the leash. "Tell the nice lady goodbye, Horse."

The animal peered up at its owner then back to Callie and wagged his tail.

"He's not one for conversation, I take it," Callie said, preparing to pull away.

"It's all in his eyes," Donna said, stepping herself and her buddy back. "Stay safe."

Callie cruised on, head swiveling, watching for issues and finding none. She spotted Buck before she found Arthur, up on a ladder working yet another set of windows. She didn't want to interrupt and just gave him a wave. If he could get to her house, he would. If he couldn't, she and Stan could manage. At least on the seaward-side windows if they couldn't get them all. Her side of Jungle Road rested six rows back from the ocean. Anything that took out her house would take out the whole island. Flooding and wind surges could hurl trees and limbs and debris to do enough damage, however, but water that got into her house that far back would mean the end of Edisto Beach.

Ahead, a house on the nine-hundred block of Palmetto, on the beach side with a clear shot of the Atlantic—which even now kicked up waves enough to deter swimmers—showed no sign of evacuating. Six cars parked beneath and in front of the property, with license plates from three different states.

A hurricane party. She'd be tickled pink if this was the only one.

She couldn't turn into the packed drive, so she paralleled the curb, letting Thomas know by mic where she was in case the party prematurely got rowdy, and she needed another hand to rein it in. As she exited, a gust whipped her face. Comfortable right now but with greater force than the norm.

Some people found watching the wind increase, the clouds gather, and the waves kick up foam exhilarating. Nine times out of ten, they'd never experienced a hurricane before.

Her phone rang, and she paused, standing at the rear end of a car with Virginia tags.

Jeb on caller ID.

Damn it, she should've called him first thing, to avoid him calling at an inopportune time. More so, however, to show she'd remembered and cared about his concerns. Bad on her.

"Hey, Son." The wind blew at her, channeled beneath the house and across the tops of the parked cars. She turned her back, trying to lessen the whoosh and whistling, then just repeated her tracks back into her vehicle.

"Hey, is this a good time?"

There really wasn't a good time, but she'd already postponed him last night. She couldn't justify putting him off again. "I'm in my car, just pulled over, so now is as good a time as any. What's up?"

"First, appears I'm in charge at Grandma's house. My marching orders are to keep track of arrivals."

"The three of us, meaning Stan, Mark, and me, won't be in until to-night. Time yet to be determined. Can't speak for anyone else."

"Is there anyone else?"

Good question. "No different than I told you last night," she said. "Probably no more than the three of us."

"Check. Sprite has been trying to call her mother, but she isn't answering."

"Probably pouting, Jeb. Miss Sophie already chewed on my butt for knowing about Sprite's close call before she did. By now, son, you ought to have a feel for that family. The Bianchis are high-spirited. They get excited. So, is that the concern? Sprite?"

This level of worry could wait until she arrived in Middleton that night. This level of worry she could live with.

"No, I've got some serious concerns about Langley."

Langley?

"The kidnapped girl who's no longer kidnapped?"

"Yes. I . . . we are not buying that she's safe or that all's-right-with-the-world spiel the dad said. Sprite keeps trying to call her, and she doesn't answer her phone."

Hmm, sometimes a girl just doesn't want to answer her phone. "Besides that, what else makes you think that she's still in danger?" Callie didn't want to discount his apprehension. The hint of alarm in his voice wasn't common for him, which meant she had to let him down gently. He ordinarily avoided interrupting her on the job, so for him to do amidst hurricane activities meant his heart was behind his words.

"She doesn't answer texts, and she isn't active on Facebook. She left things in her room she'd have taken home with her."

"Like what?" Callie looked up, watching for anyone to come out of the house she needed to check on after this call.

"Her phone charger, for one. Her earbuds charger. Her makeup. Her overnight bag." He waited for a response, then not getting the reaction he wanted, said, "Tell me there's nothing suspicious about that."

Admittedly, those were oddities that would give one pause. "Have you checked with the RA on the hall? Don't y'all have to let them know when you go home or leave campus for any serious length of time?"

"The RA heard nothing. Langley went to class and never came back, Mom. Still hasn't been seen after the dad's claim she's safe."

One thing Jeb and Sprite were not considering, however, was the idea that a normally forthright and focused individual could have a breakdown, fail a test, and get snubbed by a secret crush. Not everyone shared their thoughts, plans, and dreams, and if Langley had strayed from what everyone assumed was her focus, and had paid a price for it, she likely would be too embarrassed to admit the gaffe. Driven people hated being seen as flawed. Especially college-aged kids under the thumbs of their parents.

A pre-med twenty-year-old, whose father was a well-admired sur-geon, certainly clicked neatly into that category. "Do you know her dad?"

"No, but we know Langley."

"Yes, but have y'all called her dad?" The girl's college friends calling to check on her made sense. Any parent would appreciate that.

"Her dad said Langley said she needed space, and she was fine."

Callie waited for Jeb to reason himself into the realization everything might just be above board.

But he didn't.

"I'm calling bullshit, Mom. We think something happened."

"Like what?"

"Not sure, but I don't like Langley disappearing right after the close call with Sprite. Stop and think. You've seen Langley's picture, right?"

"Yes." The coed was lovely. Blue eyes that contrasted with dark hair and a light complexion. If a child could appear affluent, she did.

"Don't you see the resemblance to Sprite?"

Callie paired the two in her mind.

"What if Sprite was mistaken identity? Same hall. Same dorm."

That was indeed a thought. Callie shivered at what would've hap-pened if Sprite had been mistaken for Langley. What if she'd been taken, the culprits realizing they'd erred, then had to discard her. But Sprite's father was a retired NFL player. Sophie and her children lacked for nothing. *She would've been just as good a victim.*

Langley, if kidnapped, could've been a substitute for missing Sprite.

Callie could spin what-ifs just like her son, only with more gruesome endings.

"So why wouldn't her father be looking for her unless the crisis were legitimately over, son?"

"Damn good question. But why sound the alarm then back off? This is totally out of character for Langley, too. It just doesn't feel right. It doesn't smell right. Do I have the whole story? No. But that's part of the problem, too." He took in a breath. "And during the chaos of a hurricane? What an opportunity to get away with something."

But the hurricane could just as easily sabotage kidnapping plans, too. How could they orchestrate a ransom when the coast was in the midst of an evacuation? The major roads were redirected to mostly one way, away from the Atlantic.

Though she had to admit, the storm would be a fine way to dispose of a body.

"Son," she said, catching herself before getting sucked into his machinations. "I'm not discounting you. You grew up with a seasoned detective and a US Marshall as parents. Crime-solving was as commonplace in the house as the furniture. You have skills. You have wiles. But the father saying what he did on television along with a hurricane bearing down on the city, gave law enforcement a much-needed excuse to redirect all their energies on the storm. She's not a minor child. They have bigger responsibilities now. Tens of thousands of folks are counting on them. Asking them to look at Langley's case again has to wait until after the storm is resolved and they can justify the manpower."

Silence dragged out between them.

"Jeb, listen. After Nikki comes and goes, go to Langley's house. If you're still convinced things are amiss, go to the Charleston detective who had the case with your concerns. However, like it or not, knowing what they know, they have higher priorities right now. They have no reason to challenge the dad or call him a liar when they've got nothing to go on."

More silence, and she waited for him to sort his thoughts. "What if he's lying?" Jeb said.

"Then after the storm, when Langley doesn't show up, they have their reason to reopen the case. The dad, however, would have some explaining to do."

"That's so wrong. My gut is telling me—"

"Son, your gut's probably more accurate than that of the average person, for sure, but they're not going to listen to you. Not today. And not with her parent against you."

She heard nothing but silent disappointment. "See you when you get here then," he said, the words slow and sad.

"Love you, Jeb."

"Yeah, love you, too, Mom."

Callie loved his zeal. She'd hug him hard once she reached her mother's house in Middleton.

She wished she was more like him.

Chapter 13

Callie
Late Thursday morning—day of the hurricane

CALLIE SHIFTED BACK into work mode as she navigated the cluster of vehicles beneath the beach house. The number of cars indicated a minimum of six guests.

After a couple of deep, acclimating breaths, she opened her car door and looked up again at the beach house packed full of people. No movement out front, but that wasn't unusual. Action was always in the back, facing the water.

She was forever amazed at how much stupidity factored into the stops she had to make on this beach. She hoped she was wrong, that this wasn't a hurricane party and that she'd walk into a hallway full of suitcases and people dressed to leave.

But her gut told her otherwise.

She didn't bother going to the front door. The activity would be in the back along with the alcohol, watching the storm come to town. With the wind's direction, the voices carried to her ears before she got halfway around the house.

Callie's first visual was that of a girl and a boy, each maybe twenty, facing the ocean, arms wide, emulating the scene in *Titanic*. Their unbuttoned shirts flapped behind them, chins up, singing Celine Dion with drinks in their hands.

She was up the stairs and on the back porch before they noticed her. Judging from their glazed stares, they had started drinking early, if not the night before. For sure, these were young souls made of sturdy stuff to be soused before noon.

"Hey, guys, we have a guest!" shouted the boy doing the *Titanic* pose. He dropped his arms and walked with a slight zigzag through the double glass doors to inside. Callie followed. Nobody protested.

That was because six people lay reposed across sofas, chairs, and pillows on the floor. The kitchen explained why, with a bar of half empty—some totally empty—bottles and cans. Used glasses on every piece of furniture. By the time the storm got here, they'd be nursing hangovers.

And they were in no shape to drive anywhere.

Callie took a head count. Twelve people, still fully clothed, between the ages of the couple on the back porch to the thirty-year-olds who'd made their way to beds at some point last night. She found it amazing nobody was nude.

Three of them stirred as Callie made her way from room to room. By the time she returned to the kitchen, she had three in tow as well as the guy from the porch. His girl had remained behind, crashed on the chaise, eyes closed. No point rousting her up.

"Any coffee here?" Callie asked, going through cabinets.

Porch guy said, "Like a Keurig?"

At their ages, a pod coffee maker was probably all they understood, but there wasn't one. Finally, an old Mr. Coffee showed its dusty head from behind a stash of pots and pans Callie moved around. A half can of coffee stood behind a mishmash of seasonings, along with an open wrapper of filters, the top one with roach droppings on it. She discarded the top two filters, washed the pot, and got a full pot of coffee going.

Rather than leave and assume they'd figure out how to make another pot, she hung until the carafe was full. Serving all the contents, sharing it amongst eight cups, she put on another pot.

"Here," she said, handing them out to the four in the kitchen. She took one out to the girl on the porch, nudging her awake, pouring out the remnants of her rum cocktail, and sitting her up with the black coffee.

By the time the second pot had dripped through, and the rest had been served, she had them all awake, half of them alert enough to listen, each holding a cup or thermos of caffeine.

"Look at me," she ordered.

"Isn't there any sugar?" one girl asked.

"No," Callie said. "Drink it as is. If you have aspirin, take it. After that, as much water as you can stand. In the meantime, listen."

The twelve drunks did as they were told, none of them in the best shape, but they weren't energized to do much more than they were told.

"There's a hurricane coming at midnight," she said.

"Yeah," laughed one twenty-something. "We spent good money to get this house to watch it."

Callie did some quick math in her head. "Your life is worth more than five hundred dollars, wouldn't you say?"

"We paid more than that for this place."

One of the oldest ones nudged the twenty-something. "She means per person, you idiot."

She let the sluggish joking cease, which didn't take long. "If this hurricane comes in anywhere between Savannah and Charleston, we're in for some water, wind, and rain. The right combination could wash over this porch, maybe into the house, and easily through your vehicles so you can't get off the beach."

"Shit, that's my dad's car," a girl said. "He's out of town and doesn't know I borrowed it."

"I just bought mine," complained a scrawny gentleman in only gym shorts. Callie could count his ribs.

A young lady with smudged makeup waved her coffee cup. "That's what insurance is for . . . damn it," she said, as the coffee sloshed down her arm.

"Y'all, would you please listen?" Callie said, using her outside voice, just short of her crowd voice.

The group hushed.

"Leave the beach," she said. "Sober up, pack up, and leave." She gave them a blatant once-over scan, communicating that they were in sorry shape. "By six this evening at the latest," she added. "Your heads will be cleared by then. Get home."

"What if we don't?" said the thirty-year-old, clothes wrinkled as if they'd been wadded up wet and dried.

"Then let me make copies of your driver's licenses."

The girl who'd spilled her coffee stiffened. "Why? My parents don't know I'm here."

"To identify the bodies," Callie said.

One girl started to cry.

CALLIE LATER CROSSED paths with Thomas near the marina.

"How many times have you used the driver's-license-find-the-body-talk?" he asked.

"A few," she said. "Alex didn't buy it. So maybe three?"

Thomas laughed out loud. "I win. Used it five times."

She smiled at the young man's humor. They used one of two ploys to entice people to leave. The one about identifying the body, and the other about how there would be no first responder assistance once the storm hit. The latter one was truth. The other they'd never had to use and hoped to never have to.

"You okay staying till dusk?" she said.

"Sure. I'd only be going home anyway." He rented a fifty-year-old, thousand-square-foot house on a couple acres on the marsh where he fished and perpetually worked on refinishing a boat. His place was closer to the big bridge than the beach, about fifteen miles away. Unless this were a Hurricane Hugo Category Five affair, he'd be safe through most any storm. Chances were Officer Annie was staying with him for the storm. She stayed there on the days they had off together, which Callie attempted to schedule.

Being after one in the afternoon, her stomach growled. "I'm checking on Mark. You grab lunch. Then we'll hit the streets again."

"Got six houses so far with people sticking it out," he said.

"I've got three," she said. They still had almost half the beach to cover. "Raysor radioed me saying they've got less traffic at the roadblock. Mostly people leaving. A couple of reporters were turned back." She paused. "Have you seen Alex Hanson?"

"Jungle Road is on your route, Chief, so no."

"I mean on the beach, or interviewing people. She's out here, and I want to make sure she leaves. Her grandmother and Monty have no business weathering this mess for the sake of her career. I'll check the house on my way home."

Thomas walked to the marina, hoping one of the restaurants could manage a sandwich for him, and to check how many boats remained moored. The big ones should already be relocated.

Callie got in her car and looked at texts. Stan had arrived at the house. *Good.* She cranked up and headed southeast, toward Jungle Road.

Where Dock Site Road turned into Lybrand, she continued watching for signs of those remaining behind to hopefully have a chat about the hazards of doing so. A half-dozen houses down, she noted a guy on a ladder, his buddy assisting with boards. They both looked familiar, but not in a resident kind of way.

She got out and strolled over. "Y'all renting here?" They weren't contractors she knew, and renters didn't normally do this sort of labor. But when the closest, the shortest of the two, turned, she made the connection.

"How was the date the other night?" she asked, recognizing Natalie's beau she'd served at El Marko's.

He pushed sweated dark hair out of his eyes. "Hello, um, Chief?" he said, quite sure.

With a grin she reached out for a shake. He took it strong and assured. "Yeah, I imagine seeing me there then here is a bit of a mind clash," she said. "My boyfriend owns the restaurant. By day, however, I'm police chief of the town." She glanced up at the other man on the ladder, about fifteen feet off the ground. She recognized him from somewhere, but not El Marko's.

"Kind of late to still be here, don't you think?" she asked.

"We're not leaving," he said. "And we promised the Marine we'd board a few of her houses. We had the time and were fully capable, so why not?"

Capable they were. Clearly, they kept themselves fit, and the way they addressed Janet as *the Marine* probably meant they were ex-military as well. "Y'all Marine?"

"Rangers," he said. "We each did about six years, most of it overseas."

He hadn't introduced his friend. She looked up at the other one, a big man, his muscles more pumped than even the most fit she'd seen out here. His tee fit him snugly. His jeans the same. He wore hiking boots, however, which was smart climbing a ladder. "Hello," she hollered for him to hear.

He waved.

"Y'all staying in the same house?"

"Yeah. Why?" said the man on the ground.

She waved her hand like pushing aside the fog. "Just hit me where I've seen him before. In the roadblock yesterday. He went out for groceries since Food Lion was picked bare. Said there were three of y'all."

"Yeah, our other guy isn't as social as we are. His tours of duty weren't as uneventful, if that makes sense."

It did. "Which house?" she asked.

The Ranger stiffened, then acted as if he didn't understand.

Callie clarified. "Your friend up there said he couldn't remember where y'all were renting. Figured you might."

"Oh," and he laughed a couple times, as though relieved. "Wasn't sure what was going on there for a second." He laughed again. "I make the reservations. Leonard just shows up and flexes." He laughed once again. "You've probably seen him jogging. Iron Man there can hardly stand to sit still."

"Well, he looks like he does his fair share of exercise. Where again?"

The guy shrugged and looked up Lybrand, due south, toward the beach a few blocks over. "He runs anywhere. Especially on the beach, but he might swim, might jog the roads. Can't get enough. If he's not sweating, he's bored."

"No," Callie said. "I mean your address. Where are you staying?"

"Oh, oh, oh, my bad." He looked down, shaking his head. "I'm so stupid. We're at *Seas the Day*. Arc Street. Not sure of the number. I understand houses go by names around here anyway."

A hint of something pinged at her, and she attributed it to the unusual day and urgency to make Edisto safe. "I know the house, and you're right. We like our names. Gives each house its own personality, I'd say."

"No two alike from what I've seen," he said, peering back up at his friend who waited, needing his other half to hand him a board.

She caught the gist of the mannerism. They wanted to get back to work. "Well, kudos to you for helping us out here. I'm sure Janet appreciates it."

"Janet?"

"The Marine."

"Oh, oh, yeah. Glad to help. It's not like we can swim today. Those rip tides are fierce."

Callie nodded. "Glad you see that. Well, if you're not leaving the beach, then be safe, okay?"

"Yes, ma'am." He doffed his head with an invisible top hat, and she couldn't help but grin. He seemed nice enough, and while Leonard hadn't been too social—most men at the top of a ladder weren't, he seemed nice enough as well from her discussion with him at the roadblock. They seemed capable of sound decisions.

She returned to her car, and, instead of heading right onto Jungle Road, she continued all the way to Palmetto Boulevard and took a right. About ten blocks down, she took another right on Neptune, then a left onto Arc Street. Slowing in front of *Seas the Day*, she took it in.

The windows were boarded, one car in the drive. Nothing loose littered the yard like chairs or hammocks, gnomes or flags. They'd tidied up and done their own prep, saving Janet and Arthur the trouble. For sure Janet liked these tenants. As much as she loved her nephew, one couldn't ignore her unspoken wish that he'd enlisted somewhere and developed a tougher hide. It's why she leaned on him so hard.

If anyone were to stay behind, Callie would prefer it be guys like this, not the party crew she'd tended earlier. These guys could *improvise, adapt, and overcome,* as the military saying went. That other gaggle of folks, however, would be more likely consumed by ol' Mother Nature. A bad storm would eat them like cotton candy.

Almost two p.m., and she was hungry. Neither Mark nor Stan had called.

But on her way home, she remembered telling Thomas she'd drive by Mrs. Hanson's house. At this rate it would be dinner time before she managed to get to Mark. But Mrs. Hanson had no business weathering this storm. Her house dated back to the sixties, meaning it wasn't up on stilts. So help her, if Alex was delaying her grandmother's evacuation in the name of a good storm story, Callie would be pissed. At a minimum, she'd cancel Alex's tag on her VW. She'd tell Mrs. Hanson to just drive herself off the island, and if need be, go to Beverly's place in Middleton. She was Beverly's age, and Beverly would fully understand regardless of how much she acted like she didn't.

Callie got to the Hanson house only to find nobody home. The VW was there, but Mrs. Hanson's SUV wasn't, meaning someone had taken the bigger car. Callie peered in the front windows, then again around the back. No lights on, but from the sliding glass doors, she could see a couple of suitcases in the middle of the floor, packed and ready to go.

Since she was this close, Callie made her way the two doors down to her house *Chelsea Morning,* a gust of wind shoving at the vehicle's seaward side, indicating things were picking up.

Stan's car sat in the drive.

Before taking the stairs up to the front door, she took the opportunity to tend her own place. Opening the ground-level storage affixed beneath the house, between the two parking areas, she moved items around and retrieved two shutters, placing the grill inside, putting flowerpots on her chest freezer. She closed the door and carried the shutters upstairs, her small toolbox as well, barely hooked over her crooked fingers.

Setting the shutters against the wall, she studied the rattan furniture on the porch, along with the red hanging swing. Best just move them inside.

Stan opened the door. "Wondered what the thumping and bumping was about out here. You are not installing storm shutters by yourself, are you?"

"No," she said. "But all this stuff here needs to go inside."

"Gives me something to do this afternoon," he said. "I'm about done with my place. Just finished giving Mark his lunch and was about to call you. Come eat."

She did as she told, eager to check on the Cajun. She found him standing, looking out the back window. "Seeing much wind out there?" he asked.

"Some," she said. "How are you doing?"

"Same," he said.

At least he was standing, but he didn't sound very upbeat.

Stan came inside with a rattan chair in his hands. "Where you want it?"

She ran to him and opened the door to her guest bedroom. "Anywhere in there." She followed him in, pushing the door almost closed, and she lowered her voice. "Is he getting depressed?"

"He's being a baby," Stan said. "It's an appendix, for God's sake. Does he need to lift anything? No. Is he pouting about being limited? Yes."

"Tell me you haven't been scolding him," she said, glancing at the door. Mark might be listening.

"Of course I have. It's nothing life threatening unless he doesn't follow doctor's orders."

"And yours," she added.

He chuckled. "And mine. Now, where do you want that red swing? Might need help getting that thing down."

"Bring up the ladder from downstairs," she said, returning to the hall. "You hold the weight off the swing, and I'll unhook it up top. Between us we can handle it."

She didn't care if everything else around her house blew to Bermuda, but that red swing from Seabrook's Palmetto Boulevard house, was going to be safely ensconced in her spare bedroom.

Chapter 14

Arlo
Early Thursday afternoon

THE POLICE CHIEF drove off, and Arlo felt they'd mostly survived the scrutiny.

"What do you think?" Leonard said, coming down off the ladder.

"She's good, I think. We're patriots." Arlo met his friend and slapped him on the back. "We're All-American boys. Besides that, we're working on behalf of the Marine. That's credibility."

Maybe saying it with enough zeal would make him believe it. He peered up. "Done with that one?"

"Yeah. Two more on the other side of the house and we're done."

Leonard retrieved the ladder while Arlo proceeded to the other side, reviewing the intel he'd gotten from talking with Natalie.

Police Chief Callie Morgan. Three years on the beach but a long-time visitor. Parents owned the house she lived in, owned since before the chief was born, so that sort of made her native. Well-respected, the chief had handled some crime in the small community that nobody saw coming. She had a solid past as a fifteen-year veteran detective in Boston, a major police department. Big fish in a small pond.

She had a few bodies notched in her gun, so not a person to underestimate. *Note to self: check out the local police force's creds when planning another adventure.*

"Steam's coming out of your ears," Leonard said, coming around the corner. "What is it?"

"She knows us," he replied.

"She *saw* us," Leonard corrected. "She doesn't know shit. We are two of who knows how many people out here boarding up, packing up, and hustling. My guess is she wants to be aware of the bodies she might have to look for if this storm turns vicious. Just doing her job."

"She knows where we rent now. After the storm, she'll come looking for us. To see if we're safe."

Leonard propped up the ladder, digging the base into the silt for a firm stronghold. He put a foot hard on the bottom rung to anchor deeper. "And we'll be gone."

Arlo didn't like this altered course of events. "Won't it look odd that we bragged about sticking things out, but they come back to find us gone?"

Leonard's laugh had a bass tone to it, and ordinarily Arlo liked laughing along with the big man. Most of the time they thought on the same wavelength. "Who's going to question why we left the coast during a hurricane, man? The Marine won't because she has our money. The chief won't because she has way more to worry about than us. We leave the house tidy with the keys in the realty's after-hours box, and there's nothing at all to question." He pointed to the closest shutter. "Come up behind me with that, and don't make me have to reach too far like the last one. Last thing we need is for me to fall off this damn thing and break a bone."

Arlo focused on the task at hand, but the idea that this chief was a smart cookie and an unexpected factor in their plans, gave him a nudge of discomfort.

She'd seen them. She had their first names.

They'd planned for almost everything, even the hurricane, using it to aid their clandestine campaign. They hadn't, however, planned for her.

Chapter 15

Callie
Early Thursday afternoon—less than twelve hours to hurricane

WITH THE RED swing finally on Callie's spare-room bed thanks to her on one end and Stan on the other, she accepted the sandwich and chips Stan handed her. She ate them while walking over to the Hanson house. Alex's car was parked in the drive, but nobody was there. The suitcases remained inside.

What the hell was Alex up to? Or did Callie even have to ask?

The most likely place she'd be was on the beach, the gusts blowing that long blond hair for emphasis in her forecasting what Nikki might do to Edisto Beach. She'd want the waves, too, which meant the south side where the surf kicked the hardest, and she'd know that from growing up there. But where was Mrs. Hanson? And Monty, the young man she'd adopted?

The sun now hid behind ominous clouds, the wind gaining speed. Leaves and fronds already aged and slack were shaking loose and skittering end over end across properties. No sign of land birds, but gulls zipped and maneuvered, enjoying the unusual weather.

Callie returned to her car in her drive, cranked it up, and radioed Thomas. "Keep an eye out for Mrs. Hanson's SUV. I need to know she's all right." She texted Jeb as she spoke, asking if Mrs. Hanson happened to have gone to Middleton. She'd been told it was an option for her.

If she had gone there, it meant Alex had hung around for a story. "I swear, Thomas, I'm going to confiscate Alex's decal and invalidate her as a resident. We've been patient with that girl. It's time she paid a price for her journalistic crap."

"On it, Chief." Thomas didn't argue. He understood full well how much this young woman got under Callie's skin.

Alex was a contradiction for Callie. An Edistonian but also a reporter. Callie hated reporters with a deep, deep passion. She'd disliked them enough before Michael Seabrook's days, but once one killed him, right before her eyes . . . the man she'd just come to love . . . she struggled being within a dozen yards of anyone in the profession. Alex's grandmother being such a dear made Callie give Alex a guarded pass. But if anything happened to that sweet older lady, the quicker Callie would one hundred percent despise the granddaughter.

Callie drove toward the front of town, and in passing Wainwright Realty reminded herself she wanted Janet's take on how many of her renters remained behind. The realty's windows had built-in shutters that took little effort to close and lock, and they were indeed closed. The Hummer wasn't in the front. Janet could be at her own home, tending to its safety, or any one of the dozens of houses she managed.

Callie reached where Highway 174 crossed the causeway, then veered right to start at the Pavilion and cruise down Palmetto hunting for the Hanson SUV. With so many cars gone, it should be easy to spot.

Only four blocks down, she caught the green SUV parked under a seaside rental. She pulled in behind it. Not surprising to find her so quickly. The further down the beach, the less impressive the waves would be, and the reporter in the girl would want the most profound side of Nature she could grab.

Callie checked her watch. After five. About time for all the other officers, all but her and Thomas, to vacate the beach. Marie was already gone, the station locked up. Most of the town's administrative souls should be gone. They knew the highways tended to back up with last-minute retreats, and most didn't want to get mired in the commute.

The absence of people seemed to give notice to the inanimate to take up arms. A flag left on a pole flapped with vengeance. It would be in tatters before the night was over. She ought to take it and its pole down before that flag became a missile plowing through someone's unboarded window.

Trees were turning into giants wielding swords, daring the adversary.

But Callie still had people in mind over things.

Passing beneath the house, heading straight behind the residence to the water, she didn't immediately see Alex. Didn't see anyone at first, which was good, but after a hard study up the sand, she found them. A hundred yards west, Alex stood with her back to the ocean with Mrs. Hanson supporting a camera on her shoulder. Monty held back Mrs. Hanson's hair from her face, one hand on each temple.

Callie broke into a trot. "Alex!"

But the wind swallowed up the call; no way was it reaching Alex's ears. No rain yet, so Callie's black work sneakers dug into the sand, her quads taxed, making the effort sluggish.

Only six hours, give or take, until the storm hit, and the outskirts of it would hit two or three hours sooner. The tide was half out, each wave a curling mass of power churning into the beach, six feet or more high, angry, intense, and already taking a wealth of beach with it out to sea. Damage was already happening. The storm wouldn't arrive at high or low tide, but at a stage in between, a stage heading toward high tide. Could be worse. Way worse.

A gale whipped in against her, the unevenness beneath her feet equally throwing her off balance. "Alex," Callie called, but again, the wind stripped her of the word. It took Callie getting within thirty yards of them before Monty noticed. He yelled into Mrs. Hanson's ear, who turned. Callie trotted the last few yards and held out her hands for the camera.

Mrs. Hanson looked at Alex, who held out her own hands for the camera instead, and Callie allowed the exchange.

Their clothes and hair flapped, each of them blinking at the dryness of so much fast-moving air. The temperature had started to dip.

"Take that camera and get out of here," Callie yelled to Alex. To Mrs. Hanson, she said, "Please take Monty to safety. You'll already have to deal with traffic but don't stay here. Do you have a place to stay?"

Mrs. Hanson looked to her granddaughter. "With her."

"In Charleston? You sure?"

The old woman nodded.

Callie inserted herself between Alex and her grandmother, facing the girl. They were about the same size, Callie having fifteen years on her, and Callie wished she had the discretion of speaking low, so nobody heard.

"If they get hurt, I'll hold you responsible, Alex."

"They are my family, Chief. My responsibility."

"Then take that responsibility seriously."

Callie made an impromptu decision. "I'm cancelling the beach decal on your VW. You don't have one for your other car. The one remaining belongs to your grandmother, assigned to her specific SUV."

But Alex wasn't affected. "Go right ahead, but you know I wouldn't let them get hurt."

"You might not mean to, but just you bringing them here tells me you're not that great a judge of their safety," Callie said.

Then she felt a hand on her shoulder. Turning, she saw Mrs. Hanson stood close, the hand giving her a few pats. "She's fine, Callie. We were about to leave, weren't we, Alex?" The grandmother turned to Monty. "Come on, Son. Let's head back to the car. We must leave before Miss Nikki arrives." She and the young man began making their way back.

Callie watched them stagger between the gusts and the bumpiness under their feet. Then a random rush straight off the ocean pushed the woman over, almost taking Monty down with her.

Callie ran with Alex, slowed by the unwieldiness of the camera. She assisted Mrs. Hanson up, and, with Monty on the other side, they returned to where the SUV was parked.

With the two in the car, Callie spun on the granddaughter. "That was reckless. How can you not see that?" She pointed toward the sea. "She could've twisted an ankle, broken a hip, wrenched a shoulder. Then where would you be? How many emergency rooms are open right now?"

"Like she said, Chief," the girl hollered over the rushing air, "we were about to leave."

Eyes squinted, half against the wind and half in incensed frustration, Callie monitored Alex getting in and heading back in the right direction. They went on, but Callie climbed the stairs and took down the flagpole, the flag already ripped around one grommet. She rolled it up and tucked it inside the screen door.

Then she returned to Jungle Road, so she could run by the Hanson house and make sure they had not only gotten home but promptly collected those suitcases and left. And she'd hang until they did.

WITH THE HANSONS gone, Callie made another pass on the streets, Thomas countering her movements on the other end of town.

Sophie was gone, supposedly with Buck. Callie's biological mother Sarah had left some time ago, heading to her sister's place in Atlanta. One of these days Callie was going to have to visit Atlanta with her or get that sister down here. After all, didn't that mean she had an aunt she'd never met?

Some kids acquired new stepparents, while Callie had earned herself a real mother two years ago, versus the mother she'd thought for forty years was her real one. But despite the new relative and the fact she had a fresh branch on the family tree, she hadn't made the effort, and Sarah hadn't pushed her to do so.

Maybe after the storm, a couple months or more after, because each time Edisto had such an event as this—enough storm power to be a concern but not enough to tear up the town—they still faced cleanup. They might be two-thirds through the tourist year, but that last third often made the difference for many residents' ability to pay bills.

She paid special attention to places with vehicles in the drive—maybe five percent of the properties—hunting for signs of life. Only a tenth of those had people inside. A small number but enough. She kept a map handy, ticking off those properties with human beings whom she'd need to come back and check on later. Ninety percent were residents, equipped, secured, and prepped for the night.

She reached the Arc Street house, where the trio of ex-Rangers must be hunkered down now. Their car, a rental from the looks of it, had been parked tightly beneath the house, against the door of the storage room. They'd done a good job securing anything with the potential to fly off.

While they'd staked their claim and assured Callie they were good for the duration of the storm, she wanted to give them one last chance to reconsider. She radioed Thomas first. "Did you talk to *Seas the Day*? Three tourists in there. Guys in their late thirties."

"Nope. They're all yours, Chief."

She hung up and got out, glad she wore a short bob, more manageable to ocean breezes and hurricane gales. She banged on the front door. "Anyone home?"

After hearing nothing, she almost returned to the ground to make her way around back, but the wooden door opened. She refreshed her memory, quickly remembering the man's name as Arlo.

"Chief. This is a surprise."

"Just checking on the folks remaining behind," she said, noting he wasn't inviting her in. She'd checked the screen door when she knocked, and its catch was engaged. He left it so.

"Guess that's us," he said. "Anything I can do for you?"

"Head count, please. You and Leonard and the third friend . . . who would be . . ."

"Three guys, yup. We're staying right here. Going nowhere, and all the hatches have been battened."

He'd held back on the third name. She'd love to go inside, at least confirm what the third guy looked like. "Mind if I come in?"

"One in the shower, you know, in case the water goes out. The other is getting in his last jog."

Odd. She'd never been inside *Seas the Day*. She liked being familiar with how the various houses were laid out, since the knowledge helped her in some situations. She guessed she wasn't getting that chance to see the floorplan nor check out the other renters.

"Janet Wainwright have all your names?"

"The Marine? Yeah." He waited for her to take the next step.

She had no step to make. "Well, here's my card." She held it out. He unclasped the door, took it, and reclosed it, the hasp reengaged.

"I'll be leaving soon," she said, "so you'll be on your own."

He nodded with a half shrug. "We understand, Chief. We've survived way worse than this, trust me."

He was probably right. "Well, take care. See you on the other side," she said, giving him a two-finger salute. She made her way back down the steps, Nikki whistling her way through the steps and around the house's corners.

Callie hadn't made it to her car when her phone rang. The call dropped before she could connect, and she tried to call back. Dropped again. The storm was monkeying around with service. She'd hoped it would be a while before that happened.

She did note the caller was Stan.

She backed out of the drive and took off to find him. With him responsible for Mark, she'd be happier knowing what Stan wanted, though in the back of her mind, she recognized she was running behind. Hopefully Stan just wanted to know where she was.

Time was ticking.

Chapter 16

Callie
Late Thursday afternoon—six hours to landfall

THE ATMOSPHERE held an urgency, and everything around Callie seemed to express motion. Nothing felt still. Everything held energy.

Every leaf on every kind of plant danced in a panic. Small, already half-dead branches broke loose and skittered across the road. Someone's towel and someone else's T-shirt flipped and flopped. A child's sand bucket played Kick the Can with itself until it caught in a bush. Light-weight items traveled everywhere . . . for now. Anchored items would bust loose later.

The storm was still a Category One. A tropical storm was seventy-three miles per hour and below. A hurricane was simply anything over that. Anything over forty was more than enough for damage in her opinion.

Six thirty was later than she'd planned to leave. She chastised herself for the delay, but like the captain and his ship, she felt the need to be the last to leave out of those intending to leave. Midnight was still far enough away.

Chelsea Morning came into view, her home looking naked without the outdoor furniture, signage, and pots. Mark's car, her personal car, and Stan's remained parked underneath the house. One would be left behind unless she did as Mark begged, let him drive and park his car for safekeeping at Thomas's place, then he would ride with her to Middleton.

A car was a valuable possession to lose.

She ran up the steps two at a time, unlocking the front door instead of knocking and waiting for Stan to answer. "What is it?" she asked before the door clasped shut behind her. The house smelled like a diner.

The men turned from watching out the back window toward the marsh, both with stymied looks. Stan held his phone, but not like he was making a call.

Mark noticed her sniffing and pointed at a cooler on the floor. "We cooked up the food that would go bad. What do you mean *what is it?* What is . . . what?"

A small branch hit the side of the house. All three jerked attention to that wall, as if they could see through it, expectant for another bang to follow. "Guess it's picking up out there," Stan said.

Callie dropped her chin to her chest. "Y'all . . . when Stan's calls wouldn't get through, I thought something was wrong."

He held up his phone. "Texts don't seem to be going through. Calls are iffy."

"I'm not surprised at service getting spotty. Plus, they still haven't gotten those osprey nests off the tower."

The locals had complained, but the tourists had raised holy hell at the fact the phone service company couldn't complete their 5G upgrade thanks to a pair of ospreys. They were federally protected birds. Most Edistonians didn't mind that part. The fact the phone company had dragged their feet long enough in repairing an old tower enough for a pair of ospreys to build the nest and create an issue in the first place was what angered folks. This time, however, Callie would bet money on Nikki being the bigger culprit.

"So, what did you want?" she asked.

Mark pointed to the clock on the kitchen wall, the one she couldn't see but he could. "You were due here an hour ago. You've done all you can," he said. "Let's go."

"El Marko's needs checking out, along with those stores in that mall. Was hoping to speak to Janet Wainwright to get a feel for how many tenants of hers remained. But Alex Hanson took Mrs. Hanson out on the damn beach to help shoot footage. The wind knocked her down on the way back to her car. She's lucky she didn't twist or break something. I'm so glad she's got Monty living with her now. For God's sake, Alex is just—"

"A reporter?" Mark finished, cutting off her breathless tirade while being fully cognizant of Callie's abhorrence for journalists.

"Selfish," Callie corrected.

Both men smirked, having heard the rant before, but then the wind whistled, taking their attention back to the window. Stan shook his head. "Well, you don't need to be out there. It sounds like this thing is coming quicker than expected."

"Nah," she said, coming closer to get a kiss from Mark then peer out the back of the house. Every tree bent under pressure. A trash can slowly slid in spurts down the silted path of Jungle Shores, the road that ran behind *Chelsea Morning*. All three watched as it made its way past, like a stranger seeking an uncertain address to stop at. A few pine needles had already stuck in the screen.

The men weren't far from being correct. The weather was testy.

"You got anything left to do, Stan?" she asked, thinking he may be right about leaving. The lights blinked once, twice, then managed to remain on.

He looked up at the light fixture, measuring his odds. "I have my stuff, but I forgot my charger and one other thing. Wanted to head over there. Won't take a second. Was trying to let you know."

"Then go get them," she said. "Should've already done so."

Her mic went off. "Yeah, Thomas. What you got?"

"Got a family of five on the front block of Catherine who refuse to leave until they find their dog. Could use some help. They're freaking and willing to risk the storm rather than leave without their Pickles."

"Put the fear of God in them, Thomas." While a firm demeanor was necessary, she'd hate to be in their shoes having to decide whether to leave their poor baby out in the wild with a storm bearing down. Dogs were children to so many. She'd seen it a zillion times out here, the canines treated better than a lot of kids and most spouses.

"I tried, Chief." He lowered his voice. "The kids are three, five, and eight. Two of them are bawling. The mom isn't much better. The dad thinks this is little more than a hard rain. We're at *C Turtle*, and they have no clue about hurricanes. They can't even hunt for the dog very well."

Callie rolled her eyes at Mark. *What next?*

"Go," he said. "I'm fine alone. We've got about two hours before we have to seriously pull the plug. Stan can go and be right back. You go talk that family off the ledge and get back here. The restaurant is fine. Ignore Janet for now."

Callie radioed to Thomas she'd be right there.

"Is your stuff in the car?" she asked Mark.

"Yep, and yours. Go be the hero, but not too long. We take the cooler down when we leave."

She made for the door, eager to find the mutt and get back. "Stan, come on. Do your business and get back, please."

The two of them left together, Stan turning left toward his place on Pompano, Callie going right toward Thomas's location.

Only a mile away, she reached the family's rental and bailed, hunting the yard and those on either side for Pickles searchers. She heard a child cry before she saw the father, carrying a red-faced three-year-old boy while hollering for the dog, panic etched in his forehead.

"Sir? What kind of dog is it?" she asked, not wanting to waste time nor stir the pot any more than it was.

"A Yorkshire Terrier," he said. Then he tried untangling the child from his neck and waist to hand over to Callie. "Here. I can look better without him."

But Callie backed up a step and declined. She wasn't here to babysit. "Your child. Stick together. I can look better without him." She held up all fingers on a hand. "You've got five minutes, sir. Then you leave. It's too dangerous, especially with young children. Priorities, sir."

She hoped they would find the dog and find him quick.

The father wasn't insulted, thank goodness. Quite the contrary, he acted as if what she said hadn't even registered.

"Five minutes," Callie repeated over the wind then joined the effort to find the dog. Hunched, she looked under anything and everything. In this melee, the dog would be hunkered down somewhere. While scared, its instincts would've told it a damn hurricane was on the way; the poor baby's instincts were probably way smarter than those of the humans it belonged to.

Hell, the tiny thing could be picked up and blown up in a tree before too long. Or out to sea, fast becoming a snack for a hammerhead. *Damn it*, why couldn't Pickles be something like a Doberman or German Shepherd?

After a couple of calls for the dog, she heard another voice echoing hers, Thomas. He was a house over, searching under bushes and stairs.

She met up with him. "This isn't gonna work," she said. "They need to leave or stay. We need to leave. Where's the mom?"

"Inside with the other two kids," he said. "She said somebody has to stay with them while we look." He gave her a sarcastic, disbelieving look. "She's a piece of work, Chief."

"Hell, the father isn't much better. He takes his son out here to do this? Keep looking. I'll go talk to her."

Nobody had time for this.

Callie trotted up the two-dozen steps to the porch and entered unannounced. Inside, the mother and two daughters sat on the sofa crying their eyes out. Nothing had been packed. Not one damn thing.

"Ma'am," Callie said, sitting in a tufted chair across from the huddled family. She spoke loud enough to be heard but not so loud as to scare the bejeezus out of them. "Y'all have got to pack up and evacuate. Now."

She shook her head. "You don't understand. Pickles belongs to the kids."

"But these children are your first responsibility." She reached over with a hand, taking that of the oldest. "It's okay. I'm the police chief out here. Let's put you in charge of your sister and let Mom get y'all ready to take a ride."

Callie held a soft look on the child, giving her full attention. The child hesitated, then not seeing her mother protest, did exactly as Callie told her. Callie put the oldest girl's hand in that of her sister, then led both over to the recliner. "There you go. Y'all sit there together. You," she said to the eldest, "tell stories to her. Fun stories. Happy stories. Princess stories."

"I like bugs," said the youngest.

Callie smiled. "Then your big sister can tell you fun, happy, princess stories about bugs. See how many you can think of before I get back."

That made both giggle. On that note, she rose and returned focus to the mom. As she had with the sisters, she held out a hand, and the mother took it. Callie escorted her into the bedroom and pushed the door almost closed, not wanting the children to feel locked out.

Once out of earshot, Callie turned to the mom, who stood there waiting for instruction.

"Pack up as fast as you can," Callie said. "I am not exaggerating when I say you could get hurt or killed in this storm. You could get stranded on the road if you don't hustle. I gave your husband five minutes to find the dog. You've got the same to pack. Is that clear?"

The mother seemed to need more instruction to function. "Five minutes?"

"Five minutes," Callie repeated, tapping her watch. Not that the mom could pack in that time, but the woman seemed to need a deadline.

The mom started tossing things in piles on the bed. From the drawers, from the closet, from the bathroom. Suddenly, she turned. "We're from Illinois."

Callie waited for more. When there was no explanation, she answered as best she could. "Well, that means your vacation got cut short. Not important right now."

The mom cuddled a wad of someone's clothes against her chest. "But where are we going?"

"A shelter if you must. The closest is in Walterboro, less than an hour up the road. But my suggestion is to head back home, because we'll have a cleanup to tend to after the hurricane, and you might return to no power, no water, even no rental. Just go home, ma'am."

That seemed to hit the mark, and the mother raced to the dresser, slinging items onto the bed.

The front door flew open, the knob bouncing off its rubber stopper. Callie raced to the commotion, to find Thomas standing there, the mutt in hand, both dripping.

"It's raining," he said. Then with one hand, he held up the drowned-rat-looking canine with a muddy blue ribbon knotted, having lost its bow.

The mom came running out, the girls bolted from their recliner, and the father raced in with the little boy clinging to his back. Everyone *oohed* and *aahed*, kissing and petting the terrier.

"Stop," Callie said, but when nobody listened, she mustered her crowd voice and repeated, "Stop with the dog."

Everyone froze, including Thomas. Not everyone had heard such a big voice from such a small person, but it had its effect.

"Kids, in the living room," she said, then to the girls, "Have you come up with those stories yet?"

"No . . . ma'am."

"Then there's your mission." She turned to the boy, the youngest. "Parents, take him with you and pack like there is no tomorrow, because if you don't leave soon, you might not have one."

The dad snatched up the boy and his wife's wrist and began doing as told.

Callie and Thomas ran into the kitchen and threw food items from the counter and refrigerator into whatever bags they could find since they found no cooler. By the time they'd finished, the dad came out with two suitcases in hand. He might not've been the most efficient person at the outset, but he was coming around.

Not twenty minutes later, the car was packed, children in car seats, wet dog in a towel in the wife's lap, and the husband waiting to see what else Callie would have him do.

"Just get out of here," Callie said. "Call your rental agency about what to do about your trip, but don't be surprised if it takes a couple of days for them to get their act together."

He shook her hand, rain coming down in a light steady manner, the wind pushing it in a slant, promising more to come.

"I'm thinking we're done, Chief," Thomas said, watching the taillights disappear from under an umbrella he'd pulled out not long ago over an already damp uniform.

"I'm thinking we are, too," she said. She'd forget El Marko's, as Mark suggested, then go home and retrieve the two men awaiting her. Thomas already knew to take his patrol car to safety, with the plan being drop off one car or another from her place there, too.

"Stay safe and stay in touch," she said, though Thomas had weathered more hurricanes than she had. She'd be asking him for advice here and there as this thing ran its course.

Her phone rang. Stan again. Then it stopped.

"Go on," she told Thomas, who got in his car and left. She slid into her own, not expecting to be dry until she reached Middleton, so no point worrying about moisture on her car's upholstery.

She studied the view before her, off the end of Catherine Street, toward the sea, wondering what level of destruction she'd come back to tomorrow. She was part of the investigatory team that analyzed when to reopen Edisto Beach to its business and property owners and monitor the cleanup, which would be needed regardless of the degree of damage. She sighed, already missing the boring normalcy of tourism and all its quirks and irritations.

Her phone rang again, abruptly interrupted mid-ring, not long enough for the phone to catch who called. Could be anyone right now. People checking on her, mostly. Maybe some islanders phoning for advice. But Mother Nature had yanked her authority away for the time being, along with the phone service.

She cruised Palmetto Boulevard where the weather always hit first and hardest, just to see if there was anything needing immediate attention. She would drive around to meet Jungle Road then go home.

The ten minutes felt long, but thus far no issues. She came within a visual of *Chelsea Morning*.

Stan's car wasn't there.

Chapter 17

Callie
Thursday evening—four hours to landfall

STAN WAS SUPPOSED to be at her house, waiting for her. At seven forty in the evening, he was pushing things close. All he had to do was retrieve his phone charger. Worried that maybe his car crapped out on him, or he'd flattened a tire running over debris, she continued past her house toward his. She tried calling him once, but the signal dropped seconds into the rings.

As she'd told so many people who had wanted to stay behind, there reached a point where you would be cut off from the world and be on your own. Guess that time had come.

A gust caught the side of her car as she turned onto Atlantic Street, headfirst toward the ocean. It eased, and she had little problem continuing past Dolphin Street and crossing the creek that fed off the lagoon, where she had to veer right onto Pompano. Stan lived near the dead end. He liked the seclusion and the one-mile walking distance to El Marko's as well as the one-block reach to the water.

On Pompano she watched for cars and any remaining people, grateful to find none, though all but a couple were rentals anyway. Limbs and fronds littered lots and roads.

Stan's car sat parked under his house, but the closer she got, the more her sixth sense told her something wasn't right. She'd learned to listen to it a long time ago, and her wariness piqued.

Parking beside his car, she noted nothing amiss with it. Not locked, but theft factor was low right now, so she went up the stairs.

She found the front door unlocked as well and entered. The evening light had all but disappeared due to the clouds veiling the sun, giving the day a sense of being two hours later than it was. However, Stan's porch lights weren't on, and once inside, she hesitated. No interior lights were on either.

"Stan?" she called, then again, louder, feeling guarded for reasons she could not nail down.

Nobody was in the bedroom to the left, nor in the living room past the kitchen. He wasn't anywhere in the house. She made another round, this time peering on the other side of the queen bed, around corners, and in the walk-in closet. Nothing.

She bolted outside, taking the back door, because she hadn't seen him on the porch in the front. At the railing she spotted him. He lay on the wet silt and sparse grass at the bottom of the stairs.

"Stan!" she yelled, just as a whoosh carried the word away.

In a fast trot she took the stairs, having to grasp the rail about four steps in as her foot slid off the slickness of the light rain that kept threatening to set in. It was enough to take her down and bounce her butt off the steps behind her. Standing, she tried to take the steps again but slid again, this time her hand too slippery on the railing to grip and stop a five-step descent to the landing, the back of her head taking a light hit on the way.

Without thinking of injury, she leaped up and took better care taking the second set of stairs, hopping over the last four or five steps to the ground. Stan lay only a reach away. A trash can on its side, about ten-feet distant, lay up against a collection of oleanders. She could only guess he'd tried to go out and take it in.

"Stan?" she said, easing down beside him, her own ankle giving her a twinge.

He didn't respond, the easy rain hitting his chunky face and making no difference. No telling how long he'd been out here, but his clothes were soaked; his hair stuck to him indicating he'd been on the ground more than a few minutes.

"Wake up, Stan. Please, look at me." Afraid to move him—then realizing she wouldn't be able to anyway since he weighed over twice what she did—she hunted for signs of blood, feeling his head for open wounds. She found a goose-egg lump on his skull, to the right and an inch or two back off his ear.

From there she worked down, studying for what might be a wound, a bone out of position, or ripped clothing to indicate something amiss beneath. When she touched his left leg, however, he winced, groaned, and fought to open his eyes. She jerked her hand back, not sure what she'd touched to achieve that reaction.

More groaning, then he came around. "What the hell are you doing?" he growled.

God, she was happy to hear him grump. "What's your name?"

"What the hell do you mean what's my name? And why are we out here in the rain?" He remained prostrate, tentative, with an awareness creeping in that he better not move too quickly without taking account. He looked at her, finally in focus. "What happened?"

"You fell down the stairs is my guess," she said, wiping dripping rain out of his eyes barehanded, but the rain was coming down faster than she could wipe. Not huge drops and not painfully hard, but just more. She hovered over him, hoping that it helped somewhat. "You have a knot on your head, and your groan just told me something's wrong with your left leg. Can you try to move each limb so I don't accidentally hurt something? Just a little to see what might be broken and what isn't. Hopefully you've only knocked yourself out."

He gave her a minimal nod and began with his head. He'd have to stand to determine if he'd get dizzy, but Callie would take what information she could get without him rising and making something else worse.

"Head hurts," he said, then without thinking, raised his left hand and felt the spot Callie had felt. "There."

Nothing wrong with that arm. He tried the other, his neck rotating toward it in the process.

He peered up past Callie, and his eyes widened. "Move!" he yelled.

Before she could register what he'd seen, before he could roll away, a branch in the old oak cracked loose. She heard it but wasn't fast enough to do anything about it.

The limb smacked her across the back, slamming her flat atop him, taking the breath out of her.

Opening her eyes, she gasped, the weight across her back unmanageable. She looked down at Stan, her eyes not three inches from his.

"Good God, Callie, are you all right?"

"I think so. Are you?"

"Yeah, thanks to you."

The burden was on her to rectify things, figuratively and literally.

She breathed deeply, to see how heavy the weight was. Looking to her left, she reckoned five feet of branch, six inches thick. To her right, she estimated three feet of smaller boughs. What she couldn't see fell in between, only deadly if it had whacked her just right in the head.

But it hadn't. She planted her hands on either side of Stan and flexed her shoulder blades. Moveable. Pulling to her knees in a slow effort to protect and avoid touching what she worried was Stan's broken leg, she inched up and managed to shove the branch a foot to the side. But it caught on her utility belt. She couldn't completely move out from under it without the risk of dropping it onto Stan, and whatever injury they hadn't assessed yet.

In an awkward twist, she reached one of the smaller offshoot limbs and dragged it a few inches. Then a few more. Finally, she bowed up, drew her feet beneath her, sucked in a deep breath, and mustered enough strength and torque to thrust it off.

The rain increased.

"Callie . . ."

"I'm okay," she said, having rolled over on her butt in the exertion. She wiped wet grass and sand off her hands and returned to her previous crouched position beside Stan. "Tell me, how's your back? How're your legs?"

He did a self-analysis. Nothing, nothing, then a snarl told her he'd found the damage.

It took him a few seconds to get past the pain such that he could explain. "My leg," he said, eyes closed, hand instinctively going down to touch it. "Oh my God, it's broken, Callie. No question."

"Which part?" she asked, trying not to appear anxious. She was his only hope for assistance. How many times had she told visitors and residents to not chance being left behind when first responders wouldn't be available? Yet here she set the example of what could happen. She couldn't blame Stan. He'd waited for her.

"Below the knee," he said, pain spreading into his expression and totally setting up shop.

What the hell was she supposed to do now? She couldn't move him. The fire department had vacated. She tried her phone, dialing Thomas. The call struggled then dropped. She did so three more times. Then she gave her mic a go. "Thomas, I need you at Stan's. Urgent. Please call me back."

Repeatedly she fought to get through, uncertain about what her officer might be hearing on the other end.

She tried for Mark. Why, she didn't know, except she couldn't not try. The call did the same as it had for Thomas.

It was a quarter to nine. Way too late. The weather would only worsen.

"Chicklet," Stan said, wiping rain from his eyes, then holding a hand over as a shield.

"You tell me to leave you, and I swear, I'll kick your bad leg," she said, thinking.

"You have to," he said. "The sooner the better. You might still catch Thomas before he gets far. How long before he left the beach?"

Stan was right. She'd rushed over to Stan's about the time Thomas was to leave the beach to head to his house.

He might not be gone yet.

She bolted to her patrol car. There wasn't much time. What she found dropped her stomach into her shoes.

An even bigger limb had fallen across her cruiser.

There was no chasing down Thomas now. But there was one thing she could do.

The driver's side door was half blocked with a limb about the size of the one out back, but it was still connected to the larger one that had bashed a six-inch deep crease across the roof of the car. To move one you had to move the other, unless you had a saw of some sort, and, son of a bitch, there wasn't time for that.

From the angle of the tree, she surmised that she might, however, get inside via the passenger door. Running around, slipping once, her hand on the car stopping the fall, she raced to the other side.

Yes. She squeezed inside. Instantly she flipped on the siren and blue lights. Hopefully Thomas wasn't too far gone not to hear, and if Heaven would lend a hand, he'd maybe see the SOS.

Chapter 18

Arlo
Thursday late afternoon—six hours to landfall

ONCE THE POLICE chief had backed out and headed to the end of the street, Arlo eased out onto the porch to ensure those taillights had fully left. Leonard came up behind him, beer in hand.

"Better ration those," Arlo said, watching the car turn toward a more major road and disappear. He had wanted her to see them as the least concerning as compared to the other issues she'd have with this storm. Of the few remaining behind, they would be the most adept at taking care of themselves, and the last she'd check on once the storm passed through.

Leonard peered where his buddy was looking. "Ration? We bought these beers for the storm, my friend. I see a storm. Enough said."

"We need to do better than this next time," Arlo said, turning and pushing past Leonard inside since the rain seemed to be seriously moving in.

Waving back toward the road with his beer bottle, Leonard hollered at Arlo, now inside the door. "She suspects nothing." He hurried inside as well.

The rain blew, the porch getting wetter, almost falling enough sideways to hit the house wall.

"She's seen us, what, three times?" Arlo said.

With a taste of condescension, Leonard arced a brow. "Me twice. You three times. I wasn't the one who took a date to the chief of police's boyfriend's restaurant and dared the world to see me."

Bruce came to his bedroom doorway. "Wind's blowing out there. Don't like it."

"I'm hungry," Leonard said, returning to the kitchen.

But Arlo recognized Bruce's appearance as more than just stretching his legs. His intrusion into the conversation was a sign. He was worried. The man of few words had just said enough to express concern over how the plan wasn't going exactly according to plan.

Arlo met Bruce at the doorway, knowing full well his buddy wasn't venturing past the threshold. That would put the duffle bag out of sight, and out of reach. "Need something to eat? We'll be here at least through tomorrow morning, and there're plenty of snacks, so no need to go hungry, man." Being a nondrinker, Bruce wouldn't want a beer, but he adored a certain kind of fitness drink. They made sure to take them on their adventures, because they didn't dare play the odds of whether a small or regional grocery store would carry the brand.

"Wait right there," Arlo said, as if he had to caution Bruce about leaving the duffle. He trotted into the kitchen, grabbed Bruce's favorite flavor of the drink out of the fridge, snatched a bag of barbecue pork skins, and returned. "Here. Take these for now. I'll try to cook up something quick, because I halfway expect the power to go out at any time."

Bruce took the offering, but he didn't return to his vigil beside the bed, watching the back of the property for anything or anyone that might violate the perimeter.

"What's up, man?" Arlo asked, reaching over to rest a hand on his friend's shoulder. Bruce had degrees of readiness, and this wasn't on the low end of his scale. "The storm? I know we didn't expect this, but we've adapted. I did my job. Leonard has done his . . . exceptionally well, I might add. Now we just hang while you do yours. We end this tomorrow once we reconnoiter the storm damage."

"Picking the end of an island wasn't smart," Bruce said. "One way in. One way out."

"That's what made it so beautiful," Arlo said. "Remember? Nobody would think of looking here. The other beaches were too populated. Too commercial. Too close to the city. Too many uniforms." He patted the shoulder once more. "How many times have we done this?"

"Twelve in three years and ten months," the buddy replied.

Arlo grinned. "Exactly."

"We didn't factor weather before," he said.

"Never had to."

"Should have. Our mistake."

Arlo cocked his head. "What mistake?" They'd been successful all twelve times. Seamless. Vacation, camaraderie, and income earning rolled into one.

Unexpectedly, Bruce moved into Arlo's space, his glare piercing. A laser gaze. "There's always room for error, and we cannot afford complacency. We should have considered weather. We always considered weather on our deployments."

Now Arlo understood his point. Back in the day, in the sandbox, as boring as it could be sometimes, weather was taken into account for a mission. Here in the states, they hadn't found it necessary.

Of course, they'd avoided heavy snowfall months in Idaho and rural New York. They'd avoided the hundred-and-twenty-degree months in Nevada. The rest of the states they'd visited, however, had more temperate climes and offered no obstacle. Like this one, their first in South Carolina. Demographics showed lots of relocations to the state exactly for its temperate environment. They'd even chosen September for its decline from ninety-degree-and-eighty-percent humidity days, while still being warm enough to enjoy the beach.

It wasn't until the adventure was in motion that hurricane potential reared its head. But it was only Category One. They'd endured worse dust storms.

Arlo ranked the weather as a strength. Bruce, however, wasn't fond of change, or anything that wasn't exactly per plan.

The overhead light flickered. Arlo looked up, like anyone did in their home. Silly.

Bruce, however, only stared at Arlo, unaffected by the alien sound of branches slapping the house.

Ordinarily, Arlo paid attention to Bruce's gut, instincts, and whatever you might call a skin-crawling, sixth-sense expectation. This time? Not so much.

"Buddy, it's only a Cat One. Tomorrow we'll be on the road. I promise."

Bruce returned to his post beside the bed.

Arlo told himself Bruce would settle down once the storm passed. On the way out of town, they could think about where they'd like to spend their next adventure. And yes, he'd make sure Bruce saw that they accounted for weather this time.

Chapter 19

Callie
Four hours to landfall

HER BLUE LIGHTS bounced off six houses on Pompano Street, the siren echoing from end to end of the island. The dropped tree limb across the vehicle barred some of the visual, but enough of her blues would be seen if anyone came within a couple of blocks. They would act more as the pinpoint for where they were; the siren would have actually drawn Thomas—or anyone, for that matter—from just about anywhere on Edisto Beach.

When a siren went off anywhere in the town, Callie could hear it from her house, only a couple of streets over, and she could just about identify on which street it came from. All of her officers could. She'd awoken several times from her bed, hearing the wail, calculating the locale.

Nikki hadn't quite arrived, but honestly, she wasn't sure of the passage of time. Rain fell, not pounding but hard enough. Enough to be a nuisance, to slick everything up, and to weigh trees, causing the weaker branches to fall.

Pitch dark earlier than usual. One could feel the barometric pressure dropping by the minute.

Leaving the lights and siren alive, she ran back to Stan, the rebounding lights giving a heightened sense of urgency to everything. Coming around the corner, she ran across his phone about eight feet from him where it had apparently landed when he'd toppled down the stairs. Wiping it across her wet thigh, she remembered he had a different phone service than she did. What were the odds his would work? These services shared towers. If one was out, chances were the other was as well, but she could hope his service proved the better provider.

Contrary to popular belief, though, if a phone couldn't receive signal, it still might pick up enough signal to enable 911. The trouble was that location probably couldn't be transmitted.

Rushing to him, she knelt, taken aback by what she saw, then tucking those feelings away. Clearly Stan felt the pain. No doubt the big man was taking account of his injuries in her absence. By the light of the phone, she saw he'd paled some, his brow knotted, eyes clenched. His left hand reached toward his leg and lay there, unable to reach his injury. His still arm lying on his leg, his hand shaking, it appeared he was afraid to touch the injury.

"Stan? Can you hear me?"

He nodded once, an effort. She bet she'd see beaded sweat if it weren't for the rain.

She put on a positive expression and held the retrieved device in front of him. "I found your phone. Mine isn't working, and maybe yours will. What's your PIN?"

"Just tell me," she said when he tried to take the phone, the simple movement of his arms making him wince.

"813749," he half whispered, half groaned.

The number made no sense to her, but Stan would of course have a passcode that made no sense to anyone.

She tried the password four times before the phone read the code with her hands so wet. The screen went to his page of apps, but about the time she dared think she had a chance, the one bar dropped to none, just like that.

What now?

She toggled airplane mode, hoping to snare signal from any provider again. Nothing. So she texted dispatch in Walterboro, Mark, Deputy Raysor with Colleton Sheriff's Office, and, believe it or not, her mother. One could hope.

With Stan too bulky and heavy for her to lift, she needed help. She needed a doctor, and she needed brawn. She needed the assistance she'd told everyone else on the beach would not be available once the storm made landfall.

She didn't want to leave Stan, but what option did she have?

And how would she leave? Her car was damaged, and it blocked Stan's car under the house. His was not a structure with an in-and-out drive like hers. At *Chelsea Morning*, one could drive in off Jungle Road and drive out onto Jungle Shores Road. The back of Stan's house faced the lagoon, not to mention Stan himself lay in the way, blocking that space to turn around.

That left Callie on foot. But to go where? To retrieve whom?

If she had to bet, this storm had moved in faster than expected. But it didn't matter now.

She stood in Stan's drive, looking up Pompano Street all the way to Whetsell Street at the long line of houses without lights.

No lights . . .

She ran to the storage room under Stan's house and with his phone still in her hand, she hit the light switch. Nothing. The power was out.

Washing the phone's light around the room, she found a tarp. Old, but better than nothing. Phone wedged into her wet pocket, she grabbed the tarp, and an old heavy metal cooler at least twenty years old. She ran back to Stan, tripping once over the long edge of the tarp.

"Here," she said, dropping everything. Coming around to his side, she grabbed an end of the limb that had landed on the two of them earlier, and she dragged it up toward his head and to the side. Then she rushed over to him. "Listen, I'm going to drape this tarp over you. No point in you lying here with rain in your face."

Unfolding it, she anchored the bottom two ends with rocks after trying to shove a stick through the grommets only for them to break off. Then she draped the remainder over Stan, over to the limb, and finally over his head to be tucked beneath the cooler. Folding it under the heavy cooler, she gave Stan room to breathe, with the ability to still see while arranging for the rain to roll off him along the angle toward his feet.

She knelt, lowering almost to her belly. "I can't drag you inside, Boss. If you can drag yourself, more power to you, but I'm not seeing you doing that right now. Best I can do for now."

"Where are you going?" he said.

"I have a list of people who remained behind," she said. "I'll be on foot until I can find help."

"Callie?" came a voice from behind her. She peered back over her shoulder toward Stan's car in the covered part of the drive.

Outlined by a flashlight, she made out Horse first, wearing a rain jacket of sorts with stripes of reflective tape. Behind him came Donna Baird, in a raincoat and rain hat and with some sort of leather bag in her hand, the flashlight in her other.

"Heard the siren then saw the blue lights," Donna said, scooting faster once she recognized that the tarp protected a body. "Who you got here?"

"Stan," Callie said. "I believe he broke his leg falling down the stairs. I can't lift him, and he's in some kind of bad pain."

Donna lifted the tarp enough to see him better yet keep the rain off him. He saw her, tried to smile, then gave up.

Callie asked a question she was afraid she already knew the answer to. "What can you do for him, Donna? I know you're a veterinarian, but is there anything in that bag of yours that works on a person?"

Donna hesitated, her gaze on Stan rather than Callie.

"Anything?" Callie repeated. "Both our cars are worthless, and I can't move him. Honestly, you and I couldn't move him without doing more harm than good," she said, motioning at the councilwoman's diminutive size so like her own.

Callie had been trained on a pack-strap-type carry when someone was injured, but with a leg fracture you transported them feet up, not down, to avoid pressure on the wound.

Nothing fit this. She and Donna did not have stature nor strength.

Seeing the veterinarian give a long side-eyed glance at her bag, Callie bet she'd thrown some medical items into that bag. Chances were, however, they were more like gauze, tape, and such.

"I can manage a splint," Donna said, finally making eye contact with her.

"And you have meds," Callie said. "I'm fully aware of the Good Samaritan Act, Donna. If you have the knowledge and means to assist someone, you legally can do so. What's in there that will cut some of his pain? Give him that then let's splint that leg."

Then she thought of something. "Stan? Any chance you have painkillers in the house?"

"Aspirin is all," he said and not in a strong way.

Callie wasn't surprised. Stan wasn't one for drugs. Then she thought of Mark. "Hey, I can go get Mark's meds," she said.

"No need," Donna said. "I have some oxycontin, tramadol, and gabapentin. Kept them from my practice after I retired. In the right dosages they work on both animals and people."

Resisting the urge to open the bag herself, Callie let the veterinarian come to grips with what she felt best to do for a human instead of a dog. However, she didn't have much patience to wait long.

Horse sat on his haunches, even in the drizzle, as if he did this all the time. The blue lights from the front continued flashing, giving his reflective stripes a creative pattern in the dark night.

"Tramadol," Donna finally said. "I'm more comfortable with that dosing range for an adult."

Decision made, Callie ran into the house and came back with a glass of water along with a sofa pillow. Holding his head up, she inserted the pillow while Donna administered the pain killer. "Afraid it won't take effect for a half hour," she said.

Callie pushed wet hair back from his brow. "We've got to get him to the hospital."

The first issue was finding a car. The second was having enough power to lift Stan into it.

"Can I borrow your keys?"

Donna thought a split second before reaching into her pocket and handing them over. "Where . . . who would you get to help with the lift?"

"Just leave it to me. Be back as soon as I can." She ran to the front, turned off the siren while grabbing the map with the names of those remaining behind. She left the blue lights flashing, still hoping Thomas would show. Then she cranked the engine to Donna's small four-door sedan and studied her list. Twenty houses with folks in them on the whole beach . . . out of hundreds.

On the map, she spotted whom she needed and mentally kicked herself for just now thinking of them.

She took Pompano to Atlantic Street, but instead of heading north to her place, she went south, to Palmetto, and then she floored the little sedan to Bay Point and then Arc Street. What better emergency help could she ask for than three Rangers?

She slid into their drive. No lights on this end of the beach either. Her headlights would have ordinarily announced her arrival, but the windows were boarded. She bounded up the stairs, considering her steps this time to avoid a repeat of the fall at Stan's. She already had a headache, and her right ankle told her she hadn't given it enough attention since banging it in her own fall.

She thumped on the door with her flashlight, her other hand wiping drips off to see better.

Arlo answered, briefly taken aback. "Weren't you just here?" he asked, attempting jest.

"Need your help," she said. "Let me in."

He hesitated, and she recalled him not letting her in before either. Before she could question why, he disengaged the catch and opened the screen, waving her in.

The house wasn't far off the standard half-dozen house plans of the majority of the rentals with a kitchen to the right, a living room beyond it, and two bedrooms on either side, each side with a bath. A bit more worn than the usual, but not beyond enjoyment.

"I need your help," Callie said, looking for the other two men. "All the emergency responders are gone for their own safety. I was about to leave when a member of my own party fell down the steps, and we think he broke his leg."

"Ouch," Arlo said. "So, what do you do during a hurricane for things like that?"

A rather flippant thing to say for someone accustomed to thinking on his feet under fire. "We try to get him off the island to a hospital. The trouble is my patrol car fell victim to a limb and is stranded. I borrowed a councilwoman's car to retrieve you guys. In my personal SUV I can lower the seats and stretch him in the back, but he's two hundred and twenty pounds if he's an ounce."

She kept scanning for the others. "Where's Leonard? And the other one?"

Leonard poked his head out of the bathroom, a flush in the background. "Right here. Sorry, missed the message. Want a beer?"

Too laid-back for her style. "No, and I hate to be rude, but I have an emergency. Please, the three of you, come with me and help me load this guy and his broken leg in my SUV so I can rush him to the hospital before he goes into shock . . . or worse. I have no idea how to treat a broken leg, so we get him to help."

She caught her breath, waiting for some sort of get-up-and-go.

"We'd be happy to help. Sure you don't need a beer?" Leonard asked. "You're rather . . . stressed, I'd say."

"I don't drink," she said. "Grab a raincoat if you have one. At least some sort of hat. Flashlights. Maybe gloves for grip. You guys are used to thinking quickly. Follow me. The address is on Pompano." She gave them the number. "*Gang Plank* is the name of the house. A brown-and-yellow sign."

But Leonard hadn't moved, instead exchanging some sort of unspoken communication with Arlo.

"What is your problem?" she said.

It was like they weren't listening to her, their height allowing them to peer over her head. "Best I stay," Arlo said to his partner.

"What?" Callie said. "What if it takes all three of you?"

"It won't," Leonard said, disappearing into the back left bedroom.

Arlo returned to dealing with Callie. "It's not a compound fracture, is it?"

"No idea." She wasn't understanding the plan that had been determined with such minimal words. "What is he doing?" she asked, pointing to where Leonard disappeared.

"Telling Bruce," he said. "We were handed a lot of shit in our day, and we've learned you take the tools for the job. Leonard's our muscle, and two hundred and twenty pounds is not out of his reach. Bruce is not only fit, but he's been a combat medic."

Medic? That was great. "But if you came too—"

"You use the right number for the job," he said. "Car room, for instance. Leaving one man behind in case he's needed if things go wrong. It's just what we do, ma'am. Trust us."

She'd have to. She had no choice.

Wasn't a full minute before Leonard and Bruce appeared, totes in hand containing who knew what, changed for the weather. Boots, pants, boonie hats, gloves.

Bruce went over to Arlo who spoke softly over his shoulder with a cold directness. "I mean it," Arlo said. "No compromise."

"I get it," Bruce said and headed for the door, not exactly pleased with what was going down.

Callie hadn't been introduced to this third guy, but right now manners were the least of her concerns. He'd been a medic, and how his momma raised him mattered not to her right now. He didn't seem to want to come, but she guessed the medical professional in him overrode his personal desires.

Outside, Leonard went straight for their car as the driver. Bruce didn't speak. Somehow they communicated without words.

She led the way up Palmetto, turning left on Atlantic Street. At Pompano, with an arm outside her rolled-down window, she motioned for them to take the turn, like they would need direction with the lights still throbbing at the dead end.

She, however, continued onward, taking Atlantic Street to its dead end where she turned east on her own road, her house five blocks down.

Still no house or streetlights. No cars anywhere but at her house. Sarah, Sophie, the Hansons, all gone. Mark was probably losing his mind wondering where everyone was, especially with communications down. She could, however, see small blinks of her patrol car blue lights between a few of the houses.

Mark waited on the porch by the time she reached the top of the stairs.

"What the hell, Callie?" he said, leaving the meaning open. Where had she been, where was Stan, when were they leaving? He did a double take at the strange car.

She gave him a quick peck. "Stan fell at his place. Broke his leg, we think. Donna's there. I took her car to get these big ex-military guys renting on Arc Street. One is a medic. I need to get back. I needed to swap vehicles and get my SUV to transport. No time for questions, Cajun Man. I love you."

And she was gone.

Didn't take her thirty seconds to reach Stan's.

She ran to the back where Donna and Leonard were holding up the tarp and Bruce was studying the patient.

"Callie?" Stan called, and she ran to him, going to her knees. "Renters? And this one claims to be a medic?" Stan wasn't happy. The tramadol had taken effect just enough to rally him and allow him to be grumpy. "Where's a damn ambulance?"

She looked at Bruce who didn't seem to care who saw him, spoke to him, or reacted to him. So she turned to Leonard instead.

"Bruce doesn't speak much," he said.

"Then you talk for him," she said. "This is Stan Waltham, a resident out here. He is the one hurting. So like you would with any patient, tell him what is going on instead of pissing him off."

Leonard nodded, half grinning, half apologizing, either way, seemingly understanding where Callie was coming from.

From under the propped tarp, Bruce gave his compatriot a look Callie wasn't sure was scolding or not, then returned to studying Stan's leg. She tired of this silent messaging.

"Give him a chance, Stan," she said, keeping a wary eye on the medic. She and Stan were coping with a lot of unknowns here.

"What did you give him?" Bruce asked Donna.

"Tramadol." Then she gave him the dosage.

To Stan, he asked, "On a scale of one to ten, how is your pain, ten meaning you're dying."

"Hurts like a mother—"

Bruce smiled, rain dripping from the ends of his hair down his neck. "Got it." He opened his bag and removed a syringe and a tiny medicine vial, preparing the shot. "How much do you weigh? And don't fudge on me."

Stan sighed, eager for release from the pain. "Two hundred and forty-two as of this morning."

"You've lost a few pounds," Callie joked, trying to help.

"Bite me," he said.

Callie liked the humor, but she preferred knowing what was going down under that tarp. "What is that you're giving him, Bruce?"

"Morphine," he said.

"I'll take it," Stan said. "Shoot away, Doc."

Bruce proceeded quickly, then with a pen out of his pocket, he wrote a big M on Stan's forehead, the dosage, and the time. Stan looked cross-eyed trying to see Bruce's actions.

M stood for morphine, a Schedule II drug given by doctor's prescription only. All she'd heard was the title *medic* and nothing about Bruce being a doctor. Bruce had hoarded drugs for personal use or discretionary use for selected familiars from his time overseas, but Callie wasn't calling him down for it. She needed him, and clearly, he took his dispensing seriously. He'd written on Stan's forehead to ensure whoever took over tending to him would know what they were dealing with, a habit from his work in the field. Right now, however, she didn't care if he'd stolen the drug from the President's personal physician, she'd take it. And he could paint a Rembrandt on Stan's chest for all she cared. For now, the pain was eased.

The problem might be, however, at the hospital when someone asked for details, but she'd deal with that story later when and if she had to. They had a lot of ground to cover amidst a serious and worsening storm.

The rain increased, and though the small group was protected a lot by the house behind them, the jungle-guarded lagoon in front of them, they still had to confront Nikki.

Callie glanced at her phone. Ten thirty.

Even partially protected, everyone's hair and clothes flapped, all trying to maintain a ring around the big man on the ground. Even the blue light seemed to lose its pattern, more erratic thanks to the heavy movement of the flora all around.

"Where are you taking him?" Bruce asked, having to speak louder now.

She hoped this was a *we* answer, not a *you*. She had no plan to carry Stan alone. "St. Francis in West Ashley," she said, but when Bruce shrugged in his stare at her, she remembered he was a visitor, not a local. "An hour drive under normal conditions," she corrected. "Fifty miles."

Bruce understood, as did probably everyone standing around, that one hour could mean two without much imagination. Six or more if they got run off the road in the wrong way.

He grimaced and returned attention to Stan, a stethoscope in use . . . on the leg. "Not hearing any arterial damage," he said. "Let's see what we can do to stabilize his leg for that long ride." He turned to Stan. "How're you feeling now?"

Stan gave Bruce a thumbs-up. "That's some good shit, man."

Another limb fell about ten feet from them, closer to the lagoon, but they all still jumped.

"We're running out of time, Bruce," Callie said. "How are we splinting the leg?"

Donna reached in her bag and pulled out a package. "Maybe this will work, but remember, it's made more for a big animal."

But Bruce pulled out a package of his own. "Air splint," he said. "More for people."

Donna stared over at Callie, and as Leonard and Bruce had done earlier, they shared the same thought. Who the hell was this guy?

Chapter 20

Callie
Two hours to landfall

"WHAT DO YOU mean you're not coming to the hospital with us?" Callie said, when Bruce finished with the air splint. She left the tarp over Stan and motioned for Bruce to follow her to beneath the house, next to Stan's car, to talk. Stan was dopey but still alert enough to listen, and he didn't need to hear this.

"I've already done more than I legally should. I don't need a hospital asking questions." Bruce brushed water off his face and arms. "I need to get back."

For the first time in a long while, she cursed being smaller than the average soul and dependent on bigger, burlier people. "Surely you're loading him in the SUV?"

"Of course. But we can't carry him far without fear of damage. If Leonard and I move the tree, you drive the patrol car out of the way." He touched the hood of Stan's sedan beside them. "I'll drive this one out to the curb, then we'll back your SUV in here for us to slide your man in the back."

Callie turned to ponder the huge limb on her car. "Are you sure you can lift—"

"Hey, Leonard," Bruce hollered, and Callie jumped at this quiet man being loud. "The lady wants to know if you can lift that limb off the cop car."

The rain took on a new life, the noise released like a small roar in announcement of what was to come. The wind whistled, then shouted as it met obstacles and fought to rush around them, making them raise their voices to be heard.

Leonard showed, black hair matted against his forehead and temples. "Let's get him moved," he said, heading to the patrol car, not waiting for anyone's permission.

With a hand saw found in Stan's storage room, they cut off straggling limbs that impeded lifting the main branch. The power in Leonard's biceps and shoulders pushed the saw's teeth through the wood at a rate Callie could only marvel at.

Once the small pieces were discarded, Leonard closed in on the eight-inch-thick bough. Bruce maneuvered himself on the other side of the car, up on the hood, and between the two of them, the oak's ten-foot appendage was lifted, shifted, lifted and shifted again. Finally, on a three-count, with Bruce's torque, Leonard gave it one huge heave and slid it off, down and beside the drive, leaving long deep scratches in the metal and paint.

Callie didn't wait to be told to hop in, and, thanking the angry heavens that the engine turned over, she backed the car out and parked it on the curb. Bruce had already collected Stan's keys, and he relocated the man's parked sedan. Callie leaped from the patrol car to her own SUV and drove it under the house, backing to within eight feet of Stan.

Donna had grabbed pillows and blankets from Stan's house, and as the two men orchestrated lifting Stan, Callie let down the seats to allow Donna to line the open area with the linens. Stan moaned as they moved him, but no doubt way less than he would have without the help of these three people who'd come to his and Callie's aid, and, of course, the morphine.

"I really wish you'd come with us," she said, approaching Bruce when Stan was settled. Thomas hadn't shown, and she hated the idea of taking Mark with her while equally hated leaving him behind alone. Someone stalwart was needed. No telling what could happen between there and Charleston.

Bruce, however, gave her a fast shake of his head and kept walking, returning to the wet tarp. He snatched it up and studied the grounds, as if hunting for any remaining sign of his being there. Then without a pause, he headed toward the rented sedan they'd arrived in.

"Leonard," he said, and Leonard trotted to catch up. No goodbye or social afterthought about calling on him if they needed him again.

They turned the car around in the cul-de-sac and left, hands clearly washed of the event.

Horse came over and nudged Callie's hand. She petted him once, feeling the need to caress something, and turned to the dog's owner. "Jesus, guess I ought to be glad they showed at all, huh?"

"Yeah, their red-white-and-blue personas sort of washed away in the rain, didn't they?"

"Well, they still helped a lot. Listen, I've got to rush," she said, not asking if Donna wanted to come. This ride would be a white-knuckled, bat-out-of-hell to get from point A to point B in the effort to stay a half step ahead of the storm. The councilwoman had to make her own choices about where she rode out this mess, and Callie wasn't going to ask her to ride things out in a West Ashley ER.

"Go," Donna said. "Safe travels."

Callie shook the offered hand, then after looking in on Stan, slid her wet self into her SUV and left. She pulled up to her own house, ran out, and tore up the stairs. It was then she realized the suitcases packed to leave Edisto Beach must be in the other vehicle. Too late to worry about that, and no room to add them to the SUV anyway. All she wanted was Mark. She could get both men off the island in one fell swoop, then drop into a bed at her mother's in Middleton later.

Opening the front door, she yelled, "Mark, come on. I've got Stan stabilized for now. We've got to go!"

He disappeared back into the bedroom, reappearing with an all-weather coat, ball cap, and a tote bag. He locked the door, and she held her breath as he took the stairs faster than she felt comfortable while maneuvering his game leg, which still held a bullet. She remembered how easily she'd stumbled at Stan's.

Mark hadn't buckled into his seat before Callie was back on Jungle Road, pushing the gas, seeing that she had barely more than an hour before Nikki was on top of them. At least the wind would be behind them a major part of the way.

She reached the edge of town and turned onto Highway 174. The water in the causeway was higher than normal for this cycle of the tide, but as long as she could keep the car between the lines and get across, she was good. In some places, water reached across the asphalt.

"Steady," Mark said, when one wheel caught a puddle.

She wasted none of her attention talking, instead keeping it on the road. Water pounded the roof with the occasional release of collected water from the broad tree canopy overhead. The racket filled their ears, and they stayed silent, feeling no room, no time, no reason to add words.

Pieces of trees, leafy boughs, limbs both thin and weighty sprinkled the highway. She crushed the small, veered around the larger, willing herself to feel the road through her hands on the steering wheel and her feet on the floorboard, hoping to make the best judgment calls. Thank God they met nobody, no traffic to slow her up, but the storm cast enough obstacles in her path to stiffen every muscle from fingers to the middle of her back, each primed to react.

Stan groaned from the back seat, and Mark took off his seat belt and turned to check on his friend. However, he wound up groaning even more than Stan from the twist.

"Sit down. There's nothing you can do," she said. "Stay buckled and just let him make his sounds. I don't need two patients. all right? You're baggage right now. Act like it."

He did as he was told, leaving one grip on the door handle, as if it helped.

More obstacles appeared to drive around; the road slick then slicker in spots. The night seemed so much darker than normal. Moisture from her and Stan being wet thickened the humidity in their confinement, making her cognizant of her breaths, half from fear.

Son of a bitch. There was no way to make up time, either. Speed would get them nowhere but in a ditch or upside a tree.

Structures were dark without electricity. With no opposing traffic's headlights nor the least bit of moon or starlight, she drove on in the pitch, a dangerous endeavor on a two-lane that would stretch thirty miles before reaching US Highway 17, the road taking them to the hospital. Once on that highway, she could fly. Until then, she gambled, a fine line between fast enough and too fast.

But she had to cross the big bridge first before thinking about reaching the mainland. Once across it, she had options in the case of trees down or debris in the way. Not many short-cuts, but options if a road was blocked. Until then, she took the lone road off the island, praying for passage and no surprises.

Her headlights bounced off the Edistonian. A couple of traffic cones left behind from where they'd managed the roadblock had been knocked over and wedged against the gas pumps. Then came the island post office. Good so far. Up ahead was Oyster Factory Road. They were making tracks. She was afraid to think she had this and made her goal solely reaching the big bridge.

"You're doing great," Mark said, as if reading her thoughts, then he hushed. He didn't touch her. No pat on the thigh for encouragement. His law-enforcement past had placed him in dire situations as bad or worse, and she didn't need consolation. She just needed to focus on eating up road and the diminishing time before Nikki hit. Botany Bay Road ought to be just ahead.

Suddenly her headlights bounced back at her off something solid.

"Brake!" Mark shouted about the time she did.

The car hit a puddle and went into a skid. She pumped the brakes and turned into the slide, her lights scanning across the long wide trunk of a moss-riddled live oak tree in the road as her car slowed. The vehicle rammed sideways against it, Callie's head striking her side window at the sudden stop. In a rebound, Mark's struck his. Stan rolled behind them, his yell indicating the pain had cut through the morphine.

Rain filled her lights along with the roots of the old tree. The tree had been most likely rotted enough to have weakened it from the top down, the roots having lost their grip over the years.

In a flash she flipped off her seat belt, snatched the small flashlight from her belt, and went to her knees in her seat to check on Stan.

From the looks of the bedding, he'd been slung to his side then returned to his back, only in a different spot. Her light reflected off open eyes.

"Stan?" For a half second, her heart lodged in her throat at his wide-eyed stillness.

"Chicklet?" he replied, weaker than any word she'd heard him say before.

"Sorry," she said, feeling she'd done something wrong. This two-lane highway was the only route short of boat off this island, and there was no way she could get across, through, or around this hundred-plus-year-old tree.

They weren't even a third of the way to the big bridge.

She had no resources, method, or plan to continue. Her only choice was to turn back and make Stan comfortable at *Chelsea Morning* until the first responders started calling in after Nikki had come and gone. At least she'd access to Bruce and Donna. She sure as hell wasn't riding out things here in the open.

She looked at her watch. Nikki was due within the hour.

"Buckle up, Mark." She did the same. "Stan?" she yelled over the rain getting ever louder, "I'm taking you back to my place to ride this out. We've got to get you inside a building."

She tried to tell herself he was no worse for wear when he didn't moan back.

This time, however, she raced heading toward Nikki, competing against time and the wind in her grill to get Stan someplace safe before those winds became harsh enough to push them off the road, bringing enough rain to create flood situations that would cover the highway and strand them.

Foot on the gas, hands cramping on the steering wheel, she reminded herself that she and Mark did not have the ability to carry Stan up the stairs. And to leave him at ground level was to subject him to the potential of flood waters that could sometimes sweep away a vehicle.

She risked driving faster, Mark watching her instead of the highway, remaining silent. They both realized she risked their lives in this mad dash back to town.

She did what she'd been trained to do, the best she could. Her headlights could barely make out the road ten feet ahead.

Finally, back at the causeway, water had about covered the full access, and in one place she had to guess where the road was. She focused on buildings up ahead, at least those she could make out in the dark deluge, guessing where the road was, praying her wheels pointed straight.

She got over, her road's turn just ahead. Now she prayed that nothing floated or blocked the remaining mile to her house. Thank God Jungle Road wasn't flooded.

Just as she turned onto it, with some of the driving danger eased, she realized the obvious. She was faced with getting Stan up those stairs in worse weather than before. She and Mark couldn't get the big man's deadweight out of the car, much less up two-dozen slick stairs.

In a quick decision, she raced past *Chelsea Morning*, heading west, toward Arc Street.

"Where are we going? The station?" Mark guessed, equally recognizing the issue with logistics.

"The station is on ground level . . . flood level. I'm headed to where those big guys are renting, the Rangers. I've got to convince them to come back and move Stan, maybe even stay there. We're much further back off the water than where they are anyway."

Flotsam littered yards and streets, but nothing she couldn't maneuver around. With Jungle Road being so far back off the beach, her vehicle wasn't hammered so much. Arc Street was two miles ahead, involving some zigzagging to reach it.

At the end of Jungle, she headed south on Lybrand, the storm's impact hitting her car head on. She had to avoid Palmetto Boulevard, the street that bore the brunt of any Edisto storm, so she turned onto Myrtle Street, taking it all the way to Arc.

There was no car at *Seas the Day*.

"Shit!" she yelled, then in a split second decided having any number of the three men was good enough for her. Leonard had said they only had one car. Maybe one or more of these guys remained in the house to assist. Worst-case scenario was they had headed for higher ground after all. At least for her, Mark, and Stan.

She eased through a flower bed in front of *Seas the Day*, nudging against an old sago palm in case it added support, and parked, putting her within close reach of the stairs.

She turned to Mark. "Stay here."

"Callie, you can't—"

"You and I cannot carry Stan into a house. I have no other options, Mark, other than parking us under my house and riding it out, hoping the water doesn't become an issue. But if these men move themselves to *Chelsea Morning* and remain with us, it'll not only be safer for them, but we'll have their muscle and Bruce's medical experience."

The look on her beau was one of utter frustration. She understood but didn't have time for feelings.

"If I have to lift him, I'll just have to, Callie."

That was love talking, not brains, along with his exasperation that he was limited and unable to help the two people he was closest to in the world.

A discussion for later. She left the car.

A gust immediately blew her against it, the air practically liquid between the rain and humidity. She gasped and had to cough the bits of rain she accidentally inhaled. The combo of hitting the car and coughing from her naval, reminded her of bruises on her backside and lower leg from falling on the stairs at Stan's.

She was fast turning into a mess.

"Callie!" Mark called, loud enough to be heard over the din.

But she waved a dismissive hand, hunkered down, and reached the stair railing.

With the ocean at her back, the weather pounded at her, water pouring down her collar, the temperature of those drops colder, a sure sign this was Nikki making her arrival.

Water ran into her eyes, ears, and once into her nose when she took a gasp, choking her and forcing her to stop and cough to dispel it. Finally, she reached the top. Falling against the door, she pounded a fist.

With so much competition against being heard, she went to yank open the screen, but the hasp caught it. She punched through it, unhooked, opened the screen, and pounded on the hard door. "It's Chief Callie Morgan!" she screamed. "Open the door."

Infuriated, she tried the knob. The door fell in, the wind pushing it and her with a force to send her stumbling. She slipped and sprawled across the floor, her feet sliding in the water, her hands unable to grab anything stable, until she face-planted in the entry way. The pain of her nose hitting the floor pierced into her eyes.

Chapter 21

Callie
Minutes to the storm

CALLIE PUSHED ONTO her hands, waiting for the pains shooting through her eyes to cease, for the stars in her periphery to fade. She almost cried for Mark.

"Jesus," she whispered, afraid if she stood she'd fall again. *Please, just make the pain go away.*

Suddenly there was Bruce. "Stand up," he said, practically lifting her off her feet when she gave him her hand. "What are you doing here? Thought you were at the hospital with your friend." He kicked the door closed.

Even through the pain, she noted his stiffness, the tone in his voice saying she was quite the surprise and not exactly welcome.

The blood sliding down her throat filled her mouth with the taste of it. A big swallow of wet clots suddenly did a number on her stomach, and she kept swallowing, which did nothing but worsen the feeling. Reaching toward her nose, she wanted to feel how much out of place she'd managed to shift it.

Bruce blocked her hand. "Don't touch it," he said. "Come in. Let me look at it in the–"

"Power's gone," she reminded, about the time he went for his phone, turning on its flashlight app.

"Hold this," he said, giving her the phone. "Shine it in your eyes and close them."

She listened while kicking herself, worrying about her two guys waiting in the car. They had no time for this stupid sidetrack.

Bruce gave her nose a light touch or two.

"Anything tragic?" she asked.

He touched it harder, and she winced. "No," he said. "Suggest a hospital, but it doesn't look out of place." He took his phone back. "But I'm not a doctor. I'll tape it, though."

"You're as close to medical help, hell, any help, as I've got right now. It's either you or the retired veterinarian." She motioned toward the front door. "My car is downstairs. Stan's still in it. A tree stopped us several miles up the highway, and we had no choice but to come back. I've got to get him into my house, and there's only me and my friend who just had surgery yesterday." She peered around Bruce, seeing little in the dark. No power. No moonlight. Just black with zero movement and absence of the other two. They would have checked her out by now.

As they talked, Bruce obtained a wet dishtowel from the kitchen just to the right. He handed it to her, holding another with ice to substitute for the first once she'd stemmed the flow.

"Where are Arlo and Leonard?" she asked, muffled from behind the rag. She looked around him, but he made a half step into her path. Unnecessary if they weren't there.

She tried to ignore her roiling stomach.

"They wanted to see the storm," he said.

"What? Can you call them?" she said without thinking. Of course he couldn't call them. The service on her phone was out, so his should be as well. All the phone services shared one tower. The nose had her judgment clouded. *Sonofabitch.*

But she forced herself back to her purpose and motioned to the door. "I've got two injured people in my car who need to be up and out of harm's way which means in my house. I cannot carry them up stairs." Her voice had thickened from being unable to breathe. She shifted the bloody rag to the icy one, the pain throbbing, tears still trickling regardless of how hard she tried to blink them back.

"Just let me do it," he said, putting his phone in his pocket. He meant the nose, not Stan.

Callie wondered whether the pain was keeping her from identifying the problem here. "Y'all need to be on higher ground and further back anyway. My house is safer. This end of the beach floods the most."

"Can't reach them," he said. "You know that. Besides, they're running the beach in the rain," he added. "They'll come back when things get dicey."

She stared at him like he'd grown antlers. "What?"

"It's what they do, Chief. Rangers lead the way, don't you know? Leonard has all these personal goals when it comes to fitness. He's never run in a hurricane before. Arlo went to keep him safe."

The answer was so asinine she couldn't help but think it true. Nobody made up crap like that. They'd already proven themselves an odd lot.

But truth or not, the other two weren't here, and Bruce was. She'd take what she could get. "They may find themselves having to hide out somewhere but come on. I need you. Stay at my place or come back here, your choice, but you've got to help us carry him or we're sitting out the storm in the car."

Sounding like a train, the air pushed at the house, forced to rebound and veer around the corners, giving it an eerie, almost metallic resonance as it audibly bounced and changed direction. Both listened to one corner of the front porch, then snapped attention to the other, the action almost paranormal. That must have been enough to put Bruce into action, because he turned and trotted back to his room. He returned, having grabbed what appeared to be the same bag as before since it was still damp, while carrying another tote, his go-bag of sorts. Military habit maybe.

"Brought rope, just in case," he said, lifting one of the bags. He dropped everything, pulled a roll of tape from his pocket, and ripped off a quick piece, molding it across Callie's nose.

She winced, didn't ask why he packed what he did. She was more than willing to just accept his Boy Scout ways, and she led them outside, the rag still in hand. When the wind dared to push her down to her butt, he maneuvered in front of her as a block. Needing both hands and all her faculties, she dropped the rag. Suddenly she understood the potential of rope.

At the base of the stairs, the wind growled harder. Bruce fought it to the back of the car when Callie popped the hatch while she forced herself into the driver's side. She held the door so it wasn't ripped off its hinges. Mark reached out for her hand to assist her in.

Bruce climbed into the back with Stan since the seats were down. He had one grip on the hatch with the wind's pressure beating against it, aiding closure when Callie hit the fob.

"What the hell happened to you?" Mark said loudly over the outside noise. He glanced to the back at Bruce, as if he might have had something to do with the blood oozing from Callie's nose.

"Later." Breathing heavy, blinking hard, Callie backed out and headed toward home, thinking how freaked Mark would've been if he'd seen her before the wet rag and the rain.

The two miles there felt like ten, with constant gusts slamming the vehicle. On Jungle Road some of their jerkiness eased with more rows of houses as a buffer; however, in the little time she'd been at *Seas the Day*, Nature had trashed the throughway.

"Once we get to *Chelsea Morning*, we aren't going anywhere," she said, trying to sniffle then trying not to when it hurt. Bruce would indeed have to stay with them. She couldn't hold him, but, surely, he had that much sense after seeing all of this.

She couldn't park under the house with hers and Mark's personal cars already there, so as she had at *Seas the Day*, she wedged the vehicle against the stairs, headlights almost touching the front of the storage room. This way the car had some protection and they could lift Stan out and straight up the steps.

A slam of a noise jerked their attentions around as all three exited the cruiser. A neighbor's golf cart, while maybe once braked, had not been anchored properly. It lay on its side, sliding in short slow spurts down the asphalt of Jungle Road.

"She's right on top of us," Callie yelled, opening the rear of the SUV as she ran around to the opening. "Mark," she hollered over Stan and into the vehicle. "Carry what you can up the stairs and open the door."

He did so, the aggravation in his expression saying what they didn't have time to discuss. He'd rather be helping lift Stan, but he collected items and followed direction.

Bruce grabbed blankets under Stan instead of his body and, in a quick move, slid him to the rear, taking the brunt of the rain on his back. He raised his voice. "Sorry, old man, but you're going to have to help us. The chief will be on one side of you and me on the other. Lean on me if you can."

Bruce got on the broken-leg side, Callie the other. The railings were eight feet from each other up the stairs, which meant only one of them could reinforce their stability. The other would have to rely on balance. With nothing to do with chivalry, Bruce took the railing side, serving as support as Stan leaned on him and half hopped up each step with his good leg. Bruce had a stronger grip than Callie did, and in case of a slip, he'd have the better hold on Stan. She was on her own if that happened.

Six steps up, Callie held a genuine fear that all it would take was one of those sixty-mile-an-hour blasts to topple them, end over end, onto the shells and gravel, resulting in an assortment of broken bones for more than Stan.

There was no talking in their efforts. They wouldn't be heard anyway. Rain poured like the roar of a crowd.

Mark made his way up the other side, a hard hold on his railing. He had a decent grip, but even he did a little slip number once, catching himself, making Callie's heart slam inside her chest. Then Stan slipped on his one leg.

She slipped with him.

It took all Bruce had in him to hold onto the man.

She almost let loose of Stan, so she didn't weigh them down, taking all three in a tumble. But in a reactive move, her right leg went down two steps and managed to stick the landing as Bruce stopped Stan.

"You all right?" Bruce yelled.

"Good," she yelled, reassuming her position beside Stan.

What felt forever took probably no more than ten minutes, but the three of them were soaked by the time they stood on the porch, water running in rivulets off them. Gales still pounded them in the back as they maneuvered Stan through the door inches at a time, because the three of them couldn't fit and he couldn't stand alone.

Callie kicked the front door closed. She was incredibly grateful for the sudden disappearance of the cacophony, and a sense of peace.

The closest room to the left happened to be the guest room, stacked with assorted porch furniture. Mark slid a chair and table off the closest side, letting them fall to the floor, then ran into the guest bath, grabbing towels. He looked around frantically for something more, then lifted a thick, sculpted rug of starfish from the floor to the bed.

They set a sopping Stan atop the rug in hope of saving the mattress. Callie reached to undo his Hawaiian shirt buttons. She wanted him dry. And she wanted him comfortable and still so she could study that leg better. Short of assorted grunts, he'd been mighty quiet through all of this. She prayed it was the morphine and not his deterioration.

"Let us take care of him, Callie," Mark said, motioning her out of the room.

She started to say she'd seen Stan in the buff before, but they didn't need a discussion of feelings right now. She walked out, closing the door behind her, and went to her own bathroom to disrobe and see what kind of moisture damage she'd done to her uniform's assorted tools and accouterments . . . and to study her nose.

From feel, because she could barely see via the small flashlight in her hand, the entire lot of what she wore was drenched, some of it made for wet weather, some of it not.

Thumps sounded through the wall. They were repositioning the porch furniture in the guest room, giving Stan full use of the bed, she imagined. Another thump sounded like someone, Bruce probably, moving something down the hall, making room.

A branch bounced off her glazed bathroom window. She whipped around, then felt silly. That kind of window couldn't be boarded, but that reminded her that she hadn't taken notice of the others, the bigger, thinner ones more prone to breakage. Wrapped in a towel, she ventured from the bath into her bedroom to check those windows first.

Nope. Stan couldn't install those very well by himself, not two stories off the ground, so they were exposed, thankfully facing the marsh. Clearly Buck hadn't gotten to them as he had hoped.

In Stan's effort to secure his own place and tend to Mark, he'd only been able to cover the front-porch windows on *Chelsea Morning*, on the side of the house toward where the storm would come to town. At least there was that.

It had taken both Leonard and Arlo to install those on some of Janet's rentals, but some shutters were custom and designed better, while others were little more than plywood with hooks. Hers were custom. While designed to be one-man capable, however, it usually took a particularly built man to handle the job. Climbing a ladder and holding one of those fifty-pound shutters in addition to whatever tools one may need was a wieldy task.

Still damp, she shivered, and, absent-mindedly, she sniffled again and closed her eyes at the shooting pain. Chilled to her core, she didn't dare shower, saving whatever water was in the tank for something more urgent, so she returned to the bathroom and toweled hard.

Grateful for shorter hair, she stopped toweling when it was mostly dry and set up her phone's flashlight into the mirror, giving her some visual by which to tape gauze over and under her nose. She didn't even try to look for bruises on her legs and backside from the topple at Stan's. They could wait.

Then she opted for jeans and a long-sleeved sweatshirt, fall socks, and Timberland boots. This time when she went out, she'd have a raincoat, too, because, yes, sooner or later, she'd be out in this mess again.

Though it hadn't worked before, she gave her body radio another go. Now that they were hunkered in, she needed to tell the Walterboro center where she was, stuck on the beach, and that they needed Stan to be helicoptered out if they couldn't get an ambulance through. She'd also ask them to get a call through to Middleton where Beverly, Jeb, and Sprite would be worried sick as to why she, Stan, and Mark hadn't arrived.

The radio went in and out, but she felt she got through enough of a message to relay where she was. The bit about the helicopter? Maybe. Static consumed most of her plea for them to call Middleton.

Crisis reduced to a lull now, she sat on the bed, mic in her hand, in as close to quiet as she'd had for hours.

She was the last person who should have been caught unawares on Edisto Beach with a hurricane on the loose.

Chapter 22

Callie
The storm arrives

WITH SO MUCH disturbance outside, the feeling of quiet isolation inside was huge. Like a frog hiding under a leaf, they sat in temporary relief amidst danger all around. They had a few hours to sit in this vacuum and ride this thing out.

A hurricane always came in spinning counterclockwise, which was the power they'd been suffering through. In a while, they'd experience the eye, assuming it was anywhere near Edisto and hadn't moved up the coast, but, according to the last notice Callie'd seen, they should be getting a piece of that eye. They'd then experience an hour or more of peace and creepy silence. One could stand outside, stare straight up, and maybe see the stars. That phenomenon both awed and chilled Callie. The fact that Nature could come at you baring its teeth then take a breath, giving you a beautiful side, almost making you think the menace was over, only to come back and slam you again. That backside would come in churning with the same energy the hurricane displayed, pounding as much or harder, introducing more water.

It would be dawn before this thing passed all the way through.

She thought about Donna and Horse, hoping their place was safe. Callie knew the house. It was high enough, but one couldn't predict storm surges or wayward debris traveling fifty miles per hour. Or a tree on your car, like her patrol car still parked over at Stan's.

She feared Leonard's and Arlo's cockiness and training weren't a match for Nikki, but if anyone had to be out in this thing, best it be them with all their muscle and battle savvy.

The twenty houses on her list that contained the holdovers primarily held natives. She didn't assume she had everyone on that list, but she appreciated at least knowing those. The others would make themselves apparent soon enough in the morning.

Natives would've stocked up and tied down. She hadn't planned on being here, though, so here she was unprepared. No bottled water. No extra supplies. Enough food for a few days. Mark owned the restaurant, so there were those goods, and if she had to, she'd get into the grocery store. The threat wasn't starving or doing without water. The threat was injury. Like broken legs and noses.

She returned to check on Stan. "How's he doing?" she called at the guest-room door. She tapped, and Mark let her in. Stan lay in the bed, eyes closed, breathing regular, seemingly comfortable beneath several layers of covers. Through the door, she could see his clothing hanging across shower curtain, sink, doorknob, and more, meaning he was probably nude.

Mark sat in a wicker rocker wedged in the corner. He motioned toward the window a couple feet to his left. "His dry clothes are downstairs in the other car. When the power comes back, when we can dry his clothes, when the rain stops and we can retrieve the others . . . whatever, we'll get him back into something. He's got some size on me, but if we must, we'll cram him into whatever we can of mine before loading him in an ambulance."

He stared hard at Callie, then at Bruce who'd come to the doorway and stood, leaning on the frame. Mark's skepticism covered his face, showing he needed to be brought up to speed as to who the hell this person was and how the hell she'd gotten a broken nose.

For now, however, Callie went over to the big man in his bed and laid a palm on his forehead, half feeling worried for him, and half testing for a fever. If that broken leg worsened, if he had any open wounds. . . . "Anyone check to see if he had more than the leg issue? Scratches, cuts, gashes?"

Bruce shook his head. "Light look. Scratches and bruises all over his arms where he tried to catch himself. Not certain how deep any one of them might be, but we have no idea the damage to muscle and bone in that leg. That's the main concern."

She held her phone's light to the side so as not to awaken Stan but so she could see better. "Shouldn't he be awake with the leg?" She peered down, seeing where the injured limb, nude except for the air splint, stuck out of the covers across the bed, to keep weight off it. "How'd you get his pants—"

"Cut them off," Bruce said. "And he had enough morphine in him to doze back off once everything settled down. Be glad. I don't want to have to keep pumping him full of that stuff."

She kept her sight on Stan while asking, "How much more of that stuff do you have?"

"Enough," he said, and she suspected he'd never give her the chance to glance in his bag of medicinal tools. "How's your nose?"

Even with the huge wad of bandage strapped across the middle of her face and a need to keep her mouth open to breathe, she considered her injuries minimal compared to Stan.

"It's okay, I guess," she said, taking a seat on the bed at the foot where there was more room.

He rummaged in his bag, pulling out a bottle. "Here, take—"

She held up a hand. "Don't need opioids or morphine or anything like them. I need to keep my head clear."

"It's extra-strength Tylenol," he said, holding out a couple of pills. "At least dull the edge."

She popped them in her mouth and swallowed, not bothering with water, and he used his now-free hand to wave the air and make a point. "It's the middle of the night. Shouldn't we all be sleeping? Something tells me tomorrow will be chaos."

"There's another bedroom upstairs, if you want to crash there," she offered.

He was right. There was no need to stand guard for anything at this point. No coming and going. No calls to send and take. Still, Bruce just talking, even about mundane things like places to sleep and Tylenol, gave her an odd sensation.

Frankly, he was the oddest of the three Rangers. Almost an anomaly.

With everything and everyone slowed and in waiting mode, thoughts caught up with her. She'd not served in the military, but she'd spent her entire adult life with police departments. With Boston PD large and as close to paramilitary as one could imagine, her experience gave her some insight into the ways of soldiers.

But Rangers, Seals, Green Berets, and Delta Force were different breeds. She'd met a few, even worked alongside a couple, but their ways weren't cop ways. They thought outside the box . . . preferred living outside the box. They didn't like boxes period.

Arlo seemed the most reintegrated of the three, and one could see the military in him, but nothing rang bells of anything elitist about him. Leonard was peculiar but little more than offbeat. Bruce, however, had a secrecy about him that made her wary. She smelled PTSD. They kept him tucked away. She wondered if what he'd seen as a medic in the field had left residual scars.

She stood. "You ever been in a hurricane?"

He gave a micro-shake of his head.

"Nothing we can do but wait for the worst to pass," she said. "Once we've been through the other side of the eye, I'll go to the station. We've got water bottles stored there along with radios, and along the way I'll be able to get some sense of the damage. Might take you with me, if you don't mind. We might have to clear our way here and there."

"Let's go now," he said.

"No," she replied. "It would be stupid to step in the middle of this and not expect to get hit or hurt." She waved over Stan, him being the prime example. "Nature trumps everything. You learn that on an island. Respect it or you pay."

Mark listened from the other side of the room, his interest divided between Stan and the conversation taking place on the other side of the bed. She could feel his need to talk, just without Bruce in the room.

A hard whistle zipped around the house, just behind Mark's position, but the noises weren't making them jumpy anymore. They'd become more tolerant and expectant.

But then the wind raised. A repetitive *rat-a-tat* slamming made them all jump . . . taking Bruce down into a crouch.

"What the . . . ?" Callie went to the front door and tried to peer through the smooth parts of the etched glass.

The sound started again, and she ducked as if she feared flying bullets, but the chattering sound gave her that sense. And if it did her, it surely did Mark and Bruce.

She peered through again, then eased, standing fully erect now. "It's all right," she said, and she'd have opened the door and shown them if not for the rain. "It's the mailbox out at the street. The hard wind is slapping its door open and shut. Must be the right angle to sound like a machine gun."

Yet her heart still thumped a bit harder. A glance back at Mark, and she saw his did, too. Bruce looked ready to take on somebody.

"Deep breaths, everybody," she said, then felt foolish at being unable to with her nose.

"I'm taking your offer for the bed," Bruce said, "but I think I'll crash on the couch, if you don't mind. Prefer to stay on the ground floor and aware." He pointed toward the door. "I'd rather be alert for shit like that."

Without further discussion, Bruce left, his footsteps taking him to the other end of the house but past the sofa. There were no boards on the back windows, and he seemed to have a sincere need to study the outside, walking from window to window. Callie went to the kitchen, listening, waiting until she heard sounds signaling he had situated on the sofa and relaxed. However, she wasn't so sure he wasn't doing the same as she was, listening for what he wasn't in the room to see.

She got out two glasses and filled them both with water. "Help yourself to anything in the kitchen," she said through the bar opening into the living room.

The man lay stretched out. Silent. She started to walk over and see if he heard, or rather see if he was asleep, but he'd be more aware than most. Instead, she returned to the bedroom and closed the door behind her.

Mark took the offered glass of water. "Don't trust him," he said quietly.

"Ditto," Callie said back. "But we needed him. He was Stan's savior, Mark. Twice."

"Guy's a freak," he said, leaning elbows on knees. "Come here." He motioned for her to sit on the corner of the bed right in front of him. "Careful, watch his leg."

He didn't have to tell her that, but she did as told to let him continue being Stan's overseer. She waited for him to whisper something not to be heard in the living room, but instead he raised his phone to see her face. "Jesus, that needs looking at. Headache?"

She recoiled at the light in her eyes. "What do you think?"

He shrugged with a question in his expression, needing to know how.

"I was pushed by the wind and rain, lost my balance and smashed face-first into the floor at Bruce's. Despite my radar going off, he's been nothing but helpful."

"Still," Mark said. "The hairs have been standing on my neck ever since I laid eyes on him."

"Well, he is the weirdest of the three, but I can't deny he's been a Godsend." She patted Mark on the leg. "How are you feeling? Pull any stitches in all of this?"

He shook his head, lips flat in denial that he be anything but of assistance. "I'm not going to become another casualty for you, Sunshine."

She would love his help. She would love to see him feeling needed instead of being in need. Mark was a doer, a people person, someone who adored offering himself to anyone's aid. Of all the times. . . . "I'm sorry," she said.

His look turned into a side-eyed one. "Don't you dare feel sorry for me."

"Okay, then I'm not sorry. But we all know we'd be better off if you were an able body right now."

"Well, ouch at that."

She lightly chuckled. "Can't have it both ways, Cajun." She touched his knee and rose, wincing at the stiffness setting into her backside and legs.

"What?" he asked.

No point laying more details on him about falls and stumbles. There'd be time for reminiscing and healing after Nikki had gone. Their first shower after this thing would expose all. "I'm just sore from all this," she said.

Bumps and thumps, whistles and fast thrusts of hurricane air seemed to crescendo. She thought of what everyone else in her life was doing right now, and studied Stan again, making sure he breathed steady.

A weariness settled into her bones. A weariness she hadn't wanted to settle over her until they were further down the road with this storm.

"Hey, why don't you come lay down for a bit?" she told Mark who didn't look too perky himself. "You're supposed to be recuperating. I'd hoped to have you in Mother's spare room being waited on by the kids."

"I can recuperate anywhere," he said.

"Then come do it."

Mark looked around her at Stan. He'd come to love the man as much as she did. They were an odd pair of guys, but it worked, especially since they both shared an appreciation for her.

She stroked Mark's hair. "He's medicated," she said in assurance. "If he wakes, he'll call, and we all know he can make himself heard."

She held out her hand for Mark to take, but he waved her off, wanting to handle himself by himself. Then together they eased out of the bedroom, leaving Stan's door open. In their bedroom, their own door open so they could hear their friend, they chose to remain clothed and simply lie across the spread—her gingerly in the crook of his arm, her not wanting to touch his abdomen; and him not wanting to disturb her nose.

After what seemed only seconds, Callie fought to clamor out of a groggy fog.

"Hey, Chief." Something nudged her shoulder.

"What?" she answered, opening eyes way heavier than she liked them to be. Then it all rushed back. The hurricane, Stan . . . Bruce in the house. Now Bruce standing beside her bed.

She sat up, which made Mark squint and try to make out what happened.

"We need to go now," Bruce said.

Mark sat up fast, disoriented. "Oh, geez, son of a bitch," he said, doubling over, reaching for his side.

Callie eased to sitting, touching his back. "Oh, honey, are you all right?"

He nodded but didn't speak, absorbing the pain.

The room remained jet black short of Bruce's phone in his hand. It wasn't dawn yet, or anything close to it, though it might be difficult to tell.

Then she noticed the quiet.

"Is this the eye?" Bruce asked. "It got weirdly silent."

She listened harder, then slid off the bed and scurried to the front porch. There were no breezes, just the occasional whisper of air and the distant roar of the ocean on the way to high tide.

Both men showed up behind her. She ventured down the stairs to the landing and stared straight up into the night sky . . . and saw stars.

"I never imagined," Mark said, almost under his breath. "And it must be fifteen degrees cooler."

"Yeah," Callie echoed. "Beautiful, amazing, and scary at the same time."

"But there's more coming, right?" Bruce asked, seemingly unaffected except as to what happened next.

Callie gave a scoff. "Oh yeah. We're only halfway through this thing, and with the tide higher, the second half of the show will be even more daring."

"Then let's go to the station and get your supplies," he said. "While we can. And we can go by my place and look for my guys."

As strait-laced and unfluffed as Bruce had been throughout an affair that had unfairly stolen him away, surely, he had concerns about his buds. Callie had underestimated that. Shame on her.

"We won't have long," she warned. "And if we meet obstacles or have to do much to maneuver the road, we'll turn around and come back, Bruce. This storm's second act ought to be worse, and we can't afford to be outside."

"I don't like it," Mark said, taking her by the arm. "It's still dark. At least wait until daylight."

Bruce tilted his head, like he was hearing a wrong note. "Things might be worse by then, man. We capitalize in the now we know or risk having fewer options later. I go for the now."

Callie saw both sides. But her concern hadn't even been stated. Stan. The minute this storm abated enough to send out first responders, she'd be accommodating him first and foremost. Or attempting to keep down his pain while waiting.

"Let's go," she said, heading back up the stairs for her keys, wishing to God she still had her cruiser left back at Stan's place, its hood caved in.

"Callie, wait." Mark limped up behind her, but Bruce bounded up steps two at a time, ready to go.

"Don't have time to wait," she said, trotting in, grabbing two flashlights, keys, and a windbreaker after strapping on a holster for her service weapon, extra magazines in their pouch.

When she turned, Mark stood in the bedroom doorway. "Not feeling great about this. Wait till morning."

She cinched the belt and went to him, wrapping arms around him. "We'll be fine. I've got a real Ranger at my back."

"Put him in front," he said, leaning down to kiss her hard on the forehead.

Bruce came up behind him. "Gotta go, man," he said, pausing before heading out the door.

"He's right," Callie said, letting loose. "There and back, as soon as we can."

Mark followed her. "I don't like this."

"I know," she said, halting just a second with a wink before taking the stairs down to where Bruce already waited beside the car.

She drove, Bruce not asking to. Jungle Road was littered with pieces of trees and bushes, items off porches that some hadn't policed before leaving town. One palmetto tree down, covering one lane of the road, then another that luckily fell parallel to it.

Her headlights bounced off a lot of brokenness. Greenery, mostly. In places, railings that were almost rotted anyway had finally given way, the owners now able to use insurance money to replace them. "This isn't so bad," she uttered, hoping she hadn't jinxed the trip.

One street down, the longest. Three more to go.

Not one single light. Not even a candle. At three thirty in the morning, the holdouts probably slept, saving batteries. She'd driven these streets at this time of night many times, but nothing like this other-dimension feel. It was as if they'd slid into the Twilight Zone and left the human race behind.

Lybrand Street held little more than palm fronds. Myrtle, however, was more flooded. She didn't dare drive a block further to Palmetto for fear of what she'd find . . . and the likelihood of getting stuck in relocated sand. They always had to clean up sand on Palmetto.

Finally, the administration building appeared in her headlights. An oak limb proved challenging to maneuver around, but she managed, even nudging it twice to open the way. Another lay across two of the parking places where the patrol cars usually parked. Good thing they'd been stored off the beach.

Choosing the fire chief's designated spot, she drove over branches that crackled and popped under her tires, paying attention to her lights sweeping across the property, assessing damage out of habit, curiosity, and duty.

Movement caught her eye amidst some shrubs.

"What was that?" She threw the transmission into park, freezing headlights on the spot.

"A deer?" Bruce keenly studied the shadows for whatever it was. "A dog left behind?"

She eased out, as if sacredly stirring the tomb-like atmosphere. Bruce did likewise on the other side.

The steady headlight enabled them to sweep the darkness on both sides with flashlights. Him right, and her left.

Her spotlight caught something blue. It moved then went still. "Over here," she said in a normal tone, not needing to holler in the velvet silence. Something indeed hid in the bushes to the left of the walkway leading to the police station door.

Training her flashlight, she softly treaded, the wetness of everything making her steps like slippers.

The movement happened again. A human hand raised and blocked the strong light beam.

"Oh my God," Callie said and ran to the person.

The girl looked to be eighteen or twenty. Her long black hair plastered to her, she crouched behind a bush barefoot, her face in shadow, wearing only a one-piece dress, a casual cotton, blue shift.

"Hey," Callie said softly, easing forward, crouching a little herself be closer to the poor girl's level. "Honey, I'm the police chief here. Are you all right?" Though eager to inspect the girl, Callie moved the light to the side a bit to avoid blinding her, and so the girl could see Callie's face.

"I don't know where I am," she said, before she burst into tears. "I saw a sign that said *Police*, but it was raining, and nobody was here." Her sobs intensified, contorting her face. "I didn't know what to do!"

Bruce remained silent, still, no sign of sensitivity.

Callie remained squatted in front of the girl, then dared to reach over and stroke a wet tress off her lashes. "Shhh, it's okay."

Somebody somewhere had to be out of their mind missing this girl. And Jeb was right. She did look a lot like Sprite.

Chapter 23

Arlo
The eye of the storm

"WE CAN'T SEE a damn thing in this weather," Arlo said, half wet from rain coming in the half-open side windows of the front seat. They'd gone north on Palmetto a few blocks, toward Big Bay Creek, where the marina would be if they turned right and kept going. The only lights were theirs. Nobody else was insane enough to drive around in the early hour of the storm.

"Pull over," Leonard said.

Arlo did as told, thinking Leonard had another plan, but instead the bigger Ranger got out of the vehicle, stripped himself of his shirt, and tossed it back in through the window. "Can't stand to even look at you now, man." Then he commenced jogging.

Arlo got out and sprinted to catch him. "What the hell are you doing?" His clothes soaked up the storm's rain in seconds, explaining why Leonard shed his.

Leonard ignored his friend and put more and more distance between them, an eagerness in his mission, and he could maintain the pace for hours. As long as needed.

"Stop, man!" Arlo caught up, not as eager to cover ground on foot. "Why'd we take the damn car if we aren't going to use it?"

Leonard returned and jabbed Arlo in the chest, knocking him back on his heel. "We could've left in the middle of this storm and been gone. We could've dropped off the package where we agreed, then hit the road with nobody the wiser. We've never skipped a step, lowered our guard, or made a mistake . . . until you screwed up. Every single adventure has been successful until now."

Leonard almost turned to run again, but he'd stoked his temper too much to let it go so soon. He spun back. "You volunteered us for duty. You made us known. And you lost the damn girl!"

"We're not unsuccessful. Not yet," Arlo said, before Leonard could speak his second thought. "Tell you what, and you already said it. We can't see, and we aren't driving much faster than you can run on foot. I'll use the car. You run. We'll find her."

Leonard backed up, then trotted backwards, his hard glare on his partner. He shot him the bird before turning back around for his run. He picked up speed, head canvassing side to side. It didn't take long for him to disappear into the dark and the weather.

Hard to argue with someone who's right. Best then that Arlo cover one block at a time, encircling each. No doubt Leonard had his short-wave radio in his pocket, and Arlo had his. In a minute he'd check with Bruce on his, to see if there'd been any changes, any news, any possibility the problem had rectified itself.

In the vehicle, Arlo slammed the steering wheel. He had fucked up. He'd never fucked up like this before. He wanted to blame some of this on Bruce . . . maybe, but Arlo was on watch at the time, which made him responsible. The three functioned as a unit in solving issues, but individually, you still owned up to your messes.

The girl had gotten loose. And that was totally on him.

Chapter 24

Callie
The eye of the storm

THE GIRL LOOKED thin with her dress and hair stuck to her. Water dripping off the big oak behind them and the roof around them gave auditory confirmation to the sogginess of everything around. She reared back, tucking into herself, unwilling to welcome Callie at first, then Callie remembered the bandage across her nose.

She touched the tape and forced a small giggle to lighten things. "Oh, don't mind this. I stepped in water and fell flat on my face." She dabbed it a little, showing it still tender. "This is what I get for not paying more attention to what I'm doing." She lowered her hand and smiled.

It took her a few coos and soothing words, general talk about the weather, and reassurance that she was the local police and could take care of her, before the girl at least shook less. She studied Callie, squinting, then finally softened. In a side glance, however, she tried to see what threat stood off in the dark.

Bruce remained well off to the side in the dark, and Callie welcomed that move. Out of range of the light, she pushed her hand to indicate he needed to step back more. No telling if the girl had experienced a run-in with a man or not, plus it was best to let her adapt to one person at a time. Being found in the middle of the night, in the middle of a hurricane, especially if she lost track of time and place, would have her afraid to do anything but stay cemented in place. Especially if she'd been . . . injured.

Bruce's idea to venture out during the eye had proven to be a good one. No telling what could have happened to this child amidst Nikki's wrath. The tide was higher now, close to its highest, so the next rains could cause more surge, more flooding, more unseen dangers in the dark. Being on ground level, even here, there could've been an issue, and then there was always the danger of exposure.

When the girl stood, it turned out she had nothing on but the cotton shift and a bra. No shoes, and in one quick bend in her attempt to stand, Callie noticed the girl wore no underwear.

A possible . . . horrible sense of violation snaked through her. "Come on, honey. Let's get you inside."

Langley St. James stood, keeping her head down, gaze seeming to dart this way and that. She was a tall one, six inches on Callie and kept taking peeks around her new protector into the darkness as Callie slowly drew her in. Finally, she accepted Callie's hand like a three-year-old seeking someone to trust.

She gripped it hard, like a rabbit's foot. Callie didn't want to lose the ground she'd gained, so she acted like she didn't see it.

With the door quickly unlocked, they slid inside, the flashlight still the only illumination with the power outage. Instead of parking the girl on the lobby sofa, Callie kept her at her side and talked to her like some close-knit aunt the child had known for years.

"We're gathering some batteries, more flashlights, radios, and water before going back to my house where it's off the ground and safer. Think you could help me with that?" Callie didn't wait for an answer and handed the girl a towel from the small stash of generic clothing and linens they stored in a small closet. You never knew when you had someone needing to cover up after whatever ordeal they'd endured. Usually, however, it was a child lost on the beach or some distraught individual who'd been scared witless by a riptide.

Bruce had not followed them in. Callie found that rather accommodating since this girl struggled enough in accepting Callie. Best she not deal with a strange man as well.

The not-wearing-panties thing angered Callie. A rapist on Edisto? Intolerable. He'd receive the worst of her wrath . . . once she took care of the girl . . . once she got Stan to a hospital . . . once she handled the hurricane. Hell, there was no finding a rapist amidst this mess. Chances were he was off island anyway after the evacuation. That last bit pissed her off.

An interview was needed, but Callie didn't want to push things. Safety was key, and time was limited. There was even the threat of tornados and waterspouts that commonly spawned from a hurricane's energy, causing worse damage. A hurricane having a tantrum.

She handed clothes to the girl, having had to hunt for underwear. It had been her idea to have several pairs in that closet, and this situation warranted that decision. "Here, put these dry things on in my office. It's private in there." The tie-on sweatpants and a T-shirt a size too big would suffice for now.

It took both her hands to take the clothing, and as normal as could be, Callie made the exchange gently, noting an IV hole in the crook of her arm.

In the office, she positioned a flashlight on the desk, so its beam bounced off the walls, almost giving the room the light of a decent lamp. "I'll be right back, okay?" she said, with one more adjustment to the light. "Just stay here. This is my office. It's safe."

She walked out slowly. The girl had been drugged, maybe to put her in la-la land so she couldn't identify her captors and didn't have to be fed.

She scurried through the lobby to outside where Bruce waited. "Where are you?" she whispered, not having her flashlight.

His popped back on. "I didn't think I ought to get too close—"

Callie nodded. "Agreed. She's barely accepted me close. She's traumatized, and I have no idea what about. Can you load the water? I put it on the counter. And those batteries and flashlights along with the radios. I want to get back to her."

"Sure." He rushed past to inside, spotted the water, and in a hefty display of brawn, stacked all items atop the two cases of bottled water, taking everything in one fell swoop.

Returning to her office, Callie found the girl dressed and seated in a guest chair in front of the desk, bare feet crossed at the ankles, the flashlight gripped tightly in her hands.

"Oh, darn it. I forgot something for your feet." Callie left and soon returned with flip-flops, which she dropped on the floor and positioned in front of the girl, so she could put them on herself.

With her visitor fully clothed and settled, Callie assumed the second guest chair. "Honey, do you mind if I take your picture?" She let her keep hold of the flashlight.

The girl gave a small passive shrug. Before she could change her mind, and while the light was in her hands giving her facial features the best sense of perception she could under the circumstances, Callie stole a few fast shots then made the phone disappear.

Damn, how the hell did she get out here? And who the hell brought her?

Then in that silent second, as she closed the photo app, Callie's brain remembered that the girl hadn't confirmed who she was. "Can you tell me your name?"

The girl seemed to debate whether to reveal herself.

"Honey. I am Jeb Morgan's mother, Callie Morgan. He's the boyfriend of Sprite Bianchi. You know them, don't you?"

There it was. Less fear, more acceptance. Even her shoulders dropped.

"Yes, ma'am. Sprite's in my dorm."

"There you go. Then could your name be Langley St. James?" Callie asked.

"Yes, ma'am."

Finally, words. Callie wanted to touch the girl, even hug her, but she couldn't without understanding Langley's head space, or whatever she'd endured.

"I hope you can trust me."

Langley lightly nodded.

"Okay, good then. Are you . . . hurt in any way?"

"I don't know," she said with a mild squirm, a motion that Callie worried had a serious origin.

She rephrased the question. "Do you hurt anywhere in particular?"

From a turn of her head to twist of her shoulders, Langley seemed to take stock of herself, even down to small movements ending at her flip-flops. But then she bent her arm with the fist to her chest and paused. In a silent decision, she stretched it back out and shined the beam to it.

"I don't know where this came from," she said, quickly adding, "I don't do drugs. Ask anyone. Ask Sprite!"

There was a small bruise in the crook of her left arm, and a needle mark that might've been ripped out. "I think I pulled something out when I got away." The wound was clotted, recent.

Assuming the girl didn't partake of drugs on her own, Callie had to consider she'd been doped up to make tending a kidnapped victim easier in transport, maintenance, or abuse. Maybe all three.

"Who did this?" Callie asked.

"I've tried to picture a face, a voice, but I have no idea. I've been fuzzy-headed or asleep since they took me. Someone covered my head and threw me into a vehicle. Don't ask me to describe it, then that's all I remember until my senses started coming back a little while ago when I found myself walking in the rain. How many days has it been?"

Callie had to think about that, so much had happened. "Three."

Langley's eyes went wide. "Seriously?"

"Believe so. And you woke up here on Edisto?" Callie asked, not particularly happy at doing this right now, but Langley was talking. They didn't have long to do this.

"I have to take your word we're on Edisto," the girl said.

They had until this hurricane ran its course to spend time together. During that time more details might come to mind. Callie needed an elementary understanding of what she was dealing with. Langley's kidnappers had come onto Edisto, or so she had to assume. They easily could still be here, or they could just as easily have made their escape when Langley did.

The mention of rape could wait.

Dr. St. James told everyone via news conference that his daughter had reappeared safe and sound when she hadn't. Likewise, nothing explained why St. James hadn't wanted to talk to Sprite and Jeb when they called to check on her. No wonder Sprite couldn't get a phone call through to her friend. The friend was being kept an hour away at the beach.

Jeb had said something wasn't right.

But here was not the place and now was not the time to delve further. They were on borrowed time in the middle of Nikki's literal calm before the storm.

"Come on," she said, reaching to take the light from the girl. "Let's go back to my place."

Hesitating at yet another unknown factor to judge, Langley seemed to steel herself with an inhale before concluding she must go along. "Can we call my dad?" she asked.

"One of the things I came here for was radios, to communicate better with dispatch. But let's get home first because this storm is almost on us. We'll check those radios and get a notice out. That'll at least tell everyone you're safe."

Apple and Google had enabled satellite messaging as a special thing for Hurricane Milton, but it had been a Cat Five, a deadly life changer. Nikki was only a Category One, so no such luck, Callie'd been told. A Cat One didn't do high-level damage, they thought. The most damage Edisto had ever experienced had been in the flooding aftermath of Cat Ones and Twos.

Callie rose, which made Langley rise, then the latter reached out for a hand to hold, and Callie accommodated. She led her out, the light not as bright in the lobby. In an afterthought, she grabbed a copy-paper box and threw the office's snack supplies in it. Office manager Marie was the snack queen, and her choices were exquisite. Tonight more than justified junk-food bingeing for everyone, especially this poor girl.

With a sweep of her flashlight, Callie noted the area and took Langley to the door. *Bruce must be outside, probably waiting in the car.* Callie would have to explain who he was to Langley, and deal with whatever reservations Langley had. Bruce looked nice enough, but he had a don't-get-too-close aura about him.

She locked the station door, again swept the area outside, and escorted them to her car.

Nobody there.

She shined into the car, seeing the water, batteries, radios, and such, but no sign of Bruce.

Walking Langley around to get in the car, taking no chance the girl might get a wild hair and run off, she loaded her in the front seat, closed the door, and continued scouting the immediate area for Bruce on her way to the other side. Still nothing.

She hated doing this, but he was a strapping guy, healthy in all appearances, and he could handle himself. Especially now that they were in the calm for a bit. He'd done what she'd wanted him to do, and he'd either made his way back toward her house to give Langley space or retreated to his own rental to his buddies.

One way or the other, he could find cover. He was a big boy. And this big boy had come with the first aid bag, which currently stood next to Stan's bed at her place. Callie hoped his sanctuary of choice to ride out Nikki was *Chelsea Morning*, so she could keep that bag and the person who knew how to use what was in it.

Wind brushed her damp hair, her wet clothes turning chilly, subtly warning her time ticked on. She got in the car and backed out, wishing she could see the clouds overhead and how angry they were, because she could no longer see the stars. A few fat drops hit the car, and she couldn't tell if they were from the trees or Nikki announcing she was back.

She wasn't but two miles from her house, but first, she had a drive-by to make.

But when she reached Myrtle, expecting to take a right toward the back way west to Arc Street, she met water, and from her knowledge of the topography, she'd find that much or more at each intersection the closer she got to *Seas the Day*. To go further and around via Palmetto would be worse, and to go the other direction would dead-end in Wyndham's golf-course property. This flooding consisted of salt water, pushed by the storm, a depth that would inch higher with the tide, maybe higher if Nikki got spunkier the second time around.

This is the route Bruce would take to his rental, assuming he stuck to roads.

She ventured into the water, seeing nothing deeper than six inches. Crawling, she made her way one block, then two, then three, sometimes going up in people's yards. Her familiarity with these roads gave her the gumption to keep going.

She stopped at Arc Street. Rain fell in small bursts, but not enough to block her vision. Artificial lights moved around inside *Seas the Day* a couple of houses down. Their car was back in the drive.

At least those two guys were back. When she got home, she could inform Bruce he should have no worries about his friends, unless he was with them.

She turned to Langley who studied the area like someone right off the boat onto an island never seen before. Nothing since leaving the station had registered with her.

Rain fell harder, and a gust gave a warning nudge to the cruiser.

"Let's get to my house," Callie said, turning around. It took her longer than normal to travel Jungle Road to *Chelsea Morning*, but by the time she arrived, an even harder rain awaited them.

"Come on," she said, yelling over the din when she opened her door. "You take the smaller stuff." She put an armload of the lesser items in the girl's arms. Callie grabbed the snack box. The two cases of water were too cumbersome to carry at the same time.

Mark waited at the top. Callie kicked her door shut and shouted, "Langley, that's Mark up there. He'll help you." Another reason she'd given Langley the lightweight items.

At the top Mark took her load, but Langley nervously remained outside until Callie reached her. "It's all right," Callie said. "That's my boyfriend. He owns the restaurant in town, and he's quite the good guy. He's a retired cop, so you're well protected." She realized she'd settled into speaking in singsong, but if it worked, it worked.

Mark deposited his armload inside and reappeared.

But unwilling to deal with yet another stranger, Langley panicked and ran back down the stairs.

"Wait here," Callie told Mark, then took off. "Langley, wait!" She heard the girl sobbing as she reached the bottom.

But once in the gravel-and-shell drive, Langley looked left then right, then both again, not able to see in the deluge, not sure which way was safe.

Callie caught up. She almost touched the girl and changed her mind. "Honey, I'm going to get you home. Promise." She blinked and spit with the rain coming down hard. "We just have to wait until after the hurricane, okay?"

Langley covered her face and cried.

Chapter 25

Callie
The back half of the hurricane—two hours into Nikki

WHILE THE WORLD around them wreaked havoc, Callie ventured closer, blinking away the weather in her face, and she finally touched Langley's elbow. When the girl didn't flinch, Callie came around and pulled the poor soppy creature to her, sensing a hug being the biggest thing she needed right now.

"I don't like not knowing what happened," she cried, bending down to Callie's level to cry into her shoulder.

"I know, I know," Callie said, rubbing her back, and discretely keeping her broken nose from being wedged in the hug. She gave Langley a moment, listening to the rain roar around them. Anyone held up in their home watching would think them insane standing amidst this storm in an embrace, but Langley was flighty. One step at a time.

It wasn't until a wind whipped them hard enough to knock them off-balance that Langley pulled back, squinting from the hard-hitting drops in her eyes, dripping off lashes. She said nothing when Callie took her again by the hand and escorted her to the car, retrieving the two cartons of water. She took one and gave Langley one—the goal being to distract her enough with a simple task to help her regain her senses.

At the top of the stairs, Mark tried to take a case from Langley, and Callie gave him a *no way* shake of her head. A blast of wind showered water onto the lot of them, and Langley darted inside, deciding that meeting someone new could take place indoors.

Mark looked around, assumingly for Bruce. "Where's . . . ?"

Callie gave him enough of a look to deter the query.

With the power down, the inside of the house had grown muggy feeling, but Callie'd take any place dry right now. "How's Stan?" she asked Mark as she set her case in the kitchen, next to Langley's.

"Sleeping off and on," he said, staring at her long enough to communicate there was more to address but now was not the time.

Callie told herself if something was bad wrong, he would cut to the chase, and she tried to hang onto that logic. Whether Stan was doing well or poorly, though, there was nothing they could do about it right now.

She turned her attentions to Langley, in need of comfort . . . and questioning.

Seemed Callie had accumulated three patients. She went looking for the newest who stood in the middle of the hallway, uncertain what to do.

"I'm getting you more dry clothes," Callie said, laughing a little at the repeat offer. She escorted Langley to her bedroom.

All she had was her own smaller sizes and some casual things of Mark's. She chose pajama pants and a henley shirt of his, and socks of hers. While Langley went into the adjoining bath to dry off and change, Callie did some changing of her own. She left her firearm on the dresser. Drying, cleaning, and oiling it would have to wait.

She checked the life of her phone. She'd plugged it into the car while at the station, and it had regained enough power to last her through what she hoped to be a decent-length interview.

After Langley came out of the bathroom, she waited while Callie changed the bandage on her own nose, grateful Langley couldn't see it in the dark. No telling how black and blue her face was. One eye felt more swollen than the other.

In the time it took for them to come back out, Mark had placed a juice bottle and two snacks from the box beside the recliner. Candles on the end tables and coffee table, a couple of bigger ones on the mantle—the small touches of his would take anyone's anxiety to a lower level, bless him.

"Sit right here, young lady," he said, wafting a hand like a waiter presenting a table. Then he backed away. Langley assumed her seat.

Callie hung back a second. "Tell me the real info about Stan," she said, when Mark passed her, headed back toward the guest room.

"He's feeling the pain now," he said, a furrow in his forehead she could see even through the room's shadows. "Don't be surprised if you hear him. You might want to tell her." He took a glance back. "Who the hell is she, by the way? A lost tourist?"

One might first think that. "She's Langley St. James," Callie replied. "From the news this week."

Mark didn't make the connection at first but soon did, tempering his reaction because of their guest's presence.

"Yeah," Callie said. "I've got to learn how she wound up here. Then I've got to contact the authorities. Can you make sure the radios are operational?"

He nodded and collected a couple off the table. "What about Bruce?"

"He took off," she said. "I hoped he might be here."

Mark planted a look on her that said he didn't appreciate that a damn bit.

"At least we have his first aid kit," she said.

His look took on a deeper concern. "But why would he disappear without it? That's not just Tylenol in that bag. I looked. Unless he's an MD, he has no business with that stuff, and I'm not seeing him as a doctor. A licensed one, anyway."

Callie took a half step towards Langley. "By being at the station, we were closer to his rental. Maybe he went to check on his buddies. They weren't there when I picked him up. But hey, let me tend to her first—"

"Go on. Yeah, we can talk later." He left to be with Stan.

She went to the girl, who'd chowed down on a protein bar and drank half her drink. "Let me try to contact dispatch. I'll be right back. You need a blanket?"

For security, for a chill, Callie didn't care why, but sometimes people just wanted covers between them and the world. The room was stuffy, but, surprisingly, Langley said yes, and Callie retrieved the lap throw off the sofa's arm and handed it over. Her guest tucked the still-folded blanket against her stomach and held it tight.

Callie smiled then retreated to her bedroom and checked her mic for life. *Yes.*

Something hit the window in front of her. She jumped, and a shrill laugh of wind seemed to mock her. Heart pumping a bit fast, she ventured to take a closer look. A crack. If another piece of debris hit the window that hard, that glass would give way.

This damn storm couldn't be over soon enough. There was no rescuing anyone until this shit passed through. The second edition of the storm danced outside in jest, whistling and flexing, smacking the siding, glass, and wood with big drops.

She needed a helicopter to set down at the Edistonian for Stan, as soon as possible, but that wasn't likely for an hour or two at best. She wished she could send Langley with him, but those medical choppers were cramped. They probably wouldn't take Mark either.

She attempted to call dispatch again. They answered, but static took every third word. Still, she informed them that in addition to Stan and herself, there were several of them at *Chelsea Morning*. In an added effort, knowing full well that other first responders could hear, she mentioned the tree down on the highway. Someone would jump right on that as soon as they could safely drive.

Her mic was about dead, and she didn't get the chance to mention Langley by name. Any other calls would have to be on the radios.

She went to the guest room, wanting to see for herself what Mark had been talking about. Langley had relaxed, giving Callie leeway to check on Stan.

She poked her head in the door. "Radio?" she said, as if that was her reason for coming in.

Mark handed her one. "This one should work."

She took it, her attention, however, on Stan. His eyes were open. "Hey, Chicklet."

How could she not respond to that? She rushed to him. "Hey, big man, how're you doing?"

"I'll live," he said, though his pallor said otherwise, and it must have showed in her expression. "Quit worrying. You're doing your best. It's the only way you operate."

Look at him trying to make her feel better. "I've asked for a chopper, but . . ."

"We don't get other people hurt for my benefit. It'll happen when it happens—" He ended on a moan, one that traveled all the way up from his gut.

A zing of deep concern filled her. No telling what sort of complications festered in that leg that they couldn't see. Broken bones offered a serious kind of torturing pain, especially a big one like this. She wished there was something she could do. Feeling inept, she wanted to go outside and scream.

"What's in that medical bag?" she asked Mark.

"More morphine. Bandage stuff, airway tools, PPE, stethoscope, blood pressure cuff, an assortment of opioids and pain meds, several kinds of antibiotics. Items for serious wounds. Not just a first aid kit. The meds are not over-the-counter except for maybe that Tylenol he gave you and diarrheal meds. I'm not a doctor, but it's a pretty intense bag for situations where you can't get to a doctor, or . . ."

"Or you don't want to have to call one," she finished.

Who was Bruce?

Honestly, who were all three of these guys?

Her impression thus far had been positive. Very positive. They didn't hide. On the contrary, they helped. One openly dated. One openly ran on the beach. Bruce was the most reclusive, but if he harbored the slightest bit of PTSD, he would be the one less apt to be seen in public. He'd made himself venture out with Leonard and load Stan into the car.

The men traveled together. They were protective of each other, which likely went back to their deployment days. This medical go bag, while containing items Bruce shouldn't be in possession of, felt like a kit they relied on back in the day and didn't want to do without now, to be less in need of putting themselves at the mercy of some strange medical person they didn't trust.

They seemed a very independent lot and extremely tight knit. She'd tried to attribute unusual behaviors and characters to experiences in their pasts, but her instincts told her they walked a different walk than most . . . for some reason all their own.

Whoever and whatever they were, right now she wished she had Bruce. He'd no doubt return for this all-too-necessary bag, but how long before he did? With him not being at *Chelsea Morning*, he had to be at *Seas the Day*, weathering this storm at home. He had shown concern for his friends who, in Callie's view, were insane to go out in a hurricane.

She stroked Stan's forehead. "Wish there was more I could do." Then to Mark, "At least give him three or four of those Tylenol."

But Mark didn't budge. "Already did a half hour ago, Sunshine."

God, she wished she knew how to dose up that morphine, but without that sort of training, she had no idea what dose was safe.

Stan had closed his eyes, falling into the pain, maybe even napping. She took that opportunity to exit, not wanting to leave Langley alone long . . . unable to watch Stan and be able to do nothing for him.

Mark took her hand as she walked past, kissed it, and let her go.

She returned to the living room. She ought to nap, but she had too much worry on her mind, and she wasn't losing sight of Langley. She couldn't risk another one of her panicky bolts. Also, Callie wasn't taking the risk she'd miss a return radio message telling her where to be and when. And there was still the interview.

She fired up the radio and got through better than with the waning mic. She confirmed all the facts she wasn't sure they had registered before and informed them about Langley, and that she was in good shape so nobody would freak. They told her it would be ninety minutes at best.

The storm was passing through when it came to Edisto, but it still had to make its way up the coast toward North Carolina, and it wasn't traveling fast. The swath was wide, and since transport came from Walterboro, ninety minutes was optimistic.

She signed off and sighed, staring out the back windows toward a high tide, white-capped marsh. Resigning herself to facts, she snared a water and returned to sit across from Langley who looked better than Callie felt.

"Now," she said, as much for herself as for the girl. "Let's talk about you."

Langley tensed some but not much. "Not sure what good I am."

"Oh, you might be more help than you know." Callie set her phone on the coffee table catty-cornered between them and hit record. While speaking the date and time and who was present into the recording, she watched Langley. She didn't tighten up as much or show her old signs of panic. They were good to go.

They covered her day at school first. "I was on my way home around four, after having been to the library." Her expression took on a sheepish appearance. "I was reading my phone."

Callie could give a lecture on that habit but saw no need at present. "And?"

"Someone grabbed me from behind. I mean, wrapped long, strong arms around me. Then something went over my head. I was lifted and carried into a vehicle, like being thrown on a back seat, not a van. I didn't even feel how they dosed me, but everything went black. I didn't wake up until today." She thought about that. "Can't believe it's been three whole days."

Nobody had seen the kidnapping, and no cams were in place at that area of the walk. Callie bet the college would rectify that in a hurry.

One big question was, for what purpose did they take her? And suddenly the parent walking back the public plea for assistance made more sense. The kidnappers might have directed that, telling them if they didn't Langley would never be coming home. Those were among the many details and questions the Charleston authorities would be clarifying with the parent for sure once Langley returned home.

Had they done anything to Langley? After all, she'd been unconscious, but how would she even know?

Callie asked anyway. "Do you feel like they did anything to you? Touch you? Bruise you? Change your clothes?" she hinted.

Langley dropped the recliner's leg support, the pop down sudden and forced with a *thunk*. She snatched up the flashlight Mark had left on the table. "I've got to go to the bathroom." She didn't wait for permission and fast-walked to Callie's bathroom, the one she was familiar with.

"Don't wash up, honey. You know why." She hoped that was explanation enough.

Callie put a stop to the recording with an explanation. Then she repositioned herself. Langley could not get past her without being seen. She tried to listen for the girl, but the weather prevented her from hearing much. In her attempt, however, she noted that Nature had tamed some outside.

In her wait a creepiness slunk up her spine as she thought about the realities of what may have happened to Langley. She knew exactly what the girl was doing in the bathroom.

In the emptiness, she shifted her aching backside and touched the left ankle. Her nose throbbed. An unwanted weariness tried to wash over her. They were a stone's throw from dawn, and her nap hadn't lasted an hour, tops. Langley hadn't faded as much, but then judging by the vague generalities she'd defined about her past few days, she might've gotten a ton of forced sleep.

Langley reappeared, returning to her chair, promptly grabbing the lap blanket and once again clutching it rather than spreading it out.

"You all right?" Callie asked, pushing her bottle of water closer before turning the recorder back on. "We need to flush your system of whatever they gave you. Drink."

Langley seemed not to hear, scratching at her arm for the umpteenth time. Callie turned on the recording and read in that they'd returned. "You might want to stop scratching that spot," she added.

"I keep feeling like it's there," she said, squinting in the candlelight, attempting to see the needle mark up close.

The girl's scratching could signify an IV having been aggravated, likely from the manner in which a groggy Langley pulled it out. Callie wished she knew more about drugs, to know better what to expect, to know better how to fix this girl. Unfortunately, she could talk street stuff more than prescription.

"You feel better?" she asked her guest again.

Langley stared at Callie with flat-lined lips. "I, um, had to pee."

"That's fine."

"And I wanted to, you know, check. To see if they'd . . . to check if . . ."

Callie stopped her. "Honey, it may take a doctor to tell." She had been well aware Langley had taken the flashlight with her to search herself.

"Any bruising that you can tell?"

"No. Nothing more than a bruise on my calf."

That could've happened shoving her in the vehicle or stumbling in the rain.

"Bleeding? From anywhere?"

Langley gave her head a few small shakes of no. She obviously had no trouble walking, and there appeared to be no broken or dislocated bones. Nothing from her personal area, or so she led Callie to believe.

"Are you sore . . . down there?"

Again, a shake of her head.

Callie sighed with relief. "I don't think you were raped, honey, but they'll have a doctor look you over, just in case."

She got a nod as Langley pushed back the recliner, propping her feet up.

The phone read a forty-percent charge. She'd get what information she could before going back out to the car to recharge.

Langley had to have been kept not far from the station, and either she'd been left alone in a house, or they'd stayed to endure the storm and were likely on Callie's list of names they'd roughly collected in the two days before.

"Think hard," Callie said. "Did you see or hear the ocean? Or smell the marsh? Was there anything about the house you recall. Think scents and sounds, not just visual."

"I can't think of anything."

"You escaped, though. You were coming to. Let's make this easier. Think about sound."

Langley closed her eyes, reaching into her memory. "Rain. Wind. No voices. No television."

No help. "Okay, let's shift to smells," Callie said. "Close your eyes again and take deep breaths."

Hugging the blanket, Langley inhaled deeply, letting it out slowly. Then again. "Stale cloth, like it had been stored somewhere. And pee." She reddened. "I think it was my own."

Three hard and fast knocks rattled her front door window before she could ask anything more. Callie hadn't stood to answer before they repeated. A surge of wind roared loud, making Callie hurry to the porch. Wet clothing smeared against the etched decorator glass.

"Now, please!" shouted the voice. "Before this storm whisks me off to Oz!"

Callie snatched open the front door. "For God's sake, Donna—"

Not waiting for the invitation, Donna rushed in, Horse stuck to her heels. "God's sake is right. God's having a lot of fun out there. Either that or he's awful pissed off."

Horse stood dripping on Callie's hallway rug, staring at Callie as if she were neglecting her guests.

"Don't let him do you that way," Donna said, helping herself to Callie's half bath, immediately coming out when she found it covered with Stan's wet clothing and no towels in the cabinet. "Horse has a mind-melding power, you know."

"Here, let me." Callie left and promptly returned with a towel for each of them from her own bath.

Donna began a quick dry job on Horse. "What the hell happened to your face?"

Callie hadn't exactly forgotten, but events were keeping her rather occupied on more than herself. "Slipped coming inside and my face kissed the floor." Callie took over, letting the councilwoman take care of herself.

"Broken?" Donna asked.

"Maybe. Bruce looked at it."

"Bruce?"

"Same guy who treated Stan," she said, not really wanting to get into Bruce with her. "What are you doing here? You did not need to be out in that gale."

Donna shed her frumpy London Fog-looking affair of hat and coat, taking them into the half bath since that seemed to be the place to hang clothes. She made *humph* noises as she got herself presentable enough hopefully to be allowed on the furniture. "When one's roof blows off over the room one's hiding in, one tends to hunt for another house, don't you think?"

Mark came out, having half heard the conversation. "Come again?"

"Damn typhoon robbed me of my roof. At least part of it. Enough to make the rest of it pretty damn worthless," said the retired vet.

"It's a hurricane," Mark corrected.

"Don't care what it is," Donna said, still huffing.

Langley sat frozen in her recliner, watching.

Callie finished with Horse who then sat on his haunches, waiting to see what his mistress was up to. "Go on into the living room," Callie said. "Get comfortable. That's Langley, by the way. She got lost in the storm."

That was all Donna needed to hear, at least in front of Langley. Callie wasn't sure whom she trusted with information about this girl who was supposed to have been kidnapped, then wasn't, then apparently was.

Chapter 26

Arlo
Riding out the storm

BRUCE PUSHED HIS way into *Seas the Day*, aided from a shove by the storm. He had to turn around and force the door shut. Wiping rain out of his eyes, he snapped his wrists free of the moisture, spraying the water to the already wet floor.

Arlo stood in the living-room entrance, stiff, jaw tight. "Where the hell have you been, man?" He'd been losing his mind. The quick note left behind had simply said, *Helping the chief.*

He strode up and pushed his wet buddy in the chest, itching to do way more than that. They had so much on the line now, and Bruce didn't see that? The plan had gone awry, and he had to take a break from their panic mode to be a Good Samaritan?

Arlo pushed his chest again. "What kind of stupid note was that? We had no idea where you were, what you were doing, why the house was left unguarded. Do you know what could've happened if someone had made their way in here and looked around?" In a forced exhale, he uttered, "Son of a bitch."

He and Leonard had returned from scouring the streets, soaked and frustrated . . . and unsuccessful. They'd come home to nobody, doubling their frustration, since they'd hoped she'd returned . . . but hadn't expected Bruce to not be there waiting. They'd launched into pure panic mode. Seeing Bruce return empty-handed only threw renewed energy into Arlo wanting to hit something . . . or someone.

Bruce braced himself, giving Arlo a side-eyed warning not to touch him like that again. "Don't," he said, blinking away drops running into his eyes from his hair.

He was drenched from head to shoes, trickling onto the floor, the rug already soggy from the comings and goings over the last few hours. "Don't touch me. This is on you, asshole."

Bruce released a hard nasal huff, blowing off the wrongness of this day.

Leonard came in holding a towel and threw it at him. "Did you see her?"

Bruce remained focused on Arlo. His frustration simmered under the surface, on the brink of making itself known. "Yes, I saw her. The chief has her. You have really screwed us up this time, Arlo."

"With the damn cops?" Arlo said. Slinging arms over his head, he turned away, needing something to do with himself . . . to do with this disastrous result.

"We nab them sedated, keep them sedated, and return them sedated," he said, more to himself than anyone else. "They cannot identify us. She cannot identify us."

The other two watched him finish venting his frustration.

"And what the hell do you mean *this time*, shithead. I'm the guy who holds this group together."

"The *group* holds the group together," Bruce said. "To think otherwise is to destroy from within."

No telling who Bruce quoted this time. He read endless books on behavioral science.

"He's right," Leonard said. Then to Bruce, "Did she recognize you?"

"Didn't give her a chance."

"How did she look?" Arlo asked.

"Scared and confused," Bruce said. "She looked straight at me with zero recognition."

"She saw you?" Arlo said it slightly ahead of Leonard, almost in unison.

"Not an issue," Bruce said, with no trepidation whatsoever.

Arlo's mouth stretched tight over his teeth. "The bottom line is you should have stayed here."

But Bruce turned on him. "The bottom line is we cannot afford to take our eye off the ball, which you damn well did. But we had to help the chief move her man. Otherwise, we drew more attention on ourselves. She came back and needed me to move him back into the house because the roads are blocked. I was the only one here." His mouth pinched tight. "But if we're finding fault, if you guys hadn't volunteered to help the damn Marine board up houses, we might not even be in this predicament! You made us known to this whole damn beach! The chief would not have known we existed except for that."

Each word brewed his temper to boiling. In a quick move, he started to shove Arlo back the same way he'd been shoved, but Arlo smacked Bruce's hand away.

"I'll be damned if I take all the responsibility for this fuck-up," Arlo said. "You and Leonard did not have to go off with the chief. That just put you on her radar."

"Unavoidable," Bruce said, speaking up over a fresh thrashing of the storm outside. The three remained in the entryway, no power, humidity thick from so much water coming in and no air conditioner to cope with it. "You'd made everyone aware we were here, so we got asked to assist. I'm a medic. They had nobody. And Leonard's the strongest. Just made sense. You were left to babysit. Just babysit. You had the simplest task. If you hadn't revealed us to the whole island, nobody would've thought of us, and we'd be on task."

This time Arlo swung, his shove with a fist on the end, but Leonard interceded, catching it mid-swing.

"She woke up!" Arlo yelled. "She fuckin' woke up! That's on you, man. She wasn't supposed to wake up!"

"I left you instructions. She was on an IV, for God's sake. All you had to do was dose her with what I left for you to do it with. I filled the syringe for you, for Christ's sake. A damn third grader could've done it." His complexion flushed, blood pressure clearly climbing higher with each accusation. Bruce stomped in to stand toe-to-toe with Arlo and have this out.

Leonard got out of the way for him to do it.

"You didn't stay in the room," Bruce screamed, fists at his side. Tears threatened as he vibrated head to toe, unmoored from his steadfast, normal logic.

This wasn't the everyday Bruce. This was PTSD-scarred Bruce, or the Bruce who hadn't vented in years. While Arlo was willing to have a fight, he acknowledged he wasn't ready for this fight. Not at this level.

"Arlo," Leonard warned.

"Yeah, man, I see it." Then to Bruce, he spoke on a calmer level. "Whoa, buddy, take it down a notch. I'm not the enemy."

But Bruce didn't hear, and nor was he willing to try to listen. "You didn't keep attention on her, you bastard! They need constant attention. Don't tell me you don't know that. Not after all this time. Not after all the other times."

"I . . . my bad, brother. I'm sorry."

But Bruce's temperature ran too hot. "Now we're stuck here. The main road is blocked. Things can't get much more fucked!"

Leonard reached over to touch the towel, to make some sort of friendly connection. Bruce snatched the towel back, with a roundhouse shrug of the arm holding it. The towel slapped across a clay bowl on the hall credenza, sending it sliding across the floor. It remained intact until hitting the wall, where the whole became a hundred thick pieces. That didn't distract him, though. Lenoard didn't distract him, either. Bruce remained fully homed in on Arlo.

Both of the sane men saw the line that had been crossed.

Arlo tried one more time. "Hey, I'm sorry. We'll make this right."

Bruce's voice still climbed. "I do not assume everything's stable. I do not assume anything can't go wrong." He sucked in a hard breath through his nose, now stuffy from tears, then through his mouth. It was as if he were feeding himself to take this to another level instead of getting a grip.

Arlo and Leonard moved back, putting a good eight feet of space between him and them, allowing the darkness to mute the situation and giving their compatriot his own space. Without arguing, without being within reach of him, and especially not in clear view, he'd have no fuel for this fire he so wished to burn.

No point in apologizing. No point in trying to rationalize. And no damn point in telling him he might be overstating the problem. They'd had to scramble for a course correction before, just not recently. Two, maybe three years ago he'd gone off like this. Right now Bruce's rage ranked about DEFCON 2.

"What now, huh?" Bruce screamed.

Arlo tensed, ready to take the man to the ground, if need be, and a backup nudge into Leonard told him the bigger man's muscles had hardened in preparation for the same. They wouldn't tackle him unless they had to, because that would do little more than make him madder, unwilling to give in until he became too exhausted to continue. Sometimes that could take a while.

While Nikki continued doing her thing, laughing at them being stuck in that house, all three men stood in place, primed for whatever any of them chose to throw down.

The air thickened, stuffy and hot, their frustrations only exacerbating the oppressive atmosphere.

Arlo tried to count Bruce's breaths. He remembered doing that to measure his friend's progress . . . or deterioration. There wasn't much else to go on, because Bruce didn't come down easy.

But before Arlo could get a good read on the number, Bruce wiped the towel over his head hard, gripped the fabric as if he wanted to kill it somehow, and tramped past the two to the bedroom.

Arlo and Leonard stood on guard for several minutes. Long, lingering, strained minutes, just in case Bruce came busting out, launching into another chapter of this confrontation. Again, he didn't come down easily.

Damn it, they'd covered twelve different states without issue. The girls ranged from eighteen to twenty-one. There was just something wrong with nabbing children. They chose young, trim, petite adult women because they were lightweight, easy to sedate and maintain, and easier to carry to the drop-off point.

All the guys had done was do a little homework. Pick someone wealthy, learn their child's routine, find a blind spot, hood over the head, and voila. The girl felt, saw, learned nothing until she awoke several days later at some obscure locale absent cameras once Mom and Dad dropped off the cash, an amount that the family could easily afford to lose.

The girls were always safe and sound. No harm done. Not the first bruise or scrape. Meanwhile, the Retrievers replenished their coffers. A creative way of living they'd become rather proud of.

Places without cameras were becoming more and more of a challenge, though, but they'd learned to lean toward fifty-year-old family-run eateries, hiking trailheads, and town parks in small, poor towns, always in the middle of the night. Once they used a drydock boat, and another time a corn field. Places where nobody would be. Where nobody could record. Leonard scouted those.

No witnesses. Not even the victim knew what happened, waking up to nothing more than an IV hole in their arm. Maybe a little chafed from the diapers used to avoid bathroom issues.

No need to take them in or out of the duffle that could be disposed of later.

So perfect. So easy.

Satisfied Bruce had gone reclusive on them, the two slipped to the kitchen, farthest from Bruce's bedroom, and they dared to breathe.

"This ain't good," Leonard said. "He hasn't done that in . . ."

"Two and a half years," Arlo finished.

Leonard leaned forward propped with stiff arms against the counter, back arced, head down, thinking. Arlo stood with his butt against it, opposite in stance staring out the small kitchen window they hadn't bothered securing so they'd have a good view of the storm's status.

Rain pummeled that window since it faced the ocean. Wind thrashed anything not tied down, too solid to flip, or locked into place. Every once in a while, sticks or objects flying too fast to identify, flashed by which only served to keep everyone on edge. Pressure changes gave the sense of the roof attempting to rise with mild *whoomphs* in the attic.

Arlo almost wished the roof would blow off, giving them reason to bail. Nobody would blame them.

He'd erred in judgment this time thinking the hurricane would help as a distraction, keeping people way too busy to look for a missing girl. For the most part, he'd been correct. Dr. St. James had initially gone to the police, even after being told not to. There was always a chance of that, but with the hurricane slowing things down, the guys were able to haul the good doctor back into line. One call from Leonard warned him that breaking the rules would ruin his chance of seeing his daughter again. Even more, to show good faith, the good doctor had been directed to walk things back by telling law enforcement Langley had just gone on a drama bender, needing time away from school responsibilities and family judgment to sort herself. The doctor had done well, painting his daughter with a stereotypical brush any parent could relate to. With the hurricane being within a day or so of Charleston, with police needed for roadblocks and evacuations, the detectives had been more than happy to take that obligation off their list.

Crisis averted . . . or so they thought before this current one arose.

Goddammit, Bruce was right. Arlo had dropped the ball. But that wasn't the only screw-up in this operation. "Don't forget we almost grabbed the wrong girl," he said. "I'm not the only one who errs."

"And we should've followed through with it and forgotten this doctor's daughter," Leonard said.

"We hadn't done the research. We had no idea if her family would have the money."

"We were also supposed to ride this damn storm out and be gone when everyone returned to their homes," Leonard said, looking at Arlo like Bruce had. "Now we're hunting for her. This adventure was screwed from the outset. Let's wash our hands and go. Consider her deposited and done with."

Pushing hands over his face, trying to push out the furrows in his brow that weren't going anywhere until they figured this out, Arlo listened to Leonard but still pondered options.

But Leonard wasn't satisfied with the silence. "We need to leave."

"Didn't you hear him?" Arlo said. "The road's blocked."

Beads of perspiration traveled down Arlo's temple, then more down his back. Breathing was like being underwater, the air thick. He'd underestimated the humidity of the South Carolina coast.

"What now?" Leonard said through his teeth, not wanting Bruce to hear.

"Shut up, man." Arlo pushed himself mentally deeper. "Let me think."

He didn't want to tell Leonard that he agreed with Bruce. They'd made a big mistake being so visible. Arlo dating Natalie in hindsight hadn't been the best move, either, though she'd been quite the informative talker about how things worked on this beach. But offering to board up rentals was goddamn stupid. All for the chance to screw Natalie one more time.

Something hit in staccato against the wall around the window. Leonard flipped around, going closer to peer out at the noise makers, unable to see what had been blown probably two houses down the street by now.

Arlo, however, remained locked in place, gripping the counter. They could stay as planned, leaving the beach after the storm, like anybody else who'd weathered this mess. Everyone would be too engrossed in rescue or cleanup. Or they could boogie now, with nobody holding that against them. The three of them had the strength to possibly move that block out of the road.

The former had been the plan, leaving the drugged girl at a safe place they'd pegged in West Ashley, at a small mom-and-pop restaurant affair without outside cameras. It had a recessed opening, and sooner or later someone would find her, or she'd find them.

"We've done this a dozen times," Leonard said. "This job has become a problem."

Success was based upon all three parties adhering religiously to their tasks.

"This wasn't on Bruce," Arlo said.

Leonard laughed once, his caustic manner painting him a skeptic. "You think? He's totally pissed how you screwed up. I'm with him on this, man."

For the first time, after so much success and building sufficient income for well into the future, they needed a Plan B. The old one had been discarded after a half-dozen successes proved they probably didn't need a Plan B. They'd come so far, so seamlessly. Arlo wasn't even sure that he remembered the details of Plan B after all this time.

"Do you remember Plan B?" he asked his partner.

"You mean abort?"

"I mean the details of how to abort."

Leonard only thought for a second or two. "We disappear. We don't pull another adventure for a year. And we remove all traces of us at the latest locale. Not rocket science."

"Then let's do it," he said. "I'll alert Bruce. His room needs the most attention."

He left off a comment that maybe Bruce would feel better once they disappeared, but they both understood Bruce would stew on this situation for days. He didn't catch fire easily, and likewise, he didn't cool down quickly, either.

When Leonard didn't move, Arlo recognized his friend doing the what ifs of their predicament. "She shouldn't remember us," Arlo said. "No differently than if we'd dropped her off according to plan. She never saw us, man."

But Leonard replied through a worried expression. "She came to enough to pull out an IV, discard the diaper he kept on her, and find a way to escape. Who's to say she doesn't remember this house? She had to escape it."

Arlo scowled back, in correction. "As doped up as she was? And she didn't know what part of the world she was on, much less the street and house." He pushed upright. "Let's get busy. By the time we pack and scrub down the place, the storm will have passed."

Leonard blew out an acceptance and flattened his mouth into a frown acceptance. "I don't ever want to do a beach again. You hear?"

Arlo didn't have to answer. He agreed.

But his anxiety wasn't about her recognizing them. She'd come to with nobody in the room. She'd escaped without seeing Arlo since he'd been in the bathroom . . . on his phone. From the blood spots, she'd roughly yanked out the IV, maybe so loopy she didn't remember doing it.

Bruce was anal about quality control, and he used gloves. Gloves that he disposed of in a bag he maintained and took with him when they left. Arlo hadn't. Thank God she hadn't carried the tubing with her. No point mentioning that, just another what-if tossed on the already tall pile of screwup.

"Bruce," he said, opening the door Bruce had slammed behind him. "Hey, man, we've decided to try to leave. How about you . . . ?"

Bruce wasn't there. Neither was his medical bag. Where the hell had he gone this time? What did he feel so Florence Nightingale about this time?

"Oh, shit," he uttered under his breath, remembering.

Bruce had returned empty-handed. He hadn't brought the bag back with him. *Shit!* He'd left it where he'd been most likely. "God help us," he whispered. That bag was likely at the chief's house.

As was the girl.

She'd get another chance to remember him.

And them if they went after Bruce. What now?

"Son of a bitch," he said, then yelled, "Leo! He's gone."

Leonard rushed to his side. "What? Oh, hell. How did we not see him leave? Or hear him?"

Arlo trotted to his own room. "Don't have time to answer that. Continue with Plan B. We'll pack up and clean up, then we'll grab Bruce on the way out the best we can."

Leonard ran to his room, doing the same, shouting their conversation back and forth. "I take it we're going to the chief's house?"

"Yep. That's my guess where he'll be. He didn't have his medical bag with him when he came back."

Leonard ran to Arlo's doorway, arms wide, leaning into the door frame. "How do we retrieve him from there and not double down on drawing attention to ourselves?"

Arlo turned on him. "Tell me another option, man." He walked over and smacked the man's collarbone with the back of his hand. "Tell me, huh? We can't leave without him, now, can we?" He pushed his friend. "Go. Pack. I'll do Bruce's room."

They were accustomed to packing up fast.

The bigger question was how to grab Bruce, get him to come peacefully, and make it seem like nothing was amiss. Just three guys tired of a hurricane, wanting badly to go home.

Chapter 27

Callie
Four in the morning

RUBBED DOWN TO being just damp, Horse escorted his owner to Callie's living-room sofa. His owner threw the towel on the carpet for him to sit, but after a short pause to sense all was well with Donna, he preferred strolling over to Langley, much as he had done with Callie when he'd ridden around town with her what seemed like ages ago. The girl's eyes widened at the beast of a dog choosing her.

"He only goes up to people he trusts," Donna said gently. "Hold out your hand to him."

After some hesitation, Langley did as told. As he had with Callie, he rested his big head in her hand. The girl melted at the silent acceptance.

"Did you get Stan to the hospital?" Donna asked, smiling at her dog's goodwill. "Can't say I expected to see you at home. Why take Stan and come back during the storm?" She peered around at Mark standing to the side, then must've realized the fact he'd come out of a room where the door was being kept shut. "Y'all didn't make it, did you?"

Mark thumbed to the bedroom. "He's in there. Tree blocked the road."

Donna got way more serious. "How is he?"

"The morphine wore off," Mark said. "I gave him Tylenol, but I gotta say, he's hurting. Once, I think he passed out in lieu of falling asleep. At present, he's out."

Donna snatched her attention to Callie, her question obvious.

"Yes, I got ahold of dispatch," Callie said, "and they'll be sending a chopper for him and whomever else we find badly injured. Hopefully just him, but it'll take an hour at least."

"I've got to get back to him, y'all." Mark paused his hand on the knob. "Glad you're alive and well," he said to Donna.

Callie stood. "Mark, any chance—"

He cut her off, his expression painful to see. "I don't know what to give him, Callie." Then he seemed to come to a new conclusion. "Donna, that Ranger's medical bag is still in there. What about you?"

He and Callie both set sights on the councilwoman. A vet was the closest thing they had to medical.

"Where's the damn man that goes with that bag?" she asked. "I can't confirm what's in those vials, those bottles, or if the syringes are even safe. No way I'm taking those chances."

"He ran off," Callie said. "Probably back to his place, but that's two miles away. Seeing what's in the bag, we expect him to come collect it, but when is anybody's guess." She waited for Donna to sense where they were going with this. The vet was the only option.

"It's not my medical bag. I told you I can't vouch for any medications in there."

Mark didn't care. "Stan needs help. We don't know how or what to give."

"I'm not much better educated than you are. How long till a chopper comes again?" Donna asked.

"Hour. Maybe more," Callie said for what she felt was the umpteenth time.

"I don't know," Donna said. "That's not long to have to wait."

But Mark wasn't happy with that answer. "That's forever to someone in that kind of pain."

"On that we can agree," she said.

The glass in the paneled door rattled, a regular repetitive knock unlike the randomness of hurricane winds. Hard enough for Callie to expect it to crack.

"Where's your weapon?" Mark asked.

"Everyone on this beach knows where I live," she said, going toward the door. Honestly, he was right. Her weapon didn't necessarily need to be in its routine place in the bedroom during a time like this. She could have more than a couple of visitors before all this was over. Better the weapon be on her hip than on her night table.

Mark followed Callie to the door. Donna rose to see better. Horse removed himself from beside the recliner and took up guard beside his owner. Funny how a knock any other day was a minor matter. Today, chances were, anyone knocking was at minimum a victim, at worst a threat.

Whoever was on the other side was big in size. Just seeing the shadow made Callie realize how the outside seemed a few shades lighter than before. Dawn had crept up on them. The storm was less, too.

The stranger banged again as if their life depended on it.

Callie snatched open the door. "Pound it off its hinges, for God's sake."

Bruce pushed through without invitation, his personality coming from a whole different place than when he'd disappeared from the police station. "I need to check the broken leg then get my bag and go."

She took a second glance outside for others. Bruce was a different person. Something had changed. He had someplace to be, and it wasn't here. She did note, however, that the wind had become a breeze no more than ten to fifteen miles per hour. A steady light rain fell in lieu of one with an attitude. Shades of navy blue and pansy purple enabled her to see some cloud outline. Not much, but enough to say dawn was rearing its head.

That meant first responders were on their way. The tree on 174 would be quickly managed.

"You find your two buddies?" she asked.

"Yeah." Bruce pushed his way into Stan's room.

Horse gave a lone woof from the living room, where he'd now taken up a vigil next to Langley.

"Good boy," Donna said, her focus on the arrival. "Isn't he the guy who helped load Stan?" she asked loud enough for Callie to hear in the hallway, as if she didn't care if he did, too.

Callie started to say, "Yeah, the guy with the morphine," but gave a lone nod of acknowledgement instead, because this guy had returned different, with an off way about him.

He'd been quiet and odd at Stan's house. He'd been weird on the way to the station, then mysteriously disappeared without a word. Now he displayed urgency. The man of few words had exhibited a wide array of mannerisms throughout the night, giving her an instinctive urge to stay wary. He seemed mostly good, even altruistic at times, but Callie sensed a secret compartment in that mind of his that might merit closer scrutiny and a guarded approach.

She followed him into the bedroom. Mark would be leery enough, his own instincts as keen or more than hers, but he was physically hampered if physicality became necessary.

Stan wasn't doing well, per his moans.

Bruce's bag remained on the nightstand at the right side of the bed, and it lay open, as he'd left it. He took Stan's vitals, without even an analytical *hmmm* as he moved to the leg.

Stan's color wasn't great. Even in this dimness Callie could see that.

He'd awoken when Bruce came in, as though sensing the stranger's arrival. He warily watched Bruce, with side glances over at Mark. *Don't let him get away with anything.*

"Can you stand the pain for another hour?" Bruce asked.

Stan squinted, as if weighing his answer.

"I'm asking, because they won't want you drugged up when they do their own analysis. Your numbers are up. Everything including temperature. Not a good sign." But instead of waiting for Stan to respond, Bruce turned to Callie. "Where's the chopper? I assume that's what's getting him to a hospital, which is, what, an hour from here by road?"

"The road was blocked, so yes, there's a chopper on the way. Closer. Out here on the island," she said. Had she not told him this? Maybe in the melee she hadn't.

He didn't seem to like that answer. "How blocked?" he asked. "Can we get him to the chopper?"

"Big-ass-tree-laying-across-the-road blocked," she said, maybe harder than she meant to.

"I'll manage," Stan said, without a lot of power behind his words. "I can handle it."

Callie scoffed. "You don't even know what *it* is."

"Yeah, you'd tell us you were good right up to when your heart stopped," Mark said. Then to Bruce, he said, "Use one of those antibiotics in there. Take down his fever."

"I'm not licensed for the antibiotic," Bruce replied.

"You're not licensed for half that bag, dude, so don't bullshit me."

Bruce had been freewheeling and unconcerned before about giving morphine, for God's sake, and now he worried about an antibiotic? He'd gone from feeling empowered to being leery. Something about him had changed. Maybe he didn't want to use up his stash? A stash to which Callie already questioned its legitimacy . . . and purpose.

"Give him what you think is necessary," she said. "I'll take care of whoever questions anything on the other end. Stan's care is primary. We have just under an hour. Do what you can. I'd do it, but I do not have the knowledge."

Bruce quit talking, reached into the bag, and administered the antibiotic and more Tylenol. "Keep ice on the leg," he said.

"Been doing that for hours," Mark said. "We just used the last of the ice."

An hour. Less than an hour, Callie kept telling herself. "While you're here, take a look at the girl?" Not a complete physical, not with the girl's mental state like it was. Just vitals. Maybe that place on her arm.

Bruce peered over his shoulder at Langley, then checked himself. "What do you think's wrong with her?"

Her radar pinging, Callie continued. "Someone had an IV in her arm for one thing. She doesn't remember where's she's been or who she's been with. She isn't sure she was raped, because she was unconscious the whole time, but she was found without underwear."

Bruce scowled. "I'm not checking to see if she was . . . raped."

"Not asking you to. We'll be getting her to a doctor as soon as we can, but at least give her a glance, please."

She wished she could see him better, read his reactions better than the candles and flashlights allowed. They wouldn't have the luxury of power for the rest of the day unless the power company sent out angels and miracle workers, so everything in Stan's room remained in shadows. Out in the hallway, however, the outlines of things looked keener. Lights and darks. Her etched glass in the front door was not only allowing daylight in but accenting it with hints of color.

Bruce still hesitated.

She wanted to shake him, and if that didn't work, punch him. He'd morphed into a different person since he'd helped Stan before. What had happened between the time he left the station and now? "Just take her vitals and note her arm," she asked. "I'm not a medical person. You clearly are."

This had become a small battle of wills on some miniscule scale, for reasons she couldn't see yet. She wasn't as trusting about Bruce as before. Well, yes and no. She'd detain him if he seemed to be becoming some sort of monster, but she wasn't seeing him anywhere near that level. She was, however, envisioning him as something more than he wanted to be seen. That gray area made her cautious.

He rose to leave, but instead of letting him go through first, she led, pointing him to the living room where the candles remained lit. Daylight made a weak appearance through the back windows now, too, giving a much better view of details.

Langley had become comfortable in the tufted recliner, a safe haven. Horse remained on her right side, letting her caress him. Donna remained three yards away on the couch, with her concentration shifting from the girl to this man as he approached.

He held out a small flashlight, and Langley pinched her eyes shut.

"Arm?" he asked, pointing at her left arm, the one not petting the dog.

Langley held it out.

He took a hard look, the light causing Langley to turn toward Horse and away from the bright. "Looks fine," he said, though he did go into his bag on the floor to his right, bringing out alcohol wipes and an adhesive bandage. Putting the light back into place, he cleaned and covered the spot, Langley preferring to look at Horse.

Bruce finished with the arm, acting as though finished.

"Vitals?" Donna asked, before Callie had a chance to. "Buddy, your bedside manner leaves a bit to be desired."

"Sure," Bruce said, ignoring the sarcasm. In quick movements, he took a temp, checked oxygen, and measured blood pressure. "Normal."

"Good to hear," Donna said, with a side glance to Callie.

Callie read the message. *Is it me or is this guy acting odd?*

"What's your name again?" Donna asked.

But Bruce ignored her, again. He set the bag on the chair's arm, taking care to replace everything he'd used.

Langley shifted in her chair, putting what little distance she could between her and him, but then she hesitated, and sniffed. With some reserve, she reached out, touched the medical bag, and stiffened.

Callie saw it. Donna saw it. And they saw Bruce see it.

Langley peered at Callie, with almost a plea in her gaze.

"Bruce," Callie started, but with a wide step, he grabbed the bag and maneuvered around the coffee table sitting between him and the retired veterinarian. Without stopping, he moved toward the hallway, clearly aiming to leave.

What had just happened?

Bruce had been asked to examine Langley's arm, but without being told, he'd asked to see her left. Then Langley had recoiled at the odor and tactile feel of the Army-issue bag.

If there wasn't a connection here, then Callie lived on another planet. Bruce and Langley had acted differently toward each other. He'd avoided speaking. She'd sensed something amiss she couldn't put a finger on.

Then she did.

Querying either Langley or Bruce in front of the other wouldn't work. Langley didn't remember squat, operating on her brain's instinctive memory. Bruce would deny any hint of an accusation, knowing full well there was no proof.

He'd almost reached the door.

Callie moved toward him. "Bruce, stop."

Her radio beeped, static loud, then the air cleared, calling Callie's name. She answered. "Chief Morgan." Then she told Bruce again, in a harsher tone, "Stop where you are." Now she wished she wore her piece.

Luckily, he halted, because he could've bolted, and nobody been able to catch him. He stood ready to dart out given half a chance, though.

"Chopper thirty minutes out," came dispatch. "Can you get him to the Edistonian?"

She moved to between the man and the door. "We'll do our best. On our way. Morgan out." Then to Bruce, "Let's get him to the SUV again. I assume you ran here from *Seas the Day?*"

He lifted his wet sleeves, to make a point, still, not saying much. He wasn't going to say much either, for fear Langley would recognize his voice. He'd been speaking in one and two-word sentences since he arrived.

"Chief?"

She answered the radio still in her hand. "That you, Thomas?"

"Yeah. Trying to get there, Chief. My road was blocked, but I'm finally through. Doing the best I can. Coming out on 174 now."

Bruce looked over Callie's head at the door. She shook her head at him and made a hand motion to the floor, telling him to stay put. "Thomas, we need you. Stan has a broken leg. Mark and I never made it off the beach." She left off the part about her broken nose though it throbbed like a bitch.

"Damn. Y'all okay?"

"Stan's not. The sooner the better, all right?" she said. "Chopper's due in thirty minutes for Stan, maybe less, but there's still the logistics of getting him to the Edistonian."

"I'll meet you there. Out."

The Edistonian, a convenience store and gas station, was ordinarily a straight shot. No telling what the ride was now.

Bruce tried to walk past.

"Oh, no you're not," she said, a strong hold on his wrist, not easy with his bulk and her petiteness. "We load up Stan, and that *we* includes you. Now. It'll take all of us to get him into the car."

"Your man just said—"

"That he would meet us at the chopper. We can't wait for him to arrive here then turn around and go back. Complete waste of time. I'm not even sure he has a clear road to even get to the chopper." She opened the bedroom door. "Help Mark arrange Stan so we can carry him. Drag, lift, slide, don't care. Just finagle something that gets him down the stairs, and into the car, so I can drive him to the Edistonian."

Mark heard and moved to the bed, talking to Stan, preparing him to be moved.

But Bruce remained in the hallway. "After he's loaded—"

"You're riding with me. Stan, you, and me."

"And me," Mark said.

"No, Mark. You stay here."

But Bruce seemed entrenched in place. "Not sure I can do that. I have plans."

Another voice piped up behind her. "Not sure that's wise, the three of you, Chief," Donna said. She'd seen the same reactions out of Langley that Callie had.

"I need someone strong in case we run into debris, Donna. Or they might need help getting Stan moved on the other end. I got this."

"That would mean . . ." but Donna didn't finish. Callie's look said she fully understood the risk. Donna started to return to Langley in the living room, then paused. "Want to take Horse?"

"No, thanks, Donna." There wasn't room in the car, and Callie wasn't comfortable enough with the animal to know which team he'd root for in time of need. And she damn sure didn't want to come back and tell the owner that her dog had met his demise by trying to assist.

"Let's do this," Mark said loudly from inside. Callie backed away and directed Bruce to proceed to help.

He dropped his bag with a *thunk*.

She picked it up. "I'll put this in the car and be right back up to give you a hand."

She assumed an in-charge air, keeping an eye on Bruce. She wouldn't be surprised if at any second he forced his way out and bolted.

But he'd come to her assistance twice already, and she had to bank on a third. He'd have the upper hand, but he'd had that this whole time and come through. After they delivered Stan, she wasn't sure what to do with him, or what kind of deal they'd be making. For sure he'd expect one after having been the good Samaritan.

"Come on, man," Mark shouted. "He's sitting up, but I'm not sure how much strength he's got or for how long."

Callie spoke quietly enough, not for Mark's ears. "There's something going on with you. We both know that we both know it."

Bruce stood silently peering down at her five-foot-two-ness.

But Callie had been talked down to, looked down on, and shouted down at for as long as she could remember. "Looks don't work on me. You run, and I'll pursue you. It would have to be after Stan is taken care of, but if I have to handle him by myself because you ran, I'll make it my mission to find you and make whatever this mess you're in the middle of stick."

"Maybe," was all he said.

"Yeah, you think that."

Bruce went into Stan's room, and she retrieved her sidearm and the holster, giving her a tool to use that she hoped she wouldn't need.

She functioned on empty threats, circumstantial evidence, and speculation with this man. Truth was, she wagered on the good side of Bruce, the side she'd seen, not the dark side she suspected. She had no choice.

Chapter 28

Callie
Friday morning—almost six

THE DAWN AIR held a cleansing scent, and birds even flitted here and there, as though tentatively announcing the storm was over. But on the steps of *Chelsea Morning*, frustrated, angry tears ran down Stan's cheeks as the three of them maneuvered his big, hulky self down the stairs, one short, careful move at a time.

Bruce's neck muscles bulged at handling the lion's share of the burden. Against Callie's and doctor's orders, Mark offered support to Stan's opposite side, supposedly just for balance, but all it would take was one slip and he'd go down with their big friend, ripping stitches, if not more.

Callie maneuvered down just ahead of them, tentatively taking the wet stairs. She held Stan's broken leg in a sling affair made from a sheet. Inside, after seeing the transport plan, Bruce had given him a taste of morphine, enough to relieve, but not enough to go limp. Dead weight would make things all the more difficult.

The opened rear of the SUV awaited them, and once they seated Stan on the edge, Bruce used the blanket still in the vehicle to drag him in. Stan released a loud yell at the last tug.

Callie rushed to him. "You're good. You're here now, big man." As his moans echoed, each one softer, she waited to see that he'd settled.

"Thank you, Jesus," she finally whispered when his shoulders relaxed into the morphine.

Mark came over to her. Stan's groans were undoing him. "I need to come with you," he said, his expression pinched with a hard stare at the SUV's load. "To be with Stan, to help on the other end, to help if you go off the road, to see that this guy, whoever this guy is, doesn't pull some sort of stunt and leave you high and dry . . . or worse."

"Mark."

He acted as if he didn't hear. "That bag of his alone," he uttered. "The way he's not totally with us . . . you know, not on this planet . . ."

Callie rested a hand on the side of his face and made him look at her, not at Stan. It took her two tries to get his attention off his friend. "That medical bag may have saved him, Mark. And I will get Stan there," she said. "Then I'll be back." She held up her radio. "And we have these."

"Alone with . . . him," he said with a tip of his head toward Bruce. The Ranger stood at the passenger door, waiting for Callie, not caring that he saw Mark's questioning look, and Mark not particularly caring about the fact that he saw it.

"He hasn't run. He stuck around to help," she explained. "There's a decency inside him. If he runs from me, so be it. If he comes back, that's fine, too. But I see him doing little else, Mark. Otherwise, he wouldn't even be here."

Mark didn't respond back at first. "He's not right."

She silently agreed, but this was the lot they were handed. Best thing she could do was assure Mark she'd thought this out, and that she had enough trust in the Ranger to proceed. She didn't, not really, but the situation was what it was. Stan was the most important issue.

"Plus," she continued, "Thomas is meeting me."

She suddenly realized she could see Mark better, more in color. The sun was daring to brighten things up from behind all the blue-gray clouds overhead to give life to everything. The rain was down to a periodic light drizzle. Funny how they'd quit worrying about being wet anymore.

"Gotta go—"

His arms around her interrupted the goodbye, forcing her face into his chest.

"Owww, oh my God," she hollered, as shooting lights shot into her brain, reminding both of them she had a broken nose.

He jerked her out from him. "Oh, oh, damn, Sunshine, I'm so sorry."

Tears leaking, she didn't even try to contain them. "I ought to poke you in the stitches," and she tried to laugh off the residual pulsing pain. "Come on, let me go, Cajun." She kissed him, trying to hide the fact she now had the headache from hell. "I'll check in. You take care of Langley. I feel better with a law-enforcement type like you keeping an eye on her anyway. If you need something to do, make room for Donna and Horse to stay over since their place is wrecked." Telling him instructions made her feel better and might make him worry less.

She gingerly eased the rear hatch shut, careful not to bounce things with Stan stretched out in the back, plus she wasn't too eager to move fast herself. Bruce got into the passenger side, medical bag in his lap.

Callie doubted he would leave that thing outside his reach again anytime soon.

"Let's do this," she said, cranking up.

Bruce said nothing, buckling his belt.

She headed east on Jungle Road, toward the causeway off the beach, counting her blessings at so easily navigating the flotsam and jetsam scattered about. The growing daylight drew attention to the breakage and loss. Ordinarily she'd have been canvassing the streets now, and the damage could be different further west toward the sound, but thus far, on the eastern end on the way across the causeway, things could've been way worse than they were. With no first responders having arrived to do the work of clearing, something told her people were attacking Highway 174 to open up the thoroughfare.

She didn't tell Mark that going without the Ranger was an option. She just didn't want to risk the odds of being stranded somewhere between the beach and them without help for Stan.

She was small in mass, and while strong for her size, mass mattered when taking on oaks, gums, and loblolly pines across one's path. Physics was physics.

But also, the cop in her wanted to keep one eye on this man who was still very much an unknown and a key to Langley's disappearance. Whether he was a good guy or a bad guy was yet to be seen, but Langley's reactions and Bruce's instinct to look at her left arm, accompanied with his medical knowledge, made Callie want to have him close. . . and further away from Mark and Langley. It could be that common practice was to put an IV in the non-dominant arm that he instinctively reached for, but the reason could be darker. Dangerously darker.

She prayed that didn't mean she'd be unable to reach the Edistonian.

"Stan?" she said, loud to be heard in the back. "Things aren't as torn up as we expected. I'd go by your house and check on it, but, you know, a busted leg sort of takes priority." That was her best effort at making light of the situation.

When she didn't hear a retort, she peered over at Bruce. "Check on him, please."

He undid his belt, and, with knees in his seat, he examined his patient while Callie slowly made her way across Scott Creek; the water was a couple inches across the road, but the tide was headed out. Good thing she knew this road like the back of her hand.

"We've only got a bit over a mile. That's nothing, Cap'n," she said, using Stan's old rank from back when they worked together in Boston.

"Damn it," she added under her breath, seeing an obstacle ahead. She'd spoken too soon.

Stopped in the middle of the road, she calculated maybe a third of a mile to their destination. So close . . . yet so far. "How is he?" she asked while reaching into her glovebox.

"He's in and out of it," Bruce said. "He's getting damn warm. Is this place far?"

"Almost spitting distance," she assured him as she pulled out her leather gloves.

Stan could be worse. The town's destruction could be worse. The weather, the injuries . . . everything could be worse. "Could be worse," she repeatedly mumbled to herself.

The drizzle was intermittent, and with the increasing sunlight, she could better analyze the limbs strewn across the road. They were clearly blocked, though. Big, short, thin, and stocky. Rotted and fresh. They'd all be wet and slippery to move, and there was a slew of them. Still, she gladly said a prayer there wasn't a whole tree, thinking again, *Could be worse.*

She exited the vehicle, expecting the heavy scent of pine that came with downed trees, but the swelling in her nose prevented sensory input. She sniffed again, just to see, but almost choked herself on a clot of blood. She swallowed, coughed, then spit before analyzing where to start clearing.

Beginning with the closest piece, she slung a thin, six-foot section off the asphalt and into the brush. As expected, without being told, Bruce got out and tackled the thicker, eight-foot section that weighed half as much as he did.

She was still surprised she hadn't seen anyone approach yet. People should be out, some desperately wanting to see the exteriors of their houses. First responders ought to be here. Problem might be other obstacles ahead. *Please don't let them be between here and the Edistonian.*

In the distance, a chain saw cranked up. Then another. Yes, the island was coming to life.

Her radio came through, dispatch announcing the helicopter ten minutes out.

"We're doing our best," she reported. "Road isn't open. A little help would be appreciated."

The request for help was noted, the word put out.

In fast synchronization, the two of them managed to clear a path just large enough to squeeze the vehicle through. "That's good," she shouted to Bruce, and leapt back into the SUV. He threw another limb or two aside and jumped in as she eased the car up beside him. Cringing as small branches scratched down the driver's side, she kept her attention ahead, seeing what she hoped would remain clear sailing except for leaves and small branches that would crush easily under her tires.

"Why isn't he moaning?" she said.

"Just go," he said, not wanting to say. Callie almost didn't want to know.

They'd traveled with the air conditioner on, for Stan's sake with the outside so humid and muggy, but she cranked down her window to listen for the *whomp-whomp* of a chopper. Then around State Cabin Road, almost within view of where the chopper would come in, the road proved impassable yet again.

Shit. More tree debris, heavier this time with some of the wood as thick as her waist. In a repeat performance, she threw the car in park and got out. *Shit again.* She wasn't so sure she and Bruce had the strength this time.

Grabbing the radio, she called for assistance. "We're stuck here," she reported, giving the locale, then, in afterthought, specifically asked where Thomas was.

"Thomas here, Chief. Parked at the chopper. What's your ETA?"

Thank God. "Less than a quarter mile. If you were standing in the road, you could make out our lights. Got a back I can use?"

"Ten four."

But she and Bruce proceeded, functioning without expectation of relief. Using her legs way harder than she had ever done running the beach, she gave her all to move impediments, most of them with Bruce on the other end.

Sweat or rain, she wasn't sure which, soaked her to the skin again, her underwear chafing her legs. Twice, sticks jutting out of bigger limbs stabbed her in the thigh as the cumbersomeness of the objects caused them to roll and twist out of her hands and slide against her, one cutting through the material, gouging to a depth she had no clue about other than it felt deep enough to draw blood. It didn't take half a minute for a spot of red to prove she was right.

This entanglement proved frustrating, this limb not budging while another unexpectedly did, sometimes shifting back into their way. Sweat poured in rivulets down her face, and when she glanced over at Bruce eight feet away, she saw his dripped off his chin.

A small branch hung up on another, and another. Digging with his thighs and back, Bruce gave the bigger trunk a sudden heave-ho to pop something loose . . . and it did.

Her limb was a wisp of a thing compared to what Bruce gripped ahold of, but come loose it did, the noise of it whipping through the air loud enough for Callie to hear the zing.

The whiplash of the supple one-inch-thick branch crossed squarely across her nose, down her jaw, and along her neck. A stabbing pain exploded from her eyes into her neck, taking her to one knee.

She attempted to stand, but the pain commanded too much attention. It continued long, deep, and for a second or two, she was afraid her consciousness might take a brief time out. Hearing Bruce, she couldn't connect his words enough to answer at first. The pain kept coming.

No way could she pass out. Not with Bruce an unknown and Stan unprotected.

She couldn't make her eyes stay open long enough to see Bruce. God, she wouldn't see through the tears. She knelt deeper, something telling her that raising her head would cause it to explode.

Why the hell wasn't the pain subsiding?

She went down to the other knee, eyes shut, then she leaned down, hands on the asphalt. "Jesus," she whispered. Holding her breath for some reason, all too quickly she ran out of it.

She heard Bruce before she sensed him, his panting continuing from his own exertion, and his body blocking some of the sun. "Give it time to pass," he said. "Don't touch it."

"Don't worry," she whispered, spittle dripping. *How long was this moment going to take?*

Looking up would take more pain than she was willing to invest, so she remained facing the road, spitting here and there. Finally, when she'd blinked away enough tears to halfway see, she spotted how it actually *could be worse.* "Is that my blood?" she asked, seeing dime-sized red spots dripping fast on the wet pavement.

The bandage on her nose clearly trashed, she saw it hanging soppy, half taped, and collecting an overflow of blood from what she feared was the shift of a bone. Breathing was impossible. She reached up to move the bandage gone awry. Snatching the old soppy gauze, she tossed it loose then aside. Pain zinged again, and blood started things flowing even more.

"Don't touch it, I said," Bruce reiterated, emphatically enough to make her freeze. "It's totally broken now. No doubt about it. We've gotta take a pause to temporarily fix that. Let me get my bag."

"We don't have the time," she said, lowering her voice when raising it reverberated small waves of agony through her skull.

He leaned down further, recognizing how incapacitated she was. "Then let's get you in the car. I'll drive. Let the chopper take you in, too."

"The branches," she started, as he helped her to her feet, his grip telling her how right he was when a dizzy spell tried to stumble her to the left.

A whoop of a siren jerked her to attention to look up 174, hoping the approaching vehicle was who she expected. The wave of pain from that motion only served to make her vomit. More pain. More nausea.

"Stop," Bruce said. "Take in a breath through your mouth. Slow down. Just slow yourself down, you hear me? I can't fix this, and somebody needs to get their hands on you who can. Like I said, you're going in the chopper."

"Chief," Thomas called, approaching, climbing over a few limbs. "Damn, what happened to you?"

Still half stooped, not yet having made it to the car, she pointed. "Stan . . . to the chopper."

There was still a major-enough trunk in the road to stop either vehicle from getting through. She had the thought everyone else did, but there were too many words for her to say. Was it quicker to pass him over the limbs or to dig in and clear enough room for the SUV?

Thomas gave a melancholy sigh. "We aren't lifting him over this mess, Chief." He motioned to Bruce. "Clear a path," he said, and immediately gripped one end of an oak branch, jerking with his chin for the Ranger to take the other end.

Callie stood to assist . . . then sat down when the world turned upside down.

Chapter 29

Arlo
Friday morning—storm has passed

WHILE LEONARD threw his personal duffle bag, gym bags, and groceries into the vehicle, Arlo sanitized bedrooms and baths. Especially Bruce's bedroom, their center of focus.

Arlo didn't wash the spread or pillowcases provided by the rental, something that the rental agency required. Admittedly, a hot wash would get rid of the girl's DNA, but there was no time. He crammed the bedding in Bruce's extra-large duffle still housed on the twin bed. The same duffle used to house their guest *du jour* and better contain the spread of victim DNA. The same duffle Bruce guarded while sleeping on a bedroll on the floor.

The duffle would disappear somewhere en route. Somewhere with no rhyme, reason, or connection to where they'd been, or whoever had been missing.

"Come on, man," Leonard said in the doorway. Rainwater dribbled off him, making puddles on the rental floor. "It's easing up out there, and we've gotta get going."

But Arlo was too busy, stooped on his knees and wiping the bed frame where the duffle had been, to worry about rain on the floor. They'd been seen too much this time, which meant more thorough cleaning.

Twelve times they'd mastered these adventures and distilled them down to a science. Twelve females who never saw them coming and never saw them leave. Twelve females who had no idea what had happened to them or who anybody was who'd taken them. No charges filed and no whiff of their identity was proof of said mastery.

"Arlo."

He finished the post and moved on to the area in front of the dresser. He'd already covered the baths, using enough Lysol such that he could taste it. Rental owners expected you to clean up after yourself, and Lysol made more sense than bleach. Everyone was afraid to use bleach much anymore. Bleach drew attention. Bleach might make people think of detective shows.

"Arlo, man, enough."

One more spot. Arlo changed wipes again.

The ransom the Retrievers requested was lower than the norm for kidnappers. Usually, they pegged it at three hundred thousand. Such a comfortable, low six figures meant affluent parents would lean toward paying without risking the cops. Small enough to easily afford.

He stood and tossed the latest wipes in the pile on the floor, eyeing his handiwork.

Arlo was nervous, and he didn't want to admit why. Their cover was still good. Bruce couldn't say anything without incriminating himself, but the concern was whether Bruce cared if he incriminated himself. Put *him* in jail, and he might be fine. He hated most of the outside world anyway. He could not socialize. On their adventures he remained holed up, staring out the window except when he tended the guest.

But Bruce was a wild card. The quietest, least active—and the most unreliable—of the three was loose in the world.

He had always been the cog they needed in this wheel. The Retrievers earned their living this way, and they'd done well. They were so adept with their business model that nine of the twelve kidnappings had never even made the news. Four of the parents had paid so fast it had made Arlo's head spin, shortcutting their adventure each of those times in half.

"Arlo, man, I think it's clean. Let's go."

He rose, finished with the door. Kitchen done. Bathrooms done.

He was the best at wiping things down. Leonard was the best at packing. They worked around Bruce, him always on watch while whichever girl at the time slept under the influence. As Bruce was so repetitive in reminding, he was better at standing guard. *Never assume all is well.*

Never take one's eye off the prize. Never.

Not like he had.

This one glitch was enough to make Arlo ponder if this was it. He had relaxed, and they'd paid a price. The others didn't trust him now. He could regain Leonard's trust, but who knew about Bruce, and Bruce was necessary.

Bruce would've gone after his medical bag and taken the route past the chief's residence. Any sort of traffic he ran into would be first responders, people he'd not want to share attention with.

He couldn't be far.

Surely, he wouldn't continue without them.

Leonard took the plastic bag containing the spent wipes off the floor and held it out for Arlo, who threw a double-fisted pile of wipes in the bag. "We're done."

"Yeah," Arlo said. The Marine real estate broker required everyone pay for a cleaning service to prep the house for the next tenant, an expense well appreciated.

Leonard's big hand wrapped around his friend's upper arm. "Man, settle down."

"I know. I know," Arlo said. "We've got to find him before he screws up."

"You're assuming he wants to be found."

Arlo didn't want to think that. They were close. Like thirteen years close. They needed to remain close . . . united.

He didn't want to envision Bruce as a loose end. Worse, he didn't want Leonard to see Bruce as a loose end. Leonard had hard-core black-and-white ways of dealing with problems.

"He'll come around," Arlo said in response to Leonard's intent stare. Arlo caught a whiff of the doubt taking root. "I'm not him," he said.

"Then act like it," Leonard said. "But we find him. One way or the other, we collect him. What happens then is up to him."

They'd never discussed any of the three leaving the fold. They'd never had to cross that bridge, ergo, no plan for the scenario.

Arlo couldn't totally read what scenarios Leonard had planned, but he could guess. "We need to discuss this before acting," he said. Leonard going rogue wasn't pretty. He was methodically lethal with a plan, but without one, he defaulted to simply neutralizing the threat, and he could do it and be gone with nobody the wiser. He'd been good at that in the sandbox.

Leonard made one more sweep of the house, hollering out each room as he went as Arlo hollered back, "Check." Arlo locked the house, and they left, him driving.

Arlo's primary thought leaned toward Bruce coaxing someone at the chief's house, since that was where the medical kit was, to escort him off the island.

They drove toward Jungle Road.

The drizzle sure beat the rain, and seeing color in lieu of pitch black in the heavens gave him hope. He remembered the name *Chelsea Morning*, thank goodness, because he had no idea of the actual address number, no idea of the make of car. Leonard watching one side of the road and Arlo the other, they made their way slowly, about deciding they'd missed the property until they came upon it on the five-hundred block. There were two cars in the drive. Somebody had to be home.

"Let me," Arlo said. "Stay here. Keep an eye out in case he bolts."

At the top of the stairs, he rapped on the door's etched glass, rehearsing what he would say if Bruce was there . . . and if he wasn't.

A guy in his forties answered.

He wasn't expecting a strange man.

"Can I help you?" the guy asked.

"Hello, I'm Arlo. My partner and I are hunting for our friend, Bruce. He helped with the man who broke his leg, I believe." Then he paused, looking around at the other houses. "Hope I have the right place. Chief Morgan's house?"

"You got it," he said, "but they left, taking the man with the broken leg to meet a chopper."

"Wait, Bruce went with them? We were packing to leave."

The man hesitated before answering, and it was then that Arlo remembered who this one was. He owned the Mexican place where he'd taken Natalie at what seemed like eons ago. The chief's boyfriend. He'd been a cop of some sort, per his date.

He'd be more watchful than most.

"Listen," the man said, stepping to the porch to glance down at the car they'd come in. Any good cop would take note of the make and model of someone they weren't sure about. "Not sure what to tell you." He looked Arlo over, taking in details.

He didn't invite Arlo in, and Arlo didn't want to go inside. If the chief had found that girl, she might be in there. Either that or on the way to the chopper. He wished he knew which, but to ask to come in or seek the girl in any form or fashion could spell disaster.

Arlo prayed she hadn't seen Bruce either. "We just want to pick up our friend and leave. We've had enough hurricane. So, he's gone?"

"Yes."

"Where's the chopper supposed to meet?"

"The Edistonian on Highway 174."

"How far is that?"

"Well, let me think. Maybe a mile and a half or so."

That wasn't much time. He could've beaten them there by now. "How long ago did they leave?" Arlo asked.

The man squinted. Took a pause as if needing to do clock math before finally saying, "Not sure. Probably there already."

Shit.

The man rambled through some directions before stopping and saying, "Well, you really don't need directions from me. It's hard to get lost on the only road that leads in and out of here. You'll be fine, I'm sure. Good luck." Then he closed the door. Arlo heard it latch.

That's when Arlo realized the guy had killed time, letting his girl reach the chopper without interference. Bruce was with them, and Arlo didn't like any of this situation.

Too many people knew too much about their existence, enough to question who these three guys were.

Arlo ran down the stairs, jumped into the car, and made for the highway. They needed to get out of here fast.

"He wasn't there, I take it," Leonard said, not disturbed at the speed with which Arlo took Jungle Road to the edge of town.

"Bruce's riding with her to meet a chopper, taking the guy you two helped earlier." Arlo turned left, crossed the causeway, and dared to pick up the pace, knocking sticks out of the way or running them over.

Leonard was the one who mapped everything out. He might know the way. "Do you recall a place called The Edistonian?" Arlo asked. One branch knocked underneath the car with a double thump.

"Yeah, where I first met the chief at a roadblock. Not far ahead at all. Mile maybe?"

Arlo hit the gas harder but didn't take long before he had to let up. Ahead stood a car. Before it lay trees across the road. A blue light flashed on the other side.

They'd found them.

Chapter 30

Callie
Friday morning

CALLIE DIDN'T CARE who was in the car coming up behind them; they could assist. They damn sure weren't getting by, and she damn sure wasn't letting them sit in their car and wait for the handful of those already there to open up the thoroughfare for them.

She stood from the passenger seat of her car where she'd been fighting the world spinning, cursing the fact she couldn't lift branches and assist in the clearing without becoming an even worse casualty. Just standing made her swollen nose throb, but not such that she couldn't approach these people and orient them as to how things were.

"*Jesus Christ*," said Arlo, getting out of the car.

If his reaction was an indication of her appearance, Callie was glad she had no idea how bad she looked. "The road's blocked. Glad you two showed and not some seniors with back issues. Get out here and help us, please. We have a chopper waiting just ahead for our guy in the back." She halted and then pointed to Leonard, who had exited the passenger side. "Wait. You're the strong guy who moved the tree off my car. Now we can get Stan to the choppers. Come on."

She waved an arm to draw them over, and the shock wave through her head made her really wish she hadn't.

In the woods, more chain saws cranked up. There had to be a dozen or more. Birds had come alive in the trees. The world was back in full color. Callie moved out of the way, recognizing her impotence in the face of the need for brawn. Wouldn't take ten minutes for that much back and muscle to open up a pathway.

It hadn't escaped her that Bruce had ignored his buddies the whole time. They seemed to have come to retrieve Bruce, who wasn't pleased they had. She could believe that they didn't want to be on Edisto anymore . . . who would, after this mess . . . but something was off. And if she had doubts about Bruce, then . . . or maybe not.

Was it her business? Langley remained at *Chelsea Morning* under Mark's watchful eye, and that mild connection with Bruce that the girl had flashed made Callie not quite willing to let Bruce get too far. She'd love to be able to figure that out. It could have been as simple as something about Bruce connected to a memory that had nothing to do with Bruce. Or not.

Before long, Arlo's face had sweated up. Leonard had shed his shirt to save it, and, bare-chested, he'd lifted weight that would've taken the others an extra man to budge.

"There," Arlo said, wiping hands on his jeans, smudges streaked across his cheeks and forehead.

Leonard grabbed his shirt off the car hood and slid it over his head. "Time to go. Bruce, let's boogie. We packed you up."

But Bruce remained fifteen feet away, over next to Thomas, who took note when Bruce didn't reply.

"Come on, man," Arlo said, headed toward his driver's door.

But Bruce didn't respond and, in a split second of what Callie saw as doubt, looked to her.

"Bruce, come with me," she said, going to her own passenger door. "I can't drive like this. You got us this far; you can take us the rest of the way."

To that, he did as told.

Thomas tried to get a visual cue from her, but with her poor face so distorted and changed from blood, clots, and now bruising, she knew he wouldn't be able to read any sort of message. "Meet us there, Thomas," she said and got into the car.

The chopper was ready and waiting, two medics with a gurney trying to figure out which car to meet, the pilot remaining at the controls.

"Here," Callie shouted, wishing she hadn't when she had to lower herself back down to her seat from the wave of pain.

Stan got strapped to the gurney, but he yelled for Callie before he'd let them load him.

"Thomas," she said to her best uniform, and he gave her his arm to reach Stan, unable to trust herself to walk that far without stumbling and causing that nose more trouble. She wasn't sure she could recover from another hit in the face.

"I'm here, big guy," she said.

"What the hell?" he said, his stare wide as silver dollars.

"I tripped," she said. "Go get fixed. I'll see you there."

They moved him to the chopper in a slick, synchronized fashion, lifting and anchoring him. One of the medics returned. "We have room for one more," she said, fixated on Callie. "I believe that's you."

"I'm not going without Bruce," she said.

He stood near her vehicle, attention riveted on her and Stan and the actions of the chopper crew. Arlo and Leonard, standing a few yards off, heard, and they moved toward their friend.

"Let's hit the trail, buddy," Arlo yelled over the noise.

"We're done," Bruce said to him. "I meant it, Arlo. I'm done with you guys."

Arlo looked back at Leonard in a quandary, then approached Bruce. "How are you getting anywhere without wheels? Unless you're staying here. That what you're doing?"

"Gotta go, Chief," said the medic. "And you need to be with us. That nose is bad."

"We stick together," Arlo continued, moving closer to Bruce. "We can't leave a man behind. You got no place here."

"Here could be an option," Bruce said.

Arlo glanced across the field of people. "These are strangers. You helped their buddy, but you're not one of them."

Leonard came up. "Screw this." He leaned over and spoke in Arlo's ear, and whatever it was made Arlo stiffen.

Chapter 31

Arlo

THE NOISE OF THE helicopter kept everyone from hearing each other without being within a foot or two. Leonard leaned over and growled in Arlo's ear. "Let the chopper leave, follow him out of here. Later, once they land, we put a round through him." Leonard went out of his way to avoid peering at Callie. "That cop is getting suspicious of us."

"So was the one at the house," Arlo said back.

Bruce, having kept his distance until now, marched to his partners, as if he could read their lips. He had purpose in his expression and in his walk. Nobody forced Bruce to do anything he didn't want to do.

But then there was Leonard, and if Arlo understood anything about that Retriever, it was that he rarely compromised. If the mission was at risk, he was the first primed to take the enemy down . . . whoever they had been, ally or foe. Leonard, while the smooth talker when it came to the parents and sealing the deals, would not tolerate anyone stepping outside their ranks.

"I might stay," Bruce said, his voice only loud enough to be heard by the two men over the sound of the chopper. "The chief kind of likes me."

Leonard laughed, with a side glance at Callie. "What, do you think she'll just forget about that girl she found? She'll get you to talk then lock your ass in jail. Then we'll get dragged in your wake when you run off at the mouth." He motioned with a tilt of his head to the half-a-dozen people standing around waiting. "What happened to all for one and one for all, dude?"

Arlo kept his focus on the people gathered, in particular the chief. She maintained a steely look, an unspoken sense of how she was learning more and more per second. Surprisingly, she hadn't interrupted them already, but he surmised she was waiting in order to fine-tune her judgment of them. From what Natalie had told him over quesadillas that evening, this beach police chief wasn't small-town naïve. She'd taken down a respectable number of foes, and if Rangers understood anything, it was what taking lives did to a person. It hardened them. Especially once you did it more than once. He'd heard she had.

That little midget of an officer had a reputation of making people underestimate her. And she'd painted Bruce into some sort of self-aware-ness corner.

"People, come on!" yelled the pilot.

Always the logical one, Arlo's abilities felt frayed as he lost his grip on both Bruce and Leonard. Neither trusted the other. They were dan-gerously close to a complete dismantling of the Retrievers, and he wasn't comfortable with how they might walk away without casualties.

"Bruce," Callie said, coming over, bloodied and bruised.

"I'm staying," Bruce said, for both her and Arlo to hear.

Arlo motioned with one hand for Leonard to stay back. "It doesn't work that way." For God's sake, they weren't going to jail because Bruce had grown a case of conscience.

"You're not talking me into another adventure," Bruce said, and pointed for Callie to get aboard the helicopter. She read him and returned to one of the medics.

Arlo took advantage of what could be seconds here. "How can we trust you, buddy?"

Bruce sneered. "You mean how can you trust a loose end? I heard Leonard. Hell, I can read his mind but stop and think. What evidence does any of us have on the other without going down together?"

He turned, and, the medical bag still in his hand, he ran to the chopper, spoke something in the medic's ear. After a word with Callie, a nod was given by the medic. Bruce assisted Callie into the chopper, then he jumped inside like he'd done so many times before.

"Bruce," Leonard shouted, "you son of a bitch!"

Arlo, however, only stood and watched as their team crumbled.

The helicopter lifted and banked east toward Charleston. To avoid questions, thank-yous, and just any conversation that might plant him and Leonard any further in anyone's memory, Arlo strode to their rental car. Leonard did the same, and without a word they turned around in the big field beside the Edistonian and drove back to the highway, headed north. Once they reached US Highway 17, he'd let Leonard dictate where they needed to go. He had between then and whenever they stopped for the night to talk Leonard into accepting the team was defunct . . . and that Bruce didn't warrant hunting down.

He hoped to hell he could talk him into it.

Chapter 32

Callie

THEY TOOK BOTH Stan and Callie straight in upon arrival at St. Francis Memorial. As much as Callie wanted to keep a grip on Bruce, she had no choice but to fold when doctors and staff saw her damage and smothered her with rapid attention. Before she could ask about Stan, someone wheeled him off, doped her up, did imaging of her nose, and went to work on righting it. She barely remembered worrying about whether she'd look like a boxer afterward, because with all those people up close and personal, she'd closed her eyes. She felt the snap after a lot of contemplation and false starts. Then, from meds or simply keeping her eyes shut , after a little while she seemed to lose sense of time.

She wasn't sure about the amount of that time until Bruce came into view. That confused her, since she expected to see staff, and if not them, then Mark. But her brain kicked in, and pieces fell into place. She'd fallen asleep.

"They defaulted to me as your next of kin," he said. "With the hurricane and all, and with your next of kin not readily available . . . I just sort of stepped up."

"You wouldn't be able to do the paperwork," she said, raspy and with effort to make herself heard. Her nose shouldn't have interfered with her speaking . . . but it did.

"You had ID on you," he said. "And the medic in the chopper vouched for you."

She didn't remember that.

"I told them I brought you in, was a friend, and that someone would be arriving who could do the rest."

"How's Stan?"

"Still in surgery," he said. "It's as bad as I expected."

She wondered whether he'd wind up with a permanent limp like Mark. "What did they do to my nose?" Tentatively, she brushed it with fingertips, surprised she couldn't feel it. The gauze bandaging felt an inch thick.

"They were able to manipulate it back into place. It's why you're a little woozy. Swelling won't go down for a week. They may have packed a little gauze inside, too, which they'll take out when you return," he said. "They contemplated surgery, so count your blessings."

"What?" She winced. "Oh, damn. Think I felt that."

"You're lucky," he said. "They'll release you in another hour, but they figured no hurry since you'd likely be waiting to hear about Stan."

She nodded. Her senses were easing back, with the exception of smell. Her hearing was crisper, her sight cleaner around the edges. Taste would be shot for a while, though.

"My things?" she asked, looking around.

"They took your radio. And your weapon. All is safe. You have a backup guy at Edisto, right?"

"Yeah. The guy you met." All six of her officers would report to duty, though, or rather, had already appeared, she guessed.

Then it hit her how talkative he was being with it just being him and her. Away from Langley. Away from his cohorts. Without the pressure of Stan or a hurricane, this might be the regular side of the man. She wasn't that uncomfortable with him. "What time is it?"

"Quarter to eleven."

Though totally understandable and completely unavoidable, her stomach fell at the idea she was laid up with everyone else coping with the storm's aftermath. They'd be going strong at it by now. She hadn't seen a horrible amount of damage in what little she'd canvassed in her spastic comings and goings with Stan and Langley, but the cleanup would be a pain in the ass.

Bruce sat uncommonly still, his medical bag at his side. A man at ease with whatever he decided he needed to be at ease about, and she suspected he would be so ninety percent of the time. Not too many dimensions to this man, but few were privy to what few he had.

A nurse checked in, took vitals, and smiled over at Bruce. "She'll be all right, you know." As if Callie weren't sitting there. As if he were her significant other.

"No doubt," he said, and attempted a smile, the first Callie had seen since they'd met. It looked good on him.

For a while Callie let herself rest, giving Bruce the chance to leave. She couldn't detain him. Not really. No proof, plus, look at him tending to her. She couldn't help thinking he was seeking someplace to land.

He had decisions to make. Maybe he'd made them. He had no car, but that probably didn't deter him from whatever his purpose. The Rangers' *adventure,* as they'd called their vacation back at the chopper, was over. While lying there, she attempted to piece this man together. The Langley situation was so vague, but her mind told her she wasn't far from some truth. A truth that touched Bruce.

Possibly she thought more favorably of him because he'd risked himself for others during the crucible of a hurricane. He'd taken care of Stan . . . and her. He'd risked his relationship with his friends. Had he been planning to leave them all along, or had this incident on Edisto been the deciding factor in changing direction?

He was a loner. They all were, but he seemed more so than the others. He'd let his partners take the lead, like when Leonard had done most of the talking originally when they'd gone to Stan's. From the little she'd come to know these three men, she would nail down their characters as the brawn, the brains, and the guardian. Throw a kidnapping scheme into that, and they had a system.

She raised her eyelids. "Tell me something." He hadn't moved.

"Anyone ever get hurt on your *adventures?*" she asked, using the term she'd heard one of the partners use.

"Nope."

"Anyone die?"

"Nope."

"Do they make it home?"

"Yep."

"Police get involved?"

"Not from what I hear."

"All business?" She wanted to know if the victims were an object of excitement to the men.

"Yep."

Again with the short and sweet.

She took things in another direction. "Are you really leaving them?"

"I don't see them in my future anymore, no."

She knew not to waste her time trying to get more specific. He'd dodge, give one-word responses, or not respond at all. Need-to-know logic, which she could respect. Talking when you didn't have to only benefited the person asking.

Callie thought a nurse was coming in again, but they walked by. She was in an area where beds were separated on the sides by walls, but their fronts were merely curtains. A drawn drape could erroneously give the sensation of privacy that didn't exist.

Instead of waiting until things quieted, however, she paused until events sounded busy, then she wriggled a finger for Bruce to come closer. He did.

"You almost got caught this time," she said. When he didn't immediately reply, she realized she hadn't asked him a question. Bruce didn't voluntarily divulge anything; she got that. Hopefully she'd built a small sense of rapport with him. His leaping aboard the chopper had enforced that hope. "You underestimated the hurricane in your plan," she tacked on. "You keep these *adventures* up, and sooner or later you'll underestimate something else."

Bruce said, "Interesting, Chief." No more.

But she wanted more. She'd let him escape his partners. She deserved more. "I may not be able to piece together the full story, but whether I can or not, the truth is you made a mistake. You'll make others. Regardless of your level of training, your camaraderie, or your strategy, you are human. Perfection is impossible."

There'd been an unseen wall between them through most of this ordeal, a wall that Callie guessed he maintained between him and just about anyone else. However, he leaned forward, maybe to keep quieter . . . maybe to show his willingness to respect her a pinch more.

"Hypothetically," he said, "pros don't compromise. In their duties or their social dealings, like getting involved with people like you, like Stan, like the lady with the dog; we don't let down our guard. It's how we stay alive."

She raised her brow, ignoring the small jolt of pain that came with the movement. "Maybe you'd prefer a life where you *could* settle with people . . . people like me, like Stan, like the lady with the dog. Where you wouldn't have to be so guarded."

He sat back in his chair, shaking his head. "Been there. Doesn't work."

"Yet you compromised a bit this time, Bruce." She used his name in the hope of building trust. "You sacrificed for Stan."

"You made me."

"I made you?" She laughed, regretting the pain but it was worth the effort.

Sympathy crept in for him that she hadn't expected. Maybe she could see him settling someplace. He sure seemed tired of his current life. Maybe not in an apartment somewhere, and suburbia was out of the question. He could, however, become invisible in the middle of a major city . . . or in a small shanty amidst the Edisto jungle. She had to stop herself short of making that suggestion.

People crossed that big bridge to leave their history behind. Every Edisto resident had. No telling how many Bruces lived on the beach.

He smiled again. He owned a pleasant smile. He'd feel better if he used it more.

"Wherever I wind up," he said, "my days of combat and adventures are done."

"And them?" She didn't have to say names.

"They'll need to find their own new direction, too."

Good to know, but. . . . "What if they come hunting you?"

"They won't. And I'm not going far. For now." He crossed his arms and settled back, as if he needed a nap. She envisioned him looking like this while protecting Langley during her kidnapping, watching over her. The scenario didn't feel as ominous as Callie had originally played out in her mind. It almost didn't feel criminal anymore, even though she knew better. Those meds they had her on were certainly softening her brain.

He closed his eyes, giving her permission to do the same. Signaling his acceptance of whatever the future held.

Her lids fluttered shut as she listened to nurses talk, shoes making rounds, intercom asking for this doctor and that. She counted her blessings that she smelled nothing of the horrible, sterilized scent of the place. Then she made a mental list of what to do once back on the job.

Checking on Langley would come first, whom Mark would hand over to the authorities ASAP. Callie would wind up dealing with said authorities in an investigation. But chances were slim to none of a conviction or even arrest if this affair left no evidence behind. Flashes of sensory memory like Langley'd had didn't often progress to actionable evidence or identification.

Setting aside the kidnap problem, she mentally ran through the needs of the beach. It was amazing the organization and contingency planning in place on Edisto for storms. Power would be up before she returned home. Tarps would cover damaged roofs. Contractors would be arriving in droves and already tending to the urgent cases, which she hoped were few. Insurance adjustors would be on site. This beach was so orchestrated for hurricanes that the economy would be up and running within forty-eight hours, many places within twenty-four. For a small town, Edisto Beach had its act together when it came to Mother Nature. Way better than Charleston, she liked to think.

Mark. She had to reach Mark, but she suspected he had his hands full with Langley. Everyone would be asking about her and Stan and going by the house to ask Mark. Her mind stayed all a whirl as to what should be going on in her absence. The second they released her, she could always Uber home. Not many Uber drivers liked driving all the way out to the island, but surely in light of circumstances, she could find one.

When she finally tried to open her eyes, she found it difficult. With extra effort, she managed, realizing she'd fallen asleep, and quite deeply so.

"Bruce," she started, turning her head to see if he was awake . . . only to find Mark standing at the curtain, talking to someone she couldn't see in the hall. He was talking serious, not-too-pleasant business with someone, for sure.

"Mark?"

He whipped around. "Hey, Sunshine." The shift was night and day, him flashing a smile so warm she almost teared.

Callie scooted herself more upright. "Hey yourself. When did you get here? Where's Bruce?"

Mark came to her bedside. "Good heavens, look at your face."

She recognized someone changing the subject. "I asked, where was Bruce. You were just talking to someone, and your expression wasn't . . ." Then it hit her. He was supposed to be protecting the girl. "Where's Langley?"

"Whoa. First, I just got here not ten minutes ago. Secondly, I brought Langley with me. I called the police, and they met us at the door, mainly because her father was already here. Third—"

"You handed her over without me?" Callie threw off the light sheet and thin blanket. The room tilted a smidge, but nothing like it had before. "Take me to them."

But Mark wasn't too keen on following her instruction. "They've got this," he said. "You stay here until they release you. They do want to talk to you, but after hearing you were in the ER, they said it could wait until tomorrow. They have Langley, and that's their best lead. Let them do their jobs."

Rather than argue, rather than let Langley and her keepers disappear, Callie pushed past Mark. "Take me where you left her," she said, and struck out, taking a half-dozen steps before realizing she had no idea where she was headed.

Mark trotted up to catch her, even reached her elbow to stop her, but she halted, her thoughts pulling a traffic jam. She'd been prepared to turn at Mark's touch to strike up the argument of how important it was for her to deal with the authorities . . . only for her gaze to sweep past him to Bruce leaning against the wall.

He was out of the pathway, with staff coming and going around him, but he gave her a slight smile, as if he waited. For her? For Mark to leave? Callie wasn't sure, but he blended in, and she was momentarily stymied as to why he hadn't taken off until she remembered his promise to remain close . . . *for now*.

Langley's voice severed her thoughts. Two uniforms and a plain clothes entered through the double doors, escorting the girl along with someone who could only be her father. A white coat and a nurse walked with them, steering them toward a bay of exam areas like Callie's.

Langley looked confused, wedged between her father and one of the uniforms, everyone talking over and around her. Her father directed the two hospital types to override the plain-clothes detective. Arguments and overtalk crisscrossed the girl as each person in the group claimed their discussion priority.

"That's rather messy," she told Mark, choosing to hold tight where she stood.

"Well, I called the father first," Mark said, inserting himself between Callie and someone walking past to avoid her getting bumped.

The detective spotted Mark and gave him a nod, acknowledging he knew where to find him when time came for his interview, and Mark tilted his head at Callie. The detective nodded back in understanding.

The cluster stood only six feet from Bruce.

Langley suddenly recognized him.

She bolted to him, arms out, and wrapped him in a hug. "This is one of the people who helped me on Edisto," she said.

That moved the crew toward him.

Callie waited for Bruce to tense at the presence of law enforcement. She'd interpreted him as so much of a loner who didn't interact with people, surely going out of his way not to be seen. He did not tense. He quietly accepted the hug, knowing the girl needed to take control of the questions and directives swirling around her.

Had he seriously compromised that anti-social comfort for her? For Langley?

The detective acted quicker than the others. "Who are you, sir?"

"Just a man who was on vacation until the hurricane came to town." He pointed at Callie. "I've been helping her and her friend with the broken leg, and while I was there, I cleaned up this little girl's arm. Used to be a medic back in the day."

All the heads turned to where Callie stood in a gown with bloodied spots across the chest and a thick white bandage ear to ear. "Police Chief Callie Morgan, Town of Edisto Beach," she mumbled through the thickness. "He's right."

At the sight of Callie, Langley rushed over, arms wide again, to which Callie held up a stopping palm. "Not too tight, honey."

Langley caught herself, smiled, and gave a light loose hug leaving space between them. "Thank you, Chief Morgan. I don't know what I would've done without you and Mark. You took me in."

The detective was chomping at the bit for answers. "She says you found her in the bushes in the middle of the storm. Any idea how she got there?" he asked.

"None. Just found her." Callie peered over at Bruce. In her gut, she'd read him right after all.

The detective followed her glance and went over to him. "And you . . . did what?"

Bruce had a scruffy look, and he played it up. Scratching his hair in disarray, still damp and dirty from the downed trees and rain, he shrugged. "Cleaned her arm and put a Band-Aid on it. Helped clear trees on the road. Helped load the man with the broken leg." He looked back at Callie. "Stan was his name, right?"

Callie slowly nodded, watching this man work. "That's right."

Doctor St. James approached Bruce with an outstretched hand. "Well, thank you for helping my daughter."

Bruce shrugged again. "Didn't do much, but glad to help. Glad she's home."

With that, the cluster of people moved back toward the bay of rooms, a nurse whipping back a curtain to where Langley would be tended to probably the rest of the day, with tests run above and beyond the norm. After all, she'd been gone for days, remembered none of it, and had been kept on an IV. Her physician father would accept nothing less than a full battery of tests, and law enforcement would let him.

Uniforms were stationed outside her curtain, while the detective, father, and another white coat went in with Langley.

With the hubbub reduced, Callie remained standing in the hallway. She looked over at Bruce.

He winked, turned, and walked out the double doors.

Chapter 33

Callie

"THE MINUTE THEY opened up 174, I grabbed Langley and drove here," Mark said, resuming his place in the lone chair in the ER bay while they awaited Callie's release.

Callie sat in the middle of the bed, cross-legged, still marveling at the finesse of the earlier moment. The ease by which Bruce had addressed the detective, been lauded by Langley's father, then been dismissed as irrelevant had her still in amazement . . . and somewhat of a quandary.

Mark continued chatting. "Met the police in the ER and passed her over to her father. Talk about a muddled mess. The police didn't know she was missing, the father apologized for misleading them, Langley cried unable to tell them anything except how great we all were for taking her in. The father said he just wanted it to be done and over with, but the police can't accept that nobody saw or heard the guilty party. The father paid the ransom, by the way. Three hundred thousand. Doesn't care because they released his daughter. Tell me how many times you've heard of that happening?"

Callie wondered when the money handover had been done, and which one of them had handled it around the storm. *Oh, yeah.*

Leonard. The roadblock. He'd returned from the mainland, groceries beside him in the front seat. Surely, she hadn't been that close to the ransom money.

"I'd hate to be the agent on that case," Mark continued. "No proof of anything or anyone, and the money gone. My question was why would anyone take a kidnapped victim to the beach? Especially ours. It's isolated."

"Because of what you just said," she replied. "Who would do that? Nobody would look."

Mark shook his head. "Or maybe they dumped her there in the storm, to buy time to get away."

"They could've asked for way more money, especially from a surgeon," she said.

"Agree. And I wonder if the storm helped her get loose."

So many questions without answers.

A headache ensued, and she scooted herself back to the head of the bed, raised it up, and eased her head on the pillow. Callie hadn't had the opportunity to go into depth with Mark about Langley, how she was found, the brief second of familiarity with Langley in the recliner, and she hadn't the energy to do so now.

She was aware with each second that she had rehashed details, Bruce got further away. She laid odds on Bruce having lost his share of the money which made her like him more.

She might have turned in Arlo and Leonard. They hadn't been willing to put their freedom on the line for someone badly hurt and in pain.

"You look tired," Mark said.

Now that he mentioned it, she was exhausted. No, she wasn't up to discussing Bruce with Mark right now. She could, but she didn't want to miss the finer points. Nor did she want him to make any sort of decision for her, in the guise of she was doped up or in pain. No, she'd hold a one-on-one with him tomorrow. Or some other day. A detective would visit her and likely come out to the beach to understand the lay of the land and what, if anything, Langley might recall.

She wanted her own bed as badly as a drink, but she more wanted to see about Stan. She sat up and motioned to a small cabinet where she was sure her things were stored. She'd have to wear bloody clothes home unless she wanted to leave in the gown.

Mark reached down and threw a plastic bag on the bed. "Clean clothes," he said. "Where's your sidearm?"

Where, indeed? About that time a nurse came in, with papers to sign.

"My weapon?" Callie asked, amid changing tops. "I assume it's in a safe somewhere?"

"Yes," she said. "I'll let you get dressed then lead you to it. I'd rather not handle it, if you don't mind."

Callie would rather she not handle it either. "Who took it off me?" she asked.

"Your gentleman friend," the nurse said. "He directed us to lock it up. It's hospital policy anyway, but one of our doctors has his CWP license, so we let him do it. Heavens, a gun in here is practically obscene."

Callie let her have her superciliousness, understanding full well if the woman had needed help with a dangerous type roaming these halls, she'd have welcomed the person arriving with the gun on their hip.

Many people didn't want a weapon until their lives turned upside down, and then they couldn't find a gun toter fast enough.

She finished dressing, papers in hand, but refused the wheelchair. Stan had come out of surgery, they said, and he was easing out of anesthesia. She'd be able to see him in a few minutes, a message that thrilled Mark as well.

As they waited, he filled her in on what little he knew about the beach's damage. He'd left Donna and Horse at *Chelsea Morning*, but she'd taken to the streets by the time he left, not only to check on her house, but to check on others, putting on her councilwoman hat to tend to her constituents. Horse accompanied her.

"She's good," Mark said.

"Agreed," Callie said. "That dog is a nice touch. I'm going to suggest she bring him to council meetings. Gives her an edge. A couple of those good ol' boys on the council could use some humbling."

The white uniform made her way to them. "You can come on back to see your friend now."

THE NEXT DAY Callie was at home, technically speaking, but when she wasn't coordinating cleanup and traffic, flooded and blocked streets, she was answering questions about her black-and-blue face, the swollen eyes giving her a punching-bag look. She told everyone she'd been hit by a tree, which was half right.

At noon she was to meet with the detective and show him the where and when of what had happened to Langley. She still hadn't delved into the details with Mark. They'd come home and crashed, then risen to deal with the town's needs, showered, and now waited on the front porch for the detective to arrive. He'd texted he was ten miles out.

All she could think about was where Bruce was and just how much she'd be telling Charleston law enforcement. That might depend on what Langley had been able to tell them. Regardless, she didn't think there was enough to assign culpability to a reasonable certainty per the law.

Callie's phone rang. Caller ID identified her son Jeb.

"We got to see Langley," he said.

"Surprised they let you see her so soon."

"She's being pampered, and it's what she wanted, so her mom let us. Boy, she gives you a lot of credit, Mom. That's cool."

"I just found her in the bushes and brought her home, Son."

"Still, your name was mentioned a lot. She told us all she could remember. Damn, Mom, that's creepy as hell. She gets kidnapped, then she's free, and she has no idea what happened in between? How are they going to catch the kidnappers? Grandma said they ought to hire a private investigator. She would if that were me."

No doubt she would. Jeb was her pride and joy. But she'd be wasting her money.

"Have you been able to come up with anything?" he asked.

Of course she told him no. The news services in the area would paint this as the perfect crime, which might lead to copycats, if not in South Carolina then elsewhere. That possibility made her want to tell the detective what she thought may have happened . . . but not for long.

"I hope between what happened to Langley and the attempt on Sprite that they put a cam in that blind spot," she said.

He gave a clipped laugh. "I think her father will see to that. He's rather connected."

Good deal. She hung up, satisfied her kids were informed and aware of taking care of themselves.

Copycats. She sure hoped no one would try. Assuming anyone attempted to emulate this *perfect crime*, Callie felt assured that new kidnappers would not possess the training and savvy of the ones who took Langley. They'd been a perfect-storm sort of criminal capacity and skill, in her opinion, and she'd almost bet a year's salary that they'd not go down that path again. Almost. If Bruce spoke the truth, they'd have to operate without him, and they'd be fools to attempt it alone. At least, that's what her gut said.

"You have a lot on your mind," Mark said, rocking in one of the outdoor chairs they'd returned to the porch, after having been stored in one of the bedrooms.

"I do," she said. "And I'm not sure what to do about it."

His puzzled expression showed he hadn't expected such a big unknown from her. "What about? The beach is on its way to normal, and you returned Langley to her family. What's to ponder?"

"This detective," she said.

"If you don't have details to assist him, then it is what it is, Sunshine."

The City of Charleston vehicle arrived in her drive, and the two of them headed down the stairs to meet him. After maybe two minutes of re-introductions, they got in his car and headed to the station.

"We found her here," she said, noting the bushes around the station's main door. "Barefoot, no underwear, sopping wet, and scared. She told me she saw a sign that said *Police Station* and came here hoping to find uniforms . . . in the middle of that storm. She was still a little dopey, and it's a wonder she didn't get hurt, or worse, trip and drown."

The detective studied the area, then asked Callie to take him to each of the police signs that Langley might have seen. "These houses were mostly empty I take it?"

"Yes. I have a loose list of those that weren't. Mostly residents because tenants tend to fear a hurricane and evacuate."

"I'd like that list," he said.

She'd already expected that and handed him a better copy than the handwritten one she'd used in the days of the storm. That would keep him busy. She'd offer to talk to the people herself, but Charleston PD would want to handle this high-profile case themselves. Didn't take the detective two seconds to make that clear.

Langley's return had made last night's news. Edisto's born-and-bred reporter Alex Hanson had already texted, called, and emailed Callie, having a fit about missing out on such a huge exclusive. After putting her grandmother, Mrs. Hanson, in harm's way, Alex could get over it.

Callie kept telling herself she had a beach to clean up and no time to assist with the outer edges and dregs of a case that wasn't really hers. She didn't want it to be hers. After being given carte blanche to interview, research, and backtrack the area, the detective seemed appeased, if not happy.

"Langley's worthless," he said. "Not her fault, though. Her mind is a blank between the abduction and when you found her. She can't even recall quite how she found your station except she thinks there was a sign."

"And there are three signs," Callie replied. "Three different directions."

He rubbed his eyes, frustrated. "Exactly. I can't recall how she got outside either. Just realized she was standing in the rain with crap blowing around her."

Mark had been dutifully listening, unable to add much, having come along as a potential witness, per the detective. By now they had returned to *Chelsea Morning.* "Any tenants are long gone," he reminded the man.

"Yeah." The detective pulled into the drive and turned off the engine, taking seconds to think. "They're all over my ass to solve this, but between you and me, it isn't happening."

"How's the family today?" she asked. "Are they leaning on you to solve this or—"

"Oh, hell no," he answered, his sideways look telling her he was indeed between a rock and a hard place. "On the contrary. They want to forget about it. They are *counting their blessings*, they said. They're pulling her out of school this semester to get counseling, then they are returning to normal, they said."

"Sound like tough people," Mark said.

"Well-connected people, too. If counseling doesn't bring that girl out of her fog . . . if any of these interviews don't provide us with answers . . . if the tenants that are gone don't flash us some sort of potential, we're done. Never seen anything like it."

"Would hate to be you right now," she said.

The laugh was rather loud, contained by the car. "Appreciate that, Chief."

They chatted a few more seconds, mostly about the pressure on the man. "Well, I'm here if you need me," she said, reaching for the door handle.

He said his goodbyes and pulled out of the drive to head back toward Charleston. Mark stood with his arm around her shoulder while she scratched the edge of the gauze around her nose.

"We're going to talk about this tonight, right?" he said, his loose hand cordially waving goodbye to the detective.

She just sighed, not sure she knew how to start.

Chapter 34

Callie

STAN HAD BEEN the least concerned about his mobility and assorted limited abilities when they released him from St. Francis, and once at the base of his outside stairs, he still touted that he'd be fine. He started up his steps—carefully, waving aside three different offers of assistance from those standing by.

"Let him go," Callie said. "He's stubborn. If he falls and breaks the other leg, maybe he'll learn to listen."

Thomas's stare at her was playful. "Rather harsh, don't you think?"

"You move in with him then," she replied. "Fix his meals. Help him up in the middle of the night when he needs to pee, because that's what'll happen if he breaks anything else."

Thomas gave her short shakes of his head. "No, I'm good."

"A sorry bunch of friends y'all are," Stan said, already four stairs up and even slower in his efforts. With the next step, he blew out a breath, sucking another in for the next attempt.

"I can't stand this," Mark said, going to him, offering his shoulder for the remaining climb.

Everyone watched, an audience holding its breath. Donna moved closer to Callie. "I assume we'll have assignments on visits and meals and such. If so, sign me up."

Donna had become Mark and Callie's guest resident while her house was under construction. There were no temporary, short-term rentals on Edisto, other than condos over in Wyndham, but they were on the other end of the beach.

Callie held her attention on Stan, equally on Mark who still was under strict orders not to lift anything over ten pounds for two more days. "Thomas, go help them, please. I don't need two invalids on my hands."

Her deputy trotted up, leaving Callie, Donna, and Sophie on the ground.

Sophie winced at an almost stumble. "He's an idiot. We'll have to come and go and do for him whether he likes it or not. Tell him not to lock his doors." The yoga maven believed locking doors invited negative karma.

"He's a cop," Callie reminded her. "Like me."

Sophie scoffed. "Which means y'all lock up everything in sight. No wonder he broke his leg. No wonder you broke your nose." They'd never come to a compromise on safety practices, and Callie would never fully grasp how Sophie's spiritual connection worked.

"I have the solution," Donna said. "Let him get to the top first." She grabbed a bag of groceries out of the car and began walking up, Horse behind her.

Sophie and Callie exchanged look with skeptical, furrowed brow. "Well," Callie said, "grab a bag, Soph. Don't waste a trip."

Inside, they set Stan up in his recliner, everyone moving things that might topple or get stumbled over, ensuring clean paths to the kitchen, the bedroom, and the bath. Callie opened the drapes to a double glass sliding door, letting him watch the jungle-like panorama of the undeveloped growth behind the house.

"Need some damn elevators out here," Stan grumbled.

"Insurance goes through the roof if you build one," Mark said. "Remember? Hurricanes love them, and the chutes they're in only channel water straight to the inside of the house."

Donna gave a *humph*, having learned something new. "Okay, y'all. Here's my idea."

Too antsy to stand still and wait, Sophie put groceries away. "Just ignore me while you talk," she said, though everyone fully expected her to listen.

Donna cleared her throat. Horse went to sit beside Stan, making Callie wonder if he liked tending to people in need.

"I can move in here while they repair my place," the councilwoman said.

The room seemed to freeze in time.

"What the hell?" came out of Stan first, almost in a whisper. Then he seemed to think about it again and spoke up. "Which one of you invited her to stay at *my* house?"

"Sure as hell not me," Thomas said, taking a half step back.

But Donna slid over to Stan's chair and knelt, both forearms resting on one arm of the recliner. "Totally my idea, and none of them knew I would even offer, you big dufus."

He grumbled. "*Dufus?*"

Mark turned away to hide his grin, while Callie remained transfixed, smiling, not wanting to miss any of this.

"I'll call you whatever you want to be called, but bottom line is I can take damn fine care of you," Donna said. "You have an extra bedroom, right?"

Stan glanced past her to the hallway, as if he had to check. "Um, yeah. Can't vouch for what shape it's in," he said.

Laughing, Donna rose. "I've cleaned many a kennel in my day, so I'm pretty sure I can handle the junk collections of an old man."

The whole room guffawed.

"Old?" he bellowed. "How old might you be . . . old woman?"

To that, people suppressed hard laughs that still leaked out in wind and chuckles.

To which, Donna only laughed herself. "I can cook. I can clean. I can tend to you. While that sounds rather old-fashioned, they are necessities for someone recuperating from surgery on a broken leg. Accept the help. I promise not to traipse around naked or anything."

More laughter, with Thomas trying to suppress tears. "Oh my God," he said under his breath.

Red-faced, Stan stared at the beast to his left. "What about the dog?"

"You allergic?" Donna asked.

"No."

"Then we're good. He's quiet. I feed and walk him. The worst he can be is company for you when I go out without him." She reached over and moved a stray lock out of Stan's eyes, his hair overdue for a cut. "I can even trim hair, if you believe that."

"Oh, my dear God," he grumbled turning to stare out the sliding glass doors.

Sophie reached over and laid two packs of Big Red chewing gum in his lap from the groceries, the man's habit for years. "There's more in the cabinet." Then her hands went on her hips, as she always did in making a point. "It's not like you've got to sleep with her, Stan. Not that people around here would care anyway. Hell, I slept with you."

Raucous laughter this time.

Sophie seemed proud of herself. "If staying with you doesn't bother *her*, it damn sure shouldn't bother *you*."

"Bug . . ." and he stopped himself from using the nickname he'd given Sophie when they were an item and she'd sexed him to the point he made up reasons to miss a few of their dates. "I just need a little help is all."

That made everyone soften.

"Then let her stay here," Callie said, gently, such that he could feel the tenderness she felt for him.

Stan peered over at the dog who stared back in kind, drawing a smirk from Stan . . . and a pat on the dog's head.

"There. Deal," Donna said. She grinned over at Callie. "Told you Horse manipulates people. Now, let's go get my junk out of your house and bring it over here."

THE EVENINGS WERE beginning to darken earlier with it now being October, so once the lot of them had moved in Stan's new caregiver, Callie and Mark took their coffees to the side porch, in lieu of the front—where people would drive, walk, and bike by, honking, waving, sometimes stopping to speak. The screen porch facing the empty lot next door still gave them the flavor of Edisto Beach but kept them from the public eye. They'd been known to do more than sip coffee out there once shadows fell dark enough. The chaise in the corner was rather comfortable.

The sun hadn't quite disappeared, and a lone hammer pounded the last of its nails for the day, somewhere Callie guessed to be about two blocks away.

Donna's residence had received the most damage of all the Edisto houses. Others had railings snatched from stairways and screens split by debris. Five or six houses needed roofs patched. Sand had to be relocated off several streets. Power, however, came up quickly, and in just over twenty-four hours, the beach throbbed with activity, from contractors to tourists, from residents to rental owners, each counting their blessings that Nikki had done as little as she did. Honestly, the active repairs seemed little more than what normally took place at the end of the peak tourist season, repairing what irresponsible tenants had overly used and abused in the summer.

A week after all the hubbub of Langley, Stan, and Bruce, repairs continued throughout the day, stopping in the evening when one could just enjoy living at the beach, pretending nothing had gone amiss and all was good.

After a half hour, Callie drew her feet up under her and threw a quilt over her lap. Mark rocked in the chair just within reach to her left. They relaxed, letting the night slowly catch up to them, the unspoken being that they were rather grateful for both Stan being home and safe with a new caregiver and *Chelsea Morning* only harboring the two of them now. Donna might not be able to run around naked at Stan's, but Callie and Mark could here, finally. They'd chuckled about it for a good ten minutes when they first sat down, pretending they had no responsibilities in the world.

The Charleston news community had milked the details of Langley's ordeal to the best of their abilities, but with the family not giving the kidnapping oxygen, and the authorities only echoing the fact the family didn't want their torment dredged through the media, journalists left empty-handed. They'd started moving on to other nuggets of news to satiate reader appetites.

Most of Edisto Beach's people had been gone during the storm, so nobody had first-hand knowledge of the Langley kidnapping except for Callie, Mark, and Donna. Donna didn't want dirt spread across her beloved town, especially being so fresh in one of its oversight positions, plus she hadn't been present for all the activities either.

That left Callie and Mark, and only she possessed the complete set of details.

"It's been a week," he said.

He didn't have to say *a week since what.*

"I'm worried you'll be disturbed about the choice I made," she said.

It was getting too dark to read a person. Oftentimes Callie liked discussions hidden behind the big oak tree outside, swallowed up by the darkness of the porch, where they couldn't second-guess what the other one was thinking because of the look in their eyes.

Mark hadn't stopped rocking, the mild creak coming through like a metronome. "Do you have doubts about what you did?"

Sure she'd had doubts. Then she'd had thoughts about those doubts which only undid the doubt. Then she'd start all over again. "Yes," she finally said. "But I'm not sure I'd have done anything differently."

Especially since she'd seen how adamant St. James had been about not airing his daughter's trauma. If Callie'd reported Bruce, Arlo, and Leonard, the heat in the investigation would've been taken from low to high, slinging the media into a different level of intensified frenzy. Then when a case could not be made, and she had little doubt of a case being made, fingers would've started pointing. At Dr. St. James, at the Charleston PD, even at Langley, and most likely at her and Edisto Beach. The end results would've done little more than put money in some attorney's pocket and smear a lot of good reputations.

"Tell me," Mark said. "No judgment here."

She took ten minutes to refill their coffees and build her courage, then for two hours, she spilled the timeline, the conversations Mark hadn't heard. She covered each time she'd had to make a decision one way or another. She elaborated on her choice whether to involve the Rangers, whether to let Bruce pop Stan with morphine, twice, whether to take Bruce with her to the chopper . . . and every little observation in between.

"It's not a cop's job to decide if there's enough evidence," she said. "That's what rubs me wrong."

"But there wasn't," he said.

"I honestly believe more damage would've occurred if I'd told them my suspicions and pushed them to drag everyone through the mud only for these guys to be set free and Langley to be scarred for life. No matter which way I play it out, the result winds up the same."

"Not to mention ruins your reputation and draws crazy attention to the beach with media, podcast influencers, and more," he said.

She wasn't sure whether he was trying to make her feel better or if he agreed.

But did it even matter now?

Mark rocked some more. She rewrapped her lap blanket. They'd finished their second cup of coffee, not eager for another.

"You did your best," he said. "You saved Stan, got him off the beach, and kept Langley safe. You're smarter than everyone in this equation, Callie. Go with it. Let everyone move forward."

Experienced, yes. But damn, she had to respect the skill and planning of the crime. It was as close to perfect as any she'd ever seen. And nobody was hurt. They'd done their best to pull off the job without traumatizing the victim . . . or victims, because no way they hadn't done this before. Not as seamlessly as this had gone until Hurricane Nikki.

Nobody could best Mother Nature.

"I don't like the bad guys getting away."

"You weren't thinking of the bad guys," Mark said. "You were thinking of the good. Move forward, Sunshine."

She heard him this time, and decided he was right.

The End

Acknowledgement

Love and thanks to Gary, who listens patiently to my oral edits, no matter how long it takes. He's ever there when it comes to signings, presentations, and behind-the-scenes changes to make a plot that much better. I don't know how I'd ever write a book without him, even though he'd love to add a lot more shootouts, bombs, and explosions.

Thanks to the support of my hometown Chapin family, which is quite a few. They are loyal to the core.

But also thanks to my Edisto family, my second home, and their faithful patience for the next Edisto release. I never tire of the question, "When's the next book coming out?"

Much appreciation for my editor Debra Dixon who believes in me. And also to the staff of Bell Bridge Books, who jump whenever jumping is needed, and make these books a reality.

And to every bookstore and library out there that carries my stories, thank you so very much. You are the catalysts for spreading these mysteries far and wide, and I could not exist without you.

And I continue to cherish Carey, Rosemary, and now Kiersten as they navigate the waters of taking these stories visual.

Made in the USA
Coppell, TX
18 July 2025

52070450R00146